© Sarah Julku

About the Author

JAMES L. NELSON has served as a seaman, rigger, boatswain, and officer on a number of sailing vessels. He is the author of *By Force of Arms, The Maddest Idea, The Continental Risque, Lords of the Ocean,* and *All the Brave Fellows*—the five books of his Revolution at Sea saga, as well as *The Guardship* and *The Blackbirder,* the first two books of the Brethren of the Coast trilogy. He is also the author of *Glory in the Name: A Novel of the Confederate Navy.* He lives with his wife and children in Harpswell, Maine. His website is found at www.jameslnelson.com.

The Pirate Round

BOOK THREE OF
THE BRETHREN OF THE COAST

James L. Nelson

Perennial

An Imprint of HarperCollins*Publishers*

First Perennial edition published 2003.

Designed by Bernard Klein

Ship diagram and map by James L. Nelson

The Library of Congress has catalogued the hardcover edition as follows:

Nelson, James L.
The pirate round / James L. Nelson.
p. cm. — (The brethren of the coast ; bk. 3)
ISBN 0-380-80454-9
1. Virginia—History—Colonial period, ca. 1600–1775—Fiction. 2. Plantation life—Fiction. 3. Tobacco farmers—Fiction. 4. Privateering—Fiction. I. Title.

PS3564.E4646 P57 2002
813'.54—dc21
2001051195

ISBN 0-06-053926-7 (pbk.)

05 06 07 ❖/RRD 10 9 8 7 6 5 4 3 2

To Elizabeth Clare Nelson, my beloved daughter

I am bound to Madagascar,
with the design of making my own fortune,
and that of all the brave fellows with me.

—THOMAS TEW

Acknowledgments

Thanks, as is always the case, are due many people. Thank you to Barry Clifford, Ken Kinkor, and especially Paul Perry for the information on St. Mary's on Madagascar's coast, a happy coincidence that they were researching the place—and going there—at the same time I was writing about it! Thanks as ever to Nat and Judith for all their help and support, and to Nancy Becker for the swordplay. And with deep appreciation I extend my thank-you to David Semanki at Harper-Collins and to Hugh Van Dusen, one of the last of the Renaissance men.

Author's Note

THE CHIEF targets of those who sailed the Pirate Round to the Red Sea and the Indian Ocean were the treasure ships belonging to the ruler of India, the Great Mogul, who demanded and received vast tribute from the many lands united under his rule.

The Moguls were descendant from Muslim invaders who conquered and ruled India, a largely Hindu land, from 1526 until their power waned in the 1730s. Despite their despotic rule, trade and commerce flourished under the Moguls, and the ships outbound from India with rich cargoes and then returning with the proceeds of their trading voyage were also enticing to the pirates.

Other targets of the Red Sea Rovers were the ships carrying well-heeled pilgrims to Mecca. In all, the wealth that flowed back and forth across the Indian Ocean was staggering, without parallel in the Christian world.

The Pirate Round is set in 1706–7, quite some time before anyone was overly worried about respecting other cultures. Only the staunchest moralists saw anything wrong with robbing dark-skinned non-Christians. Moralists, and the wealthy merchants who ran the various East India companies, whose lucrative trade was threatened as the Great Mogul became increasingly incensed by the depredations of European pirates.

To the pirates, and most Europeans at the time, any dark-skinned non-Christian was considered a "Moor," like Shakespeare's Othello. It was a catchall that included Muslims, Hindus, Arabs, Indians, and the people of North Africa. In this book I have retained the word and use it as it was meant in the early eighteenth century.

J.L.N.

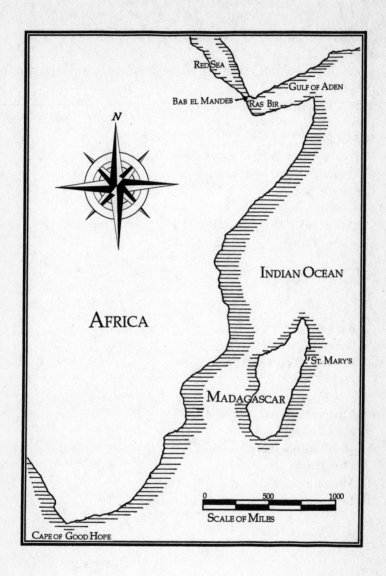

RED SEA

GULF OF ADEN

BAB EL MANDEB — RAS BIR

N

INDIAN OCEAN

AFRICA

I. ST. MARY'S

MADAGASCAR

0   500   1000

SCALE OF MILES

CAPE OF GOOD HOPE

Sails

A. Spritsail
B. Spritsail Topsail (pronounced *tops'l*)
C. Foresail or Fore Course
D. Fore Topsail
E. Fore Topgallant Sail (pronounced *t'gan's'l*)
F. Mainsail or Main Course
G. Main Topsail
H. Main Topgallant Sail
I. Mizzen Sail
J. Mizzen Topsail

Spars

1. Bowsprit
2. Spritsail Topmast
3. Foremast of Fore Lower Mast
4. Fore Topmast
5. Fore Topgallant Mast
6. Mainmast of Main Lower Mast
7. Main Topmast
8. Main Topgallant Mast
9. Mizzenmast
10. Mizzen Topmast
11. Ensign and Ensign Staff

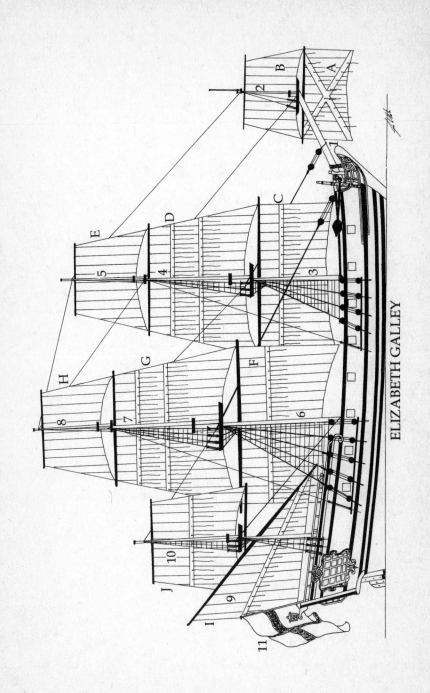

ELIZABETH GALLEY

Prologue

THE AIR was hot, the wind steady. It blew down the length of the Red Sea, funneled through the straits of Bab el Mandeb, swept over the little island of Perim, which the pirates called Bab's Key. A regular fifteen knots, but it brought no relief from the crushing heat.

The *Amity* sloop was moving well in that wind. Not her fastest, but well. She was under fighting sail, reduced canvas that would make her easier to handle during the coming action, keep her stable for laying the great guns.

Thomas Tew stood on the low quarterdeck, rigid, pressed against the weather rail. Grains of sand, swept up from the deserts of Arabia to the north and carried along on the wind, stung his face like tiny biting insects. They worked their way into his clothing, clung to the sweat that coated his body under his shirt, waistcoat, coat, and breeches.

He envied the men forward, crowded into the sloop's waist, stripped down, bare-chested, barefooted. He wished he could be in such a state of undress, but he could not. It was not for him, the captain of the *Amity*, the famous Thomas Tew, the fabulously wealthy Thomas Tew, to go into a fight dressed like a common sailor.

In fact, he was wearing his best suit of clothes, rich burgundy silks and cotton, silver buckles that gleamed so bright he could not look at them.

It was not a status he had enjoyed long. Three years before, when he had set sail from Newport, Rhode Island, with a commission to take the French factory at Goorie on the Gambia River, he had been no more than one of many, many minor privateer captains, the commander of a small sloop and sixty-odd men. Back then he had not worn such fine clothes on the quarterdeck. He had not even owned such things. He had not been wealthy, or famous.

Wealth and fame came after, and it started with the most important decision of his life, which was to not go to the Gambia at all. Rather, he called his men aft, told them that, former plans notwithstanding, there was little to be gained in Africa and great danger in gaining it. The Red Sea should be their destination, their goal the great ships that brought annual tribute to the Mogul of India from all the lands over which he ruled.

It was a plan that was greeted with enthusiasm. "A gold chain or a wooden leg," the men cried, "we'll stand by you!"

That was in 1692, and now, three years later, Tew could not help but recall that time, being as it was so very like his current situation. The Red Sea, the Great Mogul's treasure ship, the eager men of the *Amity* ready at the guns, small arms draped from sword belts and shoulder belts, pistols clutched in sweating hands.

They had searched for months, back in '92, and had seen nothing. Then, just past the straits of Bab el Mandeb, they happened on the great, wallowing treasure ship—a huge, high-sterned, gilded monstrosity, a row of great guns jutting from her slab side, three hundred dark-skinned, turban-clad soldiers protecting the riches in her belly. One well-laid broadside from her huge cannon could have swept the *Amity* from the sea, one coordinated rush of the soldiers would have trampled the meager sixty Rhode Island privateersmen underfoot.

It was folly to attack, but attack they had, blasting away with round and grapeshot, rushing up her sides, falling on the defenders like the screaming furies of hell. The three hundred who sailed in defense of the Mogul's treasure stumbled over one another to flee in the face of them. The Indian soldiers flung aside muskets and swords and lances, raced belowdecks, fell to their knees in supplication.

Fifteen minutes of inconsequential fighting and the Yankees had in their possession a fortune the likes of which had not been seen in the Western world since the heyday of the Spanish treasure ships. A hundred thousand pounds in gold and silver, gems, pearls, ivory, spices, silk. It was staggering. They sailed to St. Mary's, a tiny island off the northeast coast of Madagascar, divided the booty in the way of the pirates. Three thousand pounds sterling for every man aboard, and double that for the captain.

They made Newport in April of 1694, like Caesar returning triumphant to Rome. Tew, the little-known privateersman, was now fêted in every great house in town. He and his wife and his two daughters were the special guests of Governor Fletcher of New York. Wherever he went, men and women wanted to meet him, to hear his tales of Arabia and the East Indies. He was a celebrated gentleman. That ugly word "pirate" was rarely applied to him, and never by anyone of import.

That was nearly two years before, and here he was again. A different man—wealthy, renowned—but on board the same ship, on nearly the same patch of water, looking at a treasure ship three cable lengths away. High-sided, clumsy, heavily armed and ornate, she looked very like the one that had made his fortune.

Oh, Lord, why ever am I here? he thought.

The pressure had been overwhelming. All the young men of substance had begged him to go out again, and take them along. Servants ran away from their masters and pleaded to join in on another venture to the Red Sea. Wealthy patrons had offered to underwrite the voyage for a percentage of the profit. Thomas Tew had had eight months to enjoy his newfound fortune and the company of his wife and daughters before he had been convinced to sally forth again.

We shall take this big bastard, and then we are for Newport once more, he thought.

Tew took a few steps forward, felt the sweat running under his clothes. The pitch between the deck planks, made soft and gummy by the terrible sun, stuck to his shoes and resisted his efforts to lift his feet and move. He put his hand down on the cap rail and then jerked it away as the hot, oiled wood burned his flesh. He rested his hand on the pommel of his sword, the other on the butt of a pistol thrust into his belt.

Three years ago, three years ago . . . he had flung himself over the rail of the Mogul's ship. He could see the soldiers with their long white coats like dresses, their bound heads, dark skin, bright silk belts, falling to the deck before the attacking Englishmen. Not one of his own men lost. Not one.

No reason to think it will be different today, Tew thought, but he did not believe it. There *was* something different. It was nothing he could hold down, just a quality that this ship had that the other did not. With his glass he could see men on her decks. There was no sense of panic, no rushing about. He could not hear the sounds of frantic preparation. The ship just stood on, stately despite her ungainliness, as if the pirate sloop closing for an attack were no more than a minor annoyance, a yapping dog at the heels of an untroubled bull.

Thomas Tew was not frightened. He had been frightened before, many times, in the course of his wandering life, and he knew that this was not fear. It was something else. Concern? Apprehension? A dull discomfort in his bowels that told him he was making a mistake, that he had pushed his luck too far.

But there was nothing for it. He looked down into the waist, wondering idly if there were some way he could break off the engagement. But he could see there was not. In the faces of his men he could see lust for gold, avarice that would not be arrested.

There were sixty of them and one of him, and if he insisted that they avoid this great ship, then they would just throw him into the sea and attack her anyway. There was nothing to support his authority as captain save for the traditions and usage of the sea, and those were a pretty flimsy bulwark against greed.

He ran his tongue over his parched lips, took another step forward in anticipation of issuing an order. His throat was dry; he was afraid his voice would come out as no more than a croak. He wondered if he should ask someone to fetch him some water, if that would look like weakness on his part.

What in all hell is the matter with me?

"Reeves," he said, and his voice was like gravel, "fetch me a cup of water."

Reeves nodded—"Aye, Captain"—and hurried forward. Tew felt himself relax a bit, felt the tension ease. He looked over the Mogul's ship once more and tried to view it with disdain and derision, but he couldn't quite muster that.

It was the quiet; that was what bothered him, he realized. He could remember that first treasure ship. Two cables away, and he could hear the sailors and soldiers shouting in their mounting panic and confusion. He recalled how the Englishmen had stood firm and silent, waiting for their moment, while the Moors had degenerated into chaos.

But not now. He heard none of that now. Just silence, and it made him profoundly uneasy.

Reeves came back on the quarterdeck carrying a tin cup running over with water. Tew took the water, nodded his thanks, not trusting his voice, and drank it down in three big mouthfuls. Green with growth and warm enough to shave with, still it had a marvelous restorative effect, more than any liquor could have had at that moment, and at last he dared speak to the men. He stepped up to the break of the quarterdeck.

"Stand fast at your guns, lads! We'll give them a broadside and then lay alongside and board 'em! Scream like the damned when you go up the side—it'll scare the fight right out of 'em! You lads that was with me in '92, you'll recall!"

That little speech brought a cheer in the charged atmosphere, but Tew knew that any words from him at that moment would have had the same effect.

"*You lads that was with me in '92 . . .*" There were not more than a dozen of them. The rest had elected to stay in Newport and enjoy their wealth or had never returned at all, had remained on that island paradise of Madagascar, lounging their lives away in the tropic warmth with all the liquor and women a man could dream of.

Tew felt a sudden twinge of regret as he thought of those men back in Newport. That could have been him. He need not have lifted a finger again for the rest of his life. He could be playing with his daughters on a broad, grassy lawn, not sweating like a plow horse under the Arabian sun.

These men, this new crew, they were different. Not like the original Amitys. Those men had been a band of brothers. But these, they were fortune hunters, men out for quick riches, careless of anything else. Tew found that he resented them. They had talked him into this voyage, he was doing all this for them, and they gave not a tinker's cuss for his sacrifice.

The treasure ship was a cable length away—two hundred yards—and it was time to stop such useless thought.

"Aim for her rails, lads, sweep her deck! We've but the one broadside to clear the way for us!"

No cheering this time. With the huge ship looming over them, dwarfing them even from that distance, the men were focused entirely on what would happen in the next ten minutes. Tew saw men yawn, a sure sign of fear, saw them pretend it was just boredom. He turned his eyes outboard, ran them along the Mogul's ship.

God, she is a beastly great thing . . . Tew wondered if she was even larger than the first. She looked like a floating mountain. She was frightening to behold.

"Ready, lads . . ." Less than one hundred yards between them. In the waist the gun captains sighted down barrels, made last-minute adjustments to elevation. Such niceties would have little effect on accuracy. It was just something to do.

Tew gripped the handle of his sword and tried to fight down his rising panic. It was not something he had ever experienced before, and he did not know how to resist it. He had to give his orders precisely—and at precisely the right moment.

Fifty yards separated the ships, and from across the water, clear as a ringing bell on a still morning, came a single order, firm, decisive, in the Moorish tongue, and Tew guessed that order was "Fire!" so without thinking he, too, shouted "Fire!" down at the men in the waist.

The *Amity* fired, and the Mogul's ship fired, nearly at the same instant. Great clouds of gray smoke banked in the narrowing space between them, the roar of the guns filling the air like something tangible. The *Amity* shook underfoot as the Mogul's great guns hammered her sides, and Tew could think only, *The other ship did not fire on us . . .*

And then he felt himself pushed aside, as if the hand of God had reached through the smoke and given him the slightest of shoves. With never a thought he dropped his sword and clapped his hands over his belly, not even certain why he had done so. Then he felt a burning sensation there.

He staggered back a few steps, looked down at his hands. There was blood running over his fingers, streaming off his hands, pooling on the white deck. Bright red blood, pumping, pumping through his fingers.

He moved his hands a bit, enough to look behind them, and he could see the gleam of something else, and now he could feel it against his palms, and he knew it was not flesh.

It was his bowels, he realized. He stomach was torn away, and he was holding his guts in with his hands, and with that realization he felt the first wave of agony sweep over him.

He fell to his knees, saw the smoky, chaotic world of the *Amity's* deck swirl around him, saw faces turn toward him, heard weird voices shouting, men running aft to where he was kneeling.

No, no . . . he thought.

No, abandoning the Gambia was not the most important decision of his life. He saw that now. It was sailing again for the Red Sea, and it was with his life that he would pay for that decision.

He looked down. The deck and the red pool of blood was swimming in front of him, rushing at him, the perspective changing fast. He hit the deck, and what breath he had was knocked from him, and only then did he realize that he had fallen.

He lay there, motionless, his cheek pressed against the hot planking, looking across the deck. Such an odd angle. He could see men's shoes and bare feet, could see where a corner had been imperfectly swept, could see under the rail to the bright blue water beyond.

Oh, Lord, what a shame, to die thus . . . Visions of his wife and daughters moved like dreams through his head, the sumptuous dinners at Governor Fletcher's, the pride in his wife's face as she looked on him, the weight of his two girls on his knees—how he wished he would see all that again.

But he would not. He could feel the blood pooling under him, could taste it in his mouth, feel it slick on his hands and his cheek where they were pressed to the deck. His vision was growing dark around the edges, the sounds in his ears dull and otherworldly. The pain in his abdomen was all-consuming—it devoured him whole— and he would have writhed with the agony if he had been able to move, but he could not. For the first time he saw death as a relief, and he welcomed it and wished it would come fast.

He closed his eyes, whispered his daughters' names.

It was September 1695, when Thomas Tew died on the quarterdeck of his sloop, holding in his guts with his own hands, his stomach torn open by the freak glancing blow of a cannonball. Their famous leader dead, the men of the *Amity* panicked and surrendered with no further resistance. Their fate at the hands of the Great Mogul of India is not known.

When word of Tew's grisly death reached Newport, it might have caused some introspection, but it did not slow in the least the great wave of fortune hunters that were arming vessels and sailing the "Pirate Wind" for Madagascar and the Red Sea and then back to the colonies in America.

Thomas Tew made himself a fortune when he took the Great Mogul's ship in 1692 and secured his place in that pantheon of sea rovers long remembered, men such as Long Ben Avery and Bartholomew Roberts and Blackbeard.

But in terms of the history of seafaring and raiding, Thomas Tew did something far more important than establishing his own fame, something that would resonate for decades to follow, that would become the concern of the most powerful nations on earth.

With his one bold attack, Thomas Tew created the Pirate Round.

Chapter 1

THOMAS MARLOWE was not studying a chart of the Indian Ocean.

True, it was laid out in front of him, along with dividers and parallel rule and all those tools that a mariner might use to study a chart. A dagger, formerly the property of a lieutenant in the Spanish navy, held down the lower right corner of the rolled vellum. Holding the left corner were the sailing directions for that area, a volume he had picked up in Port Royal over ten years before, when he had first considered a jaunt against the Moors.

But he was not considering it again. It was foolhardy, unethical. It was piracy, and that was not what he did. He was not studying the chart. He assured himself of that.

He sighed, tossed the dividers aside, leaned back in the chair. August, hot and sultry in Virginia, a steamy heat after two days of rain. The windows to the library were flung open, and the lightest of breezes found its way in, rustling the papers on Marlowe's desk. Accounts that needed settling, mostly. Unencouraging reports from his merchant in England.

Marlowe ran his fingers through his shoulder-length hair, scratched his scalp. Until just the past few months he had worn it close-cropped to accommodate one of the many elaborate periwigs that his station in Virginia society had dictated he wear. Finally, a combination of creeping age (he was nearing forty), a secure position in Tidewater society, and a general disgust with the expense and discomfort of the things had led him to abandon the fashion and allow his own hair to grow back, as he had worn it in his days at sea.

With periwig gone and coat tossed over the seat of a straight-backed caned chair, Marlowe was about as comfortable as he was going to get on such a day. He stared out the window, across the wide expanse of lawn to the lush, green line of trees in the distance. It was his, all his. He felt the weight of it pushing him down.

Today was a day for packing tobacco for shipment to England. Through the open window he could hear the squeak of the lever arm used to prize the air-cured hands of tobacco into the hogsheads.

Marlowe smiled as he thought of it. When he arrived in Williamsburg in 1700, determined to give up a former life of piracy, he understood none of that. He did not know that tobacco had to be left suspended in a curing house to dry in the air after it was cut, did not know that it was bound up into little bundles called hands and then forced, or "prized" into hogsheads.

He knew only that he wanted a plantation, wanted to be lord of the manor. Money procured that. Once he owned the plantation, he set free the slaves that had come with the bargain and hired them to take care of the cultivation. That part of plantation owning, the agriculture part, did not interest him. Besides, the former slaves had forgotten more about it than he would ever know.

The squeaking stopped, followed a moment later by the peevish voice of Francis Bickerstaff saying, "No, no more. There is a finite amount these hogsheads will hold, you know. We shall blow it apart if we put one more hand in there. Affix the head now, cooper, and let us have another." He sounded like a schoolmaster lecturing a recalcitrant student.

That was hardly surprising. Bickerstaff had been a tutor to a wealthy man's children up until the moment his ship had been captured by the pirate vessel aboard which Marlowe was sailing. Marlowe had forced Bickerstaff to sail with him, to teach him to read, to speak properly, to pass as a gentleman. The two had become friends, the closest of friends, and remained so.

Bickerstaff had a curious mind, as befitted a scholar. While Marlowe was happy to ride around the plantation and enjoy his lordship over it, Bickerstaff felt the need to learn all he could about raising, curing, and selling tobacco. After five years of living at Marlowe House, he knew as much as any planter in the Tidewater. Between Bickerstaff and the freed slaves, Marlowe's plantation produced as much and as good tobacco as any plantation in Virginia or Maryland.

Thomas drew a deep breath. Along with the sounds of prizing, the breeze carried the scent of the air-dried tobacco being readied for shipment. It was the smell of money in the Tidewater. Or had been, until now, the Year of Our Lord 1706.

Now it was hard times for the once-prosperous colony. Queen Anne's War had dragged on for four years, with not the least indication that it would let up. The markets of Europe were closed to English tobacco, just when the planters in Virginia and Maryland were enjoying record yields.

Marlowe stared and pondered and idly massaged his right forearm. It had been broken four years before in an ill-advised attack on a French East Indiaman, and it still bothered him on occasion.

He had forsworn piracy, but on a few occasions since beginning his new life he had wandered close to the sweet trade—and had made a fair amount of money in doing so. That booty had carried him through the hard times, had allowed him to keep out of debt and to pay his former slaves, as he had promised them he would. But his cache of loot was nearly exhausted now, and there was little money to be made from tobacco, and he did not know what he would do.

He sighed again, glanced down at the tempting chart and its promise of fat Moorish treasure ships running down the Red Sea and through the straits of Bab el Mandeb. Somewhere off in Europe, armies were beating each other bloody to determine who would sit on the decadent throne of Spain, and it was ruining his life, like some black-magic spell cast from far off. He was accustomed to simpler problems, enemies that he could face with sword and pistol.

He realized that he was looking for just that, a way to attack his problems with steel and powder, searching for some action he could take to fight his way back to solvency. *I am still quite an unsubtle creature*, he thought.

The soft padding of feet beyond the door, the sound of his wife, Elizabeth, coming down the hall. He looked up at the doorway and then down at the chart, then up again, frozen in indecision. He did not want Elizabeth to think he was studying the thing, because he was not. But neither did he want her to catch him trying furtively to hide it from her.

In the few seconds it took him to not make a decision, the decision was made for him when Elizabeth appeared in the door, gave a light rap on the frame. "Thomas, do you have a moment?" She held in her arms the big ledger books for Marlowe House, which were her special charge.

"Yes, my dearest, of course. I was just, well . . ."

Elizabeth crossed over to the desk, glanced down at the chart that Marlowe was now rolling up with a great show of innocence. "Madagascar and the Indian Ocean?" she said. "I did not know you had such a chart."

"Yes, well, I have had it these many years. Just wondering about something. Francis and I were wondering about the size of Madagascar, you know. Turns out to be half again as long as I had thought."

"Hmm-hmm" was all that Elizabeth said. She laid the ledgers down on the desk slowly, a somber and foreboding gesture. "I have brought the accounts up to date. It is not a pretty thing, I fear."

Marlowe stared at the ledger books, hating them, as if they were to blame. He held them in the same light as he had held all books before he learned to read—as something he did not understand and therefore something to fear.

"Are we in debt?"

"No."

"Well, thank God for that at least." Debt was a death knell in the colonies. Once money was owed to merchants in England, men far beyond the reach of careful scrutiny, it was nearly impossible to get out.

It was stunning how quickly a merchant's fawning respect turned to scornful abuse once a planter owed him money.

"Yes," Elizabeth agreed. "It is something. But the funds held by the bank are nearly gone, and, I fear, the . . . ah . . . contents of your warehouse in Jamestown are all but entirely sold off. There is only the silk you were holding on to and some ivory, but we have never found much of a market for that here."

"Hmm" was all Marlowe could say to that. The warehouse in Jamestown, up the river from Jamestown, really, was known to only himself and Elizabeth and Francis Bickerstaff. It had been abandoned for years before Marlowe bought it, secretly, and it appeared abandoned still. In it he kept the booty he had gathered from his activities that, if not entirely illegal, would certainly have raised eyebrows—and questions—among those in authority.

That was the bounty that had carried them along thus far, through falling tobacco prices and rising wartime costs. And now it was gone.

Marlowe rubbed his temples. "Very well. What is to be done? I'll confess I have no notion."

"Ah, as to that . . . I did have one thought . . ."

Thomas looked up at his wife. She was displaying more hesitancy than was usual for her, and it piqued his curiosity.

"Yes?"

"Well, it seems to me there are two things that are making it quite impossible for us to realize any profit from our plantations—any of us here in the Tidewater. The first is the damned shipping rates. With the dearth of seaman and ships, we'll not pay below fourteen pounds a ton this season, which is madness. In the best of times that would eat up most of our profit."

Marlowe leaned back in his chair, laced his fingers together. "Mmm-hmm," he agreed, watching Elizabeth. She had rehearsed this speech, he could tell, so she must be coming to something interesting. Interesting enough for her to be nervous about mentioning it to her husband, a man from whom she had no secrets.

"The other thing of it is the convoys," Elizabeth continued. "All the ships gather together, we all load our tobacco aboard, and then the navy ships escort the whole lot across the ocean to London. The entire year's crop arrives on the dock at the same instant, creates an immediate glut. The damned merchants name their price, and they ain't overgenerous. There is no profit to be made with those considerations."

"Mmm-hmm. And your thought . . . ?"

"Yes, well . . . you have a great advantage over the others, you see. You, unlike most in the Tidewater, own a ship . . ."

He did that. The *Elizabeth Galley*. She was an old but solid merchantman when he bought her in '02, and he had refitted her as a privateer. He had been forced to use her in hunting down his old friend King James, after he turned pirate. And once he had returned from that unhappy mission, Governor Nicholson had insisted on having back the *Galley*'s great guns, which were property of the colony and needed for her defense, now that England was at war.

Thus unarmed, and with Marlowe's desire for cruising quashed by the horror of what he had had to do the last time he put to sea, the *Elizabeth Galley*'s rig had been sent down, and she had been moored in the freshets of the James River to keep her free of weed and teredo worm. And there she had remained.

"I do own a ship," Marlowe agreed. "Are you thinking we should get into the business of shipping?"

"Yes. The cost of manning the ship would be nothing compared to the freight rates, I shouldn't think, particularly if you were to command her."

"I'll warrant you are right about that. Seamen are hard to find, but we could fill out the crew with some of our people here." By "our people" Marlowe meant the former slaves who worked the plantation. "Some of those young fellows would make first-rate seamen, with just a bit of instruction. But that solves only half the problem. We are still faced with the glut of weed once we are in London."

"Yes, as to that . . . I had thought perhaps we could sail before the convoy. They will put to sea in three months' time. Sure we could have the *Galley* ready before that. What are you grinning about, you son of a bitch?"

Marlowe was indeed grinning, nearly laughing at this. Elizabeth had not led the most upright life before she had married him, but since then she had shunned any kind of impropriety.

"You are suggesting we become smugglers?" Marlowe asked.

"No, not smugglers. It is not illegal to sail without the convoy, if we get a permit to do so."

"But you know perfectly well that they grant permits only to well-armed ships, which we are not, not anymore. Besides, there is never enough time now to secure a permit."

"Well, I had thought . . ."

"No, no. None of your excuses. I am not saying I don't like the idea. I do. I just want you to say, 'Yes, Thomas, I am suggesting we smuggle.'"

"Thomas, damn you . . ."

"Say it . . ."

Elizabeth glared at him, then seemed to accept defeat. She deflated, flopped down in the chair facing his desk. "Yes, Thomas, I am suggesting we smuggle. There is no way around it—we are lost otherwise. I have no doubt we can carry some of our neighbors' tobacco as well. They would be as happy to beat the convoy as we would."

Thomas looked at his wife, her lovely face now touched with sadness. She was twenty-eight years old, and the first twenty-three years had not been easy for her. But together they had managed to build something good at Marlowe House. An honest, respectable life. It was something new to both of them, and there was nothing Elizabeth would not do to hold on to it.

"I think this is a capital idea," Marlowe said, and he was entirely sincere. "We might even pick up a cargo for the return voyage, perhaps buy some goods to sell when we are home again."

It was a good plan. With just a little luck they would realize enough from this voyage to keep themselves out of debt for a few more years at least.

"We may not be able to do it, in any event," Elizabeth continued. "We'll need sailors, we'll need to get the *Galley* ready for sea, which will cost money. And, of course, there are no guns aboard. We would be most vulnerable to attack."

" 'We'?"

"Yes, 'we.' Did you think you would sail off again without me?"

In fact he had, though there was no pleasure in the thought. But still . . . Elizabeth on board? "I don't know if it is quite the thing—" he began in weak protest.

"There is no helping it. You know nothing of the tobacco trade, you admit it freely. I know what our yield is, what it is worth. I do the books here. You are useless with numbers, another thing you have often admitted."

"True. But Bickerstaff—"

"Francis knows the growing and curing and prizing. He does not know the selling or bookkeeping."

That was true enough. Elizabeth had always dealt with the factors and agents once the crop was in, kept the books. Bickerstaff had probably been less involved in that part of it than even Thomas, and that was very little indeed.

The older field hands were certainly capable of seeing to the plantation without his or Elizabeth's or Bickerstaff's supervision. Marlowe House would be safe in their absence; there was no one left in the Tidewater who might wish to cause them grief. He was running out of arguments.

"There is also the point . . ." Elizabeth continued, and Marlowe could tell she had rehearsed this speech as well. He was surprised; that kind of preparation was unlike her. "Perhaps you should not be seen along the waterfront in London. One never knows when a fellow from the old days might recognize you . . ."

She did not have to say more. They both understood. One reliable witness, and Marlowe would hang for piracy. There was no pardon for his crimes.

"That is true as well," Marlowe admitted. "And there is also the point that I could not bear to be parted from you for the half a year the voyage would take."

Elizabeth smiled, her stern, businesslike demeanor melting before his words, and suddenly they were connected again, like man and wife, not partners in a merchant firm. Their love and passion for one another, which had not diminished in the least over the years, sparked between them and moved like a potent spirit.

"I had hoped you might feel that way," Elizabeth said.

"Indeed, my love, I am much buoyed by this plan. No doubt we can scrape up the funds we need to get the ship to sea, and I am equally sure our neighbors will want to get in on this. Sailors we can find—yes, my beloved, I think this is a fine idea. I shall begin at once to get things moving along . . ."

His voice trailed off, and his eyes moved unconsciously down to the rolled chart on his desk. In his mind they had already completed Elizabeth's plan, had the money in hand from the merchants in London, and now they were moving on to the next thing and the next after that.

Marlowe had made the decision even before he stood up from his desk. There was no reason to dally. Suddenly his desire to act was like a physical pressure, pushing from within. It was time to get under way.

Chapter 2

THERE WAS, unfortunately, a considerable distance between making a decision to get under way and actually getting under way, particularly aboard a ship that had not sailed in three years.

First an inspection of the *Elizabeth Galley* to assess her condition and determine her needs. Marlowe's mind was working fast now. Round up a crew, of course, that was no easy task. Secure a cargo—Marlowe House would not produce enough tobacco to entirely fill the *Elizabeth Galley*'s cavernous hold. Might as well make a little extra hauling the neighbors' weed.

"Oh, damn me," he said.

"What? Whatever is the problem?" Elizabeth asked, concerned.

"We have committed ourselves to the racing at Joseph Page's this afternoon." Marlowe was eager now to move on their plan, and he was not happy to recall this social obligation. He felt like a charging dog brought up short by its leash.

"I've wagered ten pounds on that sorrel nag of his." *Like I can bloody well afford that*, he thought. Declining to wager would place a greater tax on his appearance of wealth than ten pounds would place on his actual wealth. It was hard to gauge which was the higher price to pay.

"Yes," Elizabeth said, "and I am sure that Francis has quite forgotten as well. I'll send Caesar for him."

"No, no. I'll go fetch him myself." He smiled. "As lord of the manor, I suppose I should see what the common folk are about."

"Good, my lord. But don't be all day about it. We must leave in an hour, no more."

Marlowe pulled on his coat and grabbed up his hat and stepped out of the library and down the hallway, then out the front door that opened onto the wide porch. The warmth of the sun and the fragrance from the plantation and the woods came on him redoubled, and he stretched and breathed deep before taking the steps down to the front walk and the grassy lawn.

The flowers that Elizabeth so lovingly tended were in full bloom, great bursts of color that lined the house and the walks and spilled out of her gardens. The grass was a rich green. Birds flashed around, twittering, diving, and lighting here and there.

Everything was alive, running over with life, growing, moving. It was so different from the sea, the cold, dead sea that always stretched away in its bleak sameness. The sea moved, to be sure, moved constantly, but it was not the motion of life. It was a random, thoughtless motion that cared not a whit for what effect it had, for whom it helped and whom it killed.

So why did he miss it so?

Marlowe stepped around the side of the house. Fifty feet away, the big tobacco barn yawned open, and spread out in front of it, on the brown patch of earth where the constant traffic had worn away the grass, the big lever arm used for prizing the tobacco, various hogsheads—some full, some waiting for their hands of tobacco—the cooper's tools. But no field hands, no Bickerstaff.

Marlowe sighed. Bickerstaff was the real lord of the manor, as far as actually overseeing what went on. The field hands no longer even bothered asking Marlowe about agricultural considerations.

Bickerstaff had no doubt been called away on some business and now would have to be hunted down. Marlowe debated getting his horse. He did enjoy riding around his property, marveling at how much of it he owned. But his horse would be off somewhere else, grazing, and Marlowe decided that fetching him would take more time than just finding Bickerstaff on foot.

He continued on past the barn, over the small rise to where he could see the fields beyond. Every year they cleared a patch of forest to make way for that year's seed beds. The tree line was noticeably farther from the house than it had been when Marlowe bought the place. The former slave quarters, once dilapidated huts but now fixed up, whitewashed, and cozy, had stood huddled at the edge of the woods then, but now they were in open field.

Marlowe paused at the top of the rise and looked around. He loved the plantation, loved his lord of the manor existence.

Back in '02, when he bought the *Elizabeth Galley*, he had been restless for the sea. He had been ready for privateering—high adventure with higher returns and low risk. But instead he had spent nearly a year on his unholy mission of hunting down his friend and the former captain of his river sloop, King James, a freed slave who had turned renegade after killing the crew of a slave ship in a fit of rage.

Why did I do that, submit to the governor's demand that I go after King James? He asked himself that question often enough. The answer: to preserve this. To maintain the life he and Elizabeth had built. To avoid becoming a pariah in a society that held him responsible for what James had done. He, Marlowe, lord of the manor, had freed his slaves. The Tidewater saw that as the seminal event in King James's crime.

At the far end of the field, past the former slave quarters, Marlowe saw a little knot of men and guessed that one was Bickerstaff, so he headed out for them.

The long voyage to Africa and back had banished from Marlowe's mind any thoughts of going to sea. For three years he had genuinely enjoyed the life of a country squire.

And then, just that morning, his hands had reached unbidden for the chart of Madagascar, and he found himself staring at it, caressing it with his dividers, remembering the feel of the ship underfoot, a misty morning, stepping on deck with a landfall rising out of the ocean ahead. And then Elizabeth had haltingly laid out her plan, and suddenly Marlowe's wanderlust was awake again.

At last he came up with the group of men, Francis Bickerstaff and four of the former slaves, now hired hands, of Marlowe House. Hesiod, head man of the field hands, in his mid-twenties, strong and confident, was nodding as Bickerstaff spoke. Over his shoulder a big ax, his huge hand wrapped around the handle. He looked like a pirate.

They were deep in a discussion of the properties of various trees for use as firewood and building material and what stand they might cut next, when Marlowe interrupted them.

"Francis, how goes it here?"

"Very well, Thomas. These fellows wish to make a start of clearing wood and laying in more lumber, and we were discussing what we might cut next. Have you a preference?"

"Whatever you think best, Francis. And the prizing, how goes that?"

"Our yield has been prodigious as ever, as you know, and the fortuitous rain has given us weather moist enough for the prizing."

"Indeed." Marlowe did not realize that one needed moist weather to prize tobacco. He tucked that fact away, said, "I have come to remind you of the racing at Page's this afternoon."

"Yes, yes. Damned insufferable gatherings."

"Good, then you will attend? Here, walk with me, and I will tell you of a plan that Elizabeth has concocted."

The two men retraced Marlowe's steps to the house, and as they did, Marlowe related his discussion of that morning. He met the objections that Bickerstaff raised with the logic that Elizabeth had employed on him, and by the time they reached the house, Francis was in agreement with the idea.

Elizabeth met them on the lawn, and the stableboy brought their horses around. They mounted and rode leisurely up the Archer's Hope Creek Road, three miles to the Page plantation, and Elizabeth said, "Francis, did Thomas tell you? Madagascar is twice again as long as you had thought."

"Pardon?"

"Madagascar. Were you two not discussing it?"

"I don't recall . . ."

"Yes, well," said Marlowe.

Archer's Hope Creek Road—known locally as a "rolling road"—was packed hard by the barrels of tobacco that were rolled from inland plantations to the landing at Archer's Hope Creek. In good weather it made for easy travel, and the three were able to discuss their plans as they walked their horses north, past brown-earth fields of harvested tobacco and patches of oak and maple, lush and green.

The breeze picked up, dissipating the humidity some and making them more comfortable, though it was still too hot for real comfort, dressed as they were in their silk coats and bodice and skirts and breeches and socks, rather than in the simple attire of the working-people and slaves.

They came at last to the Page plantation, a somewhat grander version of Marlowe House. There were a hundred people there already—gentlemen and ladies, laborers, slaves, all manner of Tidewater society. Horse racing was a passion in Virginia, enjoyed with a zeal that Marlowe could not begin to muster.

In fact, few of the things that delighted his peers—dancing and hunting, cards, bowling—did much for him, though he put on a brave front when forced to participate. He enjoyed fencing and billiards at least, and had garnered something of a reputation as a hand at both.

But horse races were good venues for conducting business. None better, in fact, with the exception of the governor's balls and Sunday worship, and so Marlowe contented himself that the afternoon might not be a total loss.

"Ah, Marlowe, there you are!" Joseph Page ambled up, red-faced, blustering with excitement. He loved a horse race, particularly his own. "Mrs. Marlowe, Bickerstaff, glad you could make it."

Marlowe slid down from his horse, and a boy raced out with a step for Elizabeth. "Wouldn't miss it, Page, never in life. I've ten pounds riding on your sorrel, I trust I won't lose it?"

"Lose it? Dear God, no. I only wish our harvests were as sure of profit as your wager, sir!"

Marlowe chuckled obediently. "Indeed. And funny you should mention our harvest. As it happens, I have just this morning come upon a scheme that I think might profit us all . . ."

By the time Page headed off to mount his sorrel for the race, Marlowe had secured his and two other neighbors' tobacco for his unorthodox voyage. The risks were explained and the terms—10 percent to Marlowe for carrying charges, with Marlowe assuring indemnity for loss due to negligence but not act of God—agreed upon.

Having concluded that business, Marlowe accepted a glass of wine from Elizabeth and accompanied her to the edge of the straight quarter-mile track that Page had laid out. Scattered along the length of the track were the many people who had come out for this event. It was like the annual celebration of Publick Times in Williamsburg. In a colony so sparsely populated, the people took every opportunity to congregate.

The buzzing among the crowd grew, the sense of anticipation swirling like smoke on a battlefield. The horses reared and jostled at the wide part at the head of the track, the starter fired his pistol, and mere seconds later Marlowe was poorer by ten pounds.

Standing at the edge of the track, twenty feet away, Marlowe noticed Peleg Dinwiddie, whose expression suggested that he also had lost, and Marlowe's disappointment was forgotten. Peleg was the master of Page's river sloop, a thoroughgoing sailor man, and just the person that Marlowe needed.

"Excuse me, my dear," Marlowe whispered to Elizabeth, and then he strolled off in Peleg's direction. Dinwiddie took an inordinate—and, Marlowe thought, not entirely sincere—interest in horses. Peleg was something of a social climber, with none of the wit or grace to climb successfully. Marlowe suspected that Peleg was more interested in appearing to fancy horses, but that did not matter. It was not Dinwiddie's view of horses that interested Marlowe now.

"Peleg!" Marlowe said, approaching with hand extended. "I haven't seen you about, this past week or more."

"Been down to Point Comfort and up the York. Time of year, you know. A lot moving by water."

"Oh, and don't I know it." Marlowe paused as if in thought. Peleg had been a merchant sailor all his working life, had been a boatswain for years and then mate before retiring to the much less demanding work of captaining a river sloop.

"Peleg, you ever miss the deepwater sailing?"

"No."

"Really? Never wish to see that blue water again, nothing but the open sea, rolling away in every direction?"

"No."

"Neither do I." Thomas paused again. "It's where the real money is to be made, though."

"I went deep water all my damned life. Never made any real money."

"Ah, but did you ever go to . . . No, never mind."

"Where?"

"Well, I was going to say Madagascar, but it don't answer, because I probably am not going there now."

"Probably?" Peleg stood a bit straighter, looked at Marlowe more intensely. Marlowe imagined he could peer into Peleg's eyes and see the vision of Moorish treasure forming in his brain. "You sailing the Round?"

"No, I am sailing to England, with a load of tobacco. Sod the damned convoy, I say. The Pirate Round? No, it is just something I am toying with, not so much chance I'll do it."

"Not so much . . . but there is a chance?"

"Yes, there is a chance."

Five minutes later, Peleg Dinwiddie agreed to report aboard the *Elizabeth Galley* in two days' time.

Marlowe felt no guilt about lying to him. What he felt was the oddest sort of confusion. He did not actually know to whom he was lying. Peleg? Elizabeth? Himself?

He had made no real decisions, save for the one that would take them to London. What might happen after that, he did not know. He was acting now, not thinking.

With the scarcity of seamen in the colonies, he needed Peleg Dinwiddie's experience. He had to tell the man what he wanted to hear.

The next morning Marlowe and Elizabeth and Bickerstaff rode south to Jamestown. It was time to inspect the *Elizabeth Galley*.

They left their horses at a stable by the landing and climbed into the boat that Marlowe kept there. Thomas took up the oars—a means of transport much more familiar to him than horses—and rowed them across the slow-moving river to where the *Elizabeth Galley* was moored.

She did not look so very seaworthy then, sitting motionless in the brown water of the river. The little bit of paint that adorned her sides was peeling off, and some of the fancy carvings were dry and cracked. She had only her lower masts—fore, main, and mizzen—in place, and the shrouds that supported those masts were slack, giving the ship an overall sagging appearance.

But those things belied her true condition. When Marlowe had moored her, he had no notion of when she might sail again. But he loved her too much, and was too much of a seaman, to let her rot away.

He had had the shrouds slackened off to keep from putting unnecessary strain on mast or rigging. He sent hands aboard her every month or so to apply fresh tar and check their condition, and he knew they were as sound as when they had first been set up.

The rest of the rigging and spars had been carefully stored away, out of the weather, and he inspected them once a month. The sails were folded carefully and stored as well, and every few months they were brought out to air to prevent them from rotting. At least twice a year he had personally crawled through the lowest parts of the hull and checked for creeping rot or signs of an infestation of the teredo worm that bored itself into ships' fabric, but he found neither.

The *Elizabeth Galley* was in disuse, but she was not neglected.

And so Marlowe was not surprised to find her in fine shape when he stepped aboard. Her decks had been swept fore and aft, and what little gear she still had aboard was in good order. He could smell fresh tar on her shrouds and linseed oil on her rails and sides. He looked around and nodded his approval.

"She is spacious as a ballroom with the great guns gone," Francis observed. They had all come in through the entry port and stood in the waist, taking the ship in.

"She is that," Thomas agreed. "And that relieves us of the need to carry powder or shot, which leaves plenty of room below for all our hogsheads and our neighbors' as well. It is a good thing, really, the governor has taken our guns."

"I could almost believe you are sincere," said Francis.

Marlowe took a step inboard, letting his eye roam over the familiar deck. So many ghosts floating around that space, too. He could see the big Spaniard looming alongside as he prepared to lead the Elizabeth Galleys over the rail. He could see again the men struggling along that deck as they were blasted by the heavy guns of the French Indiaman. He could recall the sight of Whydah slipping below the horizon as he looked over that taffrail at the place where they had buried King James.

Ghosts everywhere. His entire life was haunted.

"Yes, well . . ." he said to no one in particular. "Let us inspect belowdecks. I'll wager you will be pleasantly surprised by what you find."

He would have won the wager, had any taken him up on it. The lower decks were musty and hot, having been shut up and uninhabited for so long. But they were clean and maintained, with no sign of mold or rot or vermin. That was because Marlowe had his people wash her out with vinegar on a regular basis and fumigate her with brimstone once a year.

They made their way through the hold, inspecting that lower part of the ship by lantern light. Nothing amiss. She was tight and seaworthy.

They returned to the quarterdeck, blinking in the brilliant sun, blinded after the gloom of the hold. "She is in fine shape," Marlowe announced. "And I'll warrant the rest of her gear is just as well preserved. Give me a decent crew and I will have her ready for sea in a month."

The first part of the crew was easy enough to find. Upon returning to Marlowe House, he summoned all the former slaves together and told them that he was going to sail the Elizabeth Galley to England and he needed men and would any of them like to sign on?

There were no takers among the older men, those for whom ships meant the middle passage, the six weeks of hell stuffed into the festering hold of a slaver.

But among the younger men that association was not so strong. Hesiod was the first of them to step forward. He, like several others, had been young enough then that the memory had faded. Still others had been born in the colonies and had no firsthand knowledge of that horror. They were the young, strong, adventurous types that Marlowe wanted, and twelve of them stepped forward and eagerly volunteered.

"You do not think this might be a problem?" Bickerstaff asked Thomas in a private moment. "Sure, these fellows are as capable as any landsmen, but you will have to hire genuine seamen as well. Do you think others might object to being shipmates with black men?"

"Your sailor is an altogether more liberal fellow than your landsman," Marlowe said. "I don't think they will object to any man who pulls his weight. It is not unprecedented, you know, white men and black working together on shipboard."

"Indeed? I have never seen it."

"You don't too often aboard honest ships, but aboard pirates it is common enough."

"Humph," said Bickerstaff. "That is not a precedent I might wish to follow."

Smart, able, and willing as those young black men were, they were not sailors. Marlowe set them to work transferring all of the gear in storage back to the ship—work that needed no special expertise.

At the appointed hour Peleg Dinwiddie reported aboard. With an experienced first officer to oversee the setting up of the rig, Marlowe was free to begin his campaign for the recruitment of experienced mariners, a scarce commodity in the Tidewater. He took his own sloop, the *Northumberland*, down the James River and across Hampton Roads to the small, rough port town of Norfolk, where he hoped to find sailors in a region that did not see a fraction of the shipping that the northern colonies did.

He went immediately to the taverns, the likeliest place to find not just sailors but sailors in a compliant mood. In the second loud, dark, smoke-filled, stinking tavern he entered, he found one.

The man was sitting alone at a small table. He was dressed in a linen shirt and well-worn broadcloth coat. His face was a sailor's face, lined and tanned, his hair was long and worn clubbed, sailor fashion. He might have been an ordinary seaman at one point in his career, but he looked now like a bosun or mate of a small merchantman. Perhaps a bit of privateering, perhaps a bit of piracy.

There was a quality that drew Marlowe's eye, an air of self-assurance. A certain attitude. There was nothing soft about the man; he was all sharp edges. If Peleg was something of a tame bear, this man looked like a wolf, and a hungry one. But those qualities were good, too, if they could be channeled the right way.

"Mind if I join you?" Marlowe stood in front of the small table. The man looked up, regarded Marlowe for a long moment, said nothing. Marlowe was wearing his seagoing clothes: faded blue coat, cotton waistcoat and shirt, and soft, well-worn canvas breeches. The clothes he might wear to call on the governor would not answer in a place like this.

Finally the man nodded to the other seat. Marlowe put his mug on the table and sat.

"Name's Marlowe. Thomas Marlowe."

The man nodded.

"I'm shipping a crew. Tobacco to London. You've the look of a seaman. Are you a'wanting a berth?"

The man looked up from the table, met Marlowe's eye, and then nodded, slowly. "Perhaps."

"Ship paid off? Sail without you?"

"No. I sailed in here as bosun on a merchantman bound out of Plymouth. But the master and I didn't see eye to eye, and now I'm on the beach."

"What was the matter?"

"The master was a horse's arse."

Marlowe nodded. This made things difficult. A judgment call. Perhaps the master *was* a horse's arse. Or perhaps this man was incompetent, a thief, a drunkard. But these were the risks one always took, hiring on a crew. Sailors were not tame men, not bookkeepers or dancing masters. They were the original troublemakers. It was little wonder that Jesus had picked mariners as his apostles when he wanted to stir things up.

"You shipped as bosun, eh? I've need of a bosun. Care to come aboard for the fitting out, see if you want to sail with us?"

"Tobacco to London? I guess I was keeping a weather eye out for something that was a bit more . . . lucrative."

"So am I. I had a thought to perhaps sail to Madagascar, after."

The man grinned. " 'Perhaps'? That don't sound too certain."

"It's not certain. It's the most I can promise."

What in hell am I saying? Marlowe thought. He was starting to bandy this Madagascar thing around like he had decided on it, which he had not, not at all. And even if he had, Bickerstaff and Elizabeth would never go along with it.

But he needed sailors, and they needed inducement, so there it was.

"All right," the man said at last. "I see something in you I like. I'll come aboard for the fitting out, and if we can stand each other, I'll sail as bosun with you." He grinned again. "Then we'll see what you decide."

His name was Honeyman. Duncan Honeyman, and he arrived aboard the *Elizabeth Galley* with three sailors in tow, men also looking for berths.

"Friends of yours, Honeyman?"

"Shipmates. They thought the master of our old ship was a horse's arse, too."

Marlowe nodded, looked the men over. They were a rough-looking bunch. Gold earrings; big knives worn with ease in the small of their backs; arms like gnarled tree limbs; long hair, clubbed like Honeyman wore it; wide slop trousers, patched and tar-stained. They each chewed absently on the tobacco in their cheeks. They smelled of rum and sweat. But he had seen worse, and shipped with much worse.

"Very well," Marlowe said. "I'll offer you the same terms I offered Honeyman. I'll hire you for the fitting out, seaman's wages, and if you work out, you can stay on for the voyage. Tobacco to London and back with cargo, that's all I can promise. And I'll thank you to not say more, regarding any other venture we might try."

The three men exchanged glances but made no protest. At last they all muttered their agreement.

Honeyman ran his eyes along the deck and up the lower masts. He squinted slightly, but beside that his face showed no expression. "This the crew?" he asked.

"Yes."

"They sailors?"

"Not yet. But they'll do a hard day's work. And they'll learn. Do you have a problem with that?"

"Not if you don't."

"Good. Take these men and report to Mr. Dinwiddie, on the quarterdeck there. With the black coat. He's first officer. He'll set you to work."

Honeyman nodded, and without another word he led the three men across the brow and aft. Five minutes later they were aloft, seeing the main topmast set in place, the standing rigging ganged over the masthead and set up.

For three weeks the *Elizabeth Galley's* rig rose higher as masts were stepped, yards crossed, running rigging rove through blocks and belayed at the pin rails. At the same time her hull sank deeper and deeper in the river as stores of water and food came aboard, and after that barrel after barrel of tobacco, all that Marlowe House had harvested that year and much of the harvest of the Marlowes' three closest neighbors as well.

Marlowe continued his recruitment, picking up another five able-bodied seamen, and saw to the outfitting of the great cabin and the acquisition of those things they would need for navigation.

Bickerstaff took careful inventory of everything that went aboard. Dinwiddie saw to the stowage, and Honeyman, quiet and generally surly, proved at least to be a competent bosun and was left to supervise the setting up of the rig and bending of sail.

Elizabeth kept track of the money and fretted about their funds, which were being spent at a frightening rate on stores and gear and all those things that a ship consumed before she could put to sea.

Marlowe tried to assuage her fears. He did not succeed.

The night before they sailed, the night that Marlowe should have been resting after the unmitigated labor of getting the ship ready for sea in an absurdly short time, he found himself instead pushing a wheelbarrow across the dark lawn of Marlowe House. The wheelbarrow held a shovel and an unlit lantern. He had to wonder at himself.

Old habits died hard, his need for a secret held back. He thought of a trick he had used many times at sea, dragging a sea anchor behind his ship to slow it down, give an enemy or victim a false sense of his own ship's abilities. Then the sea anchor was cut away, and suddenly his ship could move with an unanticipated speed. This was like that. The little thing held in reserve.

He pushed the wheelbarrow onto a trail in the woods, and when he was lost from sight from Marlowe House, he pulled out his tinder pouch and lit the lantern. In the light of its feeble glow he made his way down the trail to the spot of dirt he had last turned six years before.

It was not easy to find—the weeds and the shoots of young trees had grown up around it and over it—but Marlowe had been careful over the years never to let it become lost completely in the bracken.

He set the lantern down, lifted the shovel, and jammed it into the dark earth. Five minutes of digging, and the spade hit the iron-bound box, hidden under a foot of dirt. He moved the lantern closer and worked the point of the shovel around until the box was fully exposed.

Why have I never told Elizabeth about this? Or Francis?

It was not a matter of trust. He trusted them both, completely, more than he had ever trusted anyone.

Perhaps that was it. He *had* never trusted anyone, until he had met them. Perhaps he could not get past that.

He breathed deep, readied himself, and then grasped the handle of the box and pulled. He thought at first it must still be caught on something. It would not move. He tried again, and this time it yielded, just a bit, and he realized that it was just heavy as hell, which he knew. Another deep breath, he braced himself and tugged, and the box came up from the dirt. He pulled it over the edge of the hole and rested it on the ground.

He stood up, flexed his back, gulped breath, cursed his creeping age. When he had recovered from the exertion, he knelt beside the box and held the lantern close.

It was wrapped in tar-soaked canvas, which was still intact. He pulled his sheath knife, cut away the canvas, and was pleased to see that the box was not rusted through. It looked pretty much as it had when he buried it in 1701.

He fished the key from his coat pocket and worked it into the lock, which sprang open after a moment's fiddling. Marlowe took it from the hasp and paused, looked around, listened. There was nothing but the sounds of the woods at night. He swung the lid open, held the lantern up.

The gold inside the box gleamed its lustrous metallic yellow, a great jumble of gold. A few bars, but coins mostly, Spanish escudos in various denominations, doubloons and ducats of Venetian and Spanish mintage. Their origins did not matter. It was all gold.

Marlowe sat for a long moment and looked at it. Here was his financial sea anchor, and he was about to cut it away. He had been tempted often enough to dig this up, during hard times in the past few years. Yet he had always resisted, and the need had passed.

But this was different. He was at the end now. This box was all the wealth he had left, and if he did not rebuild his fortune on this voyage, then he was finished.

He closed the box and locked it, then stood and braced himself. With painful effort he hefted it up onto the wheelbarrow. He grunted through clenched teeth, felt something pop in his arm, knew whatever it was would hurt like the devil in the morning.

But it was done. The gold was on the wheelbarrow, the last of his wealth unearthed and ready to be put to use. He set the lantern and shovel beside the box, took up the handles again, and made his way back down the trail to Marlowe House.

Chapter 3

ROGER PRESS sat back in the velvet wing chair and worked the silver toothpick around with his tongue. He liked the feel of the hard, smooth metal between his lips. The toothpick was almost a part of him now, a constant companion. He gave no thought to it as he worked it into his gums, probing them till they bled. He liked the coppery taste of the blood in his mouth.

In his hand he held a snifter of brandy. He pushed the toothpick to one side, tucked it in his cheek, and sipped the liquor. Magnificent. These rich bastards drank it like water. The brandy mixed with the blood in his mouth, swirled down his throat.

Tall and thin, but not handsomely so, with big hands and feet, joints like doorknobs, his face scarred from a childhood bout of the smallpox, his teeth growing black around the edges and often painful, Captain Roger Press was not a lovely man to look on. And so the other men in that richly appointed drawing room arranged themselves in their seats, busied themselves with some little thing, and avoided his eyes.

In the uncomfortable silence he glanced down at the snifter, the knife-edge rim, the seemingly impossible delicacy of the glass. He could crush it in his hand, make it explode into a thousand glittering fragments. The thin glass probably would not even cut through his callused palms.

That would surprise them.

"Captain Press . . ." The older one broke the silence. Sir Edmund Winston. He was the owner of the house in which they sat, a grand edifice that fronted on Pall Mall. It was one of a half dozen he owned, the house he used when he was in London for the season.

Sir Edmund blathered some nonsense about how grateful they were that he could come. Press worked the toothpick in his mouth and ran his eyes over the room. Rich velvet on the walls, portraits of brooding Winstons glaring down at this coarse intruder. A carpet laid over the polished oak floor, the kind that a younger, diffident Press might have been afraid to step on.

Ten o'clock in the evening. *Four bells in the night watch.* Outside it was black night, but the chandelier overhead held enough candles that the room was brightly lit.

More money in this one room than most men I know would see in a lifetime.

And he was the guest of honor.

"Captain Press," another of them was saying. Hobkins. This one was Hobkins. Owned a Jamaican sugar plantation, did a big business in slaves and silk from the Orient. Owned a dozen ships at least. Roger pulled his eyes from the silver arranged on the sideboard and met his eyes. The man was all silk and ruffles and chins.

"Captain, as you are no doubt aware, we here represent a good portion of the shipping between England and the Moorish countries. India, the Arabian lands, the Spice Islands. Thinking of getting into China trade. But that is not your concern, of course."

Press looked long and hard at him, but the man would not flinch. He was flabby, but he was not weak. Weak men did not become as powerful as Hobkins.

Still, Press could hear the note of discomfort in his voice. Roger Press was not a subtle man. He had not gained his place through intrigue and manipulation, as these men had. He had fought and killed his way up, used and discarded men, won his present notoriety by being meaner and bolder than most, and outlasting the rest. He exuded violence, and it frightened these civilized men.

"Of course," Press agreed.

"Our problem is this, and this is where you are concerned." Another, Robert Richmond, took up the discussion. "We are suffering the most egregious depredations in the Indian Ocean. These so-called privateers, these Roundsmen, hunting after the Moorish treasure ships. The current Great Mogul is a bloody-minded heathen named Aurangzeb. Thinks the company is in league with these pirates. Even imprisoned our manager and fifty of our men till he could be convinced otherwise."

"And it's not just the Moors these rogues hunt neither," Winston continued. "The villains are attacking our shipping. British East Indiamen. It's piracy, is what it is, and it must be stopped."

"Indeed." *Set a thief to catch a thief.* Press had been as much pirate as any of those in Madagascar, and these men knew it. He had been granted a letter of marque and reprisal at the outbreak of the present war, had fought a few hard actions as a privateer, taken a few valuable and legitimate prizes. Now he was a sought-after fighting man.

Well, he would take their money and let them kiss his arse, one and all.

"Navy's not worth a damn," Sir Edmund continued. "Too busy with the rutting French to bother with the pirates in Madagascar. What we need is to make a show in the Indian Ocean. A show for this nigger Aurangzeb and for the damned pirates, too. Show them all we will not tolerate this nonsense any longer."

"But I had thought the East India Company ships were armed like men-of-war," Press said, deigning to make his first comment. "Sure they should be enough to fight pirates or Moors?" It was a question, the answer to which he already knew. But he wanted to make them say it. It would further reinforce his own invaluable stature.

"The company ships are armed, to be sure. But they are too damned weak to do any good. A drain on resources, worse than useless. Can't find any active or intelligent men to command, can't find enough men to man them like a fighting ship."

What you mean, Press thought, *is that you will not pay for enough men to man them like a fighting ship.*

"And that, Captain, is where you come in," said Hobkins.

"More brandy with you, sir?" asked Sir Edmund.

"Yes."

Sir Edmund snapped his fingers. The attending servant filled Press's snifter and then the other men's.

"We are putting together our own expedition," Sir Edmund continued, getting to the heart of the thing. "Two ships. A decent-size man-of-war and a tender, also armed. The man-of-war is a frigate, sold out of the navy. We have named her the *Queen's Venture*. And we've secured a royal commission for the hunting of pirates. Gives quite a bit of latitude."

"We reckon it makes more sense for us all to pool our resources and put together an expedition that can genuinely be effective," Richmond added.

Press nodded, sipped brandy. *You bunch of tightfisted bloody buggerers,* he thought. *You could build a fucking armada, the money you got. One rotten old man-of-war and a tender! Cheap, bloody—*

"We think you are the man to lead this thing," Sir Edmund said. "No one expects you can entirely wipe out the villains in the Indian Ocean. But we want a lesson taught, do you see? Show 'em they ain't as safe as they reckon. Go after them on the high seas and in their so-called strongholds on the island of Madagascar."

"And St. Mary's," Press interjected. "Hotbed of piracy, St. Mary's. It cannot be ignored."

"Yes, yes, St. Mary's, of course. You'll receive the same pay as the captain of an East Indiaman, plus a double share of the prize money."

"Twenty-five percent of the prize money," Press said.

"Twenty-five . . . well, now . . ." Sir Edmund blustered, looking to his fellows for support.

You fat bastards, thought Press. *You want to drive the pirates out and get richer still on prize money and plunder. Playing both ends of it, and me in the middle to do the dirty business.*

"I don't see how we can . . ." Sir Edmund said, in a tone that would admit no argument.

"Twenty-five percent or I shall bid you good day." He took the silver toothpick between thumb and forefinger, stabbed it into his gum.

More muttering, soft consultation, and then Sir Edmund said, "Very well. Twenty-five percent."

Press smiled. "You see, gentlemen, it would seem I am a pirate still!"

That joke received only weak smiles, a few uneasy glances. These men, Press knew, did not care to traffic with the likes of him, even if he was now a wealthy and famous privateersman, his clothing almost as fine as theirs. He reckoned they would burn the chair he was sitting in once he left, and toss away the glass he had used.

They despised him, feared him. Five years ago they would have seen him hanged, if he had come before the judges they controlled. But now they needed him.

That did not bother Press in the least. Being despised was nothing new to him.

For that matter, he would have taken their damned two shares if they had been more insistent. He didn't care about that either. All that really mattered was that these stupid bastards were going to give him two powerful ships and a private army and governmental permission to rampage through the Indian Ocean.

They had specifically said that he was to go to St. Mary's. That was what mattered.

"So, Captain, you will accept this commission?"

"Yes, Sir Edmund, I do believe I will."

The *Elizabeth Galley* rolled along under a perfect sky, taking the six-teen knots of wind on the quarter and plowing an easy course through the blue, blue sea.

Their heading was a little south of east, their destination Bermuda. A lovely island. Thomas had persuaded Elizabeth that they should call there en route to London. The beauty of the place aside, they needed another six able-bodied seamen at least, if they were going to sail or fight their way unescorted through the cordon of pirates and French privateers that patrolled the approaches to the English Channel.

Newport or New York might have been better choices for that, but

Marlowe did not care to put in at those places. Too many faces from the sweet trade, he argued, wandering about those waterfronts. Too many ghosts.

The wind had not failed them, and the ship worked as if she had never been laid up. The young black men from Marlowe House had labored at setting up the masts and rigging—the very best possible training—and so terms such as "topsail weather brace" and "fore course clew garnets" were perfectly familiar to them by the time they were under way. Halfway to Bermuda, and they were well advanced in their new careers as sailors.

The lookouts aloft had sighted three sail in the course of the passage, each one a potential enemy, each a potentially grave threat to the unarmed ex-privateer, but they had left each of them below the horizon. The *Elizabeth Galley* was still a fast ship.

They raised Bermuda a fortnight after getting under way, and the following morning the *Elizabeth Galley* stood in past Spanish Point. The men crowded the rails, the officers and Elizabeth on the quarterdeck, as Bermuda's Great Sound opened up before them and they swung off to the east, threading their way into Hamilton Harbor.

One of Honeyman's sailors was in the chains with the lead, another up in the foretop scouting for coral. They were quiet men and somewhat surly, like Honeyman himself, but they were thoroughgoing sailors, and Marlowe had come to rely on them during the fitting out and the crossing to Bermuda.

"Have you been to Bermuda before, Mr. Dinwiddie?" Marlowe asked the first officer as the ship crept along under fore topsail alone.

"The one time, in '89. Lovely place. I've entertained thoughts often enough of settling here, get some little enterprise or other going."

They rounded up, and Marlowe gave Honeyman in the bow a wave, and Honeyman ordered the anchor let go. It plunged into the bright blue-green water of the harbor, and the *Elizabeth Galley* came to rest.

They fired a salute to the governor, Isaac Richier, whom Marlowe knew only by reputation. Dinwiddie sent hands aloft to stow sail. Marlowe sent his compliments to Richier, along with a letter of introduction from Governor Nicholson. The boat brought back an invitation to dinner.

"Mr. Dinwiddie, I do hope you will join us at the governor's dinner?" Marlowe said. It was an offhand remark, an invitation of no great importance as far as Marlowe was concerned, and so he was surprised to find Peleg somewhat flustered at the thought.

"Dinner, you say? At the governor's?"

"Yes . . ."

"Did he . . . Surely he didn't specifically ask that I should join you?"

"No, not by name. I fear your fame has not spread this far. But he says 'any of your officers whom you would please to bring,' and I would certainly please to bring you."

"Oh, well . . ." Peleg smiled, then frowned, and then without another word dove below.

An hour later he knocked on the great cabin door, where Elizabeth and Thomas had just finished dressing for dinner. He was red-faced and sweating under a battered wig, much in need of powder, that did not quite cover all the hair he had tried to stuff under it.

He wore a red wool coat that must have been packed away for special occasions—the creases still stood out boldly where it had been folded. His breeches were a bit tighter than one might wish, and his calves were enveloped in plain wool stockings. He wore his only pair of shoes, battered and misshapen. They had not been improved by his attempt to polish them.

"Good day, Captain. Mrs. Marlowe," he said, stiff and formal, which was not his way. "I hope my appearance will do the ship credit?"

Marlowe did not know what to say. Peleg was a fine officer, a good man, and Marlowe counted him a friend. He should have guessed that Peleg was just a simple sailor, uncomfortable with formal affairs, with little sense for how to handle them.

He shook his head. *Who have I become?* Ten years before he would not have been able to muster half the social grace that Peleg was displaying. He'd been a drinking, whoring, fighting pirate; the only intercourse the Marlowe of a decade before would have had with a governor would be to stand before him at the bar and plead not guilty.

And here he was, dressed out in a tailored silk coat and embroidered waistcoat, silk stockings, shoes like polished ebony with silver buckles, giving never a thought to dining with the royal governor of Bermuda.

He did not know what to say to Peleg Dinwiddie.

Elizabeth, fortunately, was the soul of tact. There was nothing she did not understand about putting a man at ease. She breezed across the cabin in a rustle of silk and taffeta, her long blond hair swept behind. In that rough male world of the ship, she was like a shaft of light breaking through a thick cover of clouds.

She took Peleg by the shoulders, looked him up and down, and said, "Peleg Dinwiddie! I would never have recognized you, and all this time me thinking you were just a plain old sailor man!"

Peleg beamed at the praise. Elizabeth could come across as sincere as an altar boy if she wished, and Peleg never even noticed the segue as she eased his coat off and said, "I do believe the steward has my iron still hot. Let him run it over your coat and freshen it up a tad. Thomas, do you not have another pair of silk stockings?"

Half an hour of Elizabeth's ministrations, during which she gently foisted on Peleg Thomas's stockings and extra shoes and convinced him that he could go wigless (he did not, she suggested, wish to appear more formal than his captain), and Peleg looked, if not good, at least not like a man who would be subject to ridicule.

Francis Bickerstaff joined them in the waist, dressed in his usual conservative manner. Marlowe saw his eyes sweep Dinwiddie head to foot, just a glance, and though his face did not change in the least, Marlowe knew that his friend had divined the entire story in that one look.

They took the longboat over to the landing, with Duncan Honeyman as coxswain. He brought the boat up to the low stone quay, and Marlowe stepped out and gave Elizabeth his hand, and after her came Bickerstaff and Dinwiddie.

Marlowe gave Honeyman instructions for when to return, along with a stern warning to keep the boat crew away from the taverns and the bumboat men who would sell them rum. All this Honeyman received with a nod of assurance and a desultory "Aye, sir."

A carriage from the governor met them on the quay and conveyed them through the narrow, cobbled streets, lined with two-story stucco homes, verandas looking down from overhead, bright flowers spilling from boxes. It felt more Spanish than English, and it was lovely.

They came at last to the governor's house on the top of a hill that afforded them a view of the town and Hamilton Harbor. They were greeted at the door by Governor Isaac Richier himself, portly and red-faced but effusive in his welcome. The letter of introduction from Governor Nicholson had put them in good stead.

Richier swept them into the mansion, pointed out this and that, summoned servants to bring drinks, food, chairs.

They dined for two hours, going from soup to brandy and pipes, at which point Elizabeth grudgingly retired with the governor's wife and left the men alone. It was an amiable gathering, an enjoyable meal, the conversation lively if not of great import.

Richier was a fine host, able to keep the talk flowing, with help from Marlowe, who had a sailor's knack for spinning a tale, and Bickerstaff, who, if not exactly loquacious, was at least conversant on a surprising number of subjects. Even Dinwiddie managed to participate, alternating between bouts of talkativeness and periods of silent concentration on his dinner.

It was nearly midnight when they departed. They stepped into the wide foyer of the governor's mansion, walking in a companionable group. As the carriage rumbled up just beyond the tall front doors, Marlowe said, "Governor, I wonder if I might trouble you for an audience tomorrow morning. There are sundry affairs I wish to discuss, regarding the *Elizabeth Galley*." He gave Richier a smile. "Too dull to bore the present company with."

"Of course, of course. I am always available to you," Richier said. "Shall we say ten?"

"Perhaps eleven would be better, if that is not inconvenient."

"Eleven it is, then."

The carriage brought them back through the now-dark streets, to the quay where the longboat was waiting, oars shipped, the boat crew talking softly.

Marlowe stepped aboard, looked with hawk eyes for any sign of drunkenness, sniffed for the smell of rum, but he could detect none. Honeyman apparently had been as good as his word. He had resisted the temptation of the nearby taverns and had made his men do the same. It was not a test many sailors would have passed.

They settled into the stern sheets, Honeyman gave a soft order, and the boat crew pulled for the *Elizabeth Galley*. It was quiet for a long moment, and then Peleg Dinwiddie, in a voice that sounded barely contained, said, "Damn me, but wasn't that one damned fine affair! Beg your pardon, Mrs. Marlowe."

After breakfast the following morning, and discussions with Dinwiddie and Honeyman concerning supplies that still needed procuring and the best tactics for finding the half dozen seamen they needed, the three men went ashore.

Dinwiddie went off to haggle with chandlers, the few in the small town of Hamilton. Honeyman did not say specifically where he was bound, but he was on the lookout for recruits, so Marlowe guessed it was taverns and whorehouses.

Marlowe himself headed for the governor's mansion.

He found the governor in his office, a tall room, whitewashed, with windows floor to ceiling that gave the occupant a grand view of the island that was his to administer. He stood and shook Marlowe's hand, and they made their greetings, Marlowe thanking him once more for dinner.

"Delighted to have you, delighted," the governor assured him, indicating a chair in front of the desk. Marlowe sat, and the governor sat as well.

"You mentioned 'sundry affairs' last night. Is there something your ship requires, something I might be of assistance in arranging?"

"Perhaps," Marlowe said. "As to stores and such, my first officer is seeing to that. But there is one thing that is more your domain . . ."

Marlowe leaned back, crossed his legs, assumed a casual air. He had planned this moment for weeks but still was not sure what he was doing, or why.

He had not lied to Elizabeth about wanting to show her the island, but that alone would not have been enough to justify calling there.

He had, in fact, lied to Peleg and Bickerstaff about not finding enough sailors in Norfolk. He had purposely held off buying sufficient cordage and salt beef for the voyage, claimed he could not find them in the colonies, that they would have to look in at Bermuda for them. All those lies, just to arrive at this moment.

What am I doing?

"We are taking tobacco to London, as you know. Arranged one of those permits to sail without convoy. But after that, I had a thought to not return to Virginia right off. I was thinking, what with the war, perhaps privateering might be the thing—"

"Oh, privateering, yes!" The governor threw up his hands. "Everyone wants to go privateering, think they'll make their fortune." He laid his hands palms down on his desk, looked Marlowe in the eye. "You are looking for a commission, I'll warrant. Certainly I have the authority to grant a commission, like any royal governor. And I daresay I wish I could.

"I perceive you are a gentleman, sir, and not of the same kidney as some of these other villains. They get a commission and then it is 'Steer for Madagascar!' and they are pirating any vessel crosses their path. No, my dear Marlowe, I fear that the government is quite fed up with privateers, and they would not look with favor upon my granting one more commission."

Coy bastard, Marlowe thought. He reached into his coat pocket, pulled out a leather purse that was heavy enough to serve as a formidable weapon. He held it up, just for a second, then let it fall on the governor's desk. It made a heavy *chink* sound as it hit, the unmistakable tone of gold coin upon gold coin.

"Of course," Thomas said, as if Richier had never spoken, "I understand that there are certain administrative costs involved in such a thing . . ."

For the next ten minutes they did not speak. Marlowe stared out one of the tall windows at the lovely harbor, the *Elizabeth Galley* like a toy far below, while Governor Richier wrote out the commission for privateering.

Chapter 4

IT TOOK them four weeks to raise England, once the *Elizabeth Galley* cleared out of Hamilton Harbor and Marlowe set her great sweeping northerly arc of a course to cross the Atlantic.

It was with some sadness that they left that beautiful island. Their stay had lasted five days, taking on stores and giving the hands a run ashore, enough time for them all to feel some attachment to the place. Thomas and Elizabeth were daily guests of the governor's, a skilled host, and Richier invited Bickerstaff and Dinwiddie on two other occasions.

Dinwiddie, of all of them, seemed most heartbroken to leave. For the five days that they had remained at anchor, his usual active, hardworking and hard-driving spirit abandoned him. He strolled the decks like a gentleman aboard his yacht, retold bits of his memories of dining with the governor, described the mansion to the sailors, recalled snippets of droll conversation. He left the bulk of the work to the stolid William Flanders, second officer, and Honeyman, the bosun.

Honeyman, for his part, did not seem to mind, did not seem to view Dinwiddie's strange behavior as any more of an imposition than he viewed most of life.

Duncan Honeyman was an odd one; Marlowe could not seem to peg him. He had all the attributes of a whiner, a malingerer, a sullen troublemaker, except that he worked like a horse and made all those in his charge do the same.

There was no genuine fault to be found in his performance as bosun.

Nor in his recruiting efforts. He went ashore and did not return for a day and a half, and Marlowe was ready to make his displeasure known, emphatically, when Honeyman appeared on the quay with five prime seamen in tow. Marlowe did not question his techniques after that.

Five days on that lovely island, and then they rigged the capstan and heaved the anchor up from the bottom and stood out into the open sea, hearts yearning for Bermuda, heads pounding from the excesses in which they had there indulged.

With each mile made good, Dinwiddie the governor's guest settled back into Dinwiddie the first officer, the man whom Marlowe had so actively recruited. A man whose conversation with the crew consisted not of descriptions of dinner but terse orders to haul the bloody mainsheet, you damned buggers, I'll thank you to mind your work, the mainsail looks like bloody washing hung out to dry.

Their first Sunday since leaving Bermuda, and Thomas Marlowe had the pleasure of watching his crew—a contented crew, a crew of tolerable size and expertise—sprawled out along the warm deck, taking their ease on their day off.

They were almost evenly divided between black men and white, odd proportions, even among the pirates. Marlowe kept a weather eye out, waited for a spark, an angry word, a shove, waited for someone to pull a knife, growl, "I'll show you, nigger, playing the man!"

But it didn't happen, because the one thing that was most offensive to a sailor, the one thing that overshadowed race or religion or political leanings, was a refusal to do one's share of work, and in that the black men could not be faulted. They worked hard and learned fast, and the more experienced white hands had no complaints.

Still . . . as Marlowe looked across the deck he saw a divided crew.

There was no animosity that he could see, no forced racial divides, but all the black men were clustered together to larboard, near the bow, and the white men, off watch, were sitting amidships. When the trouble came, in whatever form it would, they would have to act as one clan. They would have to be the Elizabeth Galleys, not white men and black.

The next day he surprised them all. "Mr. Dinwiddie," he called the mate aft, "some of the men, I perceive, are still in their shore clothes, and that won't do. I think today we will have a 'make and mend' day."

The "some" whom he meant were the black men; the white hands were all sailors and had come aboard in their wide slop trousers and work shirts, sheath knives and neckerchiefs. The black men still wore the clothes in which they had labored in the fields at Marlowe House.

"Make and mend, aye, sir, and they'll be glad of it." A make and mend day was almost as much a holiday as was a Sunday.

"Issue out cloth and needles and thread to those that need it. Have the hands that know how to run up clothes help their watchmates who don't."

"Make and mend?" Francis Bickerstaff asked an hour later as he stepped onto the quarterdeck and joined Marlowe in observing the work going on forward. All over the deck men were paired up, the sailors helping the new men make their wide-legged slops, their work shirts cut in the seaman's way.

Marlowe knew that the former field hands would not know how to sew clothes. The deep-water sailors, however, the men who sailed ocean voyages and were used to being long out of the company of women, all were adept at the necessary chores that landsmen left to wives and daughters. Now the white sailors were patiently instructing the young black men in the tailor's arts.

"Clothes make the man, Francis, be he a gentleman or a sailor man."

And while the clothes might not, in fact, make the man, they did much to help the men make themselves. The newly minted sailors laughed at their new rigs, pretended to be unimpressed with them, felt a certain degree of embarrassment in wearing them, like they were dressing up in costumes. Hesiod, on the foredeck, his black skin sharp against his new white clothes, doing a wild parody of a sailor's hornpipe to the delight of the other black men.

But that embarrassment faded with just a few days, and soon Marlowe could see them strutting the deck with the air of old salts. Neckerchiefs appeared around their necks, sheath knives worn with casual grace behind.

By the end of the week Marlowe noticed that the men were starting to congregate more by watch than by race. They were becoming a crew now, a single unit that would work to his command.

And all for the price of a little cloth and thread.

For four weeks they plowed the North Atlantic, with never a sail sighted and nothing worse than two days of fierce rain and an uncomfortable, lumpy sea to slow their progress. The *Elizabeth Galley* reeled off an easy six and seven knots, running her easting down.

Four weeks, and Francis Bickerstaff, who had developed considerable skill in celestial navigation, worked out an evening sight and announced that, if the wind held, they would raise the Lizard the following day.

Halfway through the next day's dinner, the masthead lookout called down that he had sighted land, fine on the larboard bow. By nightfall the Lizard, the headland that formed the southwesternmost point of England, that familiar landfall to sailors inbound and outbound from the southern coast, was plainly seen from the deck.

They were in among shipping now, all manner of vessels from coasters and fishing vessels to deep-sea merchantmen, Indiamen, and men-of-war. It took them four days to skirt the coast, run through the Strait of Dover, and weather Foreness Point, where they turned west and worked their way toward the wide mouth of the Thames River.

Marlowe stood on the quarterdeck with Elizabeth at his side and pointed out the various landmarks as they passed, related tales of his life at sea as one or another place sparked a memory. He had spent enough time in those waters to be familiar with them, but not intimately so. He did not know the Thames the way he knew Jamaica or New Providence or Tortuga. It was on the Thames, however, that he had done his legitimate seafaring, and the stories were ones that he could tell without embarrassment.

"Here is Gravesend," he said, pointing over the larboard rail. "That is where I was born."

Elizabeth looked at the small cluster of buildings huddled on the grimy shore, then turned and put her arm around her husband. "I did not know that," she said softly. "How could I have not known that?"

"I am not much given to discussing it."

"So much of your life, a whole world before we met."

Marlowe pulled her closer. "My life began when we met. Everything that went before was prologue, useless stuff."

His words were not idle flattery, and Elizabeth knew it.

They anchored with the turning of the tide and twelve hours later were off again, working their way up the river, which grew narrower, more crowded, filthier with each mile made good.

For Thomas and Elizabeth and Francis it was the oddest sensation, watching that familiar shoreline slip by with London springing up around them.

They each had spent considerable time in that city, long before the odd quirks of fate had thrown them together. They all had their own memories, their own feelings that were evoked by seeing ancient, stolid London again. They were familiar with each other, they were familiar with the city, but somehow the two did not fit with one another, like two separate lives pushed together.

"How very foreign it seems," Elizabeth said in a whisper. "I have become a country girl, I reckon. I cannot fathom why anyone would ever live in such a place."

She smiled. "In faith, I thought the same thing the first time I saw the wild places in Virginia, six weeks after sailing down this very river."

They came at last to the heart of London, as far upriver as they could go, where the shipping seemed to accumulate against London Bridge, like detritus caught on a dam. Ships were tied up four and five deep along the docks, a towering jumble of masts, and moored in every open spot of water, leaving only enough room for more ships to work through the narrow channel in center stream. And weaving their way between them, like bustling servants, was a vast fleet of smaller boats under sail or pulled by oars.

As huge as the Thames was, it seemed less impressive now to people who lived alongside the great rivers that cut through Virginia—the James and the York and the Rappahannock—and it seemed that not one more ship could be wedged into that place.

They managed to find room enough to drop anchor, with two cables bent and the second bower ready to go down to moor the *Elizabeth Galley* and hold her in place in either a flood or ebb tide.

There was a wild rush of activity as the ship was made fast and sails stowed and hatches broken open, and then it was quiet, and Elizabeth and Thomas were able to survey the city from their familiar place on the deck.

Dark and filthy, loud, gritty. Once-familiar smells of sewage and smoke and cooking and blacksmithing and horses and fetid water swirled around them in a now-alien cloud. The excitement their younger selves had once felt when in the midst of all that rush of activity ashore was gone, and now they wanted only to finish their business and sail away again.

Honeyman and Dinwiddie went ashore and arranged a lighter, while Flanders began to break bulk. The next morning the lighter—a wide, flat-bottomed barge, propelled by long sweeps—came alongside, and the Elizabeth Galleys fell to with yard and stay tackles. They hauled and swayed and eased away handsomely, and one by one the casks of tobacco, which had last seen daylight in Virginia, over two thousand miles away, emerged from the gloomy hold and swung over the rail and disappeared into the lighter's guts.

It took the better part of the day to transfer the tobacco from the *Galley* to the boat. As that work proceeded, Elizabeth went over the accounts, the bills of lading, the inventory of their and their neighbors' tobacco.

"Now, recall, there is nothing illegal about our landing this tobacco," Marlowe lectured. "Permits for sailing unescorted are none of this fellow's business, and don't let him tell you otherwise. We are a month at least ahead of the convoy. Our cargo should fetch twice what it did last season. And none of his letters of credit either. Ready money. He'll have it on hand. Settle for no less."

Elizabeth slammed her account book shut, looked up at Thomas with her exasperation showing plain. "Damn it, Thomas, if you are so sure I will make a hash of it, then go see the goddamned merchant yourself!"

"Me? What an idea! Elizabeth, I have told you time enough that I cannot show my face around the waterfront, not in London, for the love of God! It is exactly where I would expect to see a familiar face. Would you have me hanged for piracy?"

"If you do not shut up, I shall hang you myself."

Before he could reply, there was a polite knock on the great cabin door, and Peleg Dinwiddie announced that the lighter was preparing to leave. It was early evening, and a mist was beginning to settle over the river, leaving the far bank obscured in shades of brown and gray.

Elizabeth draped her wool cloak over her shoulders, collected up her account books, and followed Dinwiddie topside, with Marlowe trailing behind. The decks were dark and wet with the falling mist as the three of them crossed to the gangway.

It had been explained to Dinwiddie and Flanders and Honeyman, and word had filtered down to the men, that Marlowe was wanted for piracy. Marlowe told them how he had foolishly become involved in a Red Sea scheme sponsored by powerful men within the government. How, when it all fell apart, the government men tried to put the blame on him, accused him of turning pirate, to save themselves.

It was all a fiction, of course, but believable enough, with shades of the fate that had befallen Captain William Kidd. Dinwiddie and Flanders seemed to accept the story, shocked at such perfidy, but without question. Honeyman nodded, shrugged, as if he needed no explanation and did not care why his captain could not go ashore.

Marlowe paused at the gangway, put his hands on Elizabeth's shoulders. "You will do brilliantly, I would never doubt it," he said and kissed her, then handed her down to Dinwiddie, who was already on the lighter's deck.

He watched the lighter's hands cast off fore and aft, watched the

gentle breeze lift the barge from the *Elizabeth Galley*'s side, and he felt
a deep shame that he should cower thus while his wife went ashore to
do his office, a profound regret that he had lived his life in such a way
that now he could not show his face on London's waterfront.

It was almost full dark, an hour and a half later, when a hired boat
returned with Elizabeth and Peleg. Marlowe waited at the gangway,
eager to hear of Elizabeth's triumph. But as she climbed up the boarding steps, scowling, her eyebrows held in that attitude of fury that he
knew all too well, he realized he would be hearing something quite
different.

"Whatever happened?" he asked, even as he held out his hand to
help her through the opening in the bulwark.

"That bastard will not allow me to close the deal," she said. "Bloody
stupid man. He says that since the cargo was consigned to you, you
must be the one to sign the bills of sale."

"But I consigned the cargo to you. You are my representative." This
made no sense.

"For the tobacco you own, yes. That was not the problem. It is the
crop that our neighbors consigned to us. Apparently you cannot transfer the consignment for that, since it is not your property. Bloody stupid—"

"Did you manage to strike a good deal in any event?" Marlowe was
looking for some bright spot while he searched for a way out of this.

"Yes, yes, fine . . ." Elizabeth said, but Peleg stepped through the
gangway next and said, "Ah, she was bloody brilliant, Captain! I've
never seen the like, not in all my years as a merchant seaman! Had the
rutting bastard all twisted around, got half again as much per pound as
we done on our best year before the war!" He was beaming, the admiration in his face genuine.

"What good it might do, I do not know. We cannot sell the tobacco
that is not ours, and it will be ruined if we try to bring it back to Virginia. We shall make a profit ourselves and ruin our neighbors. They
will of course demand indemnity. No, it won't do. Thomas, I am at a
loss."

"Oh, for the love of God," Marlowe said. All this because he was too craven to row two hundred yards to the shore and walk another hundred to a warehouse to sign some papers? It was absurd. "I shall just go ashore and sign the damned papers and be done with it."

Elizabeth looked up, surprised and afraid. "No, Thomas, that is not possible. You cannot do that."

Dinwiddie nodded his head. The concern on his face made him look like a big dog, of the jowly, drooling variety.

"Of course I can. This is nonsense, this crawling around like some frightened thing. It is night, there is a fog, I shall speak only to those to whom I must, sign the rutting papers, and be gone. There is never a thing to fear. Mr. Dinwiddie, pray see the gig cleared away and a boat crew told off."

"Aye, sir," Dinwiddie said grudgingly, and he lumbered off to see it done. Marlowe met Elizabeth's eyes, held them, and heard all the arguments forming in her head.

"It will be all right, my dearest," he said softly, heading the arguments off. "And we have no choice in the matter."

Marlowe went below for his coat, hat, and sword. When he returned to the deck five minutes later, the gig was floating at the bottom of the boarding steps, four men at the oars and Honeyman at the tiller. Marlowe noticed they were armed, with pistols hidden under jackets and cutlasses wrapped in canvas in the bottom of the boat. Mr. Dinwiddie's caution and efficiency.

Marlowe went down first, then Elizabeth climbed down after him, and he helped her make the difficult step into the boat while Honeyman and the crew looked discreetly away. When they were settled in the stern sheets, the bowman shoved off and the boat pulled slowly through the crowd of shipping.

"See here." Marlowe nodded to the ship under whose high stern they were passing, drawing Honeyman's attention to her. "What do you reckon she's about?"

Honeyman looked up, cast a critical and professional eye over the vessel. "*Queen's Venture* . . ." He read the gilded letters under the big stern windows. "A frigate. Older frigate, but she's flying East Indiaman's colors. Looks to be fitting out for some cruise or other."

She did that. She had about her the look of a ship readying for sea, not the worn look of a vessel just in. Her decks sported the telltale clutter of stowing down. But for all that, she looked formidable enough, her long row of shut gunports promising significant firepower behind.

"Humph," Marlowe said, and nothing more. She was a curiosity, but she was not his affair.

They pulled up at last to the slick, wet granite steps that emerged from the water and led through a break in the stone seawall up to the cobbled road that ran along the river. Again Marlowe stepped out first and offered his hand to Elizabeth. They climbed the steps together, and Marlowe said, "You must show me the way, dear, you being so familiar with these streets."

They reached the road, paused as Elizabeth got her bearings, and then a voice—gruff, slurred—asked, "Got bags, guv'nor, which I can carry for you?"

Marlowe turned without thinking, said, "No, my man, we are just—"

Eyes met, Marlowe's and the old man's. A wrinkled, leathered face, a smooth gash of a scar across his cheek. The man was a sailor, or had been. They paused, and something passed between them.

It was not recognition, not on Marlowe's part, just some vague familiarity. In the dim light of the sundry lanterns that lit the waterfront, in the mist turning rapidly to fog, they held one another's eyes for a second, less than a second. Then Marlowe turned fast, took Elizabeth's arm, hurried off down the road.

It is not bloody possible, he thought. *The first bloody face I see?*

It was nothing, it was his imagination, he assured himself. All these old broken sailors, they all looked alike. He had known a dozen men who looked just like that old beggar.

But those eyes, that scar. He tried to take twenty years off the face, place it where he might have seen it last.

It was not possible he could have been recognized, not by the first man he met! He hurried Elizabeth along the cobbled road until she had to ask him to slow down, ask what was the matter.

"It is nothing, dear, not a thing. Just anxious to be done with this, I reckon. And afraid the merchant's office will be closed. Do you know when they close?"

"Nine o'clock. We have an hour or better," Elizabeth said.

Marlowe glanced back over his shoulder but saw only darkness there and mist and the odd halos of lanterns glowing in the fog.

They came at last to the merchant's office, set in the front of a vast warehouse. In the common area were stationed tall desks for the harried bookkeepers and behind them a few walled-off offices for those of greater importance.

They stepped through the door, into the din, lit with the pools of light spilling from various candles and lanterns, messengers and stevedores and scriveners hurrying about, great stacks of casks and unidentifiable bundles lurking in the shadows in the back of the big building.

A clerk met them at the door. Both he and his clothing had a wilted, resigned quality. "May I help you?" he asked, and then, "Ah, Mrs. Marlowe, of course. And this would be . . ."

"Captain Marlowe," Elizabeth said curtly. "He has come to sign the bills of sale, and he does not care to waste another moment with this nonsense."

"Of course, of course," said the clerk, running his eyes over Marlowe, seeming to try to gauge how far this fellow could be pushed. "Let me inform Mr. Dickerson that you are here, sir."

The clerk disappeared into one of the offices and a moment later was back, saying, "Mr. Dickerson instructs I tell you he is grateful you could come in person, and he will attend to you the very instant he is done with the business he is on."

"Very well," said Marlowe in a tone that conveyed his feeling that this was not very well at all. He loosened his cloak, crossed his arms, gave Elizabeth an arched eyebrow, and silently they waited.

Five minutes, ten minutes, and never a sign of Dickerson.

"That son of a bitch," Elizabeth whispered. "He is doing this because he is angry about the deal I struck, I know it. I think he reckoned on getting some great bargain when you would not show up."

"If he does not see us now, then he shall get more than a bargain.

I'll cut his damned throat in another minute," Marlowe muttered. He was worried and angry and anxious to be gone, all at once.

And then the door opened, and the clatter of the streets drowned out the muted noise of the office. Marlowe turned, and there, filling the door, was Roger Press.

He stepped through, and behind him came two other men, big, rough-looking men, hands resting on cutlass pommels, but Marlowe had no eyes for them.

He looked only at Press, who stood in a relaxed attitude, arms folded, shifted his silver toothpick with his tongue, and looked back at him.

Tall, gangly, pockmarked and, to Marlowe, inexplicably still alive, Roger Press. And all that Marlowe could think was *It is not bloody possible*.

Chapter 5

THEY STOOD there, said nothing. Here it was again—that face, this background. The two did not seem to go together. Half a minute passed.

Finally Press broke the silence, saying, "Surprised to see me, I'll warrant. Fear not, I am no ghost." Then he smiled, and the toothpick waggled obscenely. "But perhaps it would be better for you if I was a ghost, eh, Barrett? What say you?"

Barrett. Even that name did not fit. Malachias Barrett, that was the name by which Roger Press knew him. His real name, before he re-made himself into Thomas Marlowe, gentleman planter.

"I'm surprised to see you alive," Marlowe said, finding his voice at last. "Now I shall have to kill you again."

Press's smile turned to a smirk. "Again? You did not kill me the first time. Nor all the others that have tried. It don't appear I can be killed."

That voice! Just the sound of it and Marlowe went reeling back seventeen years, across the Atlantic, across the Spanish Main. He felt suddenly a bit unsteady.

He saw himself once again leading a band of thirty ragged buccaneers up the narrow, cobbled streets of Nombre de Dios.

He could see the pistol in his left hand, the sword in his right, the same sword that now hung from his belt. Another brace of pistols hanging from a ribbon around his neck, slapping against his chest as he ran, his clubbed hair thumping against his back. A red sash around his waist, patched slop trousers.

Up the narrow street, walled in by two- and three-story stucco buildings, bright shutters slammed tight against the marauders. Nombre de Dios — it was not the orgy of gold and silver that it had been in Drake's time, but it was wealthy enough still to make it worth attacking and weak enough that it might fall to the sixty or so men who came from the sea to plunder the place.

Came in before dawn in longboats from the pirate ship *Fury*. Malachias Barrett, quartermaster. Roger Press, captain.

The buccaneers were shouting, firing their pistols, racing to the citadel that dominated the center of the Spanish colonial town. Faces peered from windows and quickly withdrew. Civilians with sword or pistol appeared before them, ready to defend their city, and fled or were cut down by the pirate juggernaut.

Attack the citadel, draw out the few soldiers that were there, engage them in a desperate fight, and then Roger Press at the head of the other thirty would appear from the west, plunge into the brawl, and together they would overwhelm the Spaniards. That was the plan: simple, easily accomplished, no great risk, and when they were done, Nombre de Dios would be theirs to sack at leisure.

The road ran like the spoke of a wheel to a wide central hub, in the middle of which loomed the great citadel that protected the town. Marlowe — Malachias Barrett — stopped short, and behind him his band did likewise.

The sweat soaked through his loose shirt, and he could feel the warm cobblestones through the thick, callused soles of his bare feet. He caught his breath, readjusted his sweating grip on the sword as the big doors of the citadel burst open and the soldiers with gleaming helmets and breastplates and swords and muskets charged out.

"Steady, lads, they're coming right to us!" Marlowe shouted, and from behind him came grunts, howls, jeers, curses. These men were *les boucaniers*, the Brethren of the Coast, and they were not afraid of two dozen Spaniards or ten dozen. They saw those men only as an obstacle between themselves and the riches of Nombre de Dios, the pleasure of sacking a town, and they wanted to be at them.

And Captain Press would be there at any moment, hitting the Spaniards on their flank.

An order shouted out in rapid Spanish, and the soldiers shouldered muskets. Marlowe raised his pistol, leveled it at the officer's face, twenty feet away, pulled the trigger, and saw the man's helmet plucked from his head, heard the ringing of the metal, just as the soldiers opened up with a rippling volley.

Bullets flying past, screams from behind, and then with a shout Marlowe led his men forward, wild buccaneers crashing into the Spaniards, pikes and swords flashing, pistols cracking back and forth, battle cries in Spanish and the polyglot voices of the pirates, English and French and Dutch. The noise echoed off the close buildings, seemed twice as loud.

It was a desperate fight, the Spaniards taking heart from the small number of attackers, not knowing, as Marlowe did, that Roger Press would be there soon. Men fell—Spanish, pirates—blood ran between the cobblestones as both sides fought on, neither yielding, neither advancing.

Ten minutes of that—it seemed like hours—and Marlowe began to wonder where Press was. They had landed at the same time, set off on their different routes at the same time—he should be there.

Marlowe had an indefinable sense of his men falling back, a step, another, and the Spaniards were pushing forward.

Press, goddamn your eyes, now, now!

It was not possible that the Spanish would repel them, but they were outnumbered and . . . Where was Press?

Another step back, yielding ground now to the Spaniards, who were fighting with a ferocity that Marlowe would not have expected from them. He saw one of his men go down, a Frenchman named Jean-Claude, and a big Spanish sword finished him, nearly severed his head.

"Steady, steady!" Marlowe shouted, loud as he could. He was gasping for breath, his sword beating back two and three men at a time, and he was stepping back as well. He could feel the men's resolve wavering, their fighting madness a fog burning away.

And then they were running, fleeing down the street up which they had come, and behind them the jeers of the Spanish soldiers, the most humiliating sound that Marlowe had ever heard before or since.

Down to the landing, the fifteen men who had lived through that vicious fight, panting, limping, bleeding. Humiliated and defeated.

And there was Roger Press and the thirty men who were to have hit the Spanish flank. They had found the government countinghouse, overwhelmed the guard, carted off quantities of gold and silver. They were just loading it in the boats as Marlowe's men were falling under the Spaniards' swords.

Harsh words passed between the two groups of men, weapons were brandished. After a moment of shouting it became clear that Press had lied to his men, led them to believe that the plan had been changed at the last moment, that they were not to support Marlowe's men at all.

Clear out the countinghouse and make for the ships. Let the Spaniards take care of Marlowe and the rest. Halve the number of men with whom the booty would be shared. That was Press's intention. It had almost worked.

Marlowe blinked hard, brought himself back to the warehouse, the cool, foggy night on the London waterfront. Out of the corner of his eye he saw Mr. Dickerson peer out of his office, assess the situation, then disappear again, like a weasel down its hole.

"The last time I saw you," Marlowe said, "we had marooned you for cowardice and for betraying us all at Nombre de Dios. I am sorry to see you did not die on that spit of sand. We left you with a bottle of water and a loaded pistol, as I recall. I am sorry you did not see fit to use the pistol to do the honorable thing."

Press just smirked, shifted the toothpick—*that damned toothpick!*—back and forth. He had the advantage now: two men at his back and Marlowe by himself. No need for fast talk this time, for arguments, denials, such as he had made when his own men had put him on trial.

He had tried to make it all sound reasonable, an innocent mistake.

It had not worked. The men of the *Fury* had pronounced him guilty of cowardice and theft from his shipmates, the two most heinous crimes in the pirates' code. Marooning, that had been the vote. It was the way with the Brethren of the Coast.

"No, Barrett, I did not use that bullet on myself. I waited. For eight days I roasted and starved and went near mad with thirst. I was ready to blow my brains out. Would have the next day, I have no doubt. But before I did, a ship came by and took me off."

Marlowe sighed. "Very well, Press, let us be done with this. I shall fall on my sword if I have to look at your damned smirking face a moment more. Cold steel? Pistols? Or will you have these apes murder me while you stand safely by? That would be more your manner of doing things, would it not?"

Press frowned, as if he did not understand. He took the toothpick from his mouth, held it like a conductor holding a baton. "Murder you? Cold steel? Really . . ."

"You will not go to the authorities, methinks. You would not care to hang at my side."

"Ah, but, my dear Barrett, you see, I *am* the authorities now! I have a commission from the queen herself to hunt down pirates and bring them to justice. And I do believe I have caught my very first one. Gentlemen"—he turned to the men behind him, who looked very much like pirates in their own right—"pray remove Master Barrett's sword. He and this lovely doxy will come with us."

Marlowe did not resist as one of the men unbuckled his sword and handed it to Press. He doubted very much that Press was in the employ of the queen—the days of Francis Drake and even Henry Morgan were over—but it made little difference. Press was armed, and his two henchmen were armed, and so they could do pretty much as they pleased.

There might yet be an opportunity to escape, Marlowe understood, but this was not it.

"This . . . doxy . . . is a stranger to me. She has naught to do with this."

"Oh, indeed? But I don't believe you. In any event, we will straighten that out later." Press tucked Marlowe's sword under his arm, opened the door. He jerked his head toward the man with the ill-concealed pistol. The man pushed past Marlowe and disappeared into the street.

Very professional, Marlowe thought. No chance of fleeing that way. These villains knew their business.

"Pray, come along," Press said politely.

Marlowe glanced at Elizabeth. Her lips were set, eyebrows together. He could see the fury held in check, the effort it was taking for her to remain silent. He could see her looking sharply around, looking for their chance, the opening to exploit, just as he was doing.

He gave her the slightest of nods, and she nodded back, stepped forward, through the door that Press held open. Marlowe followed and, behind them, Press and the second guard.

It was dark, and the fog had settled down on London like a thick wool blanket draped over a sleeping form. Twenty feet in any direction the wet streets and buildings disappeared in the haze. Here and there glowing ghosts of light showed where a lantern was lit against the gloom. The air was damp and pungent.

Marlowe paused, looked around—for what, he did not know. Something. Then Press gave him a push from behind, said, "Start walking. To your right. And none of your nonsense, or I shall shoot you before you are two steps gone. And I shall shoot this little bunter first. Or save her for my men."

Marlowe gritted his teeth, began to walk. Press had a knack for finding the fissure and sticking the knife in, an ability to divine the most offensive statement and then give it voice. It was no wonder that others besides Marlowe had tried to kill him.

Marlowe guessed he himself would try again, and soon.

They stepped off into the dark and fog, the one guard leading the way, then Marlowe and Elizabeth side by side, then Press and the second guard.

This is it, Marlowe thought. There would not be a better chance at escape than now, on that open road, with the *Elizabeth Galley's* boat just one hundred yards away. Three against one and he with never a weapon, but this was the main chance.

With each step Marlowe inched closer to the seawall that formed the left side of the street, a low stone wall, and beyond that a straight drop to the Thames below. He could hear the water washing against the ancient rock, but he could not see it in the fog.

Over his shoulder Press called to the guard leading the way, "Hanson, damn you, man, we have walked clean past Dock Street!"

Hanson turned, and Marlowe stumbled against a raised cobblestone, cursed, tried to regain his balance.

"Watch him!" Press shouted, saw the fake, took two quick steps forward. "Shoot him if he—"

Marlowe straightened, wheeled about, grabbed Press by the lapels of his coat, and twisted him around, nearly jerking him from his feet, slamming him into Hanson, who was pulling his gun and rushing back to grab the prisoner.

Press grunted with the impact, and Hanson staggered. Marlowe's muscles screamed in pain—Press was a strong man, and heavy. The surprise worked for a second, no more, and then Press was fighting back.

Too close to draw a weapon, Press lashed out with his long arms, wrapped powerful fingers around Marlowe's throat. Marlowe heard his sword drop from under Press's arm, clatter on the road, heard Hanson cock his pistol, heard sharp footfalls behind as the second guard rushed up.

Press's fingers were digging into Marlowe's throat, crushing his windpipe, choking the life from him, but at least he was blocking Hanson's shot.

He heard a gasp behind, and the footsteps stopped, and then a thud like a sack of flour hitting the road, and he guessed that Elizabeth had tripped up the running man.

Marlowe twisted, pushed away from Press until he was able to drive a fist up between Press's arms and into his jaw—one powerful jab, then another—and another and then he felt Press's grip weaken.

Both arms up between Press's forearms, a jerk outward, and Press's hold was broken. Marlowe could see that the big man was dazed by the blows. He grabbed Press's lapels again, twisted him around. Press's legs hit the low wall, which would have prevented a smaller man from falling but only served to trip Press up. One shove and he was over, falling in a flurry of coattails and gangly legs and arms.

Marlowe leaped to the street, heard Press hit the water as Hanson's pistol discharged, the flash bright in the fog, the bullet whizzing over-head. He snatched up his sword and tried to recall if Press could swim. A flick of the wrist and the scabbard flew off, and he drove the blade into Hanson's stomach as the man descended on him.

"Elizabeth! Get to the boat! Go! Go! Tell Dinwiddie to get ready to slip the cable!" he shouted even as he stood and pushed the sword deeper, then pulled it free and turned to face the next man.

He saw Elizabeth hesitate, one beat, two beats, unwilling to leave Marlowe behind. Ten feet away the second man. He had regained his feet after Elizabeth tripped him, sword drawn, hanging back. From the fog came more footfalls, and two more men resolved from the mist and took their place alongside the second man.

Damn him! Marlowe thought. Press had his guards, and he had two more trailing behind.

"Go!" he shouted again, and this time Elizabeth turned and fled down the road.

Three against one again. Marlowe faced them, sword drawn. The second guard pointed toward Elizabeth, running away down the street, shouted, "Stop that bitch!" and one of the new men charged after her as the other pulled a pistol from his belt.

Then everyone was moving at once. Marlowe took two big steps and flung himself at Elizabeth's pursuer as he raced past. He was in midair when the pistol went off, and he felt the bullet rip through the flesh of his upper arm, and then he and the man were rolling on the street, the impact with the cobblestones thankfully dampened by the man's body.

But that did nothing to ameliorate the agony in his arm. He shouted with the pain, rolled over, kicked his way to his feet, untwisting him-self from his cape just as the others were on him. He met the sword coming down at him with his own, held crosswise over his head, turned it aside and lunged, felt the tip bite flesh before his attacker could leap clear.

He heard a sharp yell but knew he had done no real damage. He managed to get his sword in place to beat off a lunge from the second man. He had purposely worn his big sword, his killing sword, not the ceremonial rapier, but that weapon was best wielded with two arms, and he was down to one.

Another lunge and he turned it aside, then whirled fast and kicked the man he had tackled hard in the head as he was pulling himself up from the road. Down again and Marlowe leaped away from a thrust he knew would come, turned to see the blade reaching into empty space, knocked it aside, stepped into the attacker, drove home another thrust.

He could beat one man that way, delivering a series of stab wounds that would wear him down, but not three. Three men would do that to him first, and he was already wounded worse than any of them.

He backed away, sword held ready, hilt at waist height, the tip wavering at the men's eyes like a snake. They had had enough of that blade that they would not attack headlong, but their advantage was too great for them to quit the fight.

Twenty feet . . . Marlowe thought. If he could put twenty feet between them, he could lose them in the fog. Hire a boat to bring him back to the *Galley*. But how could he win twenty feet?

And then more footfalls on the cobblestones, coming from the opposite direction, running hard, and all four men paused, listening.

Duncan Honeyman burst from the mist, two men of the boat crew behind him, and they fell on Marlowe's attackers like wolves, wet blades flashing in the muted light. Three strokes, four strokes, and it was over, the one called Hanson dead on the street, the others flinging away their weapons as they fled.

Honeyman pursued, no more than ten feet, until he was certain they were gone. Then he turned to Marlowe, and for a minute all that either man could do was gasp for breath.

When Marlowe could talk again, he said, "Elizabeth?"

Honeyman nodded and gasped, "Made it to the boat . . . told us what was acting . . . got here fast as we could . . ."

Marlowe nodded, too. "Fast enough . . ." he managed. He staggered over to the seawall, looked down at the river. Something was floating there, bobbing in the water ten feet from the stone wall. Marlowe stared at it for a moment before he recognized it. Press's hat.

Guess he couldn't swim, Marlowe thought. He pictured Roger Press sinking down into that black, filthy water, struggling to regain the surface, his long limbs thrashing out, finally gasping for breath, getting only a lungful of the Thames, and Marlowe felt not the slightest remorse.

"Bastard," he muttered. Turned to Honeyman. "Come, let's get us back to the *Galley*. Quickly."

Chapter 6

ROGER PRESS could not swim.

He felt himself go over the seawall, and he was gripped by panic, crushing panic, like being in the jaws of a beast. It seemed unreal, a horrible dream, as he plunged toward the water and then it was around him, covering him up, and even the dark, foggy night was gone, and it was all watery blackness.

He lashed out, flailed out with arms and legs, but the water kept him from moving fast, and that made him more panicked still. Then his fingertips hit something hard and smooth, the stones of the seawall, something concrete in that watery world. He clawed at them, but there was no hold to be had on the wet rock.

He clawed again, and this time his fingers found the gap between two stones, and he locked his fingertips in as best as he could, held that tiny ledge with his powerful hands and pulled himself up.

His head came out of the water, and he found he was pressed against the slime-covered wall. He reached out with his other hand, found another groove between two stones, and held on. It was the most precarious of handholds—he was supporting himself with his fingertips—but it was enough. His head was free of the water. He was breathing.

And now the river was his ally, because now it supported him. He would never have been able to hold on as he was were he hanging in air, but being more than half submerged gave him just enough help to maintain his grip.

For a long time he did not move, just clung to the rock, let the panic subside. Overhead, close overhead, he could hear the fight, heard Marlowe yelling, "Elizabeth! Get to the boat! Go! Go!"

"Doxy's a stranger to me . . ." Press's panic had cooled enough now that he ached to get into the fight. He looked up, craned his neck, hoping to see something of what was happening, but he was under some kind of overhang, the top of the seawall jutting out, a narrow cliff a foot above his head. He could see nothing but the underside of the wet rock.

He cocked his ear instead and listened. He could hear more men running, someone shouting. His reserves. They would do for that bastard.

I was always one step ahead of that stupid whoreson . . .

But then the reality of his situation came back. He was safe, but he could not stay where he was.

How the hell do I get out of this poxed river?

He would have to move, let go of his precious handhold, find another. The idea brought fresh panic. Every instinct told him to stay put, but reason told him that if he did, then eventually his grip would fail and he would sink into that black water.

The thought was enough to steel him for the next move. He grit his teeth, then carefully, carefully, let go with his right hand and, holding his weight with his left, ran his fingers along the wall until he found another fissure to which he could cling. He settled his grip as best he could, then shuffled himself along the seawall and held himself with his right hand as he found a new hold for his left.

Inch by inch, handhold by handhold, he moved along the wall. It was like a nightmare trap, the dark water just below his head, the overhang above. His fingers ached, the tips were bleeding, which only made his grip slicker and more difficult to maintain.

He realized that the fighting on the road had stopped, how long ago he could not recall. He had not heard what had happened, and at that moment he did not care.

Another inch and another. He lost his grip once and went under but managed to pull himself up again, held himself in place as he vomited from panic and from ingesting the filthy water.

He had no sense for how long it was that he crept like a lizard along the seawall. He was near exhaustion, near giving up, when the steps appeared out of the mist, just ten feet away. Ten feet. He had only to make that distance and he would not be swallowed up by the horrible, horrible river.

Inch by inch, and finally he could reach out with his long leg and touch the submerged stone, and a minute later he was lying on it. He gasped, sputtered, gagged, but it was air he was sucking into his lungs, not water. The filthy, stinking air of London. It was the sweetest smell he had ever enjoyed.

He lay on his back on the seawall steps, the Thames lapping around him, his face toward the sky, breathing, his fingers hanging limp, with no more possibility of being taken by the water.

After some time of that he began to shiver, and he knew he had to move. With a groan he pulled himself up to a sitting position, and then he stood. He ached all over from the effort and the tension of the past hour.

He had not thought that he could hate Malachias Barrett more than he had when he stood on that strip of sand seventeen years ago and watched the *Fury* sail away. A strip of sand that rose incongruously out of the ocean, one hundred feet around and barren, where he had been left to die.

Now it was twice that Barrett had bested him, humiliated him, nearly killed him. He hated him with twice the passion he had felt then. Incredible.

He staggered up the steps and through the gap in the stone wall and onto the street. It was quiet, deserted, no one moving at that time of night.

It was possible that Barrett was dead. Probable. It had been two against one, and because he, Press, was so much more clever than Barrett, there had been reserves as well. They should have done for him.

His tongue moved to work the toothpick in his lips, but of course it was not there anymore.

"Goddamn it," he muttered, then plunged his hand into his cold, wet coat pocket, hunted around through the sodden folds of cloth until he felt another. He pulled it out, thrust it into his mouth, worked it furiously with his tongue. The cool, hard metal tasted of Thames water. Press jerked it out, spit on the cobblestones, and then inserted the toothpick again.

He shuffled down the road, moving more quickly as the blood began to flow through his limbs once more. Perhaps he could find some evidence of what had happened while he was inching along the wall.

He could see something lying in the road, and as he approached, he saw it was a sword, discarded, and nearby another. He frowned, picked it up, moved on.

Through the dark and the mist he could see a shape now, and he had seen enough men lying wounded and dead to recognize one just by the dim outline. He stepped cautiously, knew the danger that a wounded man could present. He could feel his heart beating. There was every chance that this was Barrett lying dead. Or, better yet, wounded.

He stepped close, and the figure did not move, and Press could see no sign of life. He poked the man with the sword. Still nothing.

He put his foot against the man's shoulder and rolled him over. The man flopped onto his back, lifeless. Hanson.

"Son of a bitch, son of a bitch!" Press shrieked, stamping his foot in his fury, despite the pain. He hobbled off down the road, back the way he had led Barrett and his slut, back to the warehouse to which the old man had followed them.

Press had eyes all over the waterfront. All those old, broken sailors who loafed on the docks and crowded the streets of Rotherhithe. He paid them well for intelligence of note, and they kept him informed. What luck that one should have known Barrett from the old days at Port Royal.

Not so much luck, actually. The community of pirates was a small one. Like members of a tradesmen's guild, they all knew one another. And many of them were now rotting out their lives on the London waterfront.

He stepped up to the warehouse door. It was shut, but he could see lights behind the shades. Some greedy bastard up late counting his money. He pounded on the door with the pommel of his sword.

There was a shuffling of feet, and then it stopped, and then silence. Press pounded again. A voice, high-pitched with fear, called, "We are closed, sir! Pray come back on the morrow!"

"Queen's officer, please open the door!"

Another pause, then, "I am sorry, I cannot . . ."

Press paused, caught his breath, forced himself to speak calmly. "I am a queen's officer," he said in a more reasonable tone. "There was a disturbance here tonight. A man was removed under armed guard. I must speak with you about that."

He heard locks being worked on the other side of the door, and then it swung open a crack. The merchant's weasel face peered out, just visible in the light from the candle he held. He was in shirtsleeves and breeches. Not expecting company.

"Yes, how may I help you?"

"Let me in, please."

"If you don't mind, sir—" the merchant began, but Press had had enough. He lashed out with his foot, kicked the door open, sent the merchant and his candle sprawling.

He stepped into the office space, shut the door behind him. The candle had not gone out. It lay guttering on its side as Press held the point of his sword under the merchant's chin, pricking his skin for emphasis. "There was a man here with a woman, pretty thing, blond hair. His name was . . . ?"

"Marlowe. Thomas Marlowe. Captain of the ship, but he didn't want to come ashore at first and sign the papers."

"I reckon not. What ship?"

"The *Elizabeth Galley*. Just cleared in from Virginia with tobacco."

"*Elizabeth Galley*? That don't sound like the name of a merchant-man to me."

"That is the name, sir, I assure you," the merchant said. There was a note of defiance in his voice, so Press jabbed him with the sword, just enough to produce a trickle of blood, and the man was cowering and subservient again.

"Show me the ship's papers," Press demanded, and he stepped back, allowed the merchant to stand. The frightened merchant scrambled to his feet, and Press followed him into his office. A desk piled with papers, a few ship models and paintings of merchant vessels on the walls. The merchant dug through the pile, with shaking hands handed Press a sheaf.

Press took the papers, thumbed through them. He did not know much about merchantmen's documents, did not really know what he was looking at. But he saw the names Thomas Marlowe and *Elizabeth Galley*, and that was enough for him.

"Where is the ship now?"

"I don't know exactly, I swear to the Lord I don't. Moored in the river, not above a mile from here, I heard the lighterman say. Beyond that, I don't know."

Press laid the sword on the desk, grabbed the merchant by the collar, punched him hard in the face. It was agony on his fingers, but it had to be done. The point had to be made.

The merchant was on hands and knees, spitting blood. "I swear . . . I know no more . . ." he whined.

"I believe you," Press said, then kicked him hard in the stomach, sent him sprawling on his back. Grabbed him by the hair and lifted him to his feet, shoved him back against the desk.

The merchant cowered, looked up at him, shying his face away. He was certain that he was about to die. Press knew the look.

"I have people watching, do you understand?" Press said, soft, so the merchant had to really listen to hear. He nodded.

"If this Marlowe returns, you get word to me. Captain Roger Press. Any sailor that lives down here will know how to find me. Understand?"

The merchant nodded again.

"Good. And, pray understand, if he comes back and you do not alert me, I'll know. If you tell anyone what happened tonight, I'll know. And then it will go hard on you. Do you believe that?"

The merchant nodded again, and Press could see that he had indeed made a true believer out of the man.

"Good." He straightened, picked up the sword from the desk. "Good night to you, sir," he said, then stepped out of the office and out onto the street. He owned the merchant now. The little man would not cross him.

And out on the water, within a mile of where he stood, Malachias Barrett was waiting for him.

They staggered back to the boat like a tiny army in retreat, Marlowe clutching his wounded arm, one of the sailors limping with a gash on his leg, all of them winded from the unaccustomed running.

At the head of the steps one of the two remaining sailors stood guard, arms crossed, pistols barely concealed under his coat. As they approached, Marlowe could see Elizabeth in the boat at the bottom of the steps, the second seaman standing on the step, painter in hand. Honeyman had stationed them well for the defense of his wife.

They made their way down the stairs and into the boat, and wordlessly the sailors followed, cast off, leaned on their oars. Three long strokes and the seawall disappeared in the mist.

They settled in, with Honeyman holding the boat on a compass heading back to the *Elizabeth Galley*. Big ships rose out of the fog and then disappeared in the boat's black wake, a few odd sounds punctuating the night: voices from ships, something falling on a deck, the slap of rigging, the groan of a vessel's rudder moving in the gudgeons.

Marlowe caught Honeyman's eye. "Thank you, Honeyman," he said, and Honeyman nodded and looked back at the compass. No more was said, or needed to be.

At last the familiar shape of the *Elizabeth Galley* appeared through the mist. Honeyman laid the boat alongside, and Elizabeth climbed awkwardly up the steps, trying to keep her feet from tangling in her skirts, and then Marlowe climbed gratefully aboard, letting the sight and smells of his beloved ship embrace him. It was safety there. He imagined this was how a criminal felt, reaching the sanctuary of a church, or a fox reaching its den ahead of the yelping dogs.

He stepped aft to the quarterdeck. Bickerstaff and a very worried-looking Dinwiddie were there.

"Things did not go well?" Bickerstaff asked.

"Not so very well, no. Not well at all, in fact." He looked around. Honeyman had saved his life by coming to his aid, but that meant that word had not been passed to Dinwiddie to ready the ship to sail.

Marlowe folded his arms, looked down the length of his deck, tried to get his thoughts in some order. Press was dead—he had to be, or he would have gotten back into the fight—but the others, Press's men, had escaped. How much did they know of Marlowe's past? Of why Press had arrested him? Who might they tell? Did he, Marlowe, still need to flee?

If they sailed now, they would be leaving behind their tobacco and that of their neighbors. The parsimonious Dickerson was not going to pay them unless they demanded payment in person. If they did not, they would be ruined.

"Mr. Dinwiddie, what is the state of the tide?"

"On the ebb now, sir. We'll have low water in two glasses. I was just getting ready to drop the second bower to moor her."

"No, no. We need no more anchors. Let us roust up all hands, quietly, and rig the capstan. We will win our anchor and drop downriver. A mile or two, I should think." The wind was light, but they had an hour more of ebb tide that would sweep them along, a few miles at least.

That should do for now, just to see how things lay. Perhaps cover up the ship's name on the transom.

Dinwiddie passed the order. Grumbling, half asleep, the men staggered up from below and went through the paces of rigging the capstan. Marlowe saw glances shot back aft, men in huddled conversation, the signs of fear and discontent. Trouble building like thunderheads.

Goddamn it all, not bloody again, he thought.

He wondered if there would ever come a day when some worthy genius would invent a miraculous engine that would replace all sailors, so that he might never again have to suffer their whining malcontent.

"Might I inquire, Thomas, what happened ashore?" It was Bickerstaff, pulling him from his foolish reverie.

"Do you recall, Francis, when I told you of the raid I undertook on Nombre de Dios, when I was a young man? And the captain, Roger Press, who betrayed us?"

"I do. You marooned him, as I recall."

"Yes, well, he did not stay marooned. In fact, I saw him this very night. He claims to have a queen's commission, which I doubt very much. But he did have four armed men with him, which were harder to deny."

Bickerstaff began to say something else, but they were interrupted by Duncan Honeyman, coming up from the waist, taking the quarterdeck steps two at a time. "Capstan's rigged, Captain," he said in his nonchalant way. He glanced up at the rig overhead, then forward, and then in a different tone said, "Lads forward ain't happy, Captain, I got to tell you. They don't know what's acting, and they ain't happy."

Marlowe looked hard at Honeyman, said nothing for a minute. "I could care less if the men are happy or not. They have their orders. I am in command here, not you."

"Don't mistake me, Captain. This ain't any of my doing. I'm a messenger, no more."

"Indeed. Well, Honeyman, in my experience, the message usually starts with the messenger."

"Usually does. But not here. Thing of it is, sir, the men thought they was signing on aboard a merchantman, and maybe for the Red Sea. They didn't reckon on being taken in London. They don't care to hang as pirates."

"They will not hang as pirates."

"They don't know that, sir. And, respectfully, you don't neither."

Marlowe and Honeyman stood two feet apart, staring at one another. *I should have reckoned Honeyman for a sea lawyer, damn his eyes*, Marlowe thought. If Honeyman thought that coming to his aid in that street brawl would give him leave to take such liberties, he was mistaken.

But Thomas understood, and he knew that Honeyman understood, that a sailor was not a soldier. He would not risk his neck if there was no reward for it. Loyalty was a precarious thing with men who moved easily from one ship to another.

"Very well, tell the men that it is an extra shilling for every man for tonight's work."

"Very good, sir." Honeyman betrayed no reaction to this, just turned and went forward.

Bickerstaff stepped up beside him. "You must bribe the men to do your bidding?"

"If the bidding smacks of the threat of arrest, yes, I do. On the open sea I could bully them more, but I can do only so much with the shore two cable lengths away."

Marlowe paused for a moment, watched as Honeyman passed the word of his offer of a bonus, saw faces brighten considerably. "If there was nothing . . . questionable about what was acting, then the threat of being accused of mutiny would keep them in line. It is my damned luck that these villains always seem to have the upper hand because I always seem to be doing something that skirts the law."

"Your 'damned luck'? I think luck has very little to do with it, my dear Thomas. I should look more to your own natural tendencies."

"Whatever it might be, we need their cooperation. If they desert and we lose this tobacco, we are done for."

"Done for indeed. Whatever did Honeyman mean by 'maybe for the Red Sea'?"

"The Lord knows. I think that Honeyman is something of a rogue. I am sorry now I shipped him aboard."

Marlowe turned slightly until he could feel the light breeze on his cheek, glanced aloft at the rig and then over the taffrail at the vessel moored astern of them. In his mind he could see the fore topsail set aback, the helm over, the *Elizabeth Galley* turned downwind and tide. They were close to the vessel astern, but once they had pulled up to the anchor, there would be room enough for that turn.

In his mind the whole evolution was a done thing. He had now only to make the ship follow his vision.

"Mr. Dinwiddie, hands aloft to loosen tops'ls, and then let us haul up to the best bower," he called, and Dinwiddie relayed the orders. He had been impressed with the need for quiet, so he modified his volume, though his tone did not change, with the result that it sounded like listening to Peleg Dinwiddie from a far way off.

The men moved fast up the ratlines and out along the yards—a single shilling could buy a lot of pleasure along the London waterfront—and a minute later the topsails were hanging in big baggy folds under the yards.

Down to deck again, and the capstan bars were shipped and the swifter rigged and the men in place, ready to heave 'round.

Marlowe glanced fore and aft. Haul up to the anchor, set the fore topsail, break out the anchor, and away they go, lost in the fog. Find a safe place in the river to hide, and then deal with the money he was owed. Simple.

"Very well, Mr. Honeyman, heave 'round!" he called.

"Heave 'round!" Honeyman called, soft but clear, and the men began to move in their slow circle, the cable began to come in, black and dripping through the hawsepipe, and Marlowe tried to contain the very uneasy feeling churning in his guts.

Chapter 7

STUMBLING, CURSING, Roger Press ran down the road that bordered the river. Ten minutes of searching, with the fog like a veil that he could not push aside, and he managed to find one of the few hired boats still operating at that hour. The boatman was asleep on the thwarts, snoring obscenely, as was his one-man crew, until Press gave him a sharp poke with his sword.

The man bolted awake, furious and ready to fight, an emotion that died an untimely death with his first look at Press's wet, bedraggled clothing, bright sword, and pocked face, twisted in an anger that the boatman could not hope to match.

"Where to, sir?" was all he said as he snatched up his oar and gave the other man a sharp kick, venting his anger at Press on his helpless mate.

"Queen's Venture," Press said as he climbed into the stern sheets. There was no need to say more. Everyone who worked on the water knew the Queen's Venture and the cruise for which she was fitting out. Sailors, indentured servants, second and third sons of the aristocracy looking for adventure in an officer's berth—they all were flocking to Press with the hope of joining in the noble expedition and its promise of huge rewards. Press had had his pick of the best mariners in London, and that meant the best in the world.

The boat pulled through the fog, and soon Press could make out the *Queen's Venture*, growing more distinct with each pull of the oars. They rowed under the ship's high counter and then down her oiled side. Press was aware of heads peering over the rail above, a sudden burst of activity on deck as the anchor watch was informed that the captain was returning, as word was passed to Jacob Tasker, the *Venture's* first officer.

Press stared straight ahead, ignored it all.

The boatman pulled up to the boarding steps, and the younger man hooked on to the chains, and Press was up and climbing even as the boatman said, "That'll be . . . sir? A shilling, sir!"

Press stepped through the entry port into the waist. As he expected, Tasker was there, in his nightshirt and breeches, still unbuttoned. He made to speak, but Press cut him off with "Pay that whoreson in the boat and meet me aft."

He left Tasker in the waist, let him deal with finding a shilling. He stamped up the quarterdeck ladder and peered out into the gloom.

A moment later he heard Tasker pad up behind him. Without turning, Press said, "I met a pirate tonight. A murdering bastard named Malachias Barrett who goes by the name Thomas Marlowe now. I arrested him, and those idiots with me let him escape. Hanson is dead."

"Dead. Aye, sir." Tasker was smart enough not to inquire further, smart enough not to ask Press about his wet clothing or his lost hat or how he seemed to have had no part in Marlowe's escape. That was why Press had shipped him as first officer.

"Barrett is out there, on a ship. Close. And I intend to find him. I want the longboat brought alongside."

It would have to be a boat attack. Press would have liked to use the *Queen's Venture*, his powerful warship, but she was in disarray, still fitting out. They were not slated to sail for Madagascar for another three weeks. It would take hours just to get her under way.

The longboat, then. "Thirty men in the boat crew," Press continued. "Armed. Cutlasses and pistols. I want to be under way in . . ."

Press paused, cocked his ear. He could sense Tasker tensing up with the gesture, but he ignored the officer, his concentration directed entirely outboard. Some little sound had caught his ear, some familiar tone.

The *Queen's Venture's* rudder groaned below them, drowning out everything else in the muted night. And then it stopped, and then Press heard the sound again, a steady, mechanical sound.

Clack, clack, clack . . . the sound of a capstan's pawls falling into place. He had heard it a thousand times before, and he could not mistake it, the sound as much a part of his life as his own voice. It was the sound of a ship getting under way. There was only one man he could imagine who was desperate enough to up anchor and move on a black, fog-shrouded night, in a river on a falling tide.

"Damn it!" Press slammed his hand on the cap rail, bit down hard on his silver toothpick. "Get that damned boat alongside now!" he hissed between clenched teeth. "Do you not hear that? They are winning their anchor!"

"Aye, sir!" Tasker turned and ran forward, knowing better than to move at a pace slower than that. Into the waist, firing a broadside of orders, conveying both the intent and the urgency of the captain's commands.

Men ran in every direction. Handpicked, able seamen, they knew when it was time to move and move fast. Cutlasses came up from below and were handed out, pistols clipped to belts. The longboat, already in the water, pulled alongside, and the boat crew dropped into it and took up the oars.

Four minutes from the moment he gave the word, Press climbed down into the fully manned, fully armed boat. It could not have been done fast enough to please him, but neither could it have been done any faster than it had been.

"Shove off. Give way," he growled, and the boat swung away from the *Queen's Venture's* side. The long sweeps came down and caught the water, and the boat shot forward, despite its being heavily loaded with men and arms.

Press pushed the tiller over, aimed the bow in the direction of the capstan noise. He had not brought any kind of light, so he could not see the boat's compass, and he cursed that fact and he cursed the fact that they had not had time to muffle the oars. The squeaking of the looms in the rowlocks seemed like the screaming of the damned in the quiet night. He was certain Barrett would hear it and be alerted to the pending attack.

But it would not matter, Press assured himself. Surprise was not so crucial. In that light air the boat could move faster than any ship under sail. And Barrett's ship was a merchantman, twenty sailors at most. It was unlikely that they would be willing to fight and die for their captain. And even if they were, they would be no match for his band.

No, beating Marlowe was no problem. He had only to find him, to come upon this *Elizabeth Galley* on the river, and the rest would be simple. He toyed with the toothpick in his mouth, waggled it back and forth with his tongue, beat the gunnel of the boat lightly and rhythmically with his fist.

The *Elizabeth Galley* inched forward, pulled against the tide as the men at the capstan hauled her up to the anchor in preparation for getting under way.

"How much cable have you veered, Mr. Dinwiddie?" Marlowe asked, an irritable and unnecessary question.

"Cable and a half, sir. We was to moor, you'll recall."

"Yes, yes," Marlowe said, and paced away. A cable and a half, almost a thousand feet of rope to haul in. He was growing more anxious with each passing moment. The loud clacking of the capstan pawls was like some kind of torture. He was sure it was increasing in volume every minute.

Elizabeth, who had gone below seeking the privacy of the great cabin to compose herself, returned to the quarterdeck. She gave Marlowe a half smile, an expression of support, then moved to the opposite rail and stood there, quiet and unobtrusive. Thomas knew she would remain in that place, ready to help if asked, not questioning, not interfering, and he loved her for that, for knowing what he needed in every instance and giving it, willingly.

Then his mind moved on from those warm thoughts. He leaned on the rail and looked out into the night. Between the dark and the fog he could not see beyond twenty feet.

Press is dead, he thought. *If he had been able to swim, he would have got back into the fight.*

But he could not shake the gnawing worry. It was not the first time he had assured himself that Roger Press was dead.

Clack, clack, clack . . .

"Here's the splice coming aboard!" Duncan Honeyman called aft, sotto voce. The splice where the two cables were joined. That meant that they had hauled in one third of the cable they had let out. Marlowe pounded the cap rail softly with his fist.

Clack, clack, clack . . . It was like a town crier announcing that they were slipping away, and Marlowe could hardly stand to listen to it.

And then he heard another sound, a creaking, like any of a hundred creaking noises that a ship might make. But there was something about it that caught his attention, a certain rhythmic quality. What was more, it did not sound as if it came from the *Elizabeth Galley* but from somewhere out in the dark. He strained to listen.

Again, there it was. Oars in tholes, he was certain. He crossed to the other side of the quarterdeck, listing in his mind all the reasons a boat might be out at that time of night—a drunken party returning to their ship, a bumboat looking for a late-night customer, even whores being ferried out to a ship—it was not unheard of. A hundred reasons a boat might be out on the water at that hour.

He leaned on the starboard rail as the boat appeared out of the mist like some nightmare water bug, a longboat, oars double-banked, men crowded at the thwarts, just fifteen feet away before it was visible. In the stern sheets, too indistinct to see in any detail but unmistakable in his gangly form, sat Roger Press.

Marlowe stood upright, gasped as if a ghost had suddenly materialized, and then Press's voice shouted, "Backwater! What ship is that?"

The men at the capstan froze, the clacking ceased. Marlowe flailed around for an answer, but before he could grab one, Peleg Dinwiddie, standing on the gangway and looking down on the boat, answered helpfully, "*Elizabeth Galley!* Who goes there?"

"Give way," Press said to his boat crew. Then to Dinwiddie: "We are going alongside."

The Elizabeth Galleys seemed to have turned to stone. They stood, unmoving, unsure what to do, but Marlowe had no doubt.

"Cut the cable!" he shouted. No need for quiet now. "Cut the damned cable!"

Still no one moved. They remained frozen long enough for a curse to build in Marlowe's throat, and then Honeyman snatched up an ax and brought it down on the bar-taut anchor cable, one stroke, two strokes, the strands shredding with each blow.

Marlowe leaned over the rail. The longboat was ten feet away, less than its own length, the crowd of men—armed men, he could see—ready to swarm up and into the unarmed, unprepared, and untrained men of the *Elizabeth Galley*. It would not even be a fight.

"Pull! Ship oars!" Press cried. He looked up, and his eyes met Marlowe's. Press looked calm, no surprise on his face, as if he had known all along where he might find his old enemy.

The boat crew pulled hard, the boat shot forward, and the oars came up and were laid on the thwarts, out of the way, where they would not hinder the men from clambering aboard the *Galley*.

The heavy boat bumped along the *Galley*'s side, its momentum carrying it fast, the bowman standing with the boat hook and reaching for the main chains, when the anchor cable parted under Honeyman's ax. The wind and tide seized the *Galley*'s bow and swung it away. The bowman lunged, slashed at the chains, almost fell overboard as the ship turned beyond his reach.

"Set the fore tops'l!" Marlowe shouted. "Hands to the halyard, haul away! Sheet home!"

The men in the waist burst from their reverie and raced to pin rails and halyard tackle. They might not have been men-of-war's men, ready for a fight, but they were good sailors and they responded swiftly to those familiar orders.

"Haul away! Sheet home!" Dinwiddie took up the series of commands, and overhead the topsail yard began to jerk up the mast, and the men hauling on the sheets pulled the lower corners of the topsail out to the ends of the fore yard below it.

The current had hold of the *Elizabeth Galley*, turning her so fast that Press and the longboat were already astern. The boat crew, caught right at the moment of preparing to board the *Galley*, were now struggling to lay down arms and take up oars again. It was a little cluster of chaos floating on the river, and it gave Marlowe a flash of hope, like a spark from steel on flint, but no more. The current would carry them both alike, and once the boat crew was straightened out and pulling again, they would move faster than the *Elizabeth Galley* could in that light air.

"That's well!" Dinwiddie shouted, and then, "Damn me! Captain! Captain! Larboard bow!"

Marlowe looked forward. The ship astern of them, which they would have missed if they had not cut their anchor cable short, was now right in their path, the river sweeping the *Galley* into her.

"Larboard your helm! Hard over!" Marlowe shouted to the helmsmen, who shoved the tiller hard to the larboard side. Such a shift of rudder would have had a dramatic effect on a ship moving fast through the water, but now it was the water that was largely moving the ship, and the rudder did little to alter her course.

"Damn my eyes," Marlowe said as they dropped closer to the moored vessel, a slow, deliberate, graceful drift toward collision. "Shift your helm!"

The helmsmen swung the tiller in an arc across the deck, all the way to starboard. The move had done some good, Marlowe noted, had jogged the *Galley* a little way out of line with the ship astern.

The bowsprit passed the moored vessel and then the bow, not five feet off, the two ships so close it would have been a simple matter to step from one to the other. Marlowe could feel the men on deck holding their breath as they watched the anchored vessel, deserted, ghostly in the mist.

"Midships!" he called to the helmsmen, and they moved the tiller to the centerline, and Marlowe saw that he had waited a second too long. The *Galley*'s stern was too close, and just as he decided that no further jogging of the rudder could help, the ships hit, the *Elizabeth Galley*'s larboard quarter slamming into the turn of the other vessel's bow with a shudder that shook both ships, keel to truck.

Marlowe watched the damage happen, a few feet from where he was standing. The *Galley* dragged down the side of the other ship with a chorus of snapping and cracking and wrenching. He heard glass break and knew that his beloved quarter galley was smashed to splinters.

For long seconds the ships ground together as the *Elizabeth Galley* was carried past. Someone appeared on the deck of the moored ship, shouting curses, just as the *Galley* bounced off her main channel, wrenching it from her side, and then she was clear.

There seemed to be a collective sigh of relief fore and aft, a second's reprieve, and then a pistol shot rang out, and Roger Press's voice was shouting, "Bring to! Bring to for a queen's officer!"

"Set the main topsail!" Marlowe called forward, as if he and Press were arguing over who was in command of the *Galley*. The men moved to obey, but slowly, and he could see eyes glancing outboard.

"Bring to!" Press shouted again, audibly closer. "Bring to for a queen's officer, or you shall all hang!"

That had the effect Press was hoping for. The men moved more slowly still, unwilling to disobey Marlowe, but by tacit agreement working with such hesitancy that they might be construed as obeying Press as well.

"Damn your eyes! He's no queen's officer, he is a bloody pirate! Give him no thought, unless you would be cut down on deck!" Marlowe shouted, but rather than inspire the men, that only seemed to confuse them more.

Damn it! Marlowe turned, looked aft. The longboat was pulling for them with a will, the men bending to the oars, the boat more than matching the *Elizabeth Galley*'s speed. Thirty feet astern and gaining, all those men, all those weapons.

What did they have for defense? No cannon, no swivels. A smattering of muskets and cutlasses. Marlowe had intended to rely on the

Elizabeth Galley's speed to keep them out of danger. He had not thought of being overtaken by a rowed vessel.

"Damn it!" he said out loud. He heard Honeyman's voice, a menacing growl, a squealing overhead. The men were being driven to set the main topsail, but even that would not keep them out of Press's hands. Unless the wind picked up dramatically in the next two minutes, the boat would overtake them.

Bickerstaff appeared beside him. "I would not expect these men to defend the ship, Thomas. They are not sure with whom they should place their loyalty."

"You are right. I am loath to say so." *If they are loyal to anyone,* Marlowe thought, *it is Honeyman. For all the good that will do me.*

"Perhaps you should slip away," Bickerstaff suggested. "Go down the starboard side with a float as Press comes up the larboard. I do not think he will molest the others if you are gone."

"Do you think I would be so craven?"

"No, but it is a prudent suggestion, and so I thought it my duty to make it."

"And I appreciate that, but I cannot." He looked back at the boat. Almost up with the after end of the *Elizabeth Galley.*

Marlowe felt a gust of wind on his neck, and the *Elizabeth Galley* heeled a bit, and the water gurgled around the cutwater. Hope surged up as he looked astern, saw the longboat disappearing again in the mist and dark. And then the gust passed, and the ship came down on an even keel, and the sound of the water died away. They had gained fifty feet. It would take Press four minutes to make up the distance.

"Perhaps we can fend them off," Marlowe said, and then he ran down the quarterdeck and along the gangway over the waist. "Mr. Honeyman, get a gang to unlash those spars!" He pointed amidships to the top of the main hatch, where the spare yards and topmasts were stored, long, massive tapered timbers like a giant bundle of kindling. "Roust out that main topsail yard! We shall fend these dogs off!"

"Come on, come on, you heard the captain! Go! Go!" Honeyman shouted the orders, and the men reacted, casting off the lashings, arranging themselves along the length of the heavy spar. They moved to

Honeyman's orders and because Marlowe had hit on just the right degree of resistance—keeping the boarders off without bloodshed, avoid-
ing the possibility of shooting at a queen's officer, if such he was, or
being shot by one.

But they would not enjoy that neutrality for long, Marlowe understood. They might boom Press off once or twice, but then Press would
start shooting, and then the Elizabeth Galleys would have to reexamine their loyalties.

The men hefted the heavy spar, twenty-five feet long and three hundred pounds, and maneuvered it so it was lying crosswise on the ship,
ready to be tilted over the side and used like a giant poker to push the
boat away.

How long will we be able to do that? Marlowe wondered. *Not very
long.*

And then Honeyman was there, at his side, and Marlowe wondered
what fresh request the men had at that critical juncture. But Honeyman
just nodded and said, "Spar's ready for fending off, Captain." He hesitated, just a beat, and then added, "I was thinking, we might hoist it
aloft with the stay tackle. Get it more vertical." He looked Marlowe in
the eye, and there was a wicked expression on his face. "Of course, if
we do that, there's a chance we might drop it. If you get my meaning."

It took Marlowe a few seconds before he did, but when he saw what
Honeyman was suggesting, he grinned as well and said, "A fine idea,
Honeyman. Sway her aloft."

Honeyman rushed off, called, "Let us get the stay tackle on this
spar, make it easier to maneuver!"

The stay tackle, a block and tackle that hung between the masts, directly over the main hatch, was used primarily for hoisting cargo and
supplies in and out of the *Galley's* hold. Now eager hands grabbed the
end of the tackle and made it fast to the middle of the spare topsail
yard, and Honeyman shouted, "Sway away!" The men hauled together, and the long, tapered spar rose up in the air.

The longboat had regained the distance lost to the cat's-paw of
wind, was pulling over the last stretch to the *Galley's* side, twenty feet
off and closing.

Across the water Marlowe heard Press shout, "Pull, you whoresons!" though he could see the men were already pulling with all they had.

Damn it, damn it, too bloody late, Marlowe fretted as his men hauled away on the tackle and the yard rose up, up, wavering and tilting in the air.

Marlowe's eyes moved between the yard rising up overhead and Press's boat flying toward them. A pistol banged out, the ball thudded into the mainmast—Press giving the men of the *Elizabeth Galley* a taste of things to come if they did not comply—and the message struck like the bullet.

The lower end of the yard was resting on the *Galley*'s rail, pointing down at the water, and the upper end was twenty-five feet above him, pointing at the sky, the whole thing nearly vertical.

Ten feet away Marlowe saw the longboat, a dim shadow in the mist. He could make out the crew giving one last pull, the men unshipping their oars again and snatching up weapons, poised, ready to board. There was the bowman again, a dark shape, once more reaching out with the boat hook. There was Press, in the stern sheets, unmistakable. Marlowe could see him run his eyes along the *Galley*'s rail, looking, no doubt, for Malachias Barrett.

Marlowe grabbed the low end of the yard, shoved it along the rail until it was hanging directly over the place where Press's boat would strike the *Elizabeth Galley*'s side. He was astounded that Press had not yet smoked his intentions.

And in that instant, Press did. The longboat hit the *Galley*'s side with a shudder, the men poised to board, and Press shouted, "Shove off! Shove off, damn it!" and over Press's voice Marlowe shouted, "Honeyman! Let go!"

The yard jerked from Marlowe's hand as Honeyman let go of the end of the stay tackle. The huge spar plunged down, down over the side, down like a great lance aimed at Press's boat. Marlowe watched the long wooden shaft rush past, heard the sound of thin planks shattering as the lower end of the three-hundred-pound yard smashed right through the bottom of the boat and kept going.

Overhead he could just make out the end of the quivering spar as it stopped, sinking itself into the mud of the Thames.

He heard shouts of surprise, screams of outrage, saw the panicked boat crew shrinking away from the water that flooded in through the shattered bottom of the boat.

The line from the stay tackle spun through the blocks and then fell into the water. Already astern, the spare topsail yard was sticking straight up from the river like a giant pin, and skewered on that pin was the longboat that held Roger Press and his stunned, shouting men.

And then the mist enveloped them, and they were lost from sight, and only the shouting remained. In a minute that, too, was gone.

The *Elizabeth Galley* drifted on a mythic river, her own black and forlorn River Styx, alone.

Marlowe looked around the deck. The men were smiling, talking in low voices, laughing. There was no remorse for what they had done, no fear of reprisal. It had been too good a trick for any second thoughts.

Peleg Dinwiddie stepped up to him, grinning as broadly as the others. "I guess you done for them, sir," he said.

"I reckon they'll stay put, for the time being," Marlowe agreed.

"You'd said we was to drop downriver a mile or so. It'll be dead reckoning for that, sir, and not so accurate on such a night, I fear."

"Oh." Marlowe had already forgotten that plan of dropping downriver. "As to that, I reckon you may as well steer for the open sea. Our business here is done, like it or not."

Chapter 8

THE ISLAND of Madagascar in the Indian Ocean, three hundred miles off the southeast coast of Africa. As if half of Mozambique had cracked off and drifted away, fetching up at last in that place. On a chart one can see where the island would still fit clean against the African coast, snapping into place like a puzzle piece or the perfectly tooled part of some machine.

But for all that kinship to the Dark Continent, the Madagascar of 1706 was a world unto itself, supporting a culture almost entirely unique in the world. It was the advance base, the dockyard, the chandlery, the marketplace, and in many cases the home of the men who sailed the Pirate Round.

Madagascar had not been the first choice of the Roundsmen, ideal though it was in so many ways. They had first set up on Bab's Key, the little island marked Perim on the charts, at the entrance to the Red Sea. It was a perfect spot, insofar as it was at the very crossroads of the great wealth of shipping in the Indian Ocean and the Red Sea—treasure ships bringing tribute to the Great Mogul; shiploads of wealthy pilgrims bound for Mecca; the lumbering, lightly manned ships of the British, French, and Dutch East India companies.

But Perim had no water, and that was the most precious jewel of all aboard ships that were at the mercy of wind and tide. A miscalculation in that area, especially in the arid and brutally hot Red Sea countries, could result in a death more horrible than anything the pirates could inflict on their most hated enemy.

So the Roundsmen had moved their operations to Madagascar. It was over two thousand miles from their hunting grounds, but piracy was a movable profession, and what Madagascar lacked in proximity it more than made up for in other ways.

The island was lush, fruitful, with an abundance of fresh water. The climate was perfect—not sweltering, not frigid—a place where a man could pass out drunk on the ground with no fear of the weather's killing him. The natives were cowed by the power of firearms, and even if they had not been, they were far too involved with fighting among themselves ever to coordinate any real resistance to the Europeans' encroachment. Any band of pirates had only to help the local tribe in a raid against its neighbor to find themselves welcome on the island.

The native girls had much to recommend them as well. Mostly local Malagasies, they had a well-earned reputation for comeliness, with none of the Christian women's aversion to fornication nor the mercenary attitude of the whores.

So perfect a place was Madagascar, such the pirates' Eden, that many never left. They took local girls for wife, set up in trade with other Roundsmen, idled away their days in ease and drunkenness. In the entire history of piracy, only Tortuga, Port Royal in Jamaica, and Nassau would come close to rivaling Madagascar as the pirates' utopia, a place where they alone ruled.

And of all the pirate communities that developed along Madagascar's extensive coastline, at Fort Dauphin and the Bay of St. Augustin and Diégo-Suarez and Ranter Bay and lesser places, the jewel of them all was the tiny island of St. Mary's, twenty-six miles long and one mile wide, less than ten miles off the northeast coast.

It was at St. Mary's that the progenitor of the Roundsmen, Thomas Tew, first landed his massive take and divided it among his men. But

Tew was not the first white man on St. Mary's. By the time the *Amity*'s anchor splashed into the bay, St. Mary's had already been settled by an Englishman named Adam Baldridge.

Baldridge recognized the island's potential as a defensible outpost—its shallow harbor with an island like a fortress at its mouth, the vicious reefs that prevented ships from landing anywhere else but under his guns. He recognized Madagascar's ideal location as a byway from Europe and America to the Red Sea and India. He saw in the island a fine place to hide from the murder charge for which he had fled Jamaica. St. Mary's suited his every need.

Business exploded for him. Manufactured goods, rum, and naval stores poured in from England and America, plundered goods and gold and jewels from the Indian Ocean and the Red Sea, with Baldridge standing right in the confluence of all that wealth.

From his tiny outpost, carved from the jungle, Baldridge established an empire that any of those men living along Pall Mall or St. James might have envied. He built warehouses, a stockade fortress, a mansion crafted in the English style from local materials, high on a hill that gave him a grand view of all he had created. He had a harem as big as any found in the East. He ruled his island kingdom without challenge.

By 1697 Baldridge was the undisputed "King of the Pirates," even holding a personal court and adjudicating disputes from all over Madagascar.

In the end the king pushed his luck too far, sold a few too many of the local citizens into slavery, and his once-loyal people rose against him, driving him out.

He settled at last in New York and lived a long life there. He was content, but he was no longer king.

Now I am king. The thought drifted through Elephiant Yancy's mind. *I am king now.*

Elephiant Yancy sat on the wide, second-story flagstone veranda that Baldridge had built, in a grand chair carved from slabs of mahogany and inlaid with ebony and ivory detailing. He was a small man, and thus the chair itself sat on a raised section of stone that he, Yancy, had

had constructed, so that even seated he might look down on anyone standing before him.

Yancy rested his head in his hand and stared idly out beyond the low wall that surrounded the veranda. Beyond and below the house lay the town of St. Mary's, where the pirates and whores and dealers in stolen goods and tavernkeepers made their homes. It was a variable population, perhaps two thousand people at its most crowded.

To the south of the town lay the shallow harbor with its black, muddy water. At the mouth of the harbor was a small island, Quail Island, which was home to a battery of cannon and not much else. But Quail Island was perfectly situated. With his men garrisoned there, ready at the great guns, Yancy could dictate completely who came and went from St. Mary's.

From his veranda Yancy could see the southern half of the harbor. He watched as a small ship stood slowly into the anchorage, rounded up, and dropped her anchor under a backed main topsail. Wondered, with only the slightest curiosity, if she was from England or America, or if she brought mail.

He thought of Baldridge. Baldridge had created all this and had been forced to abandon it. He, Yancy, had found it, all but in ruins, had built it back up, had made it his own. Baldridge might have started the whole thing, but Elephiant Yancy, former pirate and Roundsman, had resurrected it to an even greater glory than Baldridge could have envisioned.

St. Mary's Rediviva.

He repeated that thought, worked it around in his mind the way an Arab worked his prayer beads. He didn't really believe it at all, which was why he had to keep telling himself it was true.

At length he looked down at the two pathetic creatures seated on the low chairs before him. One of them had been talking for . . . how long? Yancy did not know, had not been listening. As lord of the island, Yancy had taken it upon himself to sit in judgment in such petty disputes. It was part of the burden he had to carry as supreme ruler of the kingdom, and he accepted that, but it was still a great bother and a terrific bore.

He was king, but he was not so ostentatious as to use that title. He insisted, rather, that he be called "Lord Yancy."

"It's a lie, what he said, Lord Yancy, I swear to Jesus God it is," one of the men was protesting. "That stuff he says I stole, it was mine, it weren't never his. Except for the knife, and that I won in gaming, fair and all, and he knows it—"

"That's a lie!" the other interjected. "Son of a bitch is trepanning you, Your Honor, and I can have a dozen witnesses say that's a fact!"

Yancy sighed audibly, stared out at the harbor again. Other men might look at his wealth, his power, his harem of women, and they might be envious, but they did not understand the terrible responsibility he carried.

He looked back at the men, put thumb and forefinger under his nose, and slowly ran the tips of those fingers down his mustache, smoothing the hair and then stroking his neatly groomed goatee with his full hand. He had practiced that gesture in the mirror until he was certain he had achieved the thoughtful, contemplative look he wanted.

The two litigants were both talking at once, a jumble of sound that Yancy could not pull apart so as to hear the individual words. He waved his hand for silence, and both men stopped talking. They paused a moment, hung there in expectation. When Yancy did not speak, one of the men started in again, but the guard who stood to one side punched him in the head, and he shut up.

"I have listened to your arguments," Yancy announced slowly, even though he had not. He did not in fact even recall what their dispute was about. "You are both liars and thieves, perfidious men. I banish you both from St. Mary's. You have until sundown to leave."

There, that was the simplest solution.

Both men looked stunned, and as the guards stepped up behind them, one shouted, "Yancy, damn it, that ain't . . ."

The words died, withered under the heat of Yancy's glare.

"Lord Yancy, sir, I mean—" the man stuttered.

"You argue with my judgment? Shall I cut your hands off and *then* banish you?"

Yancy saw the guards' faces brighten at the thought, but the man shut his mouth tight and shook his head. Finally he managed, "No, my Lord . . ."

"Good. Begone."

Yancy closed his eyes, massaged his temples as the guards shuffled the two away. He hoped someone was watching, as he knew that this particular gesture gave him the look of a world-weary monarch, a man who carried a great load on his shoulders.

Elephiant Yancy was not much above five feet tall, and thin, and he had the small man's energy, but he tried not to display it. It was not fitting for one in his position.

But energy he had, and drive. He had the energy for pirating in the Caribbean, for sailing the Round. Five years before, he had stepped ashore with the small crew of his pirate sloop, the *Terror*, and taken possession of Baldridge's old haunt from the few drunks who lived there. He had the vision and energy to see it built up again to its former glory, to court trade from the American colonies and from London.

He had done all that, and now he was at the top, and he moved with the languid quality of the nobility, let others serve him. He did not rush, he did not speak quickly, as was befitting a monarch. He dressed in the clothing of a gentleman and sported great capes lined with red silk and wide-brimmed hats with long feathers trailing behind. He understood that in order for his people to respect him as lord of St. Mary's, his every action, his every word, must be lordly.

But for all his certainty about his own divine right to rule, Yancy was worried. He closed his eyes, still massaging his temples, pictured the faces of the guards. They were bored by the trial, pleased by the possibility of cutting off a man's hands, disappointed when Yancy let him go. They were a brutish lot. Their loyalty was open to question.

There were currently more than five hundred men on St. Mary's, and nearly every one was or had been a pirate, and those who had not were still of no higher moral character. They frequented the makeshift taverns along the harbor, caroused with the native girls on the beaches or in the thick jungle, spent their booty, died as broken wrecks in the dirt streets. They were his army, but how many could he really count on?

Thirty, he reckoned. Those men who had first come with him, who had helped him build this up, who had recognized his place as king of it all. He had made those men rich, had given them harems, slaves. They lived with him in the big house, surrounding him. His Praetorian Guard. They would stand by him. Of the others? A third, perhaps, would stand by him, but they would be loyal to whoever they thought wielded the most power.

The last would like to see him impaled. He had just added two more to that group.

He sighed, stood up from his chair, which he thought of as a throne but did not refer to as such. He walked across the wide veranda, his cape swishing behind in a dramatic swirl of cloth, leaned his elbows on the stone wall, looked down on the town and the harbor below.

The jungle spilled from the interior of the island right to the water's edge, as if cascading down the hillsides, a thick green waterfall of vegetation running down to the sea. Here and there the green was splotched with color, the lovely flowers that were native to the place, bougainvillea and hibiscus, the air heavy with their scent.

A dusty road ran from the center of the town below and followed the shoreline to the harbor to the south, where it terminated at a battered old dock. A boat was pulling away from the newly arrived ship to the docks, which probably meant mail. Yancy hoped there would be some good word from some quarter. He could use that.

Soft footsteps at the far end of the veranda, and a native servant announced, "Dinner, Lord Yancy. Me bring there, lord?" The servants were all Madagascar men and women, some slaves, some freemen, depending upon their station. It was Yancy's standing order that the servants announce themselves from a distance. He did not need people sneaking around behind him.

"Yes. Set it here," he said, never taking his eyes from the harbor and the boat that had now reached the dock. He could see a man get out of the stern sheets, step onto the dock, hurry along the road to the town.

The servant set down the tray and retreated quickly. Yancy glanced at the food. Cold roast beef and a pot of mustard. Bread, butter, a slice of kidney pie. A gold chalice filled with wine. It looked like the Holy Grail.

The cook was English, enticed off a visiting vessel with absurdly high wages and a small harem of his own. He was good, but that did not mean he was trusted.

Each bit of food had a small piece carefully cut away where Yancy's taster had taken his sample—cut cleanly to retain the neatness of the presentation, but cut obviously enough that Yancy knew that the food had been tested. A man as powerful as he had powerful enemies. He had to defend against assassination.

Lord Yancy reached for the bread, realized he was hungry, then stopped. What if his taster were part of a plot? He was the one person who could easily poison Yancy's food. Taste it, declare it fit, then slip some poison or other in it.

He pulled his hand back slowly, as if the food might strike out at him like a snake if he made a sudden move. He felt his appetite melt away. He tried to recall if the taster had a family, a wife, children? If so, should he arrest one or more of them, hold them as collateral, with the promise that they would be tortured to death if he died of poisoning?

He was staring at the food, trying to formulate a plan of action, when he heard boots on the cobblestone veranda, walking fast, confident. Henry Nagel, Yancy's quartermaster during his days on the account, his second in command now, his chief adviser, his lord chamberlain. No one else would dare approach so boldly. He held a canvas bag in one meaty hand.

"Ship just come to anchor, my lord," Nagel said as he approached. "Arrived from London, forty days out. Brought mail. Captain brought it ashore, right off."

Yancy turned and looked at Nagel, who stood a respectful five feet away. Nagel was the physical opposite of Yancy—a big, powerful brute of a man, a seaman and pirate through and through, but with enough insight to realize that it was brains, such as Yancy had, and not brawn like his, that made a man a leader.

"Henry, how loyal are the men of this island to me?"

"My lord," Nagel began, and Yancy could hear the placating tone in his voice.

"Tell me true."

Nagel straightened, tried to summon the words. He was the only man on the island who was not afraid of Yancy, and if his loyalty were not so far beyond question, Yancy would have had him killed. As it was, he could not imagine ruling St. Mary's without Nagel, the only man who dared tell him the truth.

"My lord, the men here, they're pirates. End of the day, they don't give a tinker's damn for any but themselves, but that ain't something you don't know. All us from the *Terror*, we what came here with you, we'd die for you and never think on it. You know that. The others? I reckon most of 'em would fight for you—if they thought there was a better than even chance you'd win against who you was fighting."

Yancy nodded. "What of our defenses? How are they?" The battery and stockade on Quail Island looked formidable indeed, with ten heavy guns trained out over the water. Any ship going in or out had to run the narrow entrance, with the big guns at point-blank range.

But the appearance was deceiving. The guns had been there since Baldridge's time. Indeed, in Baldridge's time there had been forty of them, but Yancy had sold off most of them, reckoning ten were more than enough for the job.

Those that remained had received no maintenance for years. They were blacked now and the carriages repaired, but blacking and new carriages would not prevent them from blowing apart if the metal had grown weak through age or defects in the casting. Yancy had never fired them. He did not dare.

"Well, as to that," Nagel said, "the stockade's in pretty good shape. There's some parts are rotting, but I mean to get some men on that, shore it up. Guns, well . . ."

"Yes, yes, very well." Yancy had heard enough. He was suddenly tired of that conversation. "Is this the mail?"

"Yes, yes, my lord." Nagel knew when to let a subject drop. He hefted the canvas bag and gently poured the contents onto the low stone wall. "Ain't sorted it out. Thought you would want to see it first."

"Yes, yes . . ." Yancy said, sifting through the letters that were piled on the wall. They were not all for him, of course. Some were for other denizens of St. Mary's, those well enough established to receive correspondence there, those few men who could read and write or knew someone who could read and write.

Two letters from Yancy's merchant in London, another from his merchant in Newport, Rhode Island. "Bloody thieves . . ." he muttered, setting those letters aside. They were his middlemen, and they robbed him with never a scruple, but he needed them.

He continued through the pile, separating his letters from the others. Here was a letter for Bartleby Finch, who operated one of the taverns near the harbor. Yancy had granted him permission, but still he did not trust the villain. "Let us see who is writing to this dog," Yancy muttered, and he set Finch's letter with his own.

A letter from his wife in New York; he wondered how she had smoked his whereabouts. She had been a pretty thing, the last time he had seen her, pale-skinned and blue-eyed.

His gaze wandered off for a moment, unfocused, as he thought of her. He loved the girls of his harem, every one of them, their dusky skin and dark hair. But he missed the creamy skin and soft blond hair of the white women he had known. He had had a surfeit of Malagasy girls. He longed for a woman of European blood.

Yancy shook off that thought, turned back to the letters. More nonsense from merchants, a letter from the governor of New York . . .

His hand paused in midreach as he saw a familiar seal. He lifted the letter from the pile, gently, as if it might break, and turned it over. Richard Atwood. He had not heard from him in over a year.

Atwood was one of Yancy's triumphs, a well-placed secretary within the British East India Company. Yancy sent him yearly tribute in the amount of five hundred pounds. To Yancy it was a trifle, but it was more than twice the salary that the East Indian Company paid. In exchange, Atwood forwarded along shipping schedules, naval information, intelligence on the doings of the Great Mogul. Yancy had used that information to earn back many times what he had paid for it.

He unsheathed the ornate stiletto that he always wore at his hip. The razor-sharp blade sliced away the seal, and he unfolded the letter. The paper was covered with Atwood's neat clerk's handwriting in even lines. "Lord Yancy, I trust this finds you well . . ." it began, as Atwood's letters always did. He knew to address his benefactor with respect.

As you, sir, are all too Aware, the Company has at Various times in the Past endeavored to make sundry attacks on what they perceive as the great threat of Pyrates in Madagascar. They have never met with any great success, in part, I flatter myself to think, due to my timely warnings of their pending Action, but also in part due to a want of intelligent or active officers to lead such an Enterprise.

There is now in the making another such Enterprise, but this one of a more Secretive Nature than the others. A few of the more influential members of the Company have undertaken to Outfit a private man-of-war and tender for the purpose of routing out Pyracy in Madagascar and there is reason to believe that their enterprise will meet with greater success than those past. In part this is due to their affording every request of the commander in the article of weaponry, supplies, and men, who are well paid and very numerous, and this being just the beginnings of their Preparations.

The men who are secretly arranging this Expedition, with the consent of the Queen, have hired a privateer captain well known for his active nature and in whom they place great confidence. His name is Roger Press . . .

Yancy gasped as if he had been doused with cold water, felt his hands clench, heard the crackle of Atwood's letter as he crushed it in his fist.

Press!

It was not possible. Yancy stared out over the water, but he did not see it. He saw only Roger Press's ugly, pockmarked face, that damned toothpick wagging between his lips like a little accusing finger.

No, it is not possible. Press could not have escaped . . .

But how many were there with that name? And of all of them, how many would be of such a kidney as to lead a raid against a pirates' stronghold? It was not inconceivable that Press had somehow redeemed himself, worked his way to a place of trust, at least trust enough that he might be given a secret and dangerous mission such as this.

Nagel stood patient but worried. He knew better than to ask Yancy what the trouble was.

Yancy looked at the date on top of the letter. The second of August, 1706. Almost three months past. If Press had sailed at the same time as the ship that had brought it, he could arrive any day. Even if he had not, he would not be far behind.

Yancy whirled around, put his hands flat on the low wall, looked down at the cluster of buildings below and the few figures moving around, as if he could judge from there their fidelity and willingness to fight for his kingdom.

". . . *Affording every request of the commander in the article of weaponry, supplies, and men, who are well paid and very numerous . . .*" That was what Atwood wrote. Would those villains down there stand and fight a well-armed and motivated band of mercenaries? Not bloody likely.

In his mind he saw himself racing down a strange hallway, flinging open doors, looking for the one that concealed the plan, the right action to meet this new threat. Door after door, and then he opened one and behind it was something he recognized as an idea. He studied the thing, and as he did, it resolved into a possibility. A minute's more consideration and it had become a full-fledged plan of action.

Elephiant Yancy had not become Lord Yancy by folding in panic in the face of every adversity. He had become Lord Yancy by recognizing that all adversity held in its core potential opportunity.

And here was adversity: his most hated enemy, still alive, well armed, and coming for him. But what Yancy saw was Roger Press sailing right into his arms. Roger Press, coming right to him and thinking it was all a great secret.

He straightened, turned to Nagel, but before he could speak, he was overcome by a hacking cough that doubled him over and rendered him incapable of speech for half a minute.

He looked up again, at Nagel's worried face. "The time has come, my dear Henry. To prepare for the future. We cannot tarry. Our fate will be upon us soon."

Chapter 9

THE *Elizabeth Galley* drifted on her forlorn stream for two hours, helped along by the fitful breeze. When the tide turned at last and they could make no headway against it, they anchored with the second bower and kept anxious watch astern, fearful of pursuit.

"They," in this case, did not include Thomas Marlowe. As concerned as he was—and he had more reason than any to be so—he was too exhausted to care. His arm ached terribly where the bullet had grazed him.

He stumbled below, shed coat and sword, fell facedown on the cushion-covered lockers aft. He was hardly aware of Elizabeth cleaning and dressing his wound. He tried to recall if, in his younger days, he could have taken on such activity and not have felt so spent, but he could not recall and did not really care about that either, and soon he was asleep.

He woke to find daylight coming in through the stern windows and the *Elizabeth Galley* under way, heeling slightly in what he perceived was a usable wind.

He pulled himself from the locker, staggered out the door and into the waist, then up to the quarterdeck. It was a magnificent day, bright blue skies with only a smattering of benign clouds, a breeze to drive the ship along. The brown Thames stretched away before and behind, the shores seeming to bustle past, the crowds of shipping—every type of shipping—moving in every direction, with every conceivable purpose. But the stately *Elizabeth Galley* clove a straight wake downriver, lovely, noble in her headlong flight.

"Captain . . ." A worried-looking Peleg Dinwiddie hustled up to him, even as he was trying to get his bearings. "You had said, sir, we was to make for the open sea, and the tide turned, and this blessed breeze, and you was still asleep . . ."

Elizabeth came up behind him, stepped around the portly officer, put her arm through Marlowe's. "It is my fault, Captain. I begged Mr. Dinwiddie to not disturb you, told him he should just proceed with your last order. Here I am giving commands, and me with less authority than the meanest sailor aboard."

"Never in life, my love." Marlowe kissed the proffered cheek. "You command us all. And I am grateful for the sleep, truly I am."

He looked around once more, saw that Gravesend was a mile or so astern of them. The place where he was born. He wondered if he would ever see it again.

"Oh, Lord, there is nothing like sleep to set one up again!" he exclaimed. The night before, his mood had been black and desperate. His life in ruins. But now, rested, under that perfect sky, he saw only possibilities. Now he needed only to get the others to share his vision.

By tacit consent they did not even mention their predicament for the next three days. That was the time it took to drop down the Thames, past Southend and Sheerness where the river spread out to merge with the North Sea, to double Foreness Point and turn south, past Ramsgate and back through the Strait of Dover and into the English Channel once more.

It was only there, with the *Elizabeth Galley* sailing a line almost halfway between England and France and out of sight of both, with only water and, on occasion, distant sails to be seen—sails that fled at the sight of them for fear they were pirates or privateers—did they undertake a formal discussion of their situation and what they might do about it.

Elizabeth spoke first. "Our entire cargo, in which we have invested our very last penny, is sitting in that villain Dickerson's warehouse. Our neighbors' as well, and they will expect to be paid for it, out of our purse, I reckon, if we just abandon it. And now we are every minute leaving it farther behind."

Marlowe nodded thoughtfully as he watched her. It occurred to him that she had more than a financial stake in this. It had been her idea in the first place to use the *Elizabeth Galley* as a merchantman to save on shipping rates. If it ended up being their ruin, she would have to bear the guilt.

"I fear," said Bickerstaff, "we have shipped all our eggs in a single basket, to rework the old saw. Worse, we have put other people's eggs in as well."

It was not a crowded meeting. Just Marlowe, naturally, as captain and owner, and Elizabeth, being the bookkeeper and supercargo. Bickerstaff, to whom Marlowe had looked for advice almost since they met. And Peleg Dinwiddie, who, as first officer, had a right to take part in any such discussion.

Peleg did not actually take part, of course. Marlowe never thought he would. Rather, he sat at the table, hands folded, trying to look as if he were carefully considering every point made. He nodded, twisted his fingers, frowned, smiled as the occasion warranted, but he said nothing. In the great cabin he possessed none of the authority and confidence with which he prowled the quarterdeck. He looked very uncomfortable, in fact.

"Without we are paid for our cargo, we cannot even buy the provisions we will need to return to the colonies," Elizabeth pointed out. Thomas could hear the despair creeping in around the edges of her voice. It was time to put a stop to this talk.

"The tobacco is lost to us," Marlowe said. "We may as well have dumped it in the river."

"But sure there is some way . . . ?" Elizabeth began.

"No. Perhaps if I had driven that tops'l yard right through Roger

Press's black heart, we might have been able to return. Believe me, I tried, but I fear I killed no more than the boat.

"Press will see to it that Dickerson informs him if anyone comes calling in regard to our tobacco. He will have the warehouse watched. Even if we send someone in our stead, hire an agent, it will do us no good. Anyone who looks twice at our cargo will be arrested. I do not care to think on what Press might do to someone in order that he might extract information from him."

"This Press would seem quite rabid with the thought of vengeance," Bickerstaff observed.

"He is like that. Always was, as I recall. Though it is not as if marooning him was my notion. It was a vote of the crew."

" 'Marooning him,' sir?" Dinwiddie spoke for the first time.

"It is nothing, Mr. Dinwiddie. Happened a long time ago. A . . . business decision, if you will."

"Still, I can see how a fellow might take it personal," Bickerstaff observed.

"All right, goddamn it, can we speak of our cargo?" Elizabeth said, annoyed, exasperated. "What are we to do about that?"

"Nothing," Marlowe said. "Abandon it."

"Then we are ruined."

"Perhaps. Or perhaps there is some other way that we might regain our fortune . . ."

He said the words, let them hang in the air, gave the others a moment to wonder. It was good theater, and he needed every trick he could muster.

"Very well, if you will make us beg," said Bickerstaff, "pray what is this scheme of yours, this main chance?"

"We sail for Madagascar."

Silence again as these words took hold. There was no need to explain the scheme further. No need to describe the treasure ships of the Great Mogul, the riches to be had on the Pirate Round. The four people sitting at the table in the great cabin knew all about it, as did anyone in the American colonies with any connection to the sea. The name "Madagascar" was enough to summon it all up.

"Piracy, then?" said Bickerstaff, making no attempt to disguise his disdain. "On the account?"

"Not piracy. Privateering. Stay . . ." Marlowe cut Bickerstaff off before he could make the obvious objection. "I do have a commission for privateering, my dear Francis. Governor Richier was kind enough to offer me one, and I had the foresight to accept."

"Richier offered you one? Just like that? Did he think it his duty as host? Is that a consideration he extends to all his guests?"

"Well, I may have offered him some little token, I do not recall."

Bickerstaff just looked at him, making a small shaking motion with his head, and Marlowe could see he was taken aback by what he was hearing.

After all these years, and you are still surprised by me, Marlowe thought. *But wait, my friend, it gets better yet.*

"Very well, privateering," Elizabeth said. "You have a commission, it is as legal as it is wont to be." As a young woman, beautiful and destitute, Elizabeth had been forced into prostitution. She understood the occasional need for pragmatism over loftier moral considerations. "But Madagascar is halfway around the world. We have no provisions and no money to buy them."

"Ah, as to that, I do happen to have a bit tucked away," Marlowe said. "Enough certainly to provision for the voyage."

" 'Tucked away'?" Elizabeth asked. "You mean to say you have money—specie—that I did not know about?"

"Well, yes, in fact. I buried it on the property, just after I bought it. Before we were married, ages before. Quite forgot about it, really. Just thought to dig it up before we left."

Now it was Elizabeth's turn to look stunned. Before she could speak, Bickerstaff said, "I know the Moors are considered easy game, but we have no cannon, no small arms, no powder. Sure they are not so cowardly that they will surrender to an unarmed vessel?"

"I think the small pittance I have should be enough to buy us those things. Cannon, small arms, powder—yes, I reckon we can stretch it enough that we might get what we need."

"But where? What chandler will you apply to for those articles?"

"We shall get them in Madagascar, my dear Francis! All things are to be had in Madagascar."

"Hold a moment." Elizabeth found her voice at last. "Do you mean to say that you have specie enough to provision and arm this ship? That you have all this time been in possession of enough money to do all that, and you let me think we were on the very edge of ruin?"

"Ah . . ." Marlowe stalled. From the moment he decided to dig up that hidden booty, he had envisioned this scene. It had been like watching a great storm building on the horizon, knowing it could not be avoided, that it would lash him eventually. And here it was.

"Yes, I suppose so," he said. "But I cannot tell you all my secrets, now can I? You would fast grow bored with me if I did not retain just a little mystery."

Marlowe did not think that his flip answer would placate her, and he was right. He saw her eyebrows come together, her lips purse, her arms fold, and he knew he had not yet felt the brunt of the storm. *We'll run before it under bare poles*, he thought. *There is naught else to do.*

"Well, I reckon you got this all thought out!" Peleg Dinwiddie said. His voice was loud and enthusiastic, and it startled the others, who, being wrapped up in layer upon layer of emotion and personal history and the subtleties of their relationships, had entirely forgotten that he was there.

Bickerstaff looked sharply at Marlowe. "Thomas, I find your coyness frankly offensive. Pray do not pretend you have not planned this for some time."

Bickerstaff was right, of course. Marlowe had been planning it for some time. Years. Ever since the horrible memory of his pursuit of King James had begun to fade. Ever since his fortunes had begun to ebb and his boredom and disgust with the gentry of the Tidewater, of the idle life of a lord of the manor, had begun to flood. Ever since then he had been planning this, even if he had never said so explicitly, not even to himself.

He was sick of playing the gentleman around Williamsburg. He was sick of worrying about money. He was sick of the small beer of tobacco cultivation. He was ready for a big payoff.

"Perhaps I have. And a damned good job, too. Because we would be shipwrecked, ruined, with no options, if I had not." Marlowe was growing weary of the coy act as well. "So I have steered us to a place where we might find some real money. If any of you can advise some other course, then I am pleased to listen."

The great cabin was silent, an uncomfortable, grim, angry silence, as each person's eyes shifted from one to another. Dinwiddie alone did not look angry. He looked worried, and Marlowe guessed that he was afraid someone might talk the captain out of steering for Madagascar.

But Marlowe knew that would not happen.

"No," Bickerstaff said at last, his words clipped. "No, we have no choice. That is your genius, Thomas, it always has been. You do not ask others to follow you; you maneuver them until they have no choice. You did it with the *Plymouth Prize*, you did it when we hunted for King James, and you are doing it now. I am in awe, sir, of your skill."

"I will accept your compliment, whether you meant it as such or no," said Marlowe.

"Of course, tricking us into acquiescence is one thing. Your plans are for naught if the men will not agree."

At that, Peleg Dinwiddie actually chuckled, an odd sound in such a charged atmosphere. "Oh, sir, I do not reckon you'll get much fight out of them!"

Dinwiddie was right about that. Once those in the great cabin had agreed to Marlowe's plans—or had at least yielded to the dual thrusts of logic and coercion—they made their way to the quarterdeck. Thomas could see the curious glances, the eyes following them as they climbed up the ladder aft. Every man aboard the ship understood what had taken place in London, the predicament that Marlowe was in, the fact that they were each owed money. They knew that the ship's decision makers had spent the entire morning in the great cabin, and they guessed that some word was imminent.

"Mr. Honeyman, pray assemble the men aft," Marlowe said. Honeyman nodded, called the word down the deck. Men came up from below, down from aloft, back to the after end of the waist, where they assembled, some standing, some sitting, all of them looking up at the quarterdeck like groundlings before a stage.

Marlowe looked down at them. Half of the faces looking up at him were black, and that surprised him. He did not often see the whole crew en masse, and so accustomed had he become to their odd makeup, so integrated into the shipboard life were the former field hands, that Marlowe had lost track of the fact that this was something unusual.

He had always counted the field hands as his own faction on board. He, after all, had freed them from slavery. They were the men of Marlowe House, his people, standing between him and whatever mutinous, piratical villains they might be forced to ship.

But now, looking out over the hands, he was not so sure.

The men no longer grouped themselves by race. Though they appeared to stand in a loose mob, black and white, Marlowe could see that they were in fact gravitating into their watches, starboard and larboard, each with his own, and also into that most intimate of shipboard divisions, the mess.

The clothes that the young men from Marlowe House had made new on the passage to England were now worn and tar-stained and patched. The men themselves had the loose-limbed, casual stance of the true deep-water sailor, like men possessing enormous strength of arm and endurance but not willing to waste any of it. They had the sailor's cocksure, jaunty quality. They seemed to swagger even when they were standing still.

The blacks were no longer the men of Marlowe House, they were Elizabeth Galleys now, loyal to their ship, loyal to their mates foremost. Once he could have counted on their support, but now they would be as unpredictable as any crowd of sailors.

The lower deck was the most heterogeneous workplace in the world.

"Listen here, you men," Marlowe began, an unnecessary injunction, he saw, since he already had everyone's rapt attention.

Honeyman was sitting on top of the spare spars, the hard cases that he had recruited standing around him like his own personal crew.

Sundry others of the men before the mast stood scattered around the waist. Twenty-eight men. Not a large crew, not for a pirate vessel.

"You men know what happened in London, you know we can't go back there. We would be taken, hanged for piracy, as unjust as that might be. The mariner doesn't always get justice—foremast jack or master, it makes no difference. You know that better than anyone.

"So we have a problem. Our cargo is gone. We'll see not one penny of profit for our labors. But there might be a way we can recoup our loss. Perhaps even make some profit. Perhaps even strike it rich. I propose we steer for Madagascar!"

That proposition received the response that Marlowe had expected: wild cheers, hats waved in the air, grins all around. Even the black men, who two months before probably had never even heard of Madagascar, cheered with enthusiasm, having no doubt been filled with tales of the Pirate Round by the more experienced seamen aboard.

"I take heart from your response," Marlowe said. "Madagascar it is!"

"Hold a moment, Captain!" Honeyman stood up, took a step forward.

Oh, son of a whore, Marlowe thought. *Must we hear from the sea lawyer now?*

"I'm for Madagascar, much as the next man," Honeyman began. "But it was a merchantman we signed aboard. Merchantman rules. If we are off on the Pirate Round, then it changes things."

Marlowe leaned on the rail, glared down at Honeyman. "You men signed ship's articles. You are bound by them."

"Beg pardon, sir, and pray believe I mean no disrespect," Honeyman continued, "but those was ship's articles for a trading voyage to London and back to Virginia. Off to Madagascar . . . well, that changes it. We're not bound by those articles. I say we draft articles anew, in the fashion of the Code of the Coast."

Glare as he might, Marlowe could not silence the murmur of consent that ran through the men at this suggestion.

Then Dinwiddie stepped forward, the timidity he might have felt in the great cabin entirely gone now that he stood on the quarterdeck, his natural forum, and faced the sailors below.

"Damn you, you sneaking puppy!" he bellowed at Honeyman. "Captain has given orders, and they're to be obeyed!"

Dinwiddie's was a voice that would have cowed most men, but Honeyman persisted. "The captain will be obeyed in all things. I reckon the men will agree there be no voting on captain, nor officers, which is common among the Roundsmen, as you know well, Mr. Dinwiddie. I say only we need articles."

The murmur of approval grew louder, heads nodded, eyes fixed aft. *Well, it is out of the damned bottle now, and I shall never get it back in,* Marlowe thought. *Damn that man, Honeyman—he has hoisted me by my own petard.*

Then up stepped Burgess, one of Honeyman's hard cases, his gnarled, muscular arms folded, his gold earring flashing, his head bound in a red damask cloth. "I say we votes Mr. Honeyman as quartermaster!" he called, and that brought a renewed murmur of approval.

Marlowe clenched his teeth, felt the entire thing slipping from his grasp.

A quartermaster now, and new articles.

But that was the way of the pirates—he knew it better than any on board. He had hoped to have it all ways, to be captain of a Red Sea Rover without submitting to the crude democracy of the Brethren of the Coast. But now he saw that would not happen. Seamen as a tribe were too protective of their precious rights to let him off that easily.

Would they now vote him out of his captaincy? And if so, what could he do about it? It was he, after all, who had suggested piracy in the first place.

"Very well," Marlowe said. He glanced behind him. Bickerstaff stood off to one side. He gave Marlowe a cocked eyebrow, an eloquent sermon on Marlowe's misplaced self-assurance. "Let us vote."

The polling did not take long, no more time than it took for Marlowe to say, "Who here would vote Duncan Honeyman as quartermaster?" and for every man aboard, including the former field workers from Marlowe House, to raise his hand.

That done, Honeyman stood on the main hatch, and all eyes turned from Marlowe to him. And Marlowe understood that he had just given up his supreme authority as a legitimate ship's captain for the popular rule of the pirates, and he was not happy. The quartermaster of a pirate ship was the representative of the men, the bridge between great cabin and lower deck, and now that bridge was Honeyman, the sea lawyer.

How long has he planned this moment? Marlowe wondered. *Since Norfolk, from the moment I first said "Madagascar"?*

"See here." Honeyman was talking now. "We said no vote on officers and Mr. Dinwiddie and Mr. Flanders are fine officers in any event, and Mr. Marlowe as good a captain as ever I've sailed with. I reckon we need only choose a new bosun, and we're set up proper."

They chose Burgess, as experienced and able as he was taciturn and piratical.

Honeyman and Marlowe retired to the great cabin, where they might work out the new articles in peace.

"Captain Marlowe," Honeyman began, "I want you to know I mean no disrespect, nor no challenge to your authority, by this. It's just . . . well, the way things are."

"Yes, yes," said Marlowe, impatient, wanting to be done with that distasteful job. Marlowe, the manipulator, did not care to be manipulated himself, and he had been. Played like a flute.

It took them no more than an hour to draw up the articles for the *Elizabeth Galley*. They both were familiar enough with the protocol of the pirate ship that they had only to write it down, with a little modification to fit their circumstances.

Every man to have a vote in affairs of the moment, save for those concerning the disposition of the *Elizabeth Galley*, of which Thomas Marlowe was recognized as the sole owner.

Every man to keep his piece, pistol, and cutlass clean and fit for service; any man who would desert the ship or his quarters in battle would suffer marooning; any man who would cheat his shipmates out of the value of one dollar would suffer marooning. The captain and quartermaster to receive two shares of a prize, boatswain and gunner and officers one and a half shares.

It differed from the standard agreement among the pirates in only a few points. An exception was made for Elizabeth in the clause banning all women from the ship, and the great cabin was recognized as her and Thomas's private domain, a luxury not enjoyed by most pirate captains.

Honeyman looked on these concessions as thoughtful consideration, but Marlowe considered them patronizing and demeaning, and they made him angrier still.

When the ink was dry, they took the document out to the waist, where it was read aloud, and then every man, save for Bickerstaff, signed, and those who could only make their mark did so, and Marlowe wrote their name beside.

In just half a day, and with that single piece of paper, the *Elizabeth Galley* was transformed from an honest merchantman to a Red Sea pirate.

That night Thomas Marlowe slept on the lockers aft. Elizabeth made it plain that he was not welcome in her bed.

He wondered, as he lay on his back looking out the big windows at the stars swaying overhead with the roll of the ship, how long she was likely to stay that angry. He wondered how Honeyman might be plotting to betray him, if Bickerstaff would remain forever disgusted with him and his clever manipulations.

All the plunder in the Indian Ocean would be meaningless to him if he lost the love of Elizabeth and Francis. He wondered if he had not made an enormous miscalculation.

Chapter 10

ELEPHIANT, Lord Yancy, looked around the clearing that had been hacked from the living jungle. It had been cleared years before his arrival and then left, and the jungle had quickly returned, like water rushing into a hollow in a cliff, before Yancy ordered it cleared once more. Fifteen miles along the length of the island, on winding, half-obscured paths from the great house and lands that he had by divine right inherited from Adam Baldridge. Fifteen miles through a deep ravine and then up along a knife-edge trail to the secret location, near the crest of one of the low mountains in the heart of the island of St. Mary's.

It had been a long day's hike to that place. Yancy, not as strong as he once was, had had to ask repeatedly that they stop, allow him to rest, before taking up the climb again. He waved off the others' solicitous concern.

Now, sitting on a stool in the shade, Yancy let his eyes move slowly over the small wood-and-wattle house, the high row of pickets that surrounded it, the deep, deep jungle beyond, a wall of coconut and banana and papaya. Like the big house, this smaller outpost had been built by Baldridge, and though not as opulent, it was still unstinting in the quality of the location and construction.

For the first few years that Yancy had been king on the island, he had not even known of its existence. He might never have known about that secret place had one of his Malagasy wives not made an offhand reference to it and then, on his further questioning, led him there.

It was in far worse shape than the big house, having been completely abandoned. The jungle was to a building what the sea was to a ship: left unchecked, it would work its way in, creep in through tiny openings, overwhelm and consume. The small house had been near to returning to a state of nature when Yancy found it.

Baldridge had understood the need for secret places, escape routes, clandestine entrances, the advantage of having a place to which one could get away. A place that was hidden and easily defensible. Yancy understood that as well, and he took advantage of the preparations that Baldridge had made.

He set his men to beating the jungle back once more, to repairing walls and roof and the stockade that surrounded the house. It was slow going. He could put only his most trusted few to work, because he would not reveal the existence of the place to any of the others.

It had taken months, but the place at last was set to rights. For several years it had been maintained that way, but rarely used. Yancy had no need to leave the big house. He did not wish to take his eyes off the activity on the harbor for very long.

Atwood's letter had changed that, had made it imperative that the small house be readied for occupation. The trusted few were set at it, urged on by Yancy, who expected every day to hear from his lookout at the top of the jungle-clad hills rising up behind the town that Press's ship and tender were standing into the harbor, guns run out, armed men swarming the decks.

But now it was done. Repaired, provisioned, armed. Yancy had casks of fresh salt beef and pork and dried peas stacked under cover. Barrels of powder and shot, muskets, a few swivel guns that could be mounted on the stockade. A natural spring came up right in the middle of the yard, which no doubt was why Baldridge had chosen that site.

They were ready to hold out there as long as need be. And Roger Press had not yet arrived.

"Good. Good," he said, nodding his approval. He pulled a red silk handkerchief from his sleeve and mopped his brow. Looked up at Henry Nagel, looming over him. "And the weapons, Henry? You are sure of the weapons?"

"Aye, sir. Seen every one of the muskets fired myself, just yesterday, to the number of fifty. Swivels as well. Two hundred rounds per gun."

"Good, good." They looked across the courtyard, enclosed by the stockade. Fifteen or so of the original Terrors were cleaning weapons and making repairs to the stockade and finishing up the last of the myriad details that would make the outpost comfortable and defensible.

They would need their women, too, of course, at least a portion of their harems. That would make it crowded, to be sure, but it was impossible to think of holding out for any length of time otherwise. With no women it would be like life at sea, but without the constant work or threat or hope of a prize to keep minds occupied.

The men would get restless, and resentful of having to do the menial chores of cooking and cleaning. These, after all, were the elite of St. Mary's, the founding fathers. They would not even be engaged in the tasks of repairing and provisioning the compound, were it not for the need for secrecy.

Yancy looked over the house, but his mind was still on the issue of his harem. Since receiving her letter, his thoughts kept wandering back to his first wife, the one he had left back in New York. Sometimes when he lay with one of his Malagasy wives he would close his eyes and picture her—Susan, that was her name—her lovely white skin and blond hair, like silk.

"Lord Yancy?" Nagel interrupted his reverie.

"What?" Yancy snapped, a response that would have made other men wince, but Nagel, too dumb or too unafraid, did not react, and it made Yancy suspicious.

"It's only, sir . . . do you means to hide out here? Forever, like? If I might be so bold, sir, what is your plan?"

"Plan?" Yancy coughed into his handkerchief. "I have no plan, Henry. What can we do against Press, with his great band of loyal men? These"—he indicated the others with a wave of his arm, "these are the only men I can trust. Precious few. No, Henry, I fear that all I can do is see that my beloved Terrors are safe, off in this paradise where Press cannot find you."

"Us, sir," Nagel corrected.

"Pardon?"

"Us. Where Press cannot find us."

Yancy was silent for a moment, watching the activity in the court-yard. "Oh, yes, yes. Us, of course."

Foul weather, above and below.

Seven days since the meeting in the great cabin, and Elizabeth was still sulky, still giving Marlowe only the most perfunctory of greetings, at first silent during dinner, and then abandoning dinner altogether, eating in the sleeping cabin, forcing him to sleep on the locker. Further apologies had been of no avail, attempts to cajole her out of her funk had been met with angry looks.

It seemed incredible to Marlowe that she should be so angry over one simple lie. Not even a lie, really, a mere omission of information. It was his money, his responsibility. His contrition was turning to anger as Elizabeth held tenaciously on to her grudge.

Bickerstaff, too. He did not sulk, was not the sulking kind, but neither did he try to hide the certain coolness he felt toward Marlowe.

It was something Marlowe had anticipated, something he had worked into the calculation. Bickerstaff detested pirates. Years before, when he had been Marlowe's prisoner—or, more accurately, Malachias Barrett's—Marlowe had forced him to sail in the sweet trade. But he had never forced him to commit piracy, had allowed him to stay below and out of any fight, had defended Bickerstaff against the other men on board the ship who thought him a coward.

It was not for want of courage that Bickerstaff stayed below. He was not wanting at all in that area. It was because of his moral revulsion with piracy. Marlowe knew he would not wish to sail the Pirate Round. But he knew as well that practical considerations and concern not for Marlowe's social standing but for Elizabeth's, whom he loved, would lead him to countenance it at least, if not participate.

Marlowe knew from the beginning that Bickerstaff would not be pleased to find out the extent to which he had planned out the entire thing. Still, he was surprised by how very displeased Bickerstaff seemed to be.

Honeyman went about his duties as ever, if perhaps a little less taciturn and a little more conciliatory, which only served to annoy Marlowe more. Dinwiddie grew more surly by the day, not pleased to find himself a first officer with less real authority than the quartermaster.

And overhead a thick blanket of gray cloud, through which the sun made not even the ghost of an appearance, not even a bright disk to hint at where it was. Below the solid cover, darker clouds raced along, driven fast by winds that were flowing in a direction different from that of the wind over the water.

The seas were big and growing bigger, gray, lumpy, with stark whitecaps as the tops broke on the bigger waves. The atmosphere was moody, hostile, threatening. Tense.

Marlowe sat at the table in the great cabin, stared out the salt-stained windows aft. A wet tablecloth spread across the tabletop held pewter plates from sliding around with the roll of the ship. On the plates the half-eaten meal shifted slightly with the bigger seas.

He was alone at the table. Elizabeth was in the sleeping cabin, eating, sleeping, praying that God strike her husband down—he did not know and was beginning not to care. The surfeit of ill will was numbing him to it.

Bickerstaff took his meals with Dinwiddie and Flanders and Honeyman. Marlowe guessed that they were not a particularly jovial group. Better to eat alone.

The *Elizabeth Galley* rolled hard to larboard, and the wide-bottomed tankard of wine toppled over, sending a dark red stain spreading across the already-wet tablecloth, but Marlowe could not muster the energy to do anything more than look at it, then turn back to the seas beyond his window.

They were two days out of sight of land. After having made the decision to turn Red Sea Rover, they had stood in for Penzance on

Mounts Bay, Cornwall, at the very western tip of England, to provision for the long voyage to Madagascar.

The Cornish people were well known for their casual disregard for Admiralty law. They asked no questions about the unarmed privateer victualing in that out-of-the-way port. They showed no curiosity about the Spanish gold with which Marlowe paid, just accepted it gladly.

Three days later the *Elizabeth Galley* stood out of Mounts Bay with food and water and firewood enough in her hold to see them around the Cape of Good Hope and on to Madagascar.

Marlowe sighed, abandoned his dinner for the quarterdeck. Had it been blue skies and calm seas, he might have stayed below, but the weather now was to his liking. Dark, ugly skies, cold wind, spitting rain and spray—it was like stepping right into his own confused and angry mind.

He stopped at the weather rail, turned his back to the wind. His cloak beat against his legs, and his hair, long enough finally to be bound in a queue, was flung forward over his shoulder.

The bow of the *Elizabeth Galley* went down into a trough between big seas, and the quarterdeck seemed to fly up in the air, like one end of a giant seesaw. Marlowe felt his stomach left behind as the after end of the ship rose, hung for a second, then plunged down again as the wave passed under. An odd sensation, but he had been too long at sea for it to bother him.

Dinwiddie and Honeyman and Burgess were everywhere, seeing storm gaskets passed around furled sail, double-gripping the boats, inspecting the tarpaulin covers over the hatches, rigging lifelines down the length of the deck.

As much as he thought Honeyman was vermin, a sea lawyer, and as much as Dinwiddie was becoming a malcontent, as surly as Burgess was, still Marlowe had to admit that they were seamen who knew their business. The storm that was building around them would be a bad one, he could tell. At that moment he would not have traded the first officer and the quartermaster and bosun for the cheeriest sycophants on earth.

The bow plunged down again and this time slammed into the oncoming wave, some quirk of timing that made the vessel shudder and sent a huge plume of water bursting over the fore rail, like surf against a rocky shore. Marlowe saw the water douse Honeyman and Dinwiddie, saw them hunch their shoulders against the cold deluge as they worked their way aft along the gangway and back to the quarterdeck.

"Deck's secured, sir," Dinwiddie said, loud, to be heard over the rising wind. "T'gallants?"

"Aye!" Marlowe said. It was time to get the topgallant masts and yards, the highest and weakest of the spars, down from their place aloft and stowed safely on deck. "Once you've struck them down, let us have the deep reef in the topsails. Mr. Honeyman, I reckon we have men enough to rig rolling tackles while the topgallants are being struck?"

"Aye, sir, should do."

"Very well, then. Let us get that all snugged down. I think this night will be something of a shitter."

"Reckon so, Captain!" Dinwiddie shouted, and then the two men went forward again to carry out the last of the preparations for the building storm.

Gray, dim, watery. For all the stormy afternoon the sky seemed never to achieve full daylight. The seas built, bigger and bigger, rising up around them to the level of the gunports, then the cap rails, then the quarterdeck rail, so that in the trough between the waves there was nothing but water roiling around, as if the *Elizabeth Galley* had been tossed down into a hole in the ocean.

And then she would rise again on the waves, up so high it seemed she must topple off such a fine perch, and then down once more.

The topgallant masts and yards were lowered to the deck and lashed to the main hatch. The topsails were reefed, the top half of the sail lashed to the yard from which it hung, leaving only a portion of the canvas still exposed to the wind. Rolling tackles that kept the heavy yards from slamming side to side as the ship rolled were rigged and bowsed taut. The *Elizabeth Galley* plunged on.

There was one good thing about that wind, only one, and that was that it was northeasterly, blowing the *Galley* south and west, the very direction that Marlowe wished her to go. South and west, they would cross the Atlantic almost to the continent of South America, drift through the equatorial doldrums, and then pick up the westerly trades south of the line that would fling them back across the Atlantic and around the southern tip of Africa. A long voyage. A desperate and final attempt at salvaging his gentleman's fortune.

The daylight, such that it was, was nearly gone when Dinwiddie came aft. Marlowe stepped toward the first lieutenant, expecting him to report that all was secure for the night.

The two men maneuvered toward each other, hands on the cap rail, feet spread wide to the wild heaving of the ship, the decks wet with the spray that filled the air and the intermittent showers of rain.

"Honeyman's getting a little large for his goddamned britches, Captain" was the first thing Dinwiddie yelled in his ear, over the shriek of wind in rigging. "Telling off men to rig the rolling tackles, arguing with me about the lead of the top rope, I won't stand for his nonsense!" Not exactly the report Marlowe had hoped for.

"Pray, Mr. Dinwiddie, let us see if we live through the night, and then we'll straighten it all out in the morning!" Marlowe shouted back. *As if I need any more nonsense from these motherless chuckleheads*, he thought.

"Aye, sir." Dinwiddie bit off the words, and Marlowe saw that he would require some placating.

"You are right! Honeyman needs taking down, and I will see to it. Now, are we set for the night?"

"Aye, sir, all snugged down proper! Don't know how long we can hold on to the topsails, though!"

Less than half an hour, as it turned out. The last vestiges of light were starting to go as Marlowe stood at the weather rail, looking aloft through the gloom, wondering about the topsails. He was braced against the wind as it tried to shove him forward, like temptation pushing him as he tried to resist. It was his nature to carry sail as long as he could, make every inch of distance if he was going in the right direction, but the canvas would not hold out much longer.

He had just decided it was time to take in sail, to run before the wind and seas under bare poles, when the fore topsail split. He was actually looking at the main topsail, contemplating the relative age and strength of the cloth, when he felt the wind give him a hard shove. He was pushed forward, grabbed at the rail, braced himself harder.

The *Elizabeth Galley* staggered as if she had been hit with a broadside, rolled hard to one side, the seas rolling up around her. She groaned, and the wind in the shrouds rose in pitch, and a thousand parts of her hull and rig clattered as she righted herself.

And then through all that chaos of noise Marlowe heard the telltale crack of splitting canvas, a sharp report, like a gunshot. He looked up again.

The main topsail was an unbroken field of taut, dull, wet canvas.

He bent down, looked forward and up. The fore topsail looked much the same, a sheet of light gray in a dark gray and black world. But just to starboard of the midpoint of the sail he could see the split, three feet long, from the bolt rope up. Just the one split, and for the moment it was getting no wider, as if the sail were fighting to keep itself together, just long enough for Marlowe to send help.

Honeyman was in the waist, and he also was looking at the sail. Marlowe thought to shout an order, realized Honeyman would never hear him, took a step forward—and then the sail let go.

Another crack, many times louder than the first, and when Marlowe had looked aloft again, the topsail was nothing but ribbons blowing out to leeward, long trails of canvas flogging like banners. The bolt rope, which had once reinforced the edges of the topsail, was still held in place, like the skeleton of the sail, as if it did not know that the canvas was gone.

Underfoot Marlowe felt the ship slew a bit as the balance of sail and hull suddenly changed. He whirled around, hand over hand on the rail, his eyes streaming tears as he took the wind full in the face, ready to issue orders to the helmsmen or take the tiller himself if need be.

But one of Burgess's mates, another seasoned hard case of a seaman, was at the tiller, backed up by one of the strong young men from Marlowe House, and they had shoved the tiller over, just a bit, to compensate for the change, turning just how Marlowe would have ordered them to, so he let them alone and turned his back to the wind again.

Honeyman was charging forward, Burgess at his heels, grabbing men to come with him, pushing others toward the pin rails and gesturing. *Clew it up! Clew it up!* Honeyman's meaning was clear, even from the quarterdeck.

"Good man!" Marlowe said out loud. But Honeyman was thinking only of the sail, and Marlowe had to think of the ship. The helmsmen could not hold the vessel forever with the sails out of balance. One wicked gust and she would spin beam on to the seas, and then over she would go.

"Mr. Dinwiddie!" he shouted to the first officer who had staggered up from the lee side. "We must get the main topsail off her!"

Dinwiddie nodded, nearly fell as the *Galley*'s bow, now lost in the dark, slammed into an unseen wave. He stumbled against the bulwark, grabbed hold, turned to Marlowe.

"You get some hands to the leeward gear!" Marlowe continued. "I shall see the weather clews manned! Tell Flanders to get a gang together to lay aloft and stow!"

Dinwiddie nodded again and shouted the orders back, though now Marlowe could hardly hear him for the wind, even from two feet away. He lurched off, calling, waving for men to follow, while Marlowe gathered up hands to help with the weather rigging.

They cast off clewlines and halyards and heaved away, hauling the main topsail yard down, inch by inch. Men clung to the clewlines, pulled, swayed with the bucking of the ship, slammed against the bulwark, pulled again.

At last the yard was down and the sheets were cast off and the sail was hauled up. It filled with wind and bucked and fought like a wild animal, but finally it was subdued through strength of arm and the mechanical advantage of block and tackle.

Then, one by one, the men climbed into the weather shrouds and worked their way aloft, moving slowly, a single careful step at a time, as the rolling ship tried to fling them into the sea. Up, up the main shrouds, over the main top, and up the topmast shrouds. From there it was step onto the foot ropes strung under the yards and shuffle out to where they could claw the canvas into submission.

Marlowe watched them go aloft. He had no business joining them. As captain, his place was on the quarterdeck, where he could see the entire situation, fore and aft. Indeed, it would have been a dereliction of duty for him to abandon that place and lay aloft with his men. But still, even after all the years he had had command of ships at sea, he could hardly bear to send men aloft into such peril while he remained behind.

Bickerstaff, he saw, was with them. He had been on deck through most of the day, bearing a hand, ignoring Marlowe. He worked by choice. He had no official duties on board. In fact, he was something of a nonentity, having refused to sign the ship's articles, leaving him with no vote and no right to any prize taken.

But for all that, Bickerstaff was not a man to shrink from labor, not the kind to use his status as a gentleman to avoid hauling side by side with the men, especially in a crisis such as the building storm. And so he hung from the clewlines like the others, heave and belay, and made his careful way aloft to save their precious topsail from the wind's terrible grip.

And Marlowe wished fervently that Bickerstaff would not die before he had a chance to redeem himself in his friend's eyes.

For over an hour the men fought with the main topsail. At last it was stowed and what was left of the fore topsail lashed in place and all the men back in the relative safety of the deck.

Full night was on them, complete blackness, which meant that every big sea that rolled up from the dark took them by surprise, sometimes breaking over the stern, sometimes seeming to pause in front of them so that the bow pounded into the wall of water again and again.

A wild, hellish night of mounting wind and bitter-cold spray, a night where men and gear were tossed around the deck by the capricious seas, and water coming over the bow and through the gunports in the open waist would run two and three feet high over the deck.

But still Marlowe was sanguine about it all. Years of experience told him that they were at the height of the storm, that dawn would bring a slacking of the wind, a diminishing of the seas. And they were secure now, the sails stowed away, everything on deck lashed down, the pumps working well. It was all hands on deck, too rough for anyone to get a watch below, but the men were not exhausted or starved, and they were showing what a solid and coordinated crew they had become.

The *Elizabeth Galley* was moving fast under just bare poles. The sail area that her masts and yards alone presented was enough to drive her at six and seven knots before the gale. Under their bow, over three thousand miles of open ocean. And best of all, and most unusual given the seemingly malicious nature of storms at sea, they were being driven in just the direction they wished to go.

Cold, wet to the skin, tired, throat burning from swallowing salt spray, Marlowe was still feeling largely optimistic as he struggled down the ladder to the waist and, bouncing off the doors in the alleyway, stumbled aft to the great cabin to check on Elizabeth.

He found her in her bunk—their bunk, their former bunk—flat on her back, moaning with each wild swing of the hanging bed. It took quite a bit to make Elizabeth seasick, but the storm was giving quite a bit that night.

"How are you, my dear?" he asked, trying to sound tender and sensitive, which was hard, as he had practically to yell over the cacophony of creaking timbers and the waves and the howl of the wind.

She looked up at him, her face waxy in the light of the lantern, which also swung in wild arcs, throwing crazy shadows around the small sleeping compartment. Her long hair was tangled and matted, and it looked as if she had not been entirely successful in keeping it clear while she vomited.

For a moment her expression was pleading, vulnerable, and Marlowe thought she was going to express her unfailing love for him, there on what she might believe to be her deathbed. But she did not. Instead she flopped onto her back and closed her eyes as the ship rolled and the bunk swung so hard that it thumped on the overhead.

When the *Galley* had come upright again, she said simply "Go to hell, Thomas," so soft Marlowe could scarcely hear.

Well, damn you, then. You shall be sorry, you ungrateful wench, if we all die this night, Marlowe thought, and without another word he turned and left her there.

Back down the alleyway and into the waist, past groups of men huddled in what shelter they could find. Nothing to do at the moment, no sail to trim, and the ship seemed to be standing up to the storm's onslaught. Only the helm to man and the pumps to work, and beyond that there was only to stay awake and alert, because their happy stasis could be torn away by a single rogue wave or gust of wind.

For all that black night Marlowe prowled the quarterdeck, standing sometimes in the lee of the cloth lashed up in the mizzen shrouds, sometimes talking with the helmsmen or with Dinwiddie or Honeyman to see how the vessel fared, sometimes making his way down into the waist to give the men some encouragement and to see that nothing had been overlooked. But the *Galley* was strong and well set up, and the crew he had managed to piece together was competent and able, if not so numerous as he might have wished, and all was well.

Two bells in the morning watch, five A.M., and Marlowe realized that the pumps were sounding louder. It took his fatigue-shrouded brain a moment to realize that this was due to a lessening in the wind, a diminishing in the omnipresent howl that had tormented them all the dark hours.

With that realization came the awareness that the sea was settling down a bit. It was still a mad, pitching, rolling, yawing ride through the big swells, but Marlowe realized it was not as bad as it had been an hour before, and an hour hence, he had reason to hope, it would be better yet.

Dawn came around four bells, no more than a gray version of the night, with the sun entirely hidden behind the impenetrable cloud. The sea was the color of lead, rising up all around, row after row of watery hillocks that obscured everything beyond as the *Elizabeth Galley* sank down in the space between them and then gave a brief glimpse of the horizon as she rose up again. But the menace of the night was gone, the tension that came with not knowing when the next wave would be on them or how big it might be.

Dinwiddie sent lookouts forward and to either beam, there now being some hope that they might see something, if there was anything to see. Marlowe doubted there would be. They had been running fast away from the English coast all night. Nothing was under their bow now but open water, clear to the Americas.

He sat wearily down on a quarter bitt. His legs ached, and his skin was chafed raw in several places from his salt-water-soaked clothing. He was thinking about breakfast.

Then the forward lookout shouted, "Son of a bitch!" his voice edged in panic.

Marlowe shot to his feet, leaped up on the bitt, hand on the mizzen shrouds, looking forward. Water, nothing but water.

"What is it, you poxed whoreson?" Dinwiddie shouted.

"Ship! Damn me! A wreck!" was all the lookout could splutter. The *Elizabeth Galley* came up again as the sea passed under. There, below her now, unseen in the trough of the waves until that moment, was a ship, or what was left of one.

Dismasted, half sunk, lying almost on her beam ends, her bottom toward the *Galley*, her deck on the far side. Glistening in the dull light, water breaking over her. A ship, lying at a right angle to the *Galley*, like something that had risen up from the grave, her stern under the *Galley*'s bow, directly in their path.

"Starboard your helm! Starboard!" Marlowe shouted. The helmsmen shoved the tiller over. The *Galley* began to turn as the wave passed under and the wreck rose up above them. And then the next roller had the *Galley*, driving her forward, and the two ships struck.

Chapter 11

THE GALLEY'S spritsail yard hit first, dragging across the quarterdeck of the drifting hulk, then catching in the shattered taffrail, tangling inextricably in the jagged wood, as if the dying ship were reaching out, one last desperate grasp for help.

Honeyman was at the bow, casting off the spritsail lifts and braces, but Marlowe could already feel the *Elizabeth Galley* pause as the wreck held her in its grip.

"Shift your helm!" The tiller went over again, and the *Galley* turned, just a bit. The wind and sea were driving the *Galley* fast, and now the waterlogged wreck was trying to hold her back.

He could see the bowsprit flexing under the enormous pressure, could see the spritsail yard bending, wondered what would give first.

And then the spritsail yard was torn clean away, pulling free from the bowsprit with a cracking of wood and snapping of lines. Bits of rigging whipped through the air as the big yard was wrenched off. The *Elizabeth Galley* leaped forward, out of the wreck's grip.

"Midships!" Marlowe shouted, and then the *Elizabeth Galley*'s starboard bow slammed into the wreck's transom. The ship shuddered, the waterlogged hulk as unyielding as solid rock. The cathead crumpled under the impact, and the bulwark stove in. Men ran aft as the ship dragged along the wreck, tearing itself up.

Marlowe stared, transfixed by the sight of the great round white bottom of the ship. The deck was still lost to his view, the ship listing away from the *Elizabeth Galley*.

The starboard fore channel hit next, tangled up in the battered stern section of the hulk. Marlowe could see the three forward shrouds grow taut and tauter under the strain, and then something snapped, and the shrouds went slack again, ripped apart like old twine. If even one more shroud was torn free, they would loose the mast.

The next sea lifted the *Galley*'s stern and began to shove it around. She turned sideways to the sea, pivoting on the forward section that was locked to the wreck. Broadside to the waves, a bigger sea might have rolled them over, but the waves were smaller now, choppier, and Marlowe did not see a watery end coming.

The channel wrenched free from the hulk, and the sea drove the *Galley* past, and they were downwind of the drifting menace, safe, beyond the threat.

The deck of the dead ship came into view, and Marlowe was able to see something of her in the imperfect light of that early morning. A big vessel, an Indiaman perhaps. The lee bulwarks were underwater—her hull must have been half filled. She had an hour to live, perhaps a bit more, and then she would be gone.

On the stump of her mainmast, rising fifteen feet above the deck, a British merchantman's ensign, torn to rags, set upside down. A pathetic signal of distress, as if anyone would see it or would have been able to render any help if they had.

Marlowe did not like to think of the horrible death that had attended the crew, thrashing in the bitter-cold water at night, the nightmare of every sailor.

Then, just as the big ship was disappearing from sight behind the next steep wave, one that would leave her farther beyond the *Galley*'s reach, he saw motion, color, something moving along the deck. He leaped into the main shrouds, raced aloft, eyes locked on the wreck, trying to gain some height, to see before she was lost behind the wall of water.

There were men still alive on her. He could see them, now one hundred yards away, but he could see them, crawling along the high side, waving frantically. Something white—a shirt, a fragment of sail—someone was desperately signaling.

The *Elizabeth Galley* was still nearly beam on to the waves, but the helmsmen had the tiller over, and she was turning again, so that in a moment she would once again be running away downwind.

"Helmsmen! Hold as you are!" Marlowe shouted. "Mr. Dinwiddie! The mizzen sail! Let us set it, quickly, quickly!"

Dinwiddie came running aft, a lumbering, awkward sort of run, with the more athletic Honeyman on his heels and a gang of men behind. They did not ask questions, they just obeyed, casting off gaskets and laying out the halyard, clapping on and hauling away with speed and care.

"Reef's tucked!" Honeyman shouted over the wind.

"Good! We are going to bring to!"

That order received a frown and a knitting of brows, but no more, as the men struggled with setting the sail in the howling gale. When they were running before it, the wind had not seemed so bad, but now, with the ship virtually stopped, it blew over them with all its force, pulling at hair and clothes, making the rigging hum and sing.

"Midships!" Marlowe called to the helmsmen. The mizzen yard inched up the mast, the bit of canvas that was exposed pulling hard, bellied out taut in the wind.

"Dinwiddie! Send some men forward! Set that fore staysail!"

The *Elizabeth Galley* turned until she was taking the sea and the wind on her damaged starboard bow.

"Now, helm a'larboard! There, hold her there!" Marlowe paused, gauging the feel of the ship, trying to get a sense of whether or not she was in balance, if she would stay as she was with the contending forces of helm and sail, and he saw that she would.

Honeyman and Dinwiddie were there, at his side, waiting for orders, wondering no doubt what he was thinking. The safest thing for them would have been to keep running before the storm. Instead they were stopped, hove to, with the wreck to windward and drifting down on them. Now and then it was visible from the deck, rising up on the swell, and then down again. The next wave, or the next, and she might go down and keep going, until she came to a stop in the sands' unknown fathoms below.

"There are men alive on that ship!" Marlowe pointed to windward. He thought that would explain everything, but Honeyman and Dinwiddie continued to stare.

"We are going to get them off!" Marlowe shouted again. Behind him the man coiling down the mizzen halyard shouted, "What? In this bloody sea?" as if he were part of the conversation, which he was not.

In fact, there *was* no conversation. Marlowe glared at Dinwiddie, challenging him to argue. He glared at Honeyman, daring him to make some noise about what the crew wished to do. He was ready to break them both at that point if they gave him a breath of grief, and the Red Sea be damned. But Dinwiddie just nodded, and Honeyman said, "How do you reckon to do it?"

That was the question. If they had been to windward of the wreck, they might have drifted a boat down to them. But they were downwind now, and all the tacking in the world would not get them back up to windward again.

Marlowe turned from the two men, ran his eyes along the deck and then out to windward, where he was able to catch a glimpse of the wreck before it was lost again between waves. The *Elizabeth Galley*, with her masts in place, was drifting much faster than the waterlogged hulk. If they could slow their drift, let the wreck drift down on them, pass a line somehow . . .

God, this is a stupid thing I am doing! Marlowe thought. The idea of letting an unpredictable hulk drift down on them, with that sea running and the wind howling around their ears, was insane. But he could not let those men die without trying. They were sailors. British sailors, to boot. He did not examine his motives; he knew only that he had to try.

"We must slow our drift!" he shouted, and the two men nodded. "Let us lash some of them spare spars together, put 'em over the side with a light hawser, a sort of sea anchor! That might do!"

"Aye, sir!" Honeyman shouted. "Mayhaps the wreck'll drift down on the spars. If those poor bastards yonder can reach them, they can grab on to the spars and we'll pull 'em aboard!"

Marlowe nodded as if that had been his thought all along, but actually it had not occurred to him. Still, it was perfect. Set a sea anchor in the form of the spare masts and yards, let the hulk drift down on that, let the men climb aboard the spars, and pull them over to the *Galley*. Simple.

But Marlowe was seaman enough to know that it was never that simple.

The first task was to lash the spare spars together and get them over the side. Honeyman and Dinwiddie and Burgess worked the gangs of men in the waist, lashing together the long, rounded timbers, *Elizabeth Galley*'s inventory of spare topmasts and yards and topgallant masts. They lashed them lengthwise, like a giant bundle of twigs, and rigged stops and yard tackle and stay tackle to lift the whole mess.

Halfway down the length of the spars they attached the hawser, the three-inch-thick rope that would hold the *Elizabeth Galley* tethered to the drifting mass.

The *Elizabeth Galley* would drift faster through the water than the half-submerged sea anchor made up of spare spars. If the hawser were attached to the sharp end of the spars, the ship would just pull the sea anchor through the water like a boat. But with the hawser attached to the midpoint of the spars' length, the *Galley* would be pulling the long timbers sideways, like trying to drag a ship broadside through the water, rather than bow first. The spars would thus act as a brake to slow the *Galley*'s fast downwind drift.

Simple.

The men staggered through the task, tired, battered from their long night, their footing unsure on the slick and rolling deck.

Will this be worth it, if any of my men are killed in the trying? Marlowe wondered.

Bickerstaff made his way aft. He looked drawn, pale with fatigue. "You are setting a sea anchor, or so the rumor goes, forward."

"Yes, we are. Let that hulk drift down on us."

"Do you mean to take possession of her?"

"Possession? Dear God, she will not live till the first dog watch. I have no hope beyond getting her men off!" Their conversation, like every such conversation for the past twenty hours, was carried out at shouting volume. Marlowe could feel his throat ache with the effort.

"Whatever do you hope to gain by this?" Bickerstaff asked.

Marlowe shook his head. His throat hurt too much to bother with "I don't understand you." "We can do no more than save those men!" he shouted, hoping that would answer Bickerstaff's question.

And apparently it did, for Bickerstaff nodded and went forward again, and the next time Marlowe looked, he was standing in the line of men holding the fall of the stay tackle and ready to haul away on Dinwiddie's command.

It took an hour to prepare, which was an extraordinarily short time in those abominable conditions. But in that time they had drifted a good quarter mile from the wreck, which was visible only now and again from the deck. In the maintop a lookout kept a steady vigil, shouting out every so often that it was still visible, that it had not rolled over or gone to the bottom. Yet.

Marlowe stood at the break of the quarterdeck. Below him, arrayed around the waist and foredeck, the Elizabeth Galleys stood ready. A dozen men on the stay tackle, the massive block and tackle that hung directly over the main hatch, used for lifting stores and cargo in and out. Now it would lift the spars straight up. More hands, including the cook and Bickerstaff, on the yard tackles, coming down from the ends of the fore and main yards and normally used to swing the ship's boats over the side. Now they would do the same for the sea anchor.

Honeyman and Burgess stood at the rope seized to the spars, like an umbilical cord between the sea anchor and the *Elizabeth Galley*, ready to slack that away as needed.

There would be no orders shouted. In that howling wind it was not worth trying. Marlowe pointed a finger at Flanders at the stay tackle, pointed toward the sky, and Flanders ordered his men to haul away.

Up off the hatch the bundle of spars rose, swaying wildly with the roll of the ship, while Dinwiddie passed orders to the yard-tackle men to keep it steady.

Carefully, carefully they lifted the ton of tapered and oiled wood, swayed it out over the side. At one point the *Galley* took a wicked roll, and the spars slammed into her side with an impact that was like hitting the wreck. Then they rolled the other way, and the spars swung outboard, and the yard tackles kept them there.

Out and clear of the ship, they were lowered into the water, and the tackles jerked free, and suddenly the spars were floating, like a great pile of wreckage, tethered to the *Elizabeth Galley* with the three-inch-thick hawser.

Marlowe gave Honeyman a sign to slack away, and Honeyman and Burgess let the rope slip around the fife rail and run out through the empty gunport. Marlowe watched the spars drift farther and farther, and then he made a closed-fist sign, and Honeyman took a turn of the rope around the rail and held it fast.

The *Elizabeth Galley* gave a light jerk as the sea anchor took hold and checked the ship's fast drift, holding it more or less in place as the dangerous hulk, beyond any control, drifted down on them.

And then there was nothing to do but wait.

Marlowe sent the men below to have what breakfast they could with the seas too rough to light the galley fires. Happily there was fresh meat aboard, they being only three days out of port, and so the beef that was already cooked was served out cold, along with fresh biscuits and butter. All in all a handsome meal, far better than the salted meat, which even when cooked could be as hard as shoe leather.

The men, like Marlowe, were too eager to see what was happening to remain below. They came back up through the scuttle, meat and biscuits in hand, and lined the rails, watching for signs of the hulk as one or both of the vessels rose on the waves.

They were rewarded with the merest glimpses at first, the low-lying wreck more than a quarter mile away and visible only on those occasions when both ships happened to rise at once. But soon it was evident that the sea anchor was performing famously, that the wreck was now drifting much faster than the *Elizabeth Galley*.

With every passing wave that held the wreck up like some article for sale in the market, they could see she was getting closer, and with each cable length she closed, Marlowe could feel the tension build like a storm. He could all but hear the questions rolling through the men's heads: *How will we get these poor sods off? How will we keep that wreck from running aboard us and taking us down, too? Is this bloody worth the risk?* Those questions rolled through his head as well.

For that last question, at least, Marlowe felt quite sure he had the answer. Quite sure, but not entirely.

An hour and twenty minutes after he had sent his men to their breakfast, Marlowe could see the people on the wreck distinctly through his glass. The battered ship was not more than three cable lengths upwind, visible all the time now, save for those few moments when both ships were deep in the troughs of waves.

She was hard over on her larboard side, her rounded bottom facing into the wind and sea, which broke over her as if she were a spit of land. Her deck was nearly vertical and facing the *Elizabeth Galley*; Marlowe had an uninterrupted view from the taffrail right up to the shattered end of the bowsprit.

He could see her crew, or what was left of them, up on the high side of the deck. They were arrayed along the combing of the main hatch like figurines on a shelf. One or two of them had been waving arms and that white cloth, but they could see now that the *Elizabeth Galley* had spotted them, and they had stopped waving, saving what must be the precious little energy that they still had.

Marlowe moved the glass from the deck down toward the sea, training it on the sea anchor, the bundle of masts and yards that floated halfway between the *Elizabeth Galley* and the drifting hulk. It was all but awash. At times it was lost from sight as the sea rose up between it and the *Galley*, and the three-inch hawser would seem to disappear right into the side of the wave.

The sea anchor worked because it did not move easily through the water, with the hawser pulling it sideways rather than from the pointed end. For that same reason it was going to be a son of a bitch to haul back aboard. Marlowe wished they had attached another line to one end so they could turn it perpendicular to the *Galley* and pull it back sharp end first, so it would ride through the sea like a ship's hull. He wished they had put some sort of a flag on it so the men on the wreck could see it better. But they had not, and it was too late now.

Another ten anxious minutes, and the wreck drifted down on the sea anchor, and every man aboard the *Galley* hoped the men clinging to her would see the spars, would think to jump for them, would be able to do so. The big seas battered the half-sunk hulk, crashing against her exposed bottom, causing her to roll in such a way that the watching men aboard the *Galley* clenched their fists and tensed their arms and waited for the whole thing to roll over and finish the poor bastards on her slanted deck.

Then at last the wreck was there. They could see the bundle of spars slamming against the deck of the hulk where it emerged from the sea. There was exactly one hundred yards separating the two ships, the length of cable that Honeyman had veered out. Now the men on the wreck had only to climb down to the spars and grab hold, and the Elizabeth Galleys would haul them over. In theory.

Marlowe climbed halfway up the mizzen shrouds, aimed his telescope at the distant deck. There was no way to communicate to the men there what he wanted them to do, no means of passing orders over the one hundred yards. He could only watch and hope.

He saw one of the men pointing down at the spars that thumped against the nearly vertical deck, right below where they were huddled on the hatch combing. He saw arms waving, pointing at the *Elizabeth Galley*, pointing down at the spars. They were getting the idea.

There followed what seemed to be half a minute of arguing, and then the men started to move. One of them climbed over the edge of the hatch, half sliding, half crawling down the sloping deck, down into the water that boiled over the low rail, and for a second he was lost to Marlowe's sight, and Marlowe feared he had been swept away. But he appeared again, his head and shoulders above the white, churning sea, clinging to the bundle of spars.

One after another his mates followed him, down the deck, into the sea, and then onto the sea anchor that ran from their former ship to the

Elizabeth Galley. In the *Galley*'s waist, men shouted words of encouragement, cheers that the men on the wreck would never hear. The Galleys were smiling, pounding one another on the back, relieved and exhilarated.

Don't bloody celebrate yet, Marlowe thought as he watched the last of the shipwrecked sailors slide down and take his place on the spars. Fifteen men he counted, perhaps half the original complement.

"Mr. Honeyman, heave away at the capstan!" Marlowe shouted. The wind had calmed enough that Honeyman could hear him from the waist. He waved acknowledgment and shouted an order to the men at the capstan bars, and they began to heave around, hauling the hawser in, pulling the sea anchor back to the *Elizabeth Galley*.

They moved fast at first, pulling in the slack. The hawser rose up out of the sea, streaming water, growing straighter with the pull of the capstan. More and more rope came inboard, and as it did, the men at the capstan moved more and more slowly. And then they stopped.

"Heave! Heave a pawl!" Honeyman shouted, as if his voice could push them around, but it was no use. The hawser would not come in.

"You there, you lazy bastards, lay onto that capstan!" Dinwiddie shouted, indicating every man who was not at that moment pushing a capstan bar. They ran to the capstan, jostled in to find a place, every possible inch taken up by men ready to push the big winch around.

"Good!" Honeyman shouted. "Now, heave!"

From the quarterdeck Marlowe could hear the combined groaning of the men, the rope, the capstan as they exerted tremendous pressure on the bars. The capstan came around, slowly, and one more pawl clicked into place, and then it stopped.

Marlowe climbed down from the mizzen shrouds as Dinwiddie came rushing aft. "No bloody good, Captain!" he said between heaving for breath. "We can't pull the damned thing in!"

"Son of a bitch!" Marlowe shouted out loud. The wreck was drifting down on the sea anchor. If he did not pull the men in, it could roll right over them. If he did not get the sea anchor free, the wreck would run right into the *Elizabeth Galley* and sink her as well.

The only reasonable thing to do was to cut away the damned sea anchor and the shipwrecked sailors with it. He thought of those men clinging to the spars. They had been sure of their pending death, and then like an angel from God the *Elizabeth Galley* had appeared. The sea anchor had been their path to salvation. He could not cut it away.

"Come with me," he said, and ran forward and down the ladder to the waist, grabbing the main topsail halyard for balance as the ship rolled under him, an awkward, jerky motion thanks to the restraining effect of the bar-taut hawser.

Honeyman saw him coming, came staggering aft. "We'll never haul it in!" he shouted. "Not in this sea! I—"

"If we attach a line to one end of the sea anchor, we can pull it so it is at a right angle to the ship!" Marlowe shouted, gesturing with his hands to imitate the motion of the sea anchor. "Then we will not be trying to pull it sideways but point first, like a boat going bow first through the water! It should come right in!"

"Yes," Honeyman agreed.

"Aye, but there's no line, sir. We can't float one upwind," Dinwiddie pointed out correctly.

"Right," Marlowe agreed. He turned to Burgess. "Have you a snatch block that can go over that hawser?"

Burgess paused. A snatch block was a specialized piece of equipment, a block—what a landsman might call a pulley—like any other, save that it was opened on one side so that it could be put around a line rather than having to thread the end of the line through it.

"Aye . . ." Burgess said at last. "But what . . . you ain't . . ."

"Get the snatch block over the hawser. I'll use a strop for a sort of harness, carry a line out along the hawser."

"Captain!" Honeyman and Dinwiddie protested, almost at once.

"Don't argue with me, just do it, goddamn your eyes!" Marlowe shouted.

"Let me take the line out to them!" Honeyman countered.

"No! Get the block!" Marlowe shouted, and Honeyman and Burgess raced off, and Marlowe shed his oilskins, coat, and shoes and climbed up on the bulwark, above the taut hawser, above the roiling sea.

Don't think, don't think . . . The words raced through his mind. This was one of those moments, all too frequent at sea, when one could not think about the action he was resolved to take, or he would never have the courage to do it.

It was his idea to save the shipwrecked men, his mistake not to order a line tied to the end of the sea anchor in the first place. Ultimately, it was all his responsibility.

Sending men aloft to stow sail in a howling wind was one thing—that was as much a part of the sailor's life as scrubbing the decks—but he could not expect anyone else to undertake this extraordinary danger. Not when it was his idea, and his oversight, that made it necessary.

These thoughts floated around in his head, amorphous and unformed, as Honeyman and Burgess rushed up with the snatch block and strop, a loop of rope that Marlowe would pass under his arms. He leaned out of the gunport, clapped the snatch block over the bar-taut hawser, tied it shut with spunyarn so it would not open accidentally. He hitched the strop over the hook in the block while Burgess arranged the rope that Marlowe would carry out to the sea anchor. He passed the bitter end to Honeyman, and Honeyman made it fast to the snatch block.

A swell rose up beyond the bulwark, slapped in through the gunport, hit Honeyman square in the chest and face, but he did not pause any longer than it took to spit out the water he caught in his mouth and blink it out of his eyes.

"Ready, Marlowe," he said at last.

Marlowe nodded, looked fore and aft. Nothing holding him back now, save for his powerful reluctance to plunge into that frigid water.

"All right, goddamn my eyes . . ." He reached down and grabbed the strop and slipped it over his head and shoulders and arranged it under his arms. The hawser was going slack. "Honeyman, I believe the wreck is shoving the sea anchor along. Keep tension on the hawser, take up with the capstan as you can."

"Aye," Honeyman said, and Marlowe was surprised to see the concern in his face and the faces of the others in the waist, but he had no time to ponder it. He slipped over the side.

Marlowe grabbed for the hawser as he went down but missed it, plunging into the sea, over his head, brought up short by the strop. He thrashed with arms and legs and finally got a hand on the rope overhead and pulled himself up, spluttering, gasping with big, openmouthed, wide-eyed gasps at the profound cold of the water. It was like a great weight pressing him all around, then a thousand wicked teeth biting into his flesh.

"Ahh! Ahh!" he heard himself shout, could not help it. He could hear the capstan going around, felt the slack coming out of the hawser. He clenched his teeth, reached out, and, half floating and half hanging from the snatch block, he pulled himself along.

Sometimes the sea rose up under him and floated him as high as the hawser, sometimes it dropped away below him and he found himself hanging, sliding down the angled rope at the end of the block. Yard by yard he made his way along, seemed to get nowhere, but every time he had the chance to see forward, the spars were closer, the men clinging to them more distinct, the wreck towering over them bigger, more threatening.

There was little feeling left in his hands. They seemed to cling to the hawser by their own will, or they were frozen in the gripping position, Marlowe could not tell. He wondered if he would be able to tie the rope he carried with him to the ends of the spars. If not, his effort was wasted, and he might die along with those he had hoped to rescue.

Then suddenly he was there. The spars, which he had thought were still a hundred feet away, were now just beyond his reach, fifteen wet, pale, drawn, exhausted men clinging to them. And behind them, just behind them, rising up and up from the sea, the wrecked ship from which they had come, a great edifice of dark, wet wood and broken gear, like some hideous monster rising up just to crush them beneath its mass.

Marlowe slipped out of the strop and climbed onto the spars, struggling over the slick, wet wood, straddled them, got himself as securely in place as he could. The sea anchor was rising and falling fast in the big seas, the water washing over it, a wild and precarious ride.

With numbed fingers Marlowe worked the knot out of the line that

Burgess had bent to the snatch block. He glanced over at the others riding on the sea anchor, sprawled out on their stomachs. He had the impression that they were seamen, saw wet, matted beards, long hair, tar-stained clothing.

No one spoke, no one made a move to help. They were beyond that, Marlowe could see. Beyond the point where they had the strength to help, the energy to speak, the will to do anything to save themselves beyond just clinging to the spars.

The knot came loose, and Marlowe wrapped the end of the line around his arm, realizing that if he dropped it, they were lost. On hands and knees he crawled along the rolling, bucking bundle of spars, pausing with fingers locked around the lashings as a big sea roiled up around them and the sea anchor disappeared under a foot of foam, then crawling on. Foot by foot to the far end of the spars, until at last he was as far out at the end as he could go.

The middle spar in the sea anchor was a spare main topmast, in the end of which was cut a hole for the topsail halyard to run. Marlowe carefully took the bitter end of the rope and threaded it through this hole and back. He held it in his teeth as he flexed his fingers, preparing for the difficult task of tying a bowline in the line, a job that he could have easily done with his eyes closed, were it not for the fact that he could hardly feel his hands.

He heard the sound of a wave breaking against the wreck and with it a groaning, a clatter of broken parts. His head jerked around, up. The wreck was rolling toward them, starting to go over. He paused, open-mouthed and dumb with cold and fatigue, waited for it to come down on them like the foot of an angry god. But it stopped, the deck as perfectly vertical now as it could get in that rolling world. It would not stay that way long.

Marlowe pulled his eyes from the monstrous hull over him, turned to the rope in his hands, forced himself to work the knot. His fingers were almost useless, as if they had turned to stone, and with gross moves of his hands he formed a loop, tried to get the bitter end through, but the whole thing collapsed in a heap.

Overhead the wreck groaned again. He could see it shift on the edge of his vision. He picked up the rope again, formed another loop. He had to hold the loop in one hand, thread the bitter end through and around the standing part and back, but his aching fingers would not let him do all that.

And then he felt the spars buck as if someone else was crawling across them. He looked over. One of the sailors had made his way up to him. Marlowe saw a long, tangled beard sprouting from a face that was gray with fatigue, a leather jerkin and torn shirt, slop trousers.

The man did not say anything, did not even look at Marlowe. He just picked up the bitter end of the rope, his fingers wrinkled with wet and no more usable than Marlowe's, and with awkward twists of hand and wrist threaded it through the loop that Marlowe held, around the standing part, back through the loop.

Marlowe wrapped the bitter end around his wrist, hauled it taut. An ugly, misshapen knot, something that would earn an apprentice seaman a box on the ear from any boatswain, but it would hold.

The wreck gave another groan, a creak, and the sound of tons of shifting water, and Marlowe and the men beside him looked up in horror, straight up, as the wreck was right over them, rising like a cliff. When it rolled, it would roll right on top of them.

Marlowe slid back to a wider place on the spars, had a chance to curse himself once again for not arranging a signal to tell the men on board the *Elizabeth Galley* when the line was fixed.

He stood, legs spread, half bent, a terribly awkward position, trying to balance on the rolling, twisting sea anchor. He managed one wave of his arm, and then he was forced to drop to his belly before a big sea knocked him away.

He spit out the water he had swallowed, blinked it out of his eyes, tried to muster the energy to stand again. He could feel his strength and will drifting away, like those others on the spars. A few more moments and he would not care if he lived or not. He wasn't sure he cared now.

And then the sea anchor began to turn, to twist around in the sea. Marlowe saw the line he had carried out with him come taut and rise from the water as unseen hands aboard the *Elizabeth Galley* hauled away with a will.

The spars came around until at last they were pointing directly at the *Galley*, and the men hauling the rope and the men on the capstan were able to pull them in, able to drag them through the big seas. Water washed over them, big seas came up from behind and pitched them forward, tried to knock them off, but they were moving. They were being pulled to safety.

Twenty yards, thirty yards from the wreck, and then the big, dead hulk gave another groan, the deep guttural sound of its final agony. Marlowe turned his head, looked back. The big Indiaman began to roll, over, over, her deck coming down onto the sea, her big weed-covered bottom rising up into the air, her keel exposed to the gray light of that stormy day.

The men on the spars watched, silent, as the ship came to rest, upside down, and from the place where it hit, a great surge of water careened toward them, breaking white over the swells, the ship lashing out, her final attempt to take her men down with her. Marlowe grabbed on to the nearest lashings, forced his dead fingers under the ropes, saw the others do the same, and then the wave was over them, burying them, spinning them around.

Marlowe felt himself go under, covered with water like a blanket of crushed ice. He closed his eyes, his mouth, felt himself lift off the sea anchor, tried to close his fingers around the lashing.

And then the water fell away, and he was in the air again and still on the spars. He looked around. Two of the men were gone, pulled from their raft. The big Indiaman had slipped beneath the sea, dragged them down with her.

For another five minutes they clung to the spars, and then the *Elizabeth Galley* was towering over them, not a threatening sight like the wreck but a welcome one. But for all his relief, Marlowe doubted that he had the strength to climb those high sides, and he knew the others did not. A raft of Moseses—they could see the Promised Land, but they could not reach it.

And then, like a vision, Duncan Honeyman seemed to float in front of him, coming down from the sky, as if he were flying. Marlowe could make no sense of what he was seeing. Honeyman lit on the sea anchor, soft as a bird landing, and only then did Marlowe realize that he had been lowered down on a boatswain's chair, a wooden seat on a line used to hoist men aloft to places where they could not climb.

Honeyman stepped off the boatswain's chair, moved nimbly across the bucking spars, pulling the chair with him. He set it down, grabbed Marlowe under the arms, helped him to his feet.

"You first, Captain," he said as he made Marlowe step into the chair and signaled to the men on the *Galley*'s deck to take up the strain.

Marlowe tried to protest that he should not go first. He was, after all, in better shape than the other men were, for what that was worth. But he could not seem to make his mouth work.

And then he was in the air, lifting up off the sea anchor and sailing in over the side of the *Elizabeth Galley*, into the waiting arms of his men. Here was Hesiod, a worried look on his dark face, pulling slack in the line with one hand and supporting Marlowe with the other. Marlowe had an image of him back at the plantation, ax over his shoulder. He looked even more a pirate now.

Elizabeth was there, wrapped in her boat cloak, her face a mask of concern. Marlowe wondered if she were going to scold him, tell him to go to hell. But instead she seemed to be giving orders, telling the men of the *Elizabeth Galley* what to do with the others on the spars, telling the two men holding Marlowe up to take him aft, telling Dinwiddie that he was in command.

On her word the boatswain's chair lifted off again, flew back over the water to Honeyman on the sea anchor, back for the next man and the next.

It seemed odd to Marlowe—he did not think Elizabeth had the authority to issue such orders—but she was doing it, and the others seemed to be obeying.

The men supporting Marlowe, Hesiod and Burns—one of Honeyman's hard cases—carried him under the quarterdeck and down the alleyway and into the great cabin. They stepped through the door, and the heat from the small wood stove hit him with a shock like that of plunging into the ocean. His head swam, and his knees buckled, and he would have fallen if he had not been supported by strong arms.

They set him down on the locker aft, by Elizabeth's orders, and began to strip him of breeches and waistcoat and shirt and underclothes. They dried him with rough towels, and he began to feel sensations coming back to his limbs, and he was overcome with fatigue.

"I must go back on deck," he said, a weak protest.

"Nonsense," Elizabeth said. "Mr. Dinwiddie has things well in hand. Put him in the bunk, pray." This last she said to Hesiod. The former slave hefted up the now-naked Marlowe, and he and Burns carried him into the small sleeping cabin and put him in the bunk. He stretched out full length, and they pulled the blankets over him, and he could not recall anything ever feeling so good.

The two men disappeared, and Elizabeth stood over him, looking down. "Francis told me what you did. Risking everything to save those men. Stupid, stupid, going into the sea that way," she said, but there was no anger in her voice.

Then, as Marlowe watched, she untied her bodice and let it fall and pulled down her skirts and let them pool on the floor. She lifted her shift over her head, and for a moment she stood there, naked, perfect, and then she slid into the cot with him, pressed up against him, warm and soft and so alive.

"Thomas, I swear I cannot tell if you are the biggest bastard in the world or the greatest man that ever lived."

"Somewhere in between, I should think," Marlowe muttered. He wondered if he had actually redeemed himself in her eyes, with his idiotic and ill-conceived heroism. It had never occurred to him that such might be the result.

In fact, as they had hauled him back aboard the *Elizabeth Galley*, his only thoughts had been a dull relief that it was over and the satisfaction of knowing he now had a dozen more hands to help him plunder the fabled treasure of the Moors.

Chapter 12

"HEAR ME, Yancy," said Obadiah Spelt, waving a chicken leg at the king of St. Mary's, "when I am king here, we shall have a regular army, see? Drills, uniforms, the whole thing."

Spelt took another bite and wiped his mouth with the wide sleeve of his coat, which was, incredibly, even less clean than the mouth he wiped.

Yancy just nodded and pressed his handkerchief to his mouth and coughed. Spelt was off again, spewing ideas as if he might spew dinner in the alley behind some penny ordinary. Not worth interrupting. Spelt was, after all, Yancy's handpicked successor.

The disease was still ostensibly a secret, the cancer that was eating away at Lord Yancy's guts, but rumors were spreading like yellow jack through St. Mary's.

The symptoms could not have gone unnoticed: the weakness, the coughing, the spots of blood on the handkerchief. They had first appeared a few months before, grew worse to the point where Yancy could no longer deny it, at least not to his own people, the Terrors. He could not deny that the time had come to pick a successor.

Not from among his elite. For them, the secret place in the moun-

tains. No, the successor had to come from down below, from the population who called St. Mary's home. The successor could not know
about Roger Press.

The town of St. Mary's, if such it could be called, boasted two roads,
sandy, deeply rutted, not built so much as beaten from the under-
growth. One road bordered the water, running along the shallow, open
roadstead to where it terminated at a jetty, thrust out into the harbor
bounded by shoreline on either side and Quail Island to seaward.

The other road crossed the harbor road at a right angle. It continued on up the side of the hill on which sat Lord Yancy's home. The
hill itself had been cleared years before, by Baldridge and his men, for
material to build the home and to create open ground with no cover
for a clandestine approach.

The high ground on which the house sat was really no more than a
hump at the feet of the higher hills that stood behind the town, but it
was on this hump that Baldridge had built the great house and encircled it with a wooden stockade. The road ran right to the big gate in
the stockade and through it, where it spread out like a river delta into
the acres of courtyard that surrounded the house.

The courtyard's open ground might be a place for casual amusements such as bowling or cockfighting, but it was not designed as such.
It was intended as a killing field where attacking troops, caught between the stockade and the big house, could be shot down from the
high windows and balconies. Amusement was all well and good, but
defense was primary.

It was through this gate, down this road, that the visibly ailing Lord
Yancy and his entourage made their way for an ostensible and un-
common inspection of the town. Since first occupying the big house,
Yancy had not often left it, and those forays had grown even less frequent over the past year.

Down the hill, with Yancy riding in a sedan chair and Henry Nagel
walking by his side. St. Mary's had prospered, Yancy could see that. He
thought of the few dilapidated shacks that had stood at the intersection
of the roads when he had first stepped ashore there; the dozen or so
drunken wrecks, both pirates and natives, that inhabited them; the

empty, rotting warehouses that Baldridge had left behind; the two half-sunk ships in the harbor.

The ships were gone, torn apart bit by bit to build the taverns and whorehouses that would serve the burgeoning town. Now there were half a dozen wooden buildings clustered around the crossroads and twice that number of permanent tents set up.

The population of the island fluctuated with the coming and going of the ships. There were never fewer than three hundred men there, and occasionally the number swelled to nearly a thousand. They sat at little tables outside the taverns and drank until they fell over, walked arm in arm with their whores along the harbor as if it were Pall Mall; they slept in upstairs rooms if they had been lucky in their hunting the Mogul's ships or in the alleys between the buildings if they had not.

They were pirates. Wild, ostentatious clothes, money spent as though they could dig it from the ground, utter debauch. It amused them to ape the aristocracy in their clothes and manners, but they ad-hered to none of the self-imposed public restraint of the people of quality.

And why should they? *They* were the aristocracy here, and there was no one—no lords, no kings, no army, no navy, no magistrates—to tell them otherwise. Yancy would not. For all his rule over the place, he would not upset the fine balance of things that kept the money pour-ing in. The pirates were freer than any men on earth, because they took what they wanted and they truly, genuinely, did not give a tinker's damn.

It was into this world, which had once been his world, that Yancy rode in his chair, borne by four strong native men. They moved slowly along the dusty road, and the pirates who were promenading there stepped aside and swept off their plumed hats and bowed deep with graceful and exaggerated moves, and the whores that were with them lifted their tattered petticoats and curtsied like women who still pos-sessed a tiny portion of modesty and dignity.

"Here," Yancy said, flicking his handkerchief at Bartleby Finch's Black Dog tavern, the larger of the two official taverns in St. Mary's, which stood on the northeast corner of the single crossroads.

The natives lowered the chair, and Nagel helped Yancy out, and the entourage paraded into the Black Dog. It had a low wattle ceiling supported by heavy beams — former deck beams — and had it been in London or New York or Norfolk, it would have been dark and smoke-filled.

But it was not. It was on a tropical island, and in keeping with that ideal climate, the tavern had big windows in each of the four walls, windows that were no more than square holes cut into the walls, unencumbered by glass or frames or shutters. They let in quite a bit of light, which unfortunately made the filth all the more visible. Still, the steady breeze kept the room largely free of smoke, despite the prodigious output of the many pipes clenched in rotting teeth.

Yancy's entrance produced a brief pause in the bacchanalia going on in the Black Dog, as heads turned and greetings were called out to the lord who had come down from the hill. A table was vacated, and Yancy sat wearily down. Finch appeared, twisting a towel in his hand, saying, "Lord Yancy, 'tis an honor, sir, you blessing us, like this, with Your Lordship's presence. Ale with you, sir? Or wine, or rum, sir?"

Yancy waved the man away with his handkerchief, did not waste the effort to speak. He ran his eyes over the low room. All there had gone back to whatever they were doing before he entered. He was not pleased, but he said nothing.

The Black Dog was something out of Yancy's past, the ugly, rough waterfront taverns where fearless men gathered and drank hard and became even more fearless and more dangerous.

It was not the kind of place for a man like Yancy, a small man, a man who understood that it was brains, not strength of arm, that would set someone on top. It was all strength of arm in places like this. Brains were left with the horses, hitched to the post outside.

Yancy had never liked the Black Dogs of the world. They frightened him and still would, if he had not brought his own strength of arm in the form of Nagel and the others.

So he sat quietly and watched. Watched the big men in their blustering bravado, drinking hard and scratching and spitting tobacco on the bare wooden floor and groping the whores who fed off them. Thick, matted beards covering brown faces, flecked with the black freckles of embedded powder; sailor's slops and long, sea-worn coats; ripped stockings thrust into battered shoes; crude cutlasses hanging from shoulder belts or fine swords—the bounty of some fortuitous strike, taken perhaps from the dead body of a merchantman's officer or gentleman passenger—hanging from their belts. All these things, these familiar scenes from Newport and Port Royal, those traditional pirate havens, now transported half a world away.

And he was king of it. He sat and searched the crowd and tried to find the man, just the right man, who could occupy his throne after he had made his exit. He saw many who might be right, but no one who absolutely was.

And then, through the crowd, came Obadiah Spelt. Nearly as big as Nagel, with a beard bursting like an unattended hedgerow from his face and falling almost to his belly, dark eyes peering out from the thatch, a long black coat and waistcoat that still showed some embroidery through the filth.

Spelt, mug in hand. Without asking, he sat down at Yancy's table and started to speak, and Yancy had to put his hand on Henry Nagel's arm to restrain him from beating the man to death.

"Lord Yancy, damn me!" He held out a hand that Yancy did not accept and then withdrew it as if they had shaken. "Yancy, sir, I've a proposition I've wanted to lay at yer feet, so to speak, a main chance which I think we, being gentlemen of fortune, like we are, might just find to be a profitable enterprise."

Yancy nodded as Spelt spoke, though he did not listen. Some nonsense about charging harbor fees and hiring Spelt as harbormaster or some such—it was of no interest to Yancy.

Rather, the reigning king listened to Spelt's stupidity, his high opinion of himself, the megalomania that seemed to burst from him as if he were an overstuffed sack, and Yancy thought, *You are the man for me.*

The foul weather that the *Elizabeth Galley* had endured came to a welcome end, inboard and out, and quickly. It put Marlowe in mind of how Noah must have felt, feet on dry land, looking at that great arcing rainbow.

The storm blew itself out in the late afternoon, leaving only a lumpy, irregular sea as a reminder, and over the dark hours that, too, subsided into the ocean's usual steady march of waves.

The next morning the wind was brisk, the sky blue, and it was up topgallants and all plain sail set as the *Elizabeth Galley* plunged along southwest, ever southwest, a heading she would hold until she had crossed the line of the equator and found the contrary winds in the Southern Hemisphere.

Her namesake, Elizabeth Marlowe, was recovered from her mal de mer and her conviction that her husband was a worthless, manipulative, sneaking bastard. Her awe with his daring, her appreciation of the risk he took to save the lives of strangers, gave her the leeway to reexamine her bitterness and anger. Her polarized feelings, like opposing forces that cancel one another out, gave her the chance to view her husband dispassionately.

In the end she decided that "manipulative" and "sneaky" were fair descriptions but that Thomas did not deserve "worthless" or "bastard."

He was not wrong about the wealth to be had on the Pirate Round or the extent to which it could help them in their fiscal crisis. He was not wrong about the degree of protest he would have received from her and Francis. So he had made arrangements on his own. It was his ship, his right to do so. He had not wished to involve her. She had insisted on going along.

Thomas could not have foreseen what had happened in London or known how very fortunate it would be that he had made his arrangements. In the end his clandestine activities might be the very thing to save them all. He could be damned lucky that way.

The hidden money irked her still, the anxiety she had felt over their looming poverty, while all along he had a buried treasure, just the thing that pirates were supposed to have.

The irony, of course, was that real pirates did not bury treasure, despite the romantic notions that people harbored. They spent it long before they could get it interred. It took a retired pirate to have such self-control.

In the end she was willing to forgive him his foibles. By the first dog watch of the first glorious day after the storm, it was as good between them as it had been right after they met, the morning after the first time they had made love in the tiny cabin of Marlowe's sloop.

It made her very happy to have that back again. As she stood on the quarterdeck, near him, watching him, she was very happy to not be angry with him anymore.

She thought of Madagascar and the Red Sea. If Thomas had proposed such a cruise back in Virginia, she would have scoffed at the notion, been horrified at the thought of leaving her home for so barbaric a place.

But Elizabeth was not of a docile bent; she did not suffer boredom easily. She would never admit it to Marlowe or to anyone, but in her heart she was thrilled with their pending adventure.

Bickerstaff was not so thrilled, though in *his* heart he was eager to see that strange, distant country. It was an intellectual curiosity, and if they were bound away for Madagascar and the Indian Ocean for any reason other than piracy, he would have been very excited indeed. As it was, he expressed nothing beyond an acceptance of the inevitable, like a prisoner aboard a man-of-war.

Like Elizabeth, he was happy to no longer be angry with Thomas. Marlowe's actions had proved once again his friend's essential goodness and morality. No one who would risk his life thus for strangers, men who could do him no great favor in return, could be entirely immoral, even if he could be manipulative and sneaky at times.

Once the rescued men had recovered enough from their ordeal that they could move about, Marlowe called them aft. Thirteen survivors, they crowded into the great cabin, sitting where they could, while Marlowe endured the deep-felt expression of thanks delivered by the boatswain, the ranking survivor, the man who had helped Marlowe tie the bowline on the sea anchor. One hundred years ago. It had to be that long at least.

"So, sir, I can't say nothing more, but—" the boatswain muttered. Marlowe cut him off.

"Enough said, sir. It was my duty as a seaman and a Christian," he said, and he was at least a good seaman. "Tell me, what ship was she? What happened?"

The boatswain cleared his throat. "She was the *Mayor of Harpswell*, sir, Indiaman and a good ship. We was running before the gale, deep-reefed topsails. Just getting ready to take 'em in, scud before it. We was pooped. Sea washed all the officers right off the quarterdeck, knocked the helm clean away."

Marlowe nodded. One seaman talking to another, there was nothing more that needed to be said. The ship running before the sea, a huge wave sweeping up over the stern, crashing down on the quarterdeck, "pooping" her. All the officers there washed away, killed by the sea's impact or swept overboard, the helm torn from its mounts.

With no way to steer, the ship would have rounded right up into the wind, the sails aback, and the storm would have ripped the masts out of her like saplings, left them a helpless wreck, rolling broadside to the waves. It probably took all of two minutes for her to go from being a well-found ship, running easily before the gale, to a foundering wreck with half her complement dead.

"Yes, well . . ." Marlowe said, and then he moved on to brighter topics. "I will give you all the choice of being set ashore at our next landfall or joining our company."

"Aye, sir, and pray whither are you bound, sir?"

"Madagascar."

A smile spread slowly across the boatswain's leathery face. "Oh, aye, sir?"

Ten minutes later there were thirteen new names scrawled on the ship's articles.

For five weeks they plowed their course south by west, five hundred miles or so off the West African coast, bound toward the equator, enduring the usual calms and squalls and rainstorms and fine weather. They made good time, having now a decent-size crew—near forty men—small by man-of-war standards but big for a merchantman, men who were quick and able at sail handling, so that Marlowe could make the most out of any slant of wind the Atlantic offered him.

The ship fell quickly into that steady, happy rhythm that marks a well-run ship, long at sea. Watch after watch, breakfast, dinner, supper, up spirits, lights out, the days and weeks cycled by in their floating world, and only now and again would someone look over the rail and realize that there was nothing but water surrounding them, that they had seen nothing but water beyond the confines of the ship for week upon week.

Floating under the hot sun, the wind entirely absent, they celebrated Christmas at six degrees north latitude, then in quick succession came the celebration of crossing the line and then New Year's. But the changing of the year did nothing to change their situation, and once the rum with which they celebrated the holidays had worked through their systems, once pounding heads had returned to normal, the well-established routine took up again.

Dinwiddie still made veiled complaints about Honeyman, muttered dissatisfaction at playing second to a quartermaster. Honeyman said little, made no demands, never indicated that the crew had any concerns or desire to make any changes.

It was an odd stasis. The *Elizabeth Galley* was running like any merchantman or man-of-war, with the standard hierarchy. But underlying that—for Marlowe at least and certainly for Dinwiddie and Honeyman, no doubt—was the understanding that she was not such a legitimate vessel, that they were run by articles, that with one vote the men could change it all. A happy ship, but for those aft, an uneasy contentment.

They came at last to the low latitudes, where the sun passed directly overhead and beat down on the deck and softened the pitch and the tar on the rigging. The wind grew fluky and then light and then nonexistent. With the ship rolling in the swells, not moving, with no reason to trim sail, the men were suddenly without much to do. That was never a good thing.

Marlowe would have liked to drill with the great guns, a productive use of idle hours, but of course there were no great guns. And while it was standard practice with a raw crew to pantomime the handling of powder and shot, so as not to expend those precious commodities in the early stages of training, Marlowe reckoned that pantomiming the guns themselves was a bit much.

Instead he set the men to making mock cutlasses out of wood with leather hand guards and asked Bickerstaff to train them in swordplay, which was certainly as useful and almost as entertaining, lacking only the great noise and concussion of the guns to render it entirely delightful to the seamen.

The men stood in lines in the waist, a great open space with the guns gone, and followed Bickerstaff through the various positions— lunge, recover, parry, lunge—until they were sweating completely. He drilled them until they began to stumble with fatigue, then sent them off and took the next batch, and so on.

The first dog watch rolled around, and Marlowe reckoned the men had had enough for that day, that they had earned a little amusement.

"Here, Francis," he called down to the waist, stripping his waistcoat as he did. He was dressed in a loose cotton shirt and slop trousers, barefooted—comfortable dress for the doldrums. "We have not crossed swords in many a year. What say we have a go, you and me?"

Bickerstaff looked up, smiled. "Delighted."

Marlowe stepped down into the waist, carrying a matching set of rapiers. They were thin-bladed weapons, swords made for speed. Not the weapons Marlowe would choose for real combat, but they were good for fencing and for developing speed and coordination. A cork was pushed snugly down on the wicked tip of each blade.

The men gathered around, leaving a clear patch along the starboard side. They were grinning in anticipation, as Marlowe suspected they might.

Marlowe stretched out, took a few practice lunges, thought of the several purposes this would serve. Entertainment for the men, practice for him and Bickerstaff. And it would demonstrate to all hands that he was the deadliest man aboard, an important lesson.

"En garde," Bickerstaff said, assuming his formal stance. Marlowe was much more casual about the whole thing, standing in a relaxed attitude, weapon held down. He knew that Bickerstaff would try to make him pay for his lack of formality by sticking him quick, and he was right.

Bickerstaff moved like a snake—one, two, three quick steps, rapier lunging out—but Marlowe was ready for it. He caught the blade on his own, pushed it aside, lunged, but Bickerstaff was already gone. The move drew a smattering of applause. He heard wagers being placed.

Marlowe took a more formal defensive stance now, feet at right angles, the tip of the rapier level with Bickerstaff's face. A false lunge, Bickerstaff parried, a real lunge before he recovered, but Bickerstaff knocked the attack aside once more, to Marlowe's surprise.

Now Bickerstaff was on the attack, blade flashing, and Marlowe could depend only on his reflexes to fend off the rapier. He was aware of the silence now along the deck, the men watching in awe as the weapons moved faster than their eyes could follow, only the clash of steel telling them that they were witnessing attacks, parries, ripostes.

And creeping age as well, though Marlowe hoped that only he was aware of it. Three, four times already he had seen opportunities that the younger, less weary Marlowe would have exploited to fatal advantage, but he was not fast enough now.

The same was true of Bickerstaff. One solid parry, Marlowe found himself opened, actually braced for the hard jab of cork on his chest, but Francis was not there, and by the time he was, Marlowe was ready to knock his blade aside.

So it went, back and forth along the deck, in front of a silent, watching crew. Marlowe could feel his arm grow heavy, his breath come faster.

And then Bickerstaff lunged, an awkward move—Marlowe could see he was tiring, too—and Marlowe's blade came across, sideways, caught Francis's sword in the hand guard. He twisted, wrenched the rapier from Francis's hand, and reflexively thrust, hitting Bickerstaff in the chest just as Bickerstaff's rapier clattered on the deck, Marlowe's weapon bending under the impact.

Bickerstaff straightened, smiled. "Touché," he gasped.

Marlowe stepped back, saluted with his sword. Turned to his men, ready to face whatever he might see: scorn, amusement at seeing that old man humping it up and down the deck.

But what he saw in its stead was astonishment. Mouths hung open, eyes wide. No one moved, and Marlowe reckoned they had managed to put on a decent show after all.

Good, and do not forget it, he thought as the men, led by Honeyman, burst out into applause, wild cheers, demands for losers to pay their bets. It was great theater.

Then Elizabeth stepped across the deck, picked up Bickerstaff's rapier. "Come, Captain, let me have a go at you!" she called, taking an *en garde* stance. The crew cheered again, in their high spirits.

Marlowe let the tip of his rapier rest on the deck. "Oh, Lord, woman, I am too tired for this!" he called.

"Oh, indeed? I've never heard that excuse before!" Elizabeth countered, and the men roared in laughter. Elizabeth had a flawless sense for subtle bawdiness, and the Galleys loved it.

"Very well, my wench, I shall get my weapon up for you!" It was the kind of happy camaraderie, the sort of "gentleman hauling with the men" fun that worked well, on occasion, with a happy crew.

Marlowe went *en garde* and advanced. Elizabeth was no swordswoman, and though she had played around a bit, she had very little skill with a blade. She made an awkward attempt at a lunge, and Marlowe parried, then counterattacked, but slowly enough that Elizabeth was able to step back.

She came at him again, and he let her drive him down the deck, lunge and parry, lunge and parry. Marlowe could see some potential there—Elizabeth was strong and coordinated—but she was almost entirely lacking in any type of training.

Back to the main fife rail, and then Marlowe began to press his attack. Slowly, pushing Elizabeth back the way they had come, befuddling her with his swordplay, ignoring the many chances he had to end it there. As they worked their way along the deck he had a glimpse of eager faces watching, men delighting in the display, delighting, he imagined, in this legitimate chance to stare at Elizabeth.

Marlowe pushed his wife back to the place where they had started, and then it was time to end the thing. He took a step back, lowered the tip of his rapier to the deck, presented his chest for her thrust.

She took it, too inexperienced to not fall for his trap, and as her blade shot forward, Marlowe's came up and knocked it aside. He twisted his blade around hers, caught her steel in his hand guard, and, just as he had done to Bickerstaff, he plucked the hilt from her fingers and tossed the weapon away. It clattered into the waterway, and Marlowe jabbed the corked tip of his own rapier into Elizabeth's stomach, just the lightest of touches.

"Touché," she said, smiling and breathing hard to a smattering of applause and a few good-natured boos. The men had hoped to see Elizabeth win the bout, but that was not going to happen.

"You did very well, my dear," Marlowe assured her, and Bickerstaff came up and said, "Very well indeed. You have the makings of a fine swordswoman. Perhaps you would allow me the honor of giving you regular instruction?"

"I should like that above all things," Elizabeth said. "By the time we reach Madagascar, I shall run my blade right through this arrogant bastard!"

"By the time we reach Madagascar, I will no longer be willing to cross blades with you, my dear. It would do my authority no good for the men to see me bested by my wife!"

And then Dinwiddie said, "You have no authority, Captain. 'Tis Honeyman runs the show now." Dinwiddie might have been making a joke, or trying, but it did not come across as such, and Marlowe felt his good humor deflate.

Despite the unhappy ending to that day's amusements, Bickerstaff did begin drilling Elizabeth in swordplay. It became a daily event. An hour before the men were mustered for their training, Francis and Elizabeth would meet on the deck and he would put her through her drills in his fussy, exacting way. The men would watch, surreptitiously, catching glances when they could, but Marlowe did not mind. They were stuck in the doldrums for a week, and the spectacle did much to improve the men's attitudes.

When he was done with Elizabeth, Francis would drill the crew as a whole, and sometimes Elizabeth would join in as well. They practiced footwork, blade work, offense, defense. When the men had had enough of that, Bickerstaff would set them to sparring with one another. It was a chance for action, rivalry, wagering, and exercise. It was perfectly suited to keep the men occupied.

They picked up the easterly trade winds at last, south of the line, turning their bow through ninety degrees and making their course to round the tip of Africa. Soon the *Elizabeth Galley* was bowling along, with a great line of wake stretching out astern and all sail set and straining before the wind, the constant wind. But by then the sword drills and Elizabeth's lessons had become such a part of the routine that they could not bear to give them up, so they did not. For five weeks they plowed along south by east, and they parried and riposted and lunged and had a marvelous time.

And, Marlowe had to admit, Elizabeth was becoming a hell of a swordswoman. He reckoned he could beat her still, but it would not be the simple matter it had been before.

Three thousand miles, and then the sword drills stopped as they battled their way around the stormy Cape of Good Hope, the tip of Africa, dropping as far as forty degrees south latitude and touching on that great band of wind that roared around the entire earth, nearly unimpeded in its circumnavigation.

They battled the wind and sea for a week before turning north again and covering the last thousand or so miles up into the tropical zones, even hotter now in the Southern Hemisphere summer. A week of bitter cold and high seas gave way fast to brilliant sun right overhead, hot deck planking, dripping tar. The men stripped down as far as they could with a woman aboard, and a piratical bunch they looked.

At last the dawn revealed not an empty sea but a black hump of land on the northern horizon. It seemed to rise up from the Indian Ocean as the *Elizabeth Galley* closed the miles. Madagascar, right under their bow.

Marlowe stood on the quarterdeck, Elizabeth next to him. "There it is, my love, at long last. Madagascar. Island of the pirates."

"We shall fit right in, I'll warrant. We are the greatest villains of them all."

"I reckon so. And you swaggering about with a sword on your hip."

They were silent for a moment, looking at the island, still no more than a dark line rising just the slightest bit above the horizon. Then Elizabeth said, "I have enjoyed this, Thomas, truly I have. But I am not ashamed to say I shall be glad to step off this ship, if even for a day."

"More than a day, I should think. We've a power of work to do before we can sail again."

Sail again. What an odd thought. Fetching Madagascar after so long a voyage, after all that had happened in London, seemed like an end, the closure of a voyage. The time to pay off the crew, retire to one's home, relive the adventure in tales told to one's neighbors.

It was hard to recall that the landfall in Madagascar was not that, not that at all. It was, in fact, just the beginning.

Chapter 13

THEY STOOD on the quarterdeck—Thomas, Elizabeth, Francis, Peleg, and Duncan. The others stood along the gangways and foredeck—the young black men from Marlowe House, the sailors they had recruited in the colonies and Bermuda, and the men they had saved from the wreck of the Indiaman. Disparate groups now molded as well as sailors could be molded into a cohesive unit, into the crew of the *Elizabeth Galley*.

They stood together, a band of men and one woman, who had already been through a great deal in each other's company. They stood and watched as the steep, jungle-covered shore of Madagascar moved slowly down the larboard side. But their attention was focused forward, where the island of St. Mary's, now distinct from the bigger island, waited, fifty miles away and right under the bowsprit.

None of them knew, of course, that two thousand miles astern of them, plunging along almost in the track through which the *Elizabeth Galley* had plowed her wake, the *Queen's Venture* and her tender were just encountering the first of the Cape of Good Hope's ferocity.

When last they had seen Roger Press, he had been shouting orders and curses from his longboat, which was skewered by the *Galley's* spare main topsail yard and pinned to the bottom of the Thames. For all they knew, he was there still.

They did not know that he and his men had remained in that awkward position for two hours until Lieutenant Tasker, growing worried by their absence, sent the ship's cutter in search of them.

Press returned to the *Queen's Venture*, disappeared into his great cabin. He did not say a word to anyone, and no one said a word to him. To a man, they knew better than that. He flung off his wet clothes, dressed in his silk banyan, poured a glass of rum, straight.

He stared out the big windows aft, into the blackness, and by the time he had finished his rum, Malachias Barrett was behind him.

Press was a practical man; it was what had led to his having command of such a big, well-found and well-funded vessel, a commission giving him all but carte blanche in the Indian Ocean and the Red Sea. He could fixate on vengeance with the tenacity of a bulldog, but he would not waste his life seeking it. He had no notion of where Barrett was bound, and he had no thought of flailing around the oceans of the world looking for him.

No, Barrett could wait. Barrett would not distract him from his well-planned mission. There was one other man that Press hated even more than Barrett.

He considered that, wondered if that was still true, in light of the outrages he had just suffered by Barrett's hand. He looked at his gnarled fingers, which had been systematically broken in the Grand Inquisitor's religious zeal, felt the mutilated skin on his back where the silk banyan touched it, and he knew that, yes, he hated that other man more.

Press felt his resolve strengthened again. He knew where that other fellow was. The story of his conquest of St. Mary's had finally filtered back to the London waterfront. No fruitless searching of the oceans for him; Press could proceed directly to St. Mary's, take him, kill him slowly, make himself master of all that his enemy had accumulated in terms of wealth and power. The most influential men in England had given him license to hunt Yancy down and the means to do so, and they did not even know it.

As the *Elizabeth Galley* was standing out of the harbor at Penzance,

Press had watched the last of the stores lightered out to the *Queen's Venture* and her tender, the *Speedwell*, a twenty-gun, ship-rigged sloop-of-war and a formidable vessel in her own right. As Marlowe was working his way down the hawser to the stricken Indiaman and cursing himself for his idiocy, Press was pacing the quarterdeck of the *Venture*, the rain beating on his oilskin, cursing the storm that kept them bottled up in the Thames.

They had sailed at last, the *Queen's Venture* and the *Speedwell*, bound away on a course almost identical to that of the *Elizabeth Galley*. It was a course familiar to many English seamen, given all the traffic that moved from London to the Indian Ocean in search of the tremendous wealth to be had in those lands, through legitimate means or not.

The *Queen's Venture* crossed the line of thirty-eight degrees south latitude two weeks to the day after the *Elizabeth Galley*. Like Marlowe, Roger Press was not overly concerned with the weather they might encounter in that stormy corner of the world. His ships were newly refitted, strong and tight, their rigs well set up, their crews large and well trained. They were not flimsy trading sloops but substantial men-of-war. They could endure the Cape of Good Hope. They had been fitted out to conquer empires, and that was the thing that was on Press's mind, not the rising wind and building seas.

Marlowe had no way of knowing that Press was there, two thousand miles astern, two and a half weeks of sailing, if one had any slant of luck with the weather.

Likewise he could not know that a mere forty miles ahead, on the peak of a steep hill behind the town of St. Mary's, Elephiant Yancy was staring breathless through a powerful telescope, taking in every detail of the *Elizabeth Galley* that could be distinguished through those imperfect optics. Nagel stood respectfully behind him and, even farther behind, the lookout who had first spotted the approaching ship.

There were lookouts stationed all over the island, with runners to convey word of any approaching vessel. They were natives, men who could run as if they were flying down the steep jungle paths, who would bring word as fast as was humanly possible. It was a system that

Yancy had set in place soon after assuming sovereignty over his kingdom. It was good to avoid surprise of any kind.

When a ship was spotted from such a high perch, there were a good
twelve hours at least before it might hope to enter the harbor. And now
that Roger Press was coming, Lord Yancy needed every minute he
could gain.

He had explained it to his elite, his Terrors. He would not allow
them to fall victim to that murdering bastard. He would not let Press
rob him of his final weeks on earth.

That morning he had been crouching on his veranda, a fire burning in a small fire pit, his hands and arms and leather apron soaked in
blood, when he spotted the runner.

Yancy had developed a distrust of his food taster and had executed
the man. Water was not a problem. They had on St. Mary's a unique
white gourd called a *mabibo*, which when cut open was filled with
fresh, unadulterated water. But food was another matter. He had concluded that the only way to assure the purity of his food was to kill and
cook it himself.

Every day a young pig was brought to him, and he slit its throat and
watched it die and then gutted it and took what meat he fancied and
cooked it over the fire pit. He had come to enjoy the onerous task,
liked the spray of blood from the neck of the thrashing, dying animal,
the feel of his hands in the warm, wet guts.

He stood, a hock bloody and dripping in his hand, and he saw the
man, way off, running down the mountain path, just a small dark spot
moving along the narrow scar in the jungle. He felt his senses sharpen
up, could see and hear everything clearer. He stuck the meat on the
spit, hung it over the fire, stared into the flames as he waited for the
man to report to Nagel, for Nagel to report to him.

It was a ship, inbound, clearly making for St. Mary's harbor. Nothing unusual about that, but Yancy knew that he had to assume that
every ship was Press. Atwood had mentioned a tender, probably a powerful vessel in its own right, and the lookout had seen just the one ship,
but still Yancy had to be sure.

So he cut a piece from the hock and ate it, then took off the apron and called for a bowl of water in which to clean himself. Then, because he was too weak to make the trek on foot, he called for his natives to bear him along in the chair, with Nagel at his side, making their laborious way back up the trail to the lookout's perch, a forty-minute hike up the steep, hilly path.

They reached the spot, and the others stood respectfully aside while Lord Yancy peered through the glass, then turned as he hacked into his handkerchief, then looked again.

There was not much he could see. A vessel, after the fashion of a galley, not a lumbering merchantman. No doubt armed. But smaller than the one he would have expected Press to command, and no tender to be seen.

Perhaps this was the tender. Was the main ship still beyond the horizon, lurking? Yancy straightened, frowned. Not viewed through the telescope, the ship seemed only the tiniest of smudges on the horizon. He ground his teeth.

He had to be sure, he had to be sure. He could not leave St. Mary's in the hands of his successor, the increasingly regal Obadiah Spelt, until he was certain that he had no choice. As soon as he, Yancy, was gone—dead from the cancer or off to the mountain hideout, whichever came first—Spelt would start issuing edicts as if he were passing out royal favors. He was already putting his plans in place. Yancy felt that he owed it to his people to postpone the man's despotic rule for as long as possible.

But neither could he wait too long. He would not be taken by surprise. That would not happen to Elephiant, Lord Yancy.

He coughed again and again stooped and peered through the glass.

It took the *Elizabeth Galley* the better part of the day to close with the island and then run along its northwest coast, between St. Mary's and Madagascar, to the entrance to the island's single, protected anchorage. As the hills of St. Mary's loomed above them to starboard and the narrow harbor, with Quail Island at its entrance, became evident from the quarterdeck, Marlowe decided that there was daylight enough for them to stand in.

He ordered lookouts aloft and on all quarters and a steady hand in the chains with the lead. He had a chart and sailing direction, but he put little trust in either, and so under topsails alone they crawled along.

St. Mary's was ringed with reefs and sandbars, a treacherous place. They felt their way through the single gap in the reefs, with Quail Island to starboard and the mainland and the town to larboard, until Marlowe found an open spot of still water to let the anchor go.

The anchor cable paid out, and the *Elizabeth Galley* came to a rest at last, held to the ground for the first time since leaving Cornwall. Marlowe breathed deep, taking in all the unfamiliar smells—dirt and vegetation and smoke from cooking fires and the tar and hemp smells of ships fitting out.

He could see a big house up on the hill to the north of them, surrounded by a stockade. Quail Island, too, he could see was well fortified, with heavy guns overlooking the harbor approach. A formidable defense indeed; the men in command on those guns could easily stop any ship from entering or exiting the harbor. All this was built and ruled over by a fellow named Adam Baldridge, or so he had heard, though it had been many years since he had heard a firsthand account of the doings on St. Mary's.

Regardless, through his telescope, looking up the dusty road from the dock, Marlowe could see several buildings that looked to be warehouses near the shore, and there was a swirl of activity around each. He could see men and women in the town, could hear the occasional shout or pistol shot. There were a half dozen vessels of various size in the harbor, and another hove down on the beach for breaming. They all had the unmistakable aspect of ships on the account.

Whether this was still Baldridge's kingdom or not, Marlowe did not know, but it was clearly still an active pirate enclave. It put him in mind of Port Royal, his own former haunt, before it was swallowed by the sea. He felt a vast relief lift him up, like floating in warm water.

All of his plans had depended upon his being able to buy powder, shot, and guns in Madagascar. From everything he knew of the island, this was not an unreasonable assumption, but it was an assumption nonetheless. He might well have arrived to find the Royal Navy in command of the big island and St. Mary's as well.

He had developed certain contingency plans—capture another pirate vessel and take its guns, go after the Mogul's ships by boarding alone, buy the spare guns of various other ships—but now it looked as if none of that would be necessary.

"On deck!" the lookout aloft cried. "Boat's putting off from shore and looks to be making for us!"

"Very well. Mr. Dinwiddie, I reckon we should have a side party or something. In case this is some sort of official of the town."

"These pirates," Bickerstaff observed, "are much given to aping the customs of the civilized."

"When in Rome and all that, Francis."

"Yes, well, I should think we will see precious little genuflecting and fiddling with beads and Latin prayer here."

"Precious little indeed. But still, we must do our best to give no offense."

So among Marlowe and Dinwiddie and Honeyman they managed to arrange a side party of sorts, with a dozen men on either side of the gangway. The boat pulled alongside, double-banked with twelve men in matching outfits and a big, bearded man in the stern sheets. The big man called, "Delegate from Lord Yancy of St. Mary's! Permission to come aboard?"

"Pray do so," Marlowe called back, and the big man stepped with the ease of an expert seaman from the stern sheets to the boarding steps and up. He stepped through the gangway, and the boarding party raised their swords and clashed them together overhead, making an archway of men and swords through which the delegate had to walk, a handsome effect, Marlowe thought.

"Welcome aboard the *Elizabeth Galley*," Marlowe said, extending his hand as the man passed through the twin lines of sailors. "I am Captain Thomas Marlowe. This is my first officer Peleg Dinwiddie, my quartermaster Duncan Honeyman. And this here is my wife, Elizabeth Marlowe."

The big man shook hands, nodded his greeting, did a poor job of hiding his surprise at seeing Elizabeth. He turned to Marlowe, looked him up and down, seemed to scrutinize him. "I'm Henry Nagel, I'm first officer to Lord Yancy, what is king of this place."

" 'Lord Yancy.' Is Adam Baldridge no longer lord of this island?"

At that, Nagel straightened a bit, his look part surprise, part consternation. "No, he ain't been here this ten year or more. And you're best if you don't mention that name again."

"I'll remember that," Marlowe said.

"Elephiant, Lord Yancy is ruler of this island now, and all here are devoted to him. You are, again . . ."

"Thomas Marlowe." The side party dispersed with little ceremony. Nagel ran his eyes over the ship, the casual, knowing look of an experienced seaman, first up aloft, over the rig, and then down along the deck.

"You sailing in company with a tender?" Nagel asked.

"No."

"Where are your great guns?"

"We have none. We had hoped to purchase them here. It is well known that Lord Yancy is the man to see for anything one might need."

Nagel nodded, seemed to be satisfied. He did not notice Marlowe's sudden familiarity with Lord Yancy's reputation. He, at least, seemed entirely devoted to Yancy, though Marlowe doubted if the others were any more devoted than pirates were to anything, save themselves.

"Lord Yancy will have guns to sell, if you gots gold to buy them. You're welcome to make use of the island as you need. I reckon my lord will wish to come out and greet you. You'd do well to have that side party for him, and musicians, if you got 'em. And bunting. He likes bunting."

"Thank you for that," Marlowe said, wondering what kind of lunatic this Yancy might be. He knew from personal experience the depravity that power could induce. "I would be delighted to welcome Lord Yancy aboard with all that my humble ship has to offer."

"Good. That's good, Captain." Nagel ran his eyes over Elizabeth one last time. "I'll bid you good day, then." With that, he lumbered back to the gangway, dropped easily down into the waiting boat. The boatmen shoved off, pulled for shore.

Marlowe watched them go, thinking, *Lord, I have been here for one hour, and already I am desperate to be gone.*

Chapter 14

DESPERATE HE might have been to leave St. Mary's, but Marlowe knew that being desperate did not necessarily mean being able to leave. And able he was not.

The *Elizabeth Galley* had now crossed the Atlantic three times, with never a bit of attention paid to her hull, and he knew that attention must be paid. They were taking on water, and great tendrils of weed could be seen streaming aft under the counter when the tide flowed around the hull. They would have to strip her top-hamper and careen her, run her up on the beach and roll her on her side to get at the weeds and the leaks. It was an onerous task, though not as bad as it might have been, since they had no guns to get off of her and precious little in the way of food or water left to sway out of her hold.

Marlowe was pulled from his consideration of that grim reality by a second hail from the lookout, the report of yet another boat pulling for them. Marlowe fixed the boat with his telescope. It was bigger than the last, sort of an ornamental barge with a canopy and a big ensign that he did not recognize streaming from a staff in the stern.

"This would be Lord Yancy, I'll wager," Bickerstaff said, his voice carrying the subtle flavor of irony and amusement.

"I'll wager you are right. And it will do us well to recall that, crack-brained though he might be, he is nonetheless the crackbrain who commands all of the guns past which we must sail. I think the utmost deference is called for, until such time as we are well beyond long-cannon range. Mr. Honeyman, what have we in the way of bunting?"

They managed to muster quite a bit in the fifteen minutes it took for the barge to make its leisurely way across harbor. Along with that, they rounded up what musicians the *Elizabeth Galley* could boast—a fore topman who was something of a hand with a fiddle; the cook, who was a master of the recorder; and one of the boys who had been practicing with a drum and found a natural talent with that instrument.

These few, and the men with cutlasses, made their best show as the barge drew alongside and Lord Yancy stepped slowly up and through the gangway.

Given the size of Henry Nagel, Marlowe had expected Yancy to be a hairy giant of a man, and so he was surprised at what stepped onto his deck. A small, thin man, squirrel-like, with a neat mustache and chin beard. He wore a wide hat with a great feather, like a French sol-dier of a former age. From his shoulders a cape fell nearly to the deck, lined with brilliant red silk. His clothes were immaculate. He wore a jewel-studded rapier on his waist.

"I take it I have the honor of welcoming Lord Yancy aboard the *Elizabeth Galley*?" Marlowe said, making a shallow bow.

"You do," Yancy said, never looking at Marlowe but rather darting his eyes around the vessel, not the slow, professional assessment of the seaman but rather a jerky, suspicious motion. He made to speak and then stopped as a coughing fit overcame him, and he bent over, hack-ing into a blood-spotted handkerchief. Finally he straightened again and said, "You did not salute the fort."

"Forgive me, my lord, I was unaware of the protocol of the island," Marlowe said, "and, as you can see, I have no great guns." He strug-gled to sound sincere, did not care for that kind of kowtowing. Two sentences, and already he wanted to twist Yancy's thin neck. He con-centrated on the big cannon on the island, which he reckoned were concentrated on him.

"Yes, well, do not forget again," Yancy said, and met Marlowe's eyes at last. The man was clearly sick with some ailment, and yet there was an energy about him that seemed out of place. "You wish to buy guns, I understand?"

"Yes, my lord. And powder and shot. And I would hope to careen as well."

Yancy nodded, and his eyes fell on Elizabeth, and he looked her up and down as only a man used to having supreme authority would dare do. Marlowe gritted his teeth. Yancy shifted his gaze a fraction of a second before Marlowe was about to speak.

"This is your wife?" Yancy asked.

"Yes. Lord Yancy, allow me to present Elizabeth Marlowe."

Elizabeth gave a shallow bow. Yancy shuffled across the deck with his weak gait, took up her hand, and kissed it as he bowed to her. He continued to hold it, turned to Marlowe. "Not many men would bring their wives on a Red Sea voyage," Yancy observed, his eyes drifting back to Elizabeth.

"There are not many wives such as Elizabeth," Marlowe countered.

"No indeed." Yancy finally eased her hand down, looked at Marlowe. "You will have your guns. We shall discuss price later. And you are welcome to careen as you wish. Plenty of good beach, you can see from here. You will dine with me tonight?" It did not sound like a question.

"I would be honored," Marlowe said.

"Good. Please bring your wife and whatever officers you see fit." Then he turned and climbed back down into the waiting barge with never another word.

"Well, he seems disposed to helping us, in any event," Bickerstaff observed as the barge pulled away.

"Yes, so he does." But that fact did not ease Marlowe's anxiety in the slightest measure.

By the time the sails were furled and the ship stood down to an anchor watch, there was not much left of the daylight. Marlowe and Elizabeth dressed for dinner, as did Bickerstaff and Peleg Dinwiddie, got up in the same attire he had worn to Governor Richier's dinner in Bermuda, so many months before. Fortunately, he had retained the lessons in fashion that Elizabeth had so diplomatically foisted on him, and he looked only a little bit odd as he met the others topside.

Marlowe did not think it would matter much. This was a pirate community, where the odd, the depraved, the bizarre were commonplace, even expected.

They gathered in the waist as the boat crew took their places on the thwarts, and Bickerstaff said, "Thomas, do you think it is entirely safe, bringing Elizabeth into this viper's nest?"

No, Thomas thought, but he said, "I should think it is safe. There is a sort of a code, you know, with these fellows. They are not wont to meddle with another's wife. Not when the other is willing and able to fight for her honor, as of course you know I am." That last he addressed to Elizabeth, with a bow.

"We shall trust your judgment in this, naturally," said Bickerstaff.

"And even if I am wrong," Marlowe added, "Elizabeth is now the finest blade in all Madagascar, thanks to your tutelage. I should think we might look to *her* to protect *our* persons."

They climbed down the side, and Marlowe took his place in the boat. He hoped very much that he would still be joking at evening's end. He did not point out to the others that there really was no choice but to bring Elizabeth ashore, did not point out that there was more danger to all of them, Elizabeth included, in ignoring this Yancy's wishes than in acquiescing. They could only play along and hope that things broke in their favor.

With Honeyman as coxswain, they were rowed ashore to a dubious wooden pier that jutted out like a poorly executed appendage to the dirt road that ran along the shore to the town. Marlowe stepped onto the slimy ladder, took a few rungs, turned, and helped Elizabeth up, and then Bickerstaff and Dinwiddie followed.

"You keep the boat crew sober, at least until we get back to the ship," Marlowe ordered Honeyman.

It was an interesting situation. By the law of the pirates, Marlowe could not give such an order. If his men wanted to get wild drunk, he could not stop them, not since he had agreed to turn his legitimate merchantman into a pirate ship.

But, to his relief, Honeyman just nodded and said, "Aye, Captain."

That done, Marlowe turned his attention to the town in front of him. There were two roads that he could see, no more, the one that ran from the end of the dock along the shore and another that wound its way up the hill to the stockade and the big house beyond. These crossed at a right angle and formed the town's single intersection. The roads were dirt, but not overly dusty in that wet, tropical climate.

Off to the right were the warehouses, big wood-frame buildings, a few shuttered windows on the upper floors, the remnants of paint still clinging to the weathered boards. Scattered around them coils of line, rusting anchors, piles of standing rigging stripped from some vessel or other. Bursts of bright green vegetation grew up around them and even through them, showing how they had not been moved in some time.

The two roads were busy. There were a few carts and oxen and one horse that Marlowe could see, but for the most part it was foot traffic. Pirates. They wore the dress of seamen—loose trousers, bare feet, long hair—as well as those things that marked them as men on the account—bright sashes, cocked hats with feathers jutting out, gentlemen's coats, weapons hanging off them in abundance.

They were hurrying or staggering or sitting on the road and singing or passed out, drunk. They were clustered about small, round tables on the street just outside one of the dilapidated taverns. They were promenading with local girls in European dress on their arms as if they were at the Court of St. James's. Several hundred men, Marlowe had to guess. The town might be no more than a little enclave carved from the jungle, but the spirit was Port Royal in its buccaneering heyday.

Marlowe and his party made their way up the road to the intersection, then turned and tramped uphill to the big house. They stopped at the stockade and were questioned by a pair of guards who stood at the gate. Marlowe explained who they were, and they were let to pass and continue on the one hundred yards to the main entrance of the house.

The house itself was a magnificent affair, even more extraordinary considering that it was built on a jungle island. The lower half, up to the second story, was stone, harvested from the ground and stacked uncut, but done so neatly that little mortar could be seen between each.

Above that, the structure rose two more stories, built of wood frame and stucco, in the Tudor style. A great, wide veranda jutted out over the grounds, and several of the windows had their own little verandas that looked out over the harbor. The roof was a massive field of thatch.

Marlowe paused, caught his breath, stared with admiration at the building. He wondered at the drive and vision of the man who had built it.

"That Baldridge fellow, he done this, right?" Dinwiddie asked, breaking the silence.

"Yes, I believe so," Marlowe said. "But I gather from Henry Nagel that Lord Yancy does not care to be reminded of that. Pray do not mention Baldridge again."

"No, I won't," Dinwiddie said. He sounded as if the reminder had offended him. He was growing touchier by the day.

They stepped up to the door, and before Marlowe could knock, Henry Nagel opened it and ushered them in. They entered a cool foyer that rose two stories above them, with a wide staircase running up to the second floor.

Nagel had managed to say no more than "Welcome—" when Yancy stepped into the foyer, his cape nearly dragging on the floor.

"Welcome, welcome to my home!" he said, expansive and gracious now, more vital in his own domain. "Captain Marlowe, the lovely Elizabeth, welcome." He glanced at the others, apparently could not recall their names, and said nothing. "Pray allow me to give you a tour before we eat. It is a simple, rustic place, but we must endure such to live in this tropical splendor!"

Yancy proceeded to show them the drawing room, the sitting room, the bedchambers on the second floor, shuffling from here to there, pausing to catch his breath or to indulge a coughing spell. There were a few other men in the house, those men, Marlowe guessed, that Yancy could genuinely trust. Yancy made introductions as they chanced to meet, named the others as though they were minor nobility, but they looked to Marlowe to be the same sort of rogues as wandered the streets below, if better dressed.

There were native men as well, servants, and native women, who seemed to outnumber the men three to one. The women smiled demurely, did not say anything to the strangers, and Yancy did not introduce them.

More bedchambers, drawing rooms upstairs, baths. Yancy showed them around with a pride as if he had built it all with his own hands.

It was a fine house, Marlowe had to agree, but he could also see that it was not wearing well. There was plaster flaking off walls and doorframes no longer square and mold creeping along window frames. He could see dirt accumulating in corners, broken bottles kicked aside, rooms with smashed furniture shoved into corners.

The grand house must have been magnificent when Baldridge had lived there, but those days were gone. Yancy and his pirates were the Visigoths, living among the crumbled glories of Rome.

They had dinner in the great hall, two stories tall, that made up the northeastern end of the house. Long tables ran nearly the length of the room, with Yancy's trusted friends sitting along them and native servants, silent, darting between broad-shouldered men, pouring wine, serving dishes piled with food, taking empty ones away.

The men ate with the refinement Marlowe would have expected from the Roundsmen, snatching food with their hands mostly, though some used sheath knives as well. Bones were flung aside to the half-dozen dogs that waited eagerly for scraps.

Marlowe and Elizabeth and Bickerstaff and Dinwiddie sat at the head table, flanking Yancy. No sooner had they sat than the great monster of a man sitting next to Bickerstaff—with matted, encrusted beard, smelling of rum and tobacco smoke and sweat—stood and extended his hand to Marlowe, across Yancy's face, nearly knocking Yancy over and saying, "Obadiah Spelt. Your servant, sir," with an arrogance that made it clear he considered himself to be no one's servant.

Marlowe took the hand and shook it and waited for the explosion, for Yancy's troops to fall on the villain and cut him up, but Yancy

seemed not to notice this blatant lack of respect, and neither did anyone else, so Marlowe ignored it, too. He sat again, wondered who this
fellow might be, who could get away with such disrespect. Yancy's
brother? Someone who had saved Yancy's life? Marlowe could not
guess, and he really did not care.

For a good part of the dinner Yancy brooded and said nothing and
ate nothing. It was only when the others were half done that Yancy finally called for food for himself, telling the servants specifically which
platters to take from and set on the plate before him.

After a few bites Yancy seemed to brighten a bit. He turned to Elizabeth. "Tell, me, ma'am, what think you of my little house?"

"I think it is beautiful, Lord Yancy," Elizabeth said, though to Marlowe's certain knowledge she had already told him as much three
times. "As fine as any of the great country houses of England," she lied.

"You are from England, then?"

"I was born there. My husband and I live in the colonies now, in
Virginia, where we—"

"I am from Newport, in Rhode Island, though my business has kept
me from there these many years. I do business with London now and
New York and, yes, Rhode Island."

"My husband and I grow tobacco mostly—"

"Tobacco is nothing." Yancy gave a dismissive wave of his hand.
"Growing things from the ground? That is for the last age. It is commerce now that is the only means to riches." He turned from Elizabeth, apparently done with her, looked at Dinwiddie. "You, sir, tell me
of yourself . . ."

It was one of the most bizarre dinners that Marlowe had ever endured. Yancy spoke to them each, not so much a conversation as an interview, and when he was done, he did not speak again, save to
Elizabeth.

Spelt was raving drunk, singing, shouting, throwing beef bones, but
no one seemed to notice, or at least there was tacit decision by all present to ignore him. Near the end of the meat course, thankfully he
passed out and fell on the floor, where he was allowed to remain.

At last it was over—the fruit and nuts, brandy and pipes—and Marlowe could reasonably insist that they had to return to the ship. This seemed to revive Yancy, and he stood and walked with them out of the great hall and along the wide corridors to the main door. He sat wearily in a chair by the door and closed his eyes. A moment later he opened them again and said, "I have much enjoyed your company, Captain, and that of your fine crew and, I need not say, your lovely wife." He reached out and took Elizabeth's hand and kissed it, augmenting the annoyance that Marlowe had felt all night, the result of the special attention Yancy had lavished on her.

"I trust you will visit with me again, before you sail. Tomorrow I will send Nagel down to make a deal with you for the guns. And as to careening, I shall see that you have all the help you might need. I am so very delighted by your company, I wish nothing but to aid you in any way I might."

He stood, bowed weakly, kissed Elizabeth's hand again, bade them good night as they stepped into the evening. Marlowe heard the big door close behind them, and it was a blessed relief.

The next morning, an hour after dawn, Nagel arrived in a longboat with twenty-five men. Marlowe watched it approach with some trepidation. He did not trust Yancy any more than he would trust a dog mad with rabies.

In accordance with his orders, Honeyman and the boat crew had remained sober while the rest of the men of the *Elizabeth Galley* had become insensibly drunk. After Marlowe and his party had returned, the boat crew had joined their fellows, gulping rum in an effort to catch up.

Now there was no one aboard the ship who was awake, save for himself and Bickerstaff and Dinwiddie, no one to defend the ship if it came to that. Nagel and his band could stand on the deck and bang drums, and it would be enough to induce the crew to surrender.

Fortunately, Nagel had no such bellicose intentions, and as the boat drew alongside, Marlowe could see that none of the men was armed beyond carrying a sheath knife, which was as much a part of the sailor's attire as trousers.

Nagel climbed up the side. "Morning, Captain," he said. "I come to see about selling you them guns. And Lord Yancy, he sent the men here to help you with your heaving down."

"Thank you. That is very kind," Marlowe said, and he meant it. Careening the ship was a great deal of work, even for men who were not still half drunk. Perhaps he had misjudged Yancy. Or, more correctly, perhaps his madness was not entirely of a malicious nature. He had, after all, done no more than flirt with Elizabeth, despite Marlowe's concerns. Flirting was nothing. There were few men, sane or otherwise, who could resist giving Elizabeth special attention.

Marlowe had known megalomaniacal tyrants who could be kind and helpful. It kept people off balance.

"What was you wanting, in the article of guns?"

Marlowe looked around at the empty gunports. "She was built with sixteen six-pounders in mind," he said, and even as the words left him, he thought, *They will never have that in this godforsaken jungle*.

But Nagel just nodded and said, "I don't reckon that will be a problem," and then Marlowe named a price, not an extravagant one, and Nagel accepted it with no argument or counteroffer.

Marlowe sent his cabin steward for coffee for himself and Nagel and then to rouse Honeyman and ask Dinwiddie to join them. When the officers were there, Marlowe told them that he wished to begin heaving the ship down and that Yancy had kindly sent hands to aid in that. Honeyman stared through red, half-closed eyes, nodded, and began to assemble the men.

It was a slow process, the men stumbling up from below, sitting or lying down again as soon as they reached the deck. Nagel called his men up from the boat, and between them and the Galleys they managed to slip the anchor cable, with a buoy attached to the end, and work the ship up to the beach, where, on the falling tide, it might be rolled on its side once the masts, yards, and rigging were down and the hold emptied.

By the time the *Elizabeth Galley* was in position, her men had revived enough to be of real help, and things began to happen fast. The crew that Yancy had sent were experienced seamen, and they went about their business with speed and care, driven by what motivation, Marlowe could not guess.

Still, he was glad to have them and pleasantly surprised the next morning when they showed up again, and the morning after as well. The ship was stripped of top-hamper, her hold emptied, and then a huge block and tackle was attached to the head of the lower main mast, the other end to a sturdy post on shore, and with the fall of the tackle run to a capstan, they pulled the ship over on her side until she looked like a beached whale.

When Yancy's men arrived the day after that and more came with the six-pounder guns in a lighter, it became clear to Marlowe that Yancy wanted them out of St. Mary's, and quickly. He did not know why. He did not understand why the lord of the island did not simply drive them away with the big guns. The only thing that was absolutely clear was that Yancy wanted them to leave of their own accord, and he wanted them to do it soon.

Marlowe had no doubt that he would find out the reason eventually. He did not think he would be happy with the discovery.

A week after the arrival of the *Elizabeth Galley*, Lord Yancy stood on his veranda, watching her through his glass. She was back on her anchor, her bottom cleaned and repaired, her rig set up. It seemed to glow in the late-afternoon sun. A long row of six-pounders jutted from her side. She sat lower in the water now, her hold full of gunpowder, shot, food, water. They had been treated well.

And that treatment had come at no small expense. Yancy had made a profit on the stores and the guns, to be sure, but not the kind he might have made otherwise, if he had bargained with Marlowe. The gang of men whom he had sent to help Marlowe he had paid fat wages. He had lavished Marlowe and his company with great feasts, three times now.

He sighed and shifted his glass down, away from the harbor and onto the road where the portly man was huffing his way up the road to the house.

It was all worth it, all the expense, if Marlowe would just sail away without a squabble, and after all the consideration he had been given, Yancy could not imagine he would not. With his sound ship and his guns and his hold full of stores, Marlowe was well positioned to garner enormous riches in the Red Sea. In Yancy's experience all loyalties would fall away in the face of that temptation.

Ten minutes later he saw the man pass through the stockade, and then he disappeared from view around the corner of the big house. Yancy left the veranda, went back up to his bedchamber, and sat down in a big winged chair, listless and weak.

Three minutes later Nagel knocked on the door, and Yancy, his voice weak, called, "Yes?"

Nagel cracked the door open. "Mr. Dinwiddie here to see you, sir," he said.

"Yes, pray show him in . . ."

Nagel opened the door, ushered the confused-looking Peleg Dinwiddie in, pulled up a chair for him. Yancy gestured for him to sit, and Dinwiddie did.

"Please, Henry, leave us . . ." Yancy said, and Henry nodded and left.

"I come as soon as I got your note. Lord Yancy, are you quite well?" Dinwiddie asked with real concern. Yancy had detected the man's ingenuous nature right off.

"Oh, I'm . . . no, my dear Dinwiddie, no, I am not. There is no use in hiding it . . ." Yancy paused with a hacking cough. "No, dear sir, I have not been well for some time. But now, I fear, it is got much worse."

"Lord Yancy . . . I feared this was the case. You didn't seem strong to me, if you'll forgive me being so forward . . ."

"I have tried to hide it. Put on a bold front. But just these past few days it has quite overrun me."

"I am so sorry. Is there anything I might do? You have shown us every kindness—"

"No, no, there is nothing. Think nothing of what I have done. Such kindness is just my nature, you know." He coughed again. "It is a cancer, I fear. I feel it eating away at me. There is nothing for it."

They sat in silence for a moment while Yancy regained his strength. "Peleg, if I may be so bold as to call you such . . ."

"Please, my lord, 'tis an honor."

"Peleg, I am not long for this life, and I do not regret it. But this is what I fear most. My kingdom, all I have worked for, it will all be lost, without I leave a solid man to the running of it . . ." He coughed again, dabbed his mouth with his handkerchief.

"That fellow, Obadiah Spelt, he seems the stuff of leaders."

"Oh, I had thought so as well. But I find the man is a fool and a drunk. He would never do."

"Your man Nagel, he seems a decent sort."

Yancy waved his hand again. "Henry is a good man, a good lieutenant, but he is not a captain, not fit for command. I had despaired of finding such, until your ship sailed in. And behold, you and Captain Marlowe, two men with just the qualities I need.

"But Marlowe, he is devoted to his ship, would not leave her, and I would expect no less. But you, sir . . . you have the qualities of a captain, a leader, and yet you are only second in command. And aboard one of these Red Sea Rovers, I suspect that even the quartermaster has more real authority than you. Am I right?"

Yancy could see from the look on Dinwiddie's round face that he was indeed right, that he had hit the right chord with that observation. "I could pass away in peace, Peleg, if I knew a man such as yourself had been named my successor . . ."

Dinwiddie leaned back, looked away, looked back at Yancy. Shook his head as if that would aid him in comprehension. "Do you ask me, sir . . . you wish . . . me to take over for you the running of this kingdom?"

"Yes. That is what I wish. I wish it to be yours."

"But . . . my lord . . . it is such a thing! I am flattered, more than that . . . but you have known me for just this past week . . ."

Yancy shook his head weakly. "I have not gained my place by being a fool, sir. I know men. I can take the measure of a man's character in an hour, much less a week. I can see you are the man I need."

"I—I do not know what to say . . ."

"All this island, all its riches will be yours."

"I am at a loss, sir. The *Elizabeth Galley*, and Marlowe . . ."

"They do not appreciate you as I do. But see here, I know it is a great thing to ask, a great responsibility I ask you to shoulder. You must sleep on it."

Yancy rose awkwardly, and Dinwiddie leaped up to help him. Once standing, Yancy waved him off. "You will spend the night as my guest. Come with me."

Yancy shuffled off down the hallway, and Dinwiddie followed behind. They came at last to a big door, which Yancy swung open. In the room beyond were a dozen native girls, partially clothed. Some were reclining on the big bed, some brushing their hair, some drawing water for a bath. They all looked up and all smiled with delight at the sight of Yancy and Dinwiddie.

"This is my harem, my lovely girls . . ." said Yancy. "I shall miss them most of all. But tonight, dear Peleg, they will attend to you. And in the morning you can tell me of your decision."

He gently shoved the astounded Dinwiddie into the room, then closed the door and walked back down the hall to the privacy of his terrace room. That much was done. There was no real need for him to wait on Dinwiddie's answer.

Chapter 15

MARLOWE COULD feel his control of circumstances slipping away, a little bit at a time, like water leaking from cupped hands.

The *Elizabeth Galley* was repaired and provisioned, guns swayed aboard and rigged at the gunports. Yancy's men no longer made their morning appearance. Nagel had come out and insisted they shift their anchorage closer to the harbor entrance. Dinwiddie was gone.

Marlowe's steward came up to him, stammered, "I looked all over the ship, sir, and right down to the cable tier, and Mr. Dinwiddie, he ain't aboard."

"He went ashore yesterday," Bickerstaff offered. "Early evening, I should think. I have not seen him since."

"Burgess had the boat. Says he saw one of them natives give him a letter," Honeyman added.

All of this discussion took place as the three men stood on the quarterdeck and watched the now-familiar form of Henry Nagel as he was pulled in a small boat out to the *Elizabeth Galley*.

"Well, it is passing strange," Marlowe said. "Were it any other man, I would assume he was passed out, drunk, in some whorehouse, but that doesn't seem like Dinwiddie."

Nagel's boat came alongside, and Nagel climbed aboard, with never a hail or a request that he might do so. He came back aft, smiling, nodding his greetings. But there was an edge to his manner, something Marlowe had not seen before. He wondered if it was his imagination. He felt the control slipping further from his grasp.

"Good day, Nagel, and what brings you here?" Marlowe asked.

"Lord Yancy sends me. He requests you join him for dinner, one last time, before you sail."

"Did I say I intended to sail?"

Nagel looked confused. Marlowe detected a spark of irritation. "You're all fit out and provisioned—"

"But I seem to have lost my first officer."

Nagel brightened. "Oh, Mr. Dinwiddie is Lord Yancy's guest, stayed the night in the big house. If you'll come to dinner, you'll see him then."

Marlowe nodded. "I do not care to have my people spirited away like that. You may tell Lord Yancy as much."

Nagel stiffened, folded his arms. His eyes darted up toward the battery that commanded the entrance to the harbor. Those big guns could easily sink the *Elizabeth Galley*, firing at point-blank range. They were so close that they would need only indifferent gun layers to do mortal damage.

Marlowe had noticed that there was an ensign flying from the battery's flagpole, the first time since his arrival. If that meant on St. Mary's what it did in the rest of the world, then the battery was garrisoned and ready for work.

He did not know if Nagel's glance was involuntary or an intentional threat, but he took the meaning well enough. He had come of his own accord into the wolf's lair, had accepted the hospitality of the dangerous and unpredictable beast. Now he could leave only by permission.

"Forgive me, I am not myself today," Marlowe said. "Of course I should be delighted to attend dinner with Lord Yancy."

"Good. And your officers, if they wish. And my lord would be most disappointed was he not able to personally say good-bye to your wife."

"Of course." Marlowe smiled. *Son of a bitch*.

He thought of those batteries, considered whether or not he could make a run for it. The wind was light, and the tide was flooding. He would never make it to the open sea, never get beyond the reach of the seaward guns.

"I had, as it happens, wanted to sail on the tide this evening," he extemporized, "but I would not wish to offend His Lordship with making an early departure from dinner . . ."

"I don't reckon that'll be a problem. He just wants to make his formal fare-thee-wells, and then you'll be free to leave."

Marlowe saw the big man over the side. "*Free to leave.*" There was no equivocation in that statement, as regarded who was in charge on St. Mary's, who controlled the comings and goings.

We have only to make it through the next few hours, Marlowe thought, *and then we sail.*

It was nearly slack water when they walked along the now-familiar road, up the hill to Yancy's commanding villa. They were ushered in the door by Nagel, led along to the great hall. Marlowe and Elizabeth and Bickerstaff now. Where Dinwiddie was, Marlowe could not guess, but he was relieved to see that Spelt was not there either.

We have only to make it through the next few hours, and then we sail.

Yancy sat at the head of the big table, as usual, slouched back, staring blankly at a stain on the wood. He could hear the animal sounds of his loyal band already eating. He had not made them wait for Marlowe's party. They looked as if they had no thought for anything, save wolfing down their food, but he knew they understood their parts, would play them well.

He glanced up at the sound of the big door creaking on its hinges. Marlowe stepped in, then the lovely Elizabeth, then Bickerstaff. Nagel loomed behind them, like a tidal wave pushing them along.

"Ah, welcome, welcome," Yancy said, but he could not muster his former enthusiasm. His business with them was almost at an end.

He could see his change in tone register on Marlowe's wary face.

"I thank you, my lord," Marlowe said, giving a shallow bow. Yancy gestured toward the seats that Marlowe's party had occupied on the other nights they had been his guests, and they sat down directly. Yancy snapped his fingers, and his native servants set food and wine in front of them, fast and silent as assassins.

"Your ship looks to be well set up again. I fear you will be leaving us soon," Yancy observed. He had tried to make himself sound disappointed, or at least interested, but he could not muster it. He could not manage the energy to placate people with whom he was done.

"I had hoped to, my lord, but my first officer seems to have gone missing."

There was a veiled accusation in his tone that made Yancy sit more upright and look hard at Marlowe, who returned the stare, unflinching. The two men locked eyes for a moment, Yancy angry and a bit unsettled. This man was not sufficiently cowed.

"Mr. Dinwiddie is here, in my home," Yancy said, relaxing a bit. "He is my guest. In fact, he has elected to remain here with me. I fear you will have to sail without his assistance."

Marlowe's eyes narrowed. "He has elected to remain here? Why should he do that?"

"This island has many charms to recommend it. Dinwiddie is hardly the first to wish to remain. I do not think he felt entirely appreciated aboard your ship."

Yancy could see that those words rang true with Marlowe, could see him floundering about for a reply. At last Marlowe said, "I should like to hear that from Dinwiddie's own lips, if you please."

"I do not please, Marlowe, and I do not care for your words or your tone. Do you call me a liar?"

Again the standoff, the two men holding one another's gaze. But now the others around the table, Yancy's faithful from the *Terror*, were pushing aside their plates, leaning away from the table, taking an interest in the conflict. The men who stood at intervals around the room, armed guards, folded arms or set hands on sword pommels or fingered pistols. The threat was not lost on Marlowe. Yancy watched Marlowe's eyes shift from his, watched them dart around the room, sum up the overwhelming odds.

"No, I do not call you a liar, sir. It is only my concern for my men that makes me speak so . . . hastily."

"I understand, Captain. Such sentiment is admirable, necessary even, in a leader. I feel the same way. That is why my men are so unflinchingly loyal to me." He let the implied warning hang in the air.

Dinwiddie was perfectly safe, Yancy knew, and entirely unaware that Marlowe was sitting in the great hall one floor below him.

The future lord of St. Mary's was at that moment preparing for dinner, allowing a half dozen of the girls of Yancy's harem to bathe him and rub him with oil. He might have lain with one of them, or two of them, before dinner, or he might have been too worn out from that morning and the night before to function carnally.

Yancy had had a sumptuous breakfast sent up to him a few hours after dawn, had given Dinwiddie time to enjoy it, and then had sent for him. A smiling, jovial Dinwiddie had found Yancy once more in the wing chair, a man dying of a cancer.

"Well, sir? Have you had a chance to think on it?" Yancy asked, between coughs.

"I have, my lord. You do me great honor. I feel I would be less than grateful if I were not to accept."

"Good, good. You make me happy, sir. Soon I will go off and leave you as lord of the island. I wish to be shed of my responsibilities, so that I might devote myself to my prayers."

"Of course, of course. I understand entirely," Dinwiddie said, and Yancy was pleased to see that in fact the fat man understood nothing.

Yancy sent him back to the girls, and while Dinwiddie was wallowing like a pig in his debauchery, he and Nagel made their way to Spelt's room, where the first handpicked successor to the throne was still sleeping off the night's drunk. They bound him, quickly and efficiently, and when at last the crushing pain of the ropes cutting into his wrists woke him, Nagel pressed the pillow against his nose and mouth.

Spelt squirmed, kicked, but he could not get out from under the pillow, held by Nagel's powerful arms. And all the time he was suffocating, Yancy stared into his eyes, their gazes locked. He could not let Spelt die without knowing that it was for his insults to Lord Yancy that he was being killed.

Five minutes later they left the limp, wide-eyed body on the bed. In Peleg Dinwiddie, Yancy had everything he wanted in a successor.

Marlowe, however, would not be fooled so easily as his first officer. That was why Yancy could not allow Dinwiddie to speak to him.

But Dinwiddie was the easy part. Yancy had to hope now that Marlowe, like most men, cared more for wealth and self-preservation than he did for any other consideration.

"In any event, Captain Marlowe, I do not wish to have harsh words with you. You are my guest, after all, and I believe I have shown you genuine hospitality during your stay on this island?"

"Yes, sir, you have done that. And I am grateful."

Yancy gave a wave of his hand, like shooing a fly. "It is my privilege to do so, though I fear it is that very hospitality that has lured your good Dinwiddie away. But see here, I think perhaps there is one more service I might do for you."

"Yes?"

"Well, Captain, what you propose, sailing off to the Red Sea, plundering the Great Mogul—I have a great deal of experience in such matters. It is a very dangerous business, I can assure you of that. No place for a woman. Might I suggest that your lovely wife remain here, as my guest, while you are off on your expedition? She will be quite safe, I can assure you. Safer than she would be on your ship, to be sure. You do not want to know what these barbarians will do to a Christian woman, do they get ahold of one. You might play the Red Sea Rover to your heart's content and then call again on your way home to pick up the fair Elizabeth."

All through that speech Yancy saw Marlowe's eyes narrow, saw him stiffen, saw the rage he tried to hold in check. He saw Marlowe glance around at the guards, who were inching closer, the men at the table who were watching him, some of whom had even stood up, backed away to give themselves fighting room. The threat was blatant, the choice—or lack of choice—obvious.

Yancy leaned back, watched Marlowe as the latter ran his options around in his head.

He could have Marlowe killed, of course, could have done so at any moment, could have his ship sunk or taken with one word. But he was afraid that Dinwiddie might hold in his breast some smoldering sense of loyalty. If he killed Marlowe, he might lose Dinwiddie.

That risk notwithstanding, he had to have Elizabeth. She was a gift from God. Here he had been thinking of the fine, fair girls he had left behind, and then she sailed right into his kingdom. He was smitten with her, thought of her every moment since first he ran his eyes over her perfect face and body. She was not destined to be the wife of some little no one like Marlowe. She was meant to be a queen, and so God had sent her to her king.

"Lord Yancy," Elizabeth was saying now, "I am grateful for your offer and your concern for my safety. Truly. But my husband and I have sailed these many months together, and I cannot think of our being parted now."

"No, no, it is far too dangerous for you." Yancy leaned over and patted her hand in a comforting manner. There was anger in her eyes also, but she would get over it. "You must stay with me."

"I do not wish to stay with you," she said, biting off the words.

"But you must. I am certain Captain Marlowe would agree." He looked up at Captain Marlowe, who was leaning back in his chair, running his eyes over the room, over the two dozen heavily armed men between himself and the door, assessing the chances of himself and Bickerstaff and Elizabeth fighting their way out. They would never make it, and Yancy was sure that Marlowe was never man enough to sacrifice his own life for the honor of some bunter.

"Well, perhaps you are right, my lord . . ." Marlowe extemporized, his eyes still moving around the room.

"Of course I am. You will be parted . . . two months, no more. But see here, Captain, I do believe the tide is on the ebb now and the wind fair. I think you had best take advantage of it, hmm? Nagel, will you see Captain Marlowe and Mr. Bickerstaff safe to the dock?"

"Yes, my lord," said Nagel, stepping up behind them. At some point in the past hour he had acquired a cutlass and a brace of pistols.

"Very well, then." Marlowe stood, gave Yancy a shallow bow. "I thank you again for your hospitality. Come along, Francis, we must away." He kissed Elizabeth lightly on the cheek. "You will be safe here, and I will return in a few months, my dear. Good-bye."

Elizabeth watched him go, stunned to speechlessness, but Yancy gave him a hearty farewell. He was not surprised. He knew men, and he knew that Marlowe would make the right decision.

The sun was two hours gone when Nagel returned. Yancy was waiting on the wide veranda. He nodded as he listened to Nagel's report. The big man had seen Marlowe and Bickerstaff back aboard, had insisted on taking them out himself in the longboat.

Yancy and Nagel stood silent for a moment, watching the *Elizabeth Galley* creeping out of the harbor. There was enough of a moon that they could clearly see her topsails as they filled, just a little, in the light air. The breeze and the tide carried her steadily along, past the rotten and abandoned pirate ships, past Quail Island with its garrisoned battery, until it was lost from sight in the darkness to the south.

Yancy watched until her big stern lantern winked once and then vanished behind the island. Even if he wanted to return now, he could not sail back against the breeze and the current. Marlowe was gone.

Yancy thought of the idiot Dinwiddie having his way with the harem girls, but that thought did not bother him in the least. He did not need harem girls. He had Elizabeth now. She was secure in a room down the hall, locked in and awaiting his pleasure. And what a pleasure it would be.

She would fight him, he had no doubt of that. She was spirited, not like these docile creatures native to the island. But that was what he wanted, what he needed. He craved challenge, had little enough of it as supreme ruler of St. Mary's. She would fight, and she would lose, and eventually she would be broken, like a horse, and she would be his.

He felt arousal creeping up on him, just thinking of what the night had in store.

Elizabeth stood on the small balcony that was part of the room in which she was locked. She watched the *Elizabeth Galley* creeping away.

Elizabeth Galley. The irony of the name made her sick. The thought of Marlowe standing up and graciously taking his leave of her made her sick.

It was not anger, not dismay, not confusion. None of those things could describe what she felt. It was a witch's brew of them all, boiling in her guts. She felt like running, careening off walls. She did not know what she felt. It was all too unreal. It was betrayal beyond the imaginable.

No, no. She shook off that thought. Thomas must have some plan, some trick or other in mind. He would not just leave her there. Not the Thomas Marlowe who had once thrown everything away to rescue her from a prison cell, who had killed men in defense of her honor. Thomas whose life was inextricably entwined with hers.

She watched as the *Galley*'s big stern lantern disappeared around the island, and then she knew she was alone, and suddenly she was unsure again. She turned and ran her eyes over the walls of the building, wondered if she could climb off the balcony and make some kind of escape. But the walls were smooth, there was nothing to grab, and below her a long drop to a rocky outcropping. There was nothing to do but jump to her death.

She looked down at the rocks, dull gray in the moonlight. Yancy obviously did not think she would do it, or he would not have given her access to the balcony. Perhaps she would surprise him. She wondered if the fall was really enough to kill her, or if it would just cripple her in some horrible way.

She leaned farther over the rail, even told herself to do it, but then she straightened and pushed herself back. That was not her way. If she had not killed herself yet, after all the misery she had suffered, then she was not about to do it now. Apparently Yancy *did* have her figured, just as he had had Marlowe figured.

No, it is not possible! Thomas would not abandon me!

She could not believe it, yet she knew that Nagel had escorted him to his ship, and she had seen his ship sail away.

He has to have some plan. The Thomas she knew would not leave her.

Thomas, the former pirate? His whole life is a lie, even his name. Why should I think his loyalty to me is anything more?

Thomas had sailed away, left her behind. It was hardly the first time she had been abandoned in her life, left to fend for herself. She had survived then, she would survive now. She would survive by her own wits and strength, and if indeed he had left her, then Thomas Marlowe be damned.

Chapter 16

DUNCAN HONEYMAN insisted on coming. Pleaded, in fact, and Marlowe could not have been more surprised.

Marlowe figured that his own choice was Elizabeth or the *Elizabeth Galley*. He reckoned that Honeyman would see this as his big opportunity. Dinwiddie gone to God knows where, the captain and Bickerstaff off the ship. The *Galley*, now complete with guns, powder, shot, stores, was his for the taking.

Marlowe was ready to make that sacrifice. In some way he even hoped for it, penitence for his incalculable stupidity and hubris. *"There is a sort of a code, you know, with these fellows. They are not wont to meddle with another's wife."* Lord, those words mocked him! And it did not help to recall that he had not really believed them, even as they were coming out of his mouth. He had pushed his luck clean over the brink.

Marlowe had planned on giving Honeyman temporary command, ordering him to return for them at dawn, but he never really thought Honeyman would. He figured that Honeyman would head for the horizon, leave them to rot, so his real plan was to make his way to Madagascar in the open boat with Bickerstaff and Elizabeth, once he had freed her, and find passage from there. It was a risk he had to take.

Back on board, climbing up the side under Nagel's vigilant eye, Marlowe had ordered the anchor up and topsails set. They stood out of the harbor with never a word spoken, save for those necessary to the running of the ship.

When at last they had cleared the headland, Honeyman approached. "Captain? Where's Dinwiddie? And Mrs. Marlowe?"

"Dinwiddie has elected to stay behind, or so it would seem. My wife has been kidnapped. Please see the jolly boat cleared away and over the starboard side, quiet as you can. I do not want anyone on the island to see. Bickerstaff and I are going back for my wife. You will have command of the ship until we return."

For a moment the quartermaster did not move or say anything, to Marlowe's annoyance. At last he said, "I'm with you."

"No," Marlowe said.

"There's no one at Yancy's house recognizes me. They all know you and Bickerstaff. You need me with you."

Marlowe had no argument to make. Honeyman was right. And for some reason Honeyman needed to be a part of this.

They got the jolly boat over the side, and Marlowe gave his orders to Flanders, who inherited command of the ship. Honeyman went down into the boat, Bickerstaff ready to follow, and up stepped Hesiod, cutlass and two braces of pistols draped over him, haversack at his side. His body looked as solid as a statue. "Jolly boat'll move faster with four men to pull oar" was all he said.

Marlowe looked at Bickerstaff, and Bickerstaff nodded. Among the former slaves at Marlowe House, Hesiod had been the hunter, the one who could disappear into the woods with an old smooth-bore musket and some snares and come back with game: deer, turkey, rabbit—nothing was safe from him. A good man to have, but Marlowe felt compelled to say, "Hesiod, there's a better-than-even chance we won't come back."

"Don't matter. It's Mrs. Marlowe," he said as he stepped down and took his place at the oar.

They pushed off from the *Elizabeth Galley*'s side, the vessel never slowing in her stately progression away from the harbor mouth. They let her pass, bobbing in her wake, then pulled for the shore, oars double-banked, a dark boat invisible on the dark water.

It took twenty minutes to fetch the shore. Honeyman went over the side in water up to his knees, pulled the boat farther up. Then the rest jumped out, and they dragged the boat up the deserted beach, half lifting it to keep the keel from making a grinding noise on the sand.

They let the boat down easy and then hurried across the beach to the edge of the trees and followed that toward the glimmer of lanterns that marked the pirate haven of St. Mary's, half a mile away.

Marlowe and Bickerstaff were dressed in old clothes—slop trousers and tar-stained shirts, sashes, battered cocked hats. Marlowe wore the tall boots and faded blue coat and cross belts he had saved since his days on the account. The clothes gave him a certain strength and re-assurance. It felt good to strip off the dandified attire he had worn to Yancy's dinner and to put on these old, rugged, well-worn garments. They were like armor to him; in them he felt able to fight back.

Honeyman and Hesiod were dressed in their usual garb, save for the profusion of weapons that hung from their belts and cross belts. But none of them looked in any way unique for the pirate enclave.

Four white men and one black, equals and brothers in arms. In nearly any other place on earth they would be absurdly conspicuous, but not on St. Mary's, not among the pirates. As long as they were not recognized, they would not attract notice.

They came at last to the edge of the dirt road that paralleled the harbor, where it seemed to dissolve into scrub and then jungle. Hesiod pushed ahead, peered along the road, and when he saw that it was all clear, he signaled the others.

They fought their way out of the brush, walked down the center of the road. Stealth would attract notice, but there was nothing odd about four brethren staggering along. They were one hundred yards from the intersection with the road that ran up the hill to Yancy's place. They could hear the distant sounds of the night's bacchanal: shouting and music and women's screams and gunshots.

They stopped, and Hesiod pulled a bottle of rum from his haversack, uncorked it, and they passed it around as they talked in low tones.

It would appear as the most innocent thing in the world in that place, if anyone was watching, four men sharing a bottle and a yarn.

"Stockade's pretty solid, far as I ever seen," Honeyman observed. "Don't reckon there's a break anywhere."

"I got ten fathom of rope in my haversack," said Hesiod. "If we find a dark place, we could up and over pretty easy, I reckon."

"It'll be some hard climbing to get around the back," Honeyman said. "That house was built in a damned good place, far as defending it goes."

"No," Marlowe said. His anxiety was growing to the point where he could not contain it. Every second that passed put Elizabeth in greater danger. Standing still was making him wild with fear. "No time for such fancy plans. We go right through the gate."

The others looked at him. Hesiod nodded slightly. Marlowe did not see any argument in their faces.

"We must be smart, however," said Bickerstaff. "We are outnumbered ten to one at least. It will do Elizabeth no good if we are slaughtered. It may in fact make her situation worse."

"Very well. Smart. But we go right at 'em."

Marlowe led the way down the road. He and Bickerstaff pulled their hats low over their eyes, and they all assumed a slightly unsteady gait as they made their way past the ramshackle taverns and tent whorehouses and the groups of men sitting around open fires, drinking and eating. The air was all wood smoke and expended gunpowder and meat cooking and rum and unwashed men. No one made any comment or even seemed to notice as they walked by.

Halfway up the hill Honeyman stopped. "Captain, they know you at the house, but Hesiod and me, we ain't been. What say you and Mr. Bickerstaff wait here, we'll see to them bastards at the gate?"

Marlowe hesitated. He did not want to stop. But what Honeyman said made sense. "Very well. But hurry."

Marlowe and Bickerstaff stepped off the road, standing half hidden behind a thick palm that rose up into the night. They watched the two others staggering up the road until they were lost in the dark. The gate, with the ubiquitous guards, was fifty yards away.

The night was still and the sounds of the carousing at the bottom of the hill muted, and Marlowe could hear the guard challenging Honeyman and Hesiod. It was quiet after that, and then a burst of laughter. More quiet, and then Marlowe heard a sound like the wind knocked from someone or a body hitting the ground, he could not tell. Another minute, and then Hesiod's voice from the dark: "All right, Captain" was all he said.

Marlowe and Bickerstaff stepped from the underbrush and hurried up the hill. The gate to the stockade loomed in front of them, visible in the circle of light thrown off by the lantern the guards had hung from a hook just outside the big door.

One of the guards was still standing there, in the half-alert position that Marlowe was accustomed to seeing, and he realized it was Honeyman. Another guard sat leaning against the big door, again in the relaxed attitude that the pirate sentries assumed. His eyes were open. The lantern light glinted on the blood that soaked his shirt and coat.

Hesiod, Marlowe, and Bickerstaff skirted the fall of the light and stepped through the gate, into the shadows of the stockade wall.

From that dark spot they surveyed the big house. To their left the banquet hall rose up two stories. The tall windows glowed with the light of the iron chandeliers that hung from the rough beams of the ceiling. They could hear the muffled roar of the riot taking place within, as Yancy's anointed took their nightly pleasure. On the second story there were lights burning in three rooms that they could see and two on the third.

"She may be in one of those," Marlowe said, nodding toward the windows in which lanterns or candles burned. "Or not."

"There's but one way to find out," said Hesiod. "Coming, Honeyman, or standing guard here?"

"Coming."

The four men hurried toward the house, moving along the stockade wall, keeping to the shadows. They came to the corner of the building, paused, crouching in the dark, listened for any guards walking the grounds. There was nothing beyond the revelry in the banquet hall and the revelry in the town below.

"Let me try the door," Honeyman said. He stood and walked toward the front door, not running or hiding but striding with purpose and a bit of a wobble, not like an intruder but rather a drunk who had no concerns about his right to be where he was.

Up the stone steps, and Marlowe could just see him in the shadow as he tugged at one door, then the other, then both, before turning and walking back the way he had come.

"Damn," Marlowe said softly. They would need another way in. He ran his eyes over the front of the house, pictured it from the inside, as it had been shown to him by Yancy.

"Hold! Who's that?" The voice from the dark startled him. Honeyman was no more than a shadow against the gray house. Marlowe saw him pause and turn toward the guard. Then he caught a flare of light overhead. He looked up, quick.

On the balcony attached to one of the rooms, a figure was holding a torch, a great flaming mass of fire. To Marlowe's surprise, that person was Elizabeth.

He stood, took a step forward. He did not know what to do. Shout? Remain silent? She was two stories up. She could not jump, nor could he climb up to her.

As he stood there, paralyzed with his indecision, Elizabeth turned her back to him, leaned over the edge of the balcony, and whipped the torch up in the air. It flew from her hand, tumbled end over end, slowly revolving in the air, and then landed on the thatched roof above.

The flame gutted, smoldered, and then flared as the dry thatch caught. The guard who had challenged Honeyman now forgot him completely as he ran for the door, shouting, "Fire! The damned bitch lit the damned roof on fire! Fire, there!"

Honeyman ran across the grounds, into the shadows where the others stood. He was grinning. "Men hear about this, I reckon they'll elect your wife captain in your stead, Marlowe," he said.

"I reckon she would do a better job."

Someone unbarred the big door at the guard's pounding. People came streaming out, and others came from around the building, looking up at the roof, which was now well on its way to being engulfed. Pandemonium began to sweep through the half-drunk men. Several were shouting orders, each trying to take command of the situation, no one listening to anyone else.

"Come on," Marlowe said, hurrying out of the shadows and racing along at the edge or the growing crowd. There were thirty or forty people on the grounds now—pirates, servants, women. Their attention was on the burning roof. No one noticed the four men at the edge of the light.

Marlowe paused, ten feet from the door. Circling the crowd unnoticed was one thing, but going inside was another. He braced himself, ready to make his move, when Nagel, like a wild bull, burst through the door, pulling up his breeches as he ran, his booming voice trampling the buzz of excitement and the orders that were flying around the yard.

"Here, you motherless bastards!" he roared. "With me! Get buckets! Get axes! We have to cut the roof away before it sets the whole goddamned house ablaze!"

He waved his arm, turned, and charged back into the house, and the others charged in behind. Now they had someone to lead them, and it would not be long before they had the blaze contained.

The last of the men in the yard rushed past, and then Marlowe and the others joined them, running in through the door at the tail of the crowd, hats pulled low, hands on pistol butts.

Across the high foyer and up the stairs, Nagel led his mob, and the four men from the *Elizabeth Galley* followed, lost in the chaos.

At the far end of the hall there was a rough ladder that led up and under the thatch, and Nagel bounded up it, heedless of the danger that the fire might present, and behind him the bolder of Yancy's men followed. Sloshing buckets appeared and were handed along.

"This way, I think," Marlowe said, and they pushed their way through the crowd toward the open hall beyond.

Marlowe looked up the corridor in one direction, then another. Doors lined the way, three on one side, three on another. He was turned around in the house, could not guess in which of the rooms he had seen Elizabeth. He grabbed Bickerstaff by the arm. "Take Hesiod, start looking in those rooms!" He pointed across the hall. "Honeyman, with me, here!"

They pushed past the pirates, the servants, the wives, and down the hall. Bickerstaff pushed open the far door, shouted, "Fire! Clear out! Fire!" as he searched the space for Elizabeth.

Marlowe tried the far door on his side, but the room was dark and empty, as far as he could see. He moved to the next, lifting the heavy latch, swinging it open.

The room was lit with a smattering of candles, giving it a dreamy, soft quality. In the middle of the room stood a big four-poster bed, draped with shiny, gauzy material. Two women were there on the bed, naked, their long black hair falling over brown shoulders. They looked up at the intrusion, and one of them propped herself on her elbow, unabashed. They gazed at Marlowe with little curiosity, as if they had no interest in what would happen to them next.

Between them, in the bed, lay Peleg Dinwiddie, flat on his back, snoring. There were various glasses and bottles and pipes scattered around the room and on the bedside table and in the bed itself. Dinwiddie's big belly rose and fell with his breath. It seemed to glow white in the light of the flames.

Marlowe crossed the room quickly, grabbed Dinwiddie's shoulder and shook it, hard.

"Peleg! Peleg!" he said in a whisper, as loud as he dared. "Peleg, wake up!"

At last the big man moaned, opened a bleary eye, looked up at Marlowe. There was no recognition in his face. "Peleg, it's me. Marlowe. Come, we have to go!"

"Marlowe?"

"Yes, yes, come along . . ."

Dinwiddie rolled his head away. "Sod off, you bastard . . ."

Marlowe paused, unsure if he had heard correctly. "What?"

Dinwiddie rolled his head back, looked up into Marlowe's eyes. "I said 'sod off.' Let that whoreson Honeyman take my place, never had any goddamned respect—"

"Peleg, you cannot stay here. Come with me, we'll sort this out."

"Sod off, bastard. Treat me like a fucking lord here . . ."

"Marlowe," Honeyman called from the door. "We ain't got much time . . ."

"Right." He looked down at Dinwiddie. "Son of a bitch . . ." There was no way he could carry him out of there. Perhaps he really did wish to stay. Marlowe did not know where his duty lay.

"Marlowe!" Bickerstaff was at the door. "There is a room at the other end of the hall, seems to be where the fire is centered!"

That had to be Elizabeth. He could not waste any more time with Dinwiddie. "Very well, I shall sod off," he said, then turned and hurried from the room, shut the door on his former first officer, who was already asleep once more.

Marlowe and Honeyman and Bickerstaff pushed down the hall, still unnoticed in the pandemonium. And now the hallway was filling with smoke, which served to further hide them.

Down the hall, and Hesiod was standing guard beside the door. "Locked" was all he said.

Marlowe looked back but still no one was paying him any attention in the commotion and the dark and the smoke. He kicked at the door, felt it yield under his boot. Kicked again, then Honeyman stepped up and kicked it, and it swung open, and they plunged through.

It was like stepping through the gate to hell. The fire had spread across the thatch above that room, had dropped to the plaster ceiling overhead and burned clean through. The entire ceiling was ablaze, and in the middle of it a great charred hole looked right up to the burning roof overhead.

Marlowe stumbled into the room, hand over his face. It was brightly lit by the flames, but he had trouble seeing through the thick smoke, which gagged him and made his eyes water.

"Elizabeth!" he shouted, thinking he would not be heard over the roar of the fire. "Elizabeth!"

The others followed him in, and Honeyman slammed the door again, leaving them in their brilliant, hot, smoking inferno.

"Elizabeth!"

And then from across the room, a voice high-pitched with controlled terror: "Thomas? Thomas?"

Marlowe stumbled across the room, stepping around the burning bits of thatch and fallen lath and plaster that were setting the floor and the carpets ablaze. Out onto the small balcony, and there he found Elizabeth, pushed back against the railing, where there was some relief from the smoke that rolled out the door. Her face was black with soot, white lines cut down her cheeks by tears.

He grabbed her, hugged her. "Are you all right? Did Yancy . . ."

"I have not seen him since you left! Oh, Thomas!" She threw her arms around him, hugged him tight. "I was so afraid you were—"

"What? You never thought I would really leave you?"

"No, never, I never thought that." The building shuddered. Something overhead gave way, and the room flared as more flames sprang up. "I fear I have killed us all, with my stupid act!"

"No, no. We would never have gotten to you if you had not set the fire!"

And then over the din of the fire and the shouts of those fighting it, Marlowe heard a shrill shout of surprise and outrage and fury.

Through the smoke Marlowe could see the door pulled open. The draft swirled the smoke away, sucking it out of the room, and Yancy stood in the frame, a big ax in his hand.

Honeyman, who was by the door, jerked a pistol from his belt, raised it, cocked the lock, pointed it at Yancy as Yancy swung the ax. It caught Honeyman's hand, knocked the pistol away, and opened up a wide red gash. Honeyman shouted, grabbed his hand as Yancy pulled back to cleave his head in two.

As the ax arced toward Honeyman's skull, Hesiod bounded across the room, grabbed his shoulder, pulled him back, and the blade came down into thin air. Marlowe was surprised. He did not think the weak little man had it in him.

Now Bickerstaff was there, his sword striking like a snake, and it caught Yancy's arm before Yancy could move away. Yancy screamed, as much in outrage as in pain, raised the ax again.

Yancy and Bickerstaff faced off, sword against ax. Marlowe saw the telltale waver as Bickerstaff prepared for a feint, then a lunge, which would have killed Yancy.

But before he could strike, the building shook again, the sound of the fire like thunder, and overhead a section of the ceiling sagged down, splitting and spitting fire out from the cracks as it fell. Yancy leaped for the door, and Bickerstaff leaped back into the room, and a ton or more of beams and plaster and thatch fell in, making a flaming wall between them.

Yancy shouted, flailing at the fire with his ax, trying to cut his way through. Marlowe charged into the room, grabbed Bickerstaff's arm, pulled him back toward the balcony and what fresh air it might afford their aching lungs and burning throats and streaming eyes.

Now what the hell will we do? Marlowe wondered.

He stumbled out onto the small balcony, crowded now with Elizabeth and Hesiod.

"Where's Honeyman?" he shouted, glancing fearfully back into the burning room, but Hesiod nodded to the ground.

Marlowe looked down. The rope that Hesiod had brought in his haversack was looped through the legs of a table wedged against the balcony wall and the two ends flung over the edge. On the ground, Honeyman held both ends of the rope in one hand, a pistol in the other, watching for anyone who might approach.

Hesiod turned to Elizabeth. "You next, ma'am," he said.

Elizabeth looked down at the ground and shook her head. "I can't do that," she said.

"Mind if I help, Captain?" Hesiod asked, and Marlowe had no more than nodded when Hesiod bent over and grabbed Elizabeth around the waist, then straightened with her over his shoulder.

"Son of a bitch! Put me down, goddamn your eyes!" Elizabeth shouted, her long hair trailing on the balcony, her rear end up in the air. She was furious, but she retained enough sense to refrain from struggling as Hesiod stepped over the balcony rail, wrapped his free arm and his legs around the rope, and fell to the ground in a controlled plummet.

"Strong son of a bitch" was all Marlowe said as he waited for Hesiod to reach the ground and set the fuming Elizabeth down before he gestured for Bickerstaff to follow.

Bickerstaff hit the ground, and Marlowe looked back toward the door. The room was engulfed. He could not see past the wall of flame, which meant that Yancy, if he was still there, would not see their egress. He would think they had burned to death if he did not guess they had a rope.

Marlowe put his leg over the rail, grabbed the rope. It had been years since he had done anything like this, and it was with some difficulty and burned palms that he finally reached the ground. Hesiod grabbed one end of the rope and hauled away, unreeving it from the table jammed in the balcony. It fell free and came down in a pile at his feet, and he coiled it quick.

"Let's go," Marlowe said.

The yard was well lit by the great bonfire that was the roof, but the few people standing there and gawking up at the flames did not notice them or did not care who they were. It was one of the great advantages of the pirate community. Curiosity was not encouraged.

They made their way out the gate and down the road, the flickering light of Elizabeth's fire nipping at them as they hurried along. Down through the center of town and down the road running along the harbor and at last to the beach with never a challenge. No one even spoke to them.

Marlowe helped Elizabeth into the boat, and then the four weary men pushed it out into the water and clambered in over the gunnels. They took up oars and with never a word spoken they fell into their easy rhythm, pulling away from St. Mary's, pulling for the open sea. The flames of Yancy's mansion were like a distant lighthouse, but it looked to Marlowe as if those fighting the fire were at last getting it under control.

He turned on the thwart, smiled at Elizabeth, then looked past her, out to the open sea. The *Elizabeth Galley* should have stood on for an hour, then come about and beat back to the island, to the extent that she was able. Marlowe did not hope to see her in the dark. They would have to wait until first light to find her and close with her.

That was if she was there. He wondered if perhaps Flanders would cross him, betray him, sail off with the ship. That thought had never occurred to him till now.

Chapter 17

IT DID not start well, the short and unhappy reign of Lord Dinwiddie I of St. Mary's.

He woke, confused and distressed, having suffered through a series of disturbing dreams of the kind that come in the half-awake hours of early morning. His head pounded whenever he moved. His throat was dry and ached in patches.

With a groan he rolled over, and his hand came down on warm, pliant flesh. The girl they called Lucy, asleep beside him. He had lain with her several times over the past few days, days that were now a blur of drinking and eating and copulating.

It had been the very paradise about which he had on occasion fantasized, during those times when his thoughts strayed from his immediate duties and his limited imagination swept him away. He had always considered those dreams of pagan abandon to be his darkest, deepest-held secret. Now he was living them.

He opened his eyes—another of those duties he knew he had to perform. The late-morning sun was streaming around and through the sheer curtains that hung in front of the room's single window. In those places where the light penetrated unimpeded, it looked like rods of gold as it passed through all the dust that swirled around.

He became aware of the acrid smell of charred wood, like a fire that has died in a fireplace but more pervasive.

And the quiet. He realized that it was very quiet, which it generally was not in that place where the pirates made their home.

He closed his eyes again. He had dreamed of Marlowe. Marlowe telling him to come, looking at him with disdain. In the dream he had told Marlowe to sod off, and it felt good and bad all at once. He had dreamed other things as well, unpleasant things that all swirled together in a great stew of emotions and left him unsettled.

There came a knocking at the door, and the rhythm had a subtle insistency about it. Dinwiddie realized that it was knocking that had woken him up.

"Come," he croaked. The door opened, and light streamed in from the hall, which seemed odd to Dinwiddie, since there were no windows there. Nagel was standing in the doorway, just a dark outline against the brilliant light at his back. He stepped into the room, and then Dinwiddie could see him better. He looked somber.

Dinwiddie struggled to sit up, pushed Lucy out of bed. The young woman stood and padded off, entirely naked, but neither Dinwiddie nor Nagel paid her any attention.

"You look damned hangdog this morning," Dinwiddie said as he waited for the pounding in his head to settle.

"It is a sorry day. A right sorry day indeed," Nagel intoned.

"Why? What has happened?"

"It's Lord Yancy. I reckon the fire was too much for him."

"Fire?"

"The fire. Last night. You didn't know?"

Dinwiddie shook his head.

"Burned half the damned roof. Nearly done for the house. Come." Nagel nodded toward the open door.

With some effort Dinwiddie stood up and shuffled across to the chair, over which he had thrown the silk banyan that Yancy had given him. He pulled that on, wrapped it around his girth, and followed Nagel out into the hall.

It looked like the aftermath of some terrible battle. The sunlight, which Dinwiddie had been at a loss to explain, poured in through the ceiling and the roof above, half of which was burned away so that there was only the charred rim outlining their view of the sky. The tops of the walls were charred as well, and the formerly white plaster was black with soot. Water stood in puddles all over the floor, and the hall was littered with blackened bits of timber that had fallen from the roof.

"Dear God . . ." Dinwiddie said. "How did it start?"

"Don't know. Started on the roof. Took us three hours to get it out, and we nearly didn't. You didn't hear none of it?"

Dinwiddie shook his head. *Lord, I must have been some far in my cups to sleep through this.*

"What was that you said, about Lord Yancy?"

Nagel shook his head sadly. "Lord Yancy, bold fellow he is. He was fighting the fire with us, leading the job, like was his way. Struggled for two hours, even though he ain't strong. Finally he just collapsed. We thought he was dead, with . . . the cancer . . . you know. But he wasn't, just overcome. But he ain't long for us, I don't reckon."

"Where is he? I must go to him."

Nagel shook his head again. "He knows it's his time. He asked to be carried away, to his secret place, where he can pray and such. He said to tell you you're lord of the island now. All this is yours. And 'Godspeed,' he says."

Dinwiddie looked at the big pirate in front of him. His head pounded harder, and he felt a surge of panic. *Lord of the island? Dear God, whatever do I do now?*

"Marlowe? Is he here? Is the *Elizabeth Galley* still at anchor?"

"No, and good riddance, I say. When the fire broke out, we sent word to Marlowe, asking would he help with putting it out. 'No,' says he, 'and with the tide making, won't we just be on our merry way.' There's gratitude, for all that Lord Yancy done for him."

"Humph," Dinwiddie said. He thought of the wrecked Indiaman they had encountered, Marlowe hanging from that hawser, working his way out to the stranded sailors. Tried to reconcile that image with the Marlowe that Nagel had just described.

"Very well, then, sod Marlowe," Dinwiddie said, and then he found himself flailing around for what he might say next. He was lord of the island. He would have to do something. Wouldn't he?

"Beg your pardon, my lord," Nagel said, "and not wanting to be too forward or nothing . . . but Yancy, he asked would I stay here and be your aide, like. Like I done for him. He wanted to be here, to tell you what he knows about ruling the island, but he hasn't the strength. Don't reckon he'll live till morning next."

"Oh. No, I would not reckon it too forward, was you to help me . . ." Dinwiddie said, and the realization that Nagel would be there, enforcing his authority, helping with the unfamiliar, gave Dinwiddie a new confidence.

Suddenly he felt not as if he were standing in the burned-out remains of a hallway on a strange island full of outlaws but rather as though he were standing on the quarterdeck of a ship, in command, the crew forward ready to jump to his command. His headache was gone.

"I think first we had best get some hands to this roof, get it repaired. And the ceiling as well. Round up a gang and get them right on that. And I'll need my breakfast. Turn the cook out."

"Aye, sir," said Nagel with a smirk. Dinwiddie caught the expression, guessed that the man was happy to have someone in charge again, someone who knew how to give commands without equivocation. Happy that Yancy had chosen a successor worthy of the office.

By noon of that day Dinwiddie was dressed, fed, and growing increasingly angry. Nagel had managed to round up all the men he could to work on the roof, a total of three. Nor did they turn to with much of a will. They moved at a near sleepwalking pace, cutting away the charred bits of the beams and pulling out the unusable thatch.

The servants and the girls from his harem that he had ordered to clean the hall were doing better at least. The water had been mopped up, the walls washed down, the chunks of debris cleared away. Save for the great hole in the roof, the hall looked much as it had when he had retired with his girls the night before.

He stood on the veranda looking out at the harbor. The *Elizabeth Galley*, which he was accustomed to seeing at her anchorage, was gone. It seemed as if there was a hole in the vista.

It seemed as well that there were a few other vessels that had sailed. He had never taken a real count of the ships at anchor, so he was not certain, but it seemed as if there were fewer now. Occasionally he looked back at the roof. There was little happening there.

"I got some more hands, should be on their way," Nagel said, stepping from the house and crossing the veranda.

"Where the bloody hell is everyone?" Dinwiddie asked. The big house had always seemed crowded with people.

"Some of the men, they wanted to be with Lord Yancy in his last hours," Nagel said. "They'll be back . . . after. You gots to remember, most of them what lives in the house, they sailed with Yancy from the colonies, like me. But if Yancy says they are to follow your orders, you can count on it they will."

"Humph." Dinwiddie did not care for that so much, nor did he care for Nagel's still referring to Yancy, who had abdicated, as "Lord" Yancy. But he did not feel he should be a stickler on the point, not with Yancy about to draw his final breath. In fact, Dinwiddie reckoned he would start off easy on his men.

"I understand full well, Nagel," he said. "Such loyalty is admirable, damn me if it ain't. Let us do this. You tell those fellows working on the roof to just get the burned bits cleared away and then stand down for the day. Get back at it first thing in the morning."

"Very good, my lord. That'll sit well with 'em."

The next morning found quite a large gang of men eating their noisy breakfast in the great hall. Twenty at least, all come to work on the roof, per Dinwiddie's command. He was gratified to see them as he staggered into the big room, half asleep still, his eyes burning.

"This is good, this is good," he said to Nagel, who stood when he entered and held the chair for him.

"Aye, my lord. But news that will make you sad, I fear. Lord Yancy, he passed in the night. Over the standing part of the foresheet he went, but with rum enough in his belly to make the pain bearable. We buried him, first light, up where he'll have a fine view for eternity. These fellows"—he nodded toward the men who were wolfing down their cold roast beef and bread and butter and ale—"sat vigil with him. Now they are here to work, what with their vigil done."

"Good, good," said Dinwiddie, taking a tentative sip of ale and waiting to see how it would settle in his stomach. The men at breakfast, with their lively banter and ribald jokes, mouths overflowing with food that sprayed across the tabletop as they talked, did not seem to be in any deep mourning for their former lord and master.

Honor among thieves and all that. As the ale cleared his head a bit, Dinwiddie thought of how he would whip them into a real company, how they would be more grieved by *his* passing, were it to happen.

He drank another glass, and that gave him the strength to eat something, and that made him feel even more revitalized. Time to get to work.

Lord Dinwiddie slammed his hands on the table, palms down, with a loud smacking sound calculated to stop the conversations and gain everyone's attention, but no one seemed to notice, and the loud talk did not pause for even a beat. He slammed his hands again, with the same results.

He scowled, made ready to bark out his unequivocal displeasure, when Nagel shouted, "Here, you great sons of whores, listen here!"

With that, the pirates fell silent and turned and looked at Nagel, who said, "Lord Dinwiddie, he wishes to say something to the gentlemen."

"Thank you, Nagel," Dinwiddie said, standing. "I reckon we're finished with our breakfast. There's a power of work to be done. Roof to repair and then the batteries to overhaul, the stockade to repair." He fell easily into the role of command, after more than a decade as mate and master aboard merchantmen. "Damned lot of work and no time to waste. So right now I want you men up on the roof. You know what to do. I'll be up to inspect your work directly."

To his annoyance the men just sat there until Nagel barked "Go!" and then they stood and shuffled out. Soon there was only himself and Nagel in the hall.

"They're villains and rogues, my lord. Pay them no mind," Nagel said. "They'll learn."

"Oh, they will, I'll see to that. And I think you had better get up there with them, Nagel. It will not serve discipline for them to see you lounging about."

"Aye, sir," Nagel said, but Dinwiddie could see that he was not happy about it. Still, it had to be done. Nagel could not be allowed to get too big for his britches. That was just what Marlowe had allowed to happen aboard the *Elizabeth Galley*. He had let Honeyman start to think he was some kind of an officer, and the whole thing had broken down. That sort of thing would not happen on St. Mary's.

Nagel left, and Dinwiddie climbed back up to the second floor and out onto the wide veranda, which was becoming his favorite place to sit and think. There were still great splashes of blood on the flat stones where Yancy had slaughtered his daily pig. Dinwiddie had to wonder at the sanity of someone who would do such a thing.

He stood at the low wall and looked down at the harbor, the green jungle, the hibiscus and bougainvillea. There were two more vessels getting under way, bound off for the Red Sea, no doubt. It was more activity than he had seen yet in the three weeks that he had been there, and he wondered if Marlowe's example had spurred these others.

After a few hours of contemplative thought and a light midmorning meal, he made his way down the hall to inspect the work on the roof. He was not happy with what he saw, and he said so. He ordered the repairs that had been done thus far be torn away and redone.

The next morning none of the men returned to work. Dinwiddie set the servants to repair the roof, but they proved even less competent or willing than the pirates. Soon they, too, began to melt away.

By the fourth day of his reign there were only half a dozen servants, a third of his harem, and four sodden pirates still living in the big house that Adam Baldridge had built. But Lord Dinwiddie was not discouraged. Rather, he took comfort from the situation. The men that Yancy had trained were unreliable—rogues and villains. They were not the stuff of which he would make the core of his empire, the nucleus of his dynasty.

He would recruit fresh blood from the incoming ships. He was a wealthy man now, with all that he had inherited, and he would grow wealthier still as he developed and grew the trade that Yancy had begun. New men, who would be loyal to him. He would greet each arriving ship, impress them with his status, his power, his sovereignty over the island.

He would start immediately. In fact, a lookout had just come down from the high peak that rose to the east of the harbor. He had asked for Nagel, but when Dinwiddie explained to him how things now lay, he gave his report to the new lord. Two ships, hull down. A big vessel and her tender, it appeared.

Dinwiddie thanked the man for the information and sent him back up the mountain to watch the vessels' approach. He summoned his servants, that they might begin their preparations for the newly arriving vessels, the first guests that Dinwiddie would entertain as lord of St. Mary's.

Yancy and Nagel stood on another peak, to the north of the harbor, and alternately looked through a powerful glass at the same pair of topgallant sails, the hulls of the vessels below them still lost beyond the horizon.

Yancy nodded. "It must be him. The big ship, the tender—it must be him."

For one who had ostensibly died of cancer, Yancy seemed remarkably fit. He was pacing, punching his fist into his open palm, looking again and again through the glass. He felt as if his nerves were charged through with St. Elmo's fire.

On the day they recruited Spelt, Yancy let Nagel understand that the cancer was a fraud. He had no choice. Nagel would not be pleased to see someone besides himself chosen as successor otherwise.

The night of the fire in the roof he had let the other Terrors in on the secret. He apologized, after a fashion, yet assured them that he had no choice but to fool them. The ruse had to be perfect. Everyone—Dinwiddie, the hangers-on at the house, the people in the town—they all had to genuinely believe in Yancy's death.

Together, Yancy and his men had retreated to the mountain hideout, this time with Yancy leading the way, not lagging behind, racked by his ersatz disease. Yancy had not dared leave the running of the island to Spelt, but Dinwiddie was so exactly the man that Yancy had hoped to find that he knew it was time to go.

And none too soon, as it happened.

It had been months since he had received the letter from Atwood. Months of planning and agonizing and waiting. But now the moment had arrived. Press was there, in the offing.

And I am here, ready for him.

Press would have been preparing as well, of course, would have been focused on this moment as intensely as had Yancy, but there was a difference, and Yancy knew it. Press thought he had surprise as a weapon. He did not know he was compromised. That put the real surprise in Yancy's camp, which made it much more potent by far.

"Good bloody thing he showed up now," Nagel grumbled. "The lads won't go back, long as that horse's arse is there."

"Oh, they would go back." Yancy looked sharply at Henry Nagel. "If I told them to, you had better goddamned believe they would go back. If I ordered them to." Yancy was not pleased with the abandonment of Dinwiddie, stupid chucklehead though he might be. He, Yancy, had ordered his men to act loyal to their new lord, and they had managed only one day of it. He was not pleased.

It was lucky for them that Press happened to show up at that moment and bring an end to their charade. Had he not, Yancy would have made them return to the big house and show some real contrition to Lord Dinwiddie. He needed Dinwiddie in place.

He held Nagel with his hawk stare, saw the contrition that he expected, that he demanded. "I do not care to have my orders ignored," he continued. He had to drive the point home. "This is a delicate thing. If you villains start acting of your own accord, then Press will kill us all. Is that clear?"

"Yes, my lord. And the men, they know it, too."

"Good." Yancy was silent for a long moment, and then in a more contemplative tone he added, "Press is a very difficult man to kill. Many have tried. I tried, and I failed.

"The joke of it is, I saved him, too. Found him marooned on a strip of land, near death, and I saved him. He sailed with us for half a year,

and then he tried to betray me, to usurp my position as captain, get the
men to vote me out.

"I turned him over to the Spanish authorities, who were looking for
him. He had led a raid on Nombre de Dios, you see. The Spanish
turned him over to the Inquisition. How he ever escaped from them I
cannot imagine, but I reckon his time with them weren't pleasant. And
now, now he will have his revenge, or he will die trying."

Yancy looked up at Nagel. "It is up to us, my dear Henry, to see it is
the latter."

I failed . . . Yancy thought. How many times had he said those
words? he wondered. Not very many. In fact, he could think of no instance, other than his attempt at delivering Press up to a painful death,
where those words might apply.

And then he thought of Elizabeth Marlowe. He had failed there.
She was not with him, not submitting to his carnal needs. He had
failed to take her.

That being the case, he was pleased to think of her dead. Nagel had
told him that the room was well burned out, nothing but the charred
remains of the furniture and the walls. But Nagel did admit, after questioning, that they had not actually found charred bodies, and while
that could just mean that they were burned up entirely, Yancy did not
think so. He had seen men burned; they did not generally burn away
to nothing.

He pushed those thoughts out of his mind. They were not productive. He had real concerns that needed his attention.

"Nagel, you must get out of your fine clothes and don the garb of a
drunken Roundsman. I need you to take up a place in the town, keep
an eye on what is going on. You know people, you can find out all that
is happening. Keep me informed."

"Aye, sir. And, my lord, when do we move on this bastard, this Roger
Press?"

"The moment he makes a mistake, my dear Henry."

Chapter 18

THE SIGHT of St. Mary's rising before him, the long green coast of Madagascar stretching away to larboard, did much to restore Roger Press's equilibrium. For weeks now he felt as if his head were spinning around, as if he were in an uncontrollable plummet. But now everything had stopped.

The *Queen's Venture* and her tender had encountered chronic and uncharacteristic calms around the Cape of Good Hope. That stretch of ocean between the bottom of Africa and the bottom of the world was well known for its wild weather. A surfeit of wind was most often the problem, not a lack of it.

But a lack of wind was what Press's expedition had found. After being hurled by strong gales and big seas past thirty-eight degrees south, the storms seemed to blow themselves out, leaving the two ships wallowing in the long ocean rollers and moving in little bursts with the occasional cat's-paw of a breeze.

They lost a week and a half at least, floating around south of the cape, and it made Press wild with impatience and anxiety. There were no real time constraints, of course. Yancy did not know they were coming; there was no reason for Press to think he would miss him. But all the logic in the world could not keep at bay his desperation to be moving again.

At last the breeze had filled and stayed that way, driving them along, around the Cape of Good Hope, northeast to Madagascar. Forward motion was more soothing to Press than all the rum, all the laudanum he could have ingested.

He stood alone at the weather rail of the quarterdeck, contemplatively rolling his silver toothpick back and forth, back and forth across the roof of his mouth. Silent, taciturn, and angry, he had been that way for the past three weeks.

He was still silent and taciturn. But now he was no longer angry.

"Mr. Tasker," he said in a conversational tone, and the first officer, always in a state of high readiness, raced across the deck.

"Sir?"

"Let us clear the ship for action. Load but do not run out the great guns. Men will remain at quarters. And let us have the East Indiaman bunting aloft."

"Aye, aye, sir!" A minute later the ship was a bustle of activity as the large, disciplined, and well-trained crew turned to, clearing away all of those bits of gear and temporary structure that did not involve bringing the ship into battle.

The sea chests and hammocks and hanging tables belowdecks were flung down into the hold. The flimsy walls of the officers' cabins were broken down and stowed away, the furniture and paintings, the rugs and bunks and cushions and other amenities of the great cabin carefully carted below and stowed in a dry place in the hold so that the men at the guns in the great cabin area could work them unimpeded.

At the forwardmost end of the ship, way out on the little round spritsail top, two hands were bending and hoisting the ensign of the Honorable British East India Company, a flag consisting of red and white horizontal stripes with the red Cross of St. George on a white field in the canton. At the very aftermost part of the ship, two more hands were bending a flag onto the ensign staff, similar in design to that on the spritsail topmast but three times the size. At fore, main, and mizzen mastheads long red and white horizontally striped pennants whipped around in the blessed breeze.

Two hundred yards off the starboard quarter, the *Speedwell* showed the same bunting. Her master, Israel Clayford, Press's first officer during the privateering days, was well acquainted with his plans for St. Mary's. They had had plenty of opportunity to discuss them as they wallowed off the Cape of Good Hope.

Press trusted Clayford as much as he had ever trusted any man. Clayford was a vicious brute, driven entirely by his two base needs: lust and avarice. Press understood what drove the man, and so he could predict Clayford's behavior. Press knew that Clayford regarded him as the quickest means to his own ends.

They stood on through the morning and into the afternoon, St. Mary's growing larger before them, St. Mary's at last. If there was anyone watching from the island—and Press knew there would be—the two ships would look to be East Indiamen, heavily armed and lightly manned, posing no threat. Yancy would not fire on them with his shore batteries. He would think them too valuable as trading partners or prizes for him to drive them away.

By midafternoon the open roads and small island at the head of the harbor at St. Mary's were under their bows, and the two ships stood in, furling sail as they went, never giving any indication of their bellicose intentions.

Press ran his glass over the big house on the hill. Built by Adam Baldridge a decade or so before. Now the home of the upstart Elephiant Yancy, or so he was told by several reliable informants.

Not taking bloody good care of it, he mused. He could see that there had been a fire there, and not so long ago. A good part of the thatched roof was gone in a great charred hole.

Yancy. He had wanted to get his mangled fingers around that prancing little bugger's neck for ten years. And now he would, and he would enjoy it.

Past the island and its abandoned battery and in toward the anchorage, the nearly deserted anchorage, to a place one hundred yards from the shore where they dropped their hooks, ship, and tender, and came at last to a stop in three fathoms of water.

"On deck! Boat's putting off!" the lookout called, jerking Press from his contemplation of the dearth of shipping in the harbor.

He had envisioned St. Mary's as crowded with vessels—Roundsmen, merchantmen, smugglers—all those who knew how to profit from the sea-lanes. He was going to pull Yancy out like a rotten mast from a ship's hull, put himself in his place. Press would enjoy his portion of the extraordinary wealth that flowed through the island. And all of it funded by those fat, rich bastards in London.

He had expected more in the way of commerce, there in the harbor.

Bloody stupid Yancy, run it right into the ground, I wouldn't fucking doubt, Press thought as he found the approaching boat with his glass. *Well, I shall just have to fix what he has made a hash of.*

The boat was pulled by four men with no apparent enthusiasm for their work. A fifth man sat in the stern sheets, but he was still too far away to see. It might well be Yancy, and that meant that he could not let himself be seen. He did not want to spoil all the fun.

"Tasker, see to some kind of side party. Whoever this is, welcome him with some sort of ceremony. I shall watch from aft."

With that, Press hurried back under the quarterdeck, back to the point where the bulkhead to the great cabin would have been had the ship not been cleared away, fore and aft. From there he could see the waist and the gangway, but no one out in that bright sunlight could see him in the gloom.

He waited while Tasker assembled a side party, going about the business with more care and efficiency than Press had intended. At last Press heard the boat bump alongside, and Tasker called his men to attention in two rows, making something of a path from the gangway to the middle of the waist.

A portly man stepped through the gangway, nodding his approval of the side party in a supercilious way. Press moved forward, still keeping to the shadows. It was not Yancy, that was certain. A bigger man than Yancy, lacking Yancy's nervous, squirrel-like motion.

The man stepped through the ranks of drawn-up men, up to Tasker and took Tasker's outstretched hand. Tasker said something that Press could not hear, but the fat man let go of the lieutenant's hand and lifted his arms in an expansive gesture and boomed, "Welcome! Welcome, all, to my St. Mary's!"

Who is this bloody horse's arse? Press thought. Tasker, playing his role well, began to accept the welcome, but Press stepped quickly forward, his long legs rushing him along, silver toothpick clenched in his teeth.

"Who the hell are you?" he demanded of the fat man, who could not hide his surprise at Press's sudden appearance, his antagonistic manner.

"I, sir, am Dinwiddie. Peleg Dinwiddie. I am lord of the island of St. Mary's."

That declaration earned a smile from Press. "Not any bloody more, you're not," he said, and before the confused and increasingly nervous Dinwiddie could respond, Press said, "Where is Yancy?"

"Yancy? Yancy is dead, if you must know—"

"Goddamn it!" Press stepped toward the fat man, but the row of sailors for the side party partially blocked his way. Press grabbed the nearest man, shoved him to the deck. "Dismissed, you whoresons!" he shouted, and the two straight lines of the side party fell apart as the men scattered.

Press grabbed Dinwiddie by the collar of his fine coat, pulled him across the deck until they were inches apart. Press towered over Dinwiddie. He was looking down into the man's bloodshot eyes when he once again asked, "Where is Yancy?"

"Yancy is dead!" Dinwiddie insisted again, and then, spluttering with outrage, he grabbed Press's wrists with strong hands—seaman's hands—and shouted, "Get your damned hands off me, you bastard, or I shall have you in irons!"

Another smile, and Press jerked Dinwiddie sideways and shoved, and Dinwiddie fell to the deck at his feet. He made to stand, but Press kicked him hard in the stomach, the face, the stomach again.

Dinwiddie lay gasping, blood flowing from his mouth. Press leaned low.

"How long have you been lord of St. Mary's?" He said it with a sarcastic flourish.

Dinwiddie had to think. "Four days," he said at last.

"Where is Yancy?"

"Dead . . ."

"When did he die?"

"Four days ago."

"You know where he is buried?"

"No."

Press straightened, looked out over the water, toward the big house. Could it be true? It was entirely possible.

But to die four days before they made landfall? Four days before he, Press, could arrive and kill him? A terrible irony, if it was true.

Once again Dinwiddie was struggling to get up, and once again Press kicked him to the deck. He would give this idiot another hour of such treatment, and if, after that, he was still alive and still insisting that Yancy was not, then perhaps he would believe him.

An hour later, with blood splattered in wild patterns across the deck, Press had to put a finger to Dinwiddie's neck to check if he was alive. He frowned, felt around, and finally located a pulse.

Dinwiddie looked soft and fat, but that appearance was misleading. He was a strong man, with a strong constitution. He had remained conscious for most of the time that Press had beaten him and kicked him around the deck, to the great amusement of the men watching from various corners of the *Queen's Venture's* deck and lower rig. The few times he had passed out under the treatment, a bucket of seawater had revived him, and he had endured more.

But for all of that time Press could not elicit any answer about Yancy save the insistence he was dead.

He took his finger from Lord Peleg Dinwiddie's neck, stood up straight, the bleeding, motionless bulk at his feet, and looked across the harbor at the big Baldridge house.

Perhaps Yancy *was* dead. There was no question that this idiot Dinwiddie thought so. Press had taken him well past the point where he would have continued to lie.

He looked down, surprised to see the boat that had taken Dinwiddie out to the *Queen's Venture* still floating alongside.

"What the bloody hell are you doing?" Press demanded.

"We was told to wait. Lord Dinwiddie told us wait for him," said the man at stroke oar.

At that Press laughed out loud. "I'll see to 'Lord' Dinwiddie, never you fear."

"We're owed a shilling for our service," the stroke oar insisted next.

"What!?" Press shouted. Such audacity was not to be suffered. "Get out of here, you son of a bitch, or I will shoot each one of you motherless bastards!"

The men in the boat needed no more encouragement than that. They shoved off, laid into the oars, pulled for the dock from which they had come.

Press watched them go. "Tasker!" he called out, and before the lieutenant could reply, he said, "We will be going ashore. Every able man is to go with the shore parties. Muskets and cutlasses."

He climbed back up to the quarterdeck, sat brooding as Tasker assembled his private army, preparing them to storm the island. He would tear the town apart looking for Yancy. If it turned out the bastard *was* lucky enough to be dead, he would have to find out where he was buried, dig him up, have a look at the whoreson's face. Leave him for the crows. That was the only way he could be certain.

He would be sorry to have missed the chance to kill him, slowly. He prayed that from the depths of hell Yancy would know that he, Press, was enjoying all the things that Yancy had worked so hard to build.

At last the boats from the *Queen's Venture* and the boats from the *Speedwell* were manned and loaded with armed sailors milling about between the two ships, waiting. Press stepped down from the quarterdeck. His steward stood ready with his sword and his brace of pistols, and he put them on with a slow, ritualistic precision.

He looked down at Dinwiddie, who was starting to stir. "We'll take that with us," he said, pointing toward the former lord of the island, then climbed down into the stern sheets of the longboat. With no more than a nod he ordered the boat under way, and behind them the other boats fell in, and the small army of invasion, their own scaled-down Norman Conquest, pulled for the shore.

Press kept a sharp eye for any signs of anything. He had left no more than a skeleton crew aboard each ship, but he was not concerned with their being taken while he was ashore. He could see the batteries on Quail Island, or so the chart called it. Whoever commanded those guns commanded the entrance to the harbor, and by day's end he intended to command those guns.

Up to the rickety, half-rotten dock, and Press climbed out and stepped ashore, walked down the wooden pier toward the road, slowly waggling the toothpick in his mouth.

He looked around, thought, *Here I am.*

From the sitting room at Pall Mall to standing on the island as his own army unloaded behind him. Magnificent. The big house, the batteries, the high hills, the warehouses—all his. Press felt closer to happiness and contentment and satisfaction than he had felt in many years.

It took fifteen minutes for the men to land and assemble, because Press had a big army with him, over two hundred strong. When at last they were formed up in columns as respectable as could be expected from sailors, Press stepped off, heading up the dirt road that led to the town, and met with the road that led uphill to the house. They passed through what must be considered the center of St. Mary's: a few dilapidated buildings, some big tents, and off to the left a few warehouses.

Lining the street, the men and women of the town watched them pass. Sailors, pirates, whores, and natives, they did not interfere or even say a word. To a person, they had the look of a population that had seen much already, that was not impressed with the new arrivals, that knew to mind their own business and run before any new gale that blew through the island.

They had no reaction to Press, and Press had no reaction to them as they tramped uphill. Rather, his attention was focused entirely on the house, alert for any possible trap. He looked sharp for movement of any kind—the glint of sun off steel, smoke, anything. But there was absolutely no indication that the house was occupied.

Up and through the gate to the stockade, which hung open. Up the path to the house, and never a challenge, never a word, save for a hungry-looking dog that barked and barked at the new arrivals until someone shot it.

Press pushed open the front door, stepped inside alone, looked around. The house was lovely, or had been once. It was in disrepair now. It had the look of a place that was patched up rather than cared for.

There was none of the musty smell of disuse. Press's keen nose caught the scents of men and food and smoke and excrement. The bitter smell of charred wood hung in the air. But for all that, there did not seem to be a person there.

"Tasker!" The lieutenant was at his side. "Divide the men up under the other lieutenants. Clayford's men with him. Spread out, search every inch of this place. Keep a care for traps. Lieutenants report to me."

"Aye, sir."

Press stepped farther into the house. Tasker was capable of organizing the search, so he did not even listen as the first officer gave his orders to his juniors, assigning each a division of men and a section of house.

There was a big staircase that led up to a second floor. Press ran his hand over the richly carved banister and looked up. It was an odd feeling, like walking around Atlantis perhaps, after one had spent a lifetime searching for it. Baldridge must have been an extraordinary man. It was revolting to think of Yancy in that place, a pretender to such glory. He, Press, was the natural heir to the island.

He headed up the stairs, taking each slowly, listening to the sounds of his men searching the house, waiting for the sound of a fight, taking in everything that he could see.

Up to the second floor, and he could see where the hall came out on a landing that opened onto a wide veranda. He walked through the doors, which hung open, and across the flagstones to the low wall that edged the space. From there he could look down on the harbor, on his ships floating placidly, on all of his new kingdom. Magnificent.

He stood there for some time, and one by one the junior lieutenants came to report that they had found nothing, save for half a dozen drunk pirates, who were paraded before Press, and two dozen servants and native girls. The pirates he ordered flung from the house. He had a good idea of the capacity in which the natives, men and women, had served Yancy, and Dinwiddie, he supposed. He and his men could make use of them in the same capacity. They were told to stay.

Along with the occupants, the searchers found the kitchen and the larder and the liquor stores, and soon Tasker was seeing to food and drink and the men were finding their place in their fine new home.

Press and Clayford sat on the big veranda, drinking rum, saying nothing. From that vantage point Press could see the hundred men he had detached as they stormed buildings and tents in the town below, pushing people into the street, searching for Elephiant Yancy. He could hear screams and the occasional gunshot.

He had instructed them that they were not to be polite or gentle. Weakness would not locate Yancy; courtesy would not reinforce the truth that he, Roger Press, was now in charge.

Press pulled his eyes from the town and considered the flat stones that paved the veranda. There were great swaths of dried blood on the stones that had been imperfectly washed away, and Press was wondering about those. Was this the result of something Dinwiddie had done? He could not imagine.

The thought of Dinwiddie conjured up the fat face in his mind, and he found something tugging at him. That face, there was something about it that he recognized, but vaguely, one of those memories that might have been a dream or might have been real.

Stupid fat bastards, they all look alike, Press thought, but he found he could not dismiss it that easily.

"Pass the word for Tasker," he said to the man who stood sentry near the veranda door, and he heard the name echoing around the house. A minute later Tasker was there.

"Lieutenant." Press looked up at him from the chair in which he sat, his spindly legs thrust out before him, already at home. "That imbecile, Dinwiddie, was he brought ashore with us?"

"Aye, Captain. Lieutenant Block, he found some prison cells, down at the western foundations to the house, and we locked him up there."

"Good, good. Bring him to me."

Ten minutes later Dinwiddie was kneeling in front of him. Press looked hard at the man's face, but he had beaten him so badly there was little recognizable about it now. He tried to picture the face as he had seen it when first Dinwiddie came aboard. Cursed himself for making such a mess out of the bastard.

He pulled the toothpick from his mouth, used it as a pointer. "Tell me your name again," Press demanded.

"Peleg Dinwiddie . . ."

"How did you get here?"

"First officer on a privateer, sailing the Round . . ." His voice cracked as he spoke. His tongue moved over parched, battered lips.

"Who was the captain?"

Dinwiddie paused and spit blood on the veranda. He looked up at Press with one eye. The other was swollen shut. "Thomas Marlowe."

Press felt as if he had been punched in the stomach. He jerked upright.

Now he remembered! He had seen Dinwiddie's fat, stupid face peering down from the side of Marlowe's ship a second before that topsail yard had plunged through the bottom of the boat. It was no wonder that his memory of Dinwiddie had a dreamlike quality. That whole affair still resonated like a nightmare.

Press settled back into a more relaxed posture. He stretched his legs, assumed the proper degree of cool, put the toothpick back in his mouth, and rolled it with his tongue.

"Would you like a drink of water, Dinwiddie?" he asked, his tone pleasant.

Dinwiddie nodded, so hard it looked painful. "Dear God, yes, water, please . . ."

"Very well. But first, please tell me about Thomas Marlowe? Why he is here, where he has gone? Tell me all. I insist."

Chapter 19

FOR TWO days the high mountains of Madagascar lingered on the southern horizon, visible from the deck of the *Elizabeth Galley*, a threatening presence, as if the horrors of that place were somehow trailing behind the ship. And then dawn of the third day broke, and the sea was empty on every quarter, and the Galleys felt a sense of relief that none of them vocalized, but of which each was aware.

They made their course north by east, following a slant of wind that would take them far out into the Indian Ocean. There they would wear around and make a long board for the Gulf of Aden and then on to the narrow straits of Bab el Mandeb, that bottleneck into the Red Sea through which much of the wealth of the Moorish nations passed.

The *Elizabeth Galley* was a happy ship, perhaps happier even than she had been before. Marlowe had not realized how Peleg Dinwiddie's gloomy discontent had cast a pall over the vessel.

Nor had he realized the extent to which Dinwiddie had become dissatisfied, and so he was surprised at what he considered Dinwiddie's betrayal.

"You cannot honestly think the man betrayed you?" asked Bickerstaff, his incredulity genuine. It was the morning they found that

Madagascar was lost from their view and themselves on the quarter-deck, discussing the events of the past week. They had not talked about it before then.

"I certainly do. The man deserted, abandoned his responsibility."

"But sure you can see how he felt abandoned himself. Honeyman had more real authority than he did, even though Peleg had agreed to ship as second in command."

"That is the way of the Roundsmen. I could do nothing about it. Dinwiddie wanted to sail the Pirate Round, and that is a part of it. Ship's articles, vote of the men, all of it. I do not love it any more than he did, but I accept it."

"Ah, yes, but it is also the way of these 'Roundsmen,' as you style them, or pirates if one prefers to eschew euphemism, that any may leave the company if he so desires. Allegiance to none, a short life and a merry one, and all of that. That is what Dinwiddie did, no more."

"Humph," said Marlowe. "Well, damn you and your roundabout logic."

At that, Bickerstaff shrugged and smiled. There were certain kinds of dueling at which Marlowe would never best him.

The men forward were happy to be free of Dinwiddie's brooding and to labor under the more benign rule of now–First Lieutenant Flanders. They were also happy because the hull was clean and repaired and the ship provisioned with food and water, both freshly put down, and the magazine held barrels and barrels of gunpowder and the shot locker was full.

Before Madagascar there had been the nagging fact that they had left from England, bound away for the hunting grounds of the Red Sea, with never a cannon on board with which to hunt. That had been the source of much concern and considerable discussion fore and aft, heated debate between those who thought that it would be no great difficulty to procure guns and those who believed that it could not be done.

But now they had them. Sixteen fine six-pounders, the King's mark on each of their black barrels, arranged starboard and larboard, housed with identical tackling and equipment, standing silent like soldiers on sentry duty. The once-great expanse of deck seemed crowded now with their presence, but no one was complaining. The sight of those big guns did more to improve spirits than anything Marlowe could think of, save for the capture of the Great Mogul's treasure ship. And now that they had the guns for the job, that possibility did not seem so very remote.

North by east, and then the *Elizabeth Galley* was turned to a course more like north by west as they pricked off the miles on the chart. The sun was blistering hot, melting caulking on the decks and making the tar drip from the rig, making it soft to the touch so that hands and feet and clothes were smeared with the black stuff when the men came down from aloft. But the breeze was steady, and that mitigated the heat some, and the forward motion it gave them kept them in good humor.

They were seventeen days out of St. Mary's, with Raasiga Caluula, the cape forming the southern entrance to the Gulf of Aden, bearing due west and two leagues distant, when they sighted the first sail.

Excitement ran through the company, and it did not diminish much with the discovery that the vessel was a dilapidated fishing boat not worth the bother of stopping. They were near the Red Sea, the legendary hunting grounds. The men of the *Elizabeth Galley* could practically smell the wealth.

They came up with several more fishing boats as they worked their way into the gulf and one larger sail, which they pursued but lost in the night. Still, the enthusiasm only grew stronger as they felt the presence of the land around them, the hot dry air off the desert, the gritty sand borne on the wind. It was all tangible proof of their being at last at the place they had all dreamed of being: the Red Sea, the Moorish countries, the place of the Red Sea Rovers.

There was something particularly foreign and exciting about the heat and the dust and the strange color of the sea as they drew closer to the land. They all felt it. They were in a very distant place, far from the gray, cold Europe or the green, wooded America that they knew. And somehow, because they were not a part of that place, because it was so unreal, they had a sense of invincibility, as if one could not be killed in so exotic a land.

The men donned their loose shirts and slops, their red sashes and bright cloths around their heads and strutted the deck, ready to conquer the Moors. It took a truly extraordinary place to make experienced seamen feel the lure of the exotic.

Twenty days out from St. Mary's, and the lookout called down another sail, right ahead, and once more the men cleared the ship for action. It did not take long. The men kept the *Elizabeth Galley* in a state of general readiness. This was not a deep-sea voyage. They were in among the Moorish shipping now. They had to be ready at all times.

That fact aside, Marlowe, standing on the main topmast crosstrees, did not think it was a Moorish ship he was looking at through his glass.

It was not a ship at all, in fact, but a brig, under easy sail, making way with no apparent destination in mind. She looked European, or colonial. She flew no flag.

"I believe this is one of us," Marlowe said offhandedly to the lookout standing on the crosstrees on the other side of the topgallant mast.

"Cap'n?"

"This brig. I reckon she is a Red Sea Rover, here on the account."

The lookout nodded. "I'll keep a sharp eye, then. You know what villains them pirates be."

Marlowe shut his telescope, made his way back to the quarterdeck, repeated his suspicions to Honeyman and Flanders and Bickerstaff. "We must speak her, see what news," he added. "Perhaps she has got wind of some treasure ship or one of these fat fellows carrying pilgrims to Mecca."

"Maybe she will want to work with us. In consort, like," Flanders suggested.

"Or maybe she'll reckon us as good a prize as a Moorish ship and try and take us," Honeyman added.

"Also a possibility," Marlowe said. "We will go to quarters, approach this fellow with caution. And grape over round shot in the great guns, I should think."

Elizabeth made one last attempt to coax her hair into looking like something she would consider presentable, but the heat and the dry air and the months of washing in salt water had rendered it as unco-operative as new ten-inch cable. Finally, disgusted, she bound it up in a ribbon and then found a square of red silk and tied that around her head. She looked at the results in the mirror and smiled.

"I do believe I have become a pirate myself," she said out loud.

She had come aboard the *Elizabeth Galley* in Virginia carrying with her all her social decorum and strict adherence to proper dress and manners and the protocol of society. During all of her poor, abused childhood, during the years she had been a high-paid doxy, she had dreamed of the day when she would have respectability and standing. She had them now, in Virginia, and she would not yield them gladly.

The sea, however, is the enemy of propriety, and soon Elizabeth found herself slipping.

At first it was her shoes. She had tried to walk while under way with the silly, impractical footwear that was the rage in London and thus, six months later, the rage in the colonies. Featuring pointed toes and big, chunky heels with leather soles, they presented a greater threat of injury to her on a rolling deck than all the raging seas and flying shot she might encounter.

She did away with the shoes in favor of her slippers, which were bet-ter, despite her initial embarrassment at being seen on deck in such footwear. She imagined that everyone was looking at her, snickering.

It took her a few days to realize that no one gave a tinker's damn what she wore on her feet—or anywhere else, for that matter.

For all the voyage to England and then the hasty departure, her gen-eral suit of clothing served her well: jacket, straw hat, bodice, apron, and simple skirts. But once they had left the cold behind and the men began to strip further and further, Elizabeth began to feel cumber-some, overdressed.

The slippers went first. She loved the feel of the hot, smooth planks under her bare feet. And suddenly she found that she was surefooted when moving on the deck and no longer felt as if she were going to slip and break her neck with every roll of the vessel.

It was not long after that when the lessons in swordplay began, and she discovered that she could hardly move with all the clothing she had. The bodice was next to go, and from the few surreptitious glances she caught from the men, she did not think this would meet with any vocal disapproval.

It was a treat to live without the bodice's confines, and she felt a new freedom of movement as she parried and riposted with Bickerstaff on the weather deck. The apron went after that, and then she was down to her shift and a single skirt, and for the first time since getting under way she was comfortable and able to move freely. Had there been even one other woman present, she would have felt abashed, humiliated, like some cheap punk or fishmonger. But there on board the Red Sea Rover she felt a kind of freedom she had never before enjoyed.

She looked at herself in the glass, at her thick blond hair tied back, the red cloth tied over it. She smiled, grabbed up a red sash, tied it around her waist. It looked good, a bold touch that accentuated her figure. She picked up one of Marlowe's pistols and stuck it in the sash. Perfect.

If all of the sailors forward, who had roamed great portions of the world, were still enchanted with the strangeness of these Moorish waters, then Elizabeth, who for all her wild and unsettled life had never seen anything beyond Portsmouth and London and Williamsburg—and Boston, which was the worst of the lot—found herself being drawn into the thing with double the force.

She crossed the great cabin, stepped out under the quarterdeck. Her legs felt strong and muscular, the result of months and months of walking on a rolling deck. It no longer bothered her to step in the warm pitch and feel it cling to her feet and leave little black marks on the deck as she walked. The bottoms of her feet were hard and most unladylike, but she loved the feel of strength and agility she had walking barefoot across the hot deck planks.

She climbed up to the quarterdeck, where Marlowe and Honeyman and Bickerstaff were in conference, all looking forward and on occasion ducking to see under the foot of the mainsail. She ducked, too, looked forward, and her eyes—now accustomed to such things—caught the flash of sail, square-rigged, before the Elizabeth Galley plunged down and the foresail smothered the horizon.

"What ho, gentlemen?" she asked.

The three heads turned in her direction, and the men smiled. "Look at you, my dear," said Marlowe, "as vicious a pirate as ever sailed the Spanish Main or the Pirate Round!"

"I am that. Now, what of this sail?"

"It is a brig, and I'll warrant it for European or American. I do believe it is a pirate, though they shall run scared when they take one look at you."

"And if not," Bickerstaff said, "I do believe you have progressed in your blade work enough that you might take on the lot of them."

For the rest of the morning they closed with the vessel, which continued on its slow course for an hour or so and then hove to, not making any attempt to meet up with the *Elizabeth Galley*, but not running either. They were like strangers meeting on a dark road, approaching warily, each ready to fight or flee or exchange pleasantries, however things developed.

Elizabeth remained on the quarterdeck, looking occasionally at the brig, and as she did, an odd thought occurred to her. She knew little about ships, could rarely tell one from another, but there was something familiar about that one, something that sparked a memory.

It did not seem possible, there, half a world away from Virginia, that it could be the brig she was thinking of, but still the thought nagged at her. She borrowed Thomas's telescope, stared at the strange vessel, now no more than a mile distant. There was nothing she saw that lessened her suspicions.

They drew closer, and more and more detail was revealed, and Elizabeth grew silent as she grew certain she was right. *Lord, what in hell are the chances?* she wondered. If she was right, she did not think this would be a very comfortable meeting. At least not for her.

It could not be . . . what are the chances? But of course those piratical fellows tended to gravitate toward the same spots: Port Royal, Nassau, the Red Sea. Birds of a feather. Perhaps it was not so great a coincidence.

The sun was near its zenith by the time the *Elizabeth Galley* hove to, half a cable length from the brig. The unknown vessel was definitely colonial built, probably from Massachusetts, most likely from Scituate, or so the speculation went among the more experienced hands who stared across the water at her. Elizabeth did not know. She would not necessarily have known that the vessel was a brig if she had not been told. But the different levels of the deck, the red and yellow paint scheme on her sides, the odd sort of female figurehead—those things she did recognize.

Then, from across the water, a voice hailed them through a speaking trumpet. "What ship is that?"

Marlowe picked up his own trumpet. "*Elizabeth Galley*, out of Virginia! What ship is that?"

"*Bloody Revenge*, out of the sea!" came the reply. That name, that voice with the slightly insouciant tone.

"Thomas, it's Billy Bird," Elizabeth said.

"Pardon?"

"The captain of the *Bloody Revenge*. It is Billy Bird. I believe you know him."

Marlowe looked at her, an odd expression on his face. "I did know a Billy Bird, back in Port Royal. A somewhat showy fellow. This is the same Billy Bird?"

"I believe it is."

"But however do you know him? How do you come to know his ship?"

Elizabeth sighed. She had been somewhat sketchy about her activities of a few years back, while Thomas had been chasing around the Atlantic after his old boatswain-turned-outlaw, the freed slave King James. Billy had taken her to Boston aboard that very brig and helped her find the root cause of the persecution waged against the former slaves of Marlowe House. But she and Billy Bird went much further back than that.

"I have known Billy for years, Thomas. From back in Plymouth. And then, when you were gone after King James, and Dunmore was hunting us, Billy was there to help. Perhaps this is not the time to go into it," she added, and her tone was sharper than she had intended.

She looked at him, all defiance, daring him to question her, to ask,

"In what way did you know him? Is he a former lover? When last did you lie with him?" but he did not. Marlowe had enough unsavory history of his own to understand he had no right to call hers into question.

In fact, she and Billy had found themselves in bed together on several occasions, as much out of mutual loneliness and affection as any kind of eternal love. But that was long before Elizabeth had met Thomas, and though Billy had made every effort to taste her sweet charms again, she had rebuffed him.

And Billy, true friend that he was, had accepted the rebuff, had helped her anyway, to the point of putting his own life in great danger on several occasions.

"Well, my dear, perhaps you had best speak to him." Thomas held out the speaking trumpet.

Elizabeth looked into his eyes. Her past was like the silted bottom of a clear, still pool, ready at any time to be swirled up, to make the clear water black. She feared censure, suspicion, condemnation. She kept a wary lookout for it, and she was ready to meet it with rage. But it was not there. She could see nothing disingenuous in Thomas's remark or his manner. She took the trumpet.

"Billy Bird? Is that you, you villain?"

There was a pause, and then, "Aye? And who are you?"

"Elizabeth Marlowe!"

A much longer pause followed that revelation, and then Billy's voice again, saying, "Well, damn my eyes, come aboard, come aboard! And bring your rogue of a husband, if you must!"

They put the jolly boat into the water, and Elizabeth and Thomas and Bickerstaff and Honeyman went across, where they were greeted with great enthusiasm by Billy Bird, captain of the sometime pirate brig *Bloody Revenge*.

Billy was in many ways the polar opposite of Marlowe: loud, buoyant, exuberant, and flashy. Elizabeth guessed that he had hurried below and shifted his clothing as they were rowing over. He was dressed in his usual cape with the red silk lining—oddly like Lord Yancy's, Elizabeth thought—and a silk shirt and breeches, red stockings, shoes with gold buckles, and a vast, wide-brimmed hat with a big plume trailing off it.

While Marlowe came aboard with a pleased but subdued greeting, Billy Bird grabbed his hand and pumped and slapped him on the back and said, "Damn my eyes! I have not seen you since Port Royal was swallowed up by the sea! Your name is somewhat altered, but the face is the same, if a bit more weather-beat! But, damn me, you look good, sir, damned good!" Elizabeth wondered how she could love both these men when they were so very different.

"And you, Billy. I am pleased to see you so well," Thomas said, shaking Billy's hand. "I am aware that you rendered my wife some service a few years back, and I am grateful for it."

Billy waved off the thanks. "It is nothing. Nothing I would not do for two old friends."

Elizabeth felt like a harp string, stretched to near breaking, quivering with tension as she scrutinized each look, each word, the tone in which every phrase was couched. She was looking for currents below the words: jealousy, hints of cuckoldry, anger, suspicion. She had done nothing wrong—she assured herself of that—nothing she could not tell Marlowe, but that fact did not calm her.

She was aware of her husband's potential for violence. More than one man who had insulted her had died for it. She hated to think what he might do to someone he thought had lain with her.

Nor was Billy Bird to be trifled with, despite his sometimes sophomoric nature. She had seen him take on two men at once with cold steel and best them both. She thought she might snap from the tension.

And then Billy turned to her, smiled, reached out his arms, and hugged her. She hugged him back, with somewhat less enthusiasm. Looked over Billy's shoulder at Marlowe, who gave her a comic raised eyebrow and a smile, and she felt her tension ease away, lessened but not gone.

Finally Billy released her, held her out at arm's length. "Dear God, look at you! Whatever has Marlowe done? When last I saw you, you were a proper lady, mistress of a great household, and now you are reduced to a common pirate!"

Elizabeth glanced down at herself, her red sash and bare feet. She still had the pistol stuck in the sash. She flushed with embarrassment. "One must be ready, Billy. One never knows what villains and rogues one will meet on the high seas."

Billy laughed. "Right, right you are! Now, come and have dinner with me! You will remember Mr. Vane, the quartermaster, and Black Tom and all these sundry rascals," Billy presented them as they stepped aft toward the great cabin.

They spent the next few hours over dinner and wine in there, while boats pulled back and forth between the two ships, and the encounter turned into a great bacchanal. The men of the *Elizabeth Galley* slaughtered a cow they had taken with them from St. Mary's. The men of the *Bloody Revenge* brought over copious amounts of rum and wine. They mixed up a grand rumfustian, and every one of them proceeded to get roaring drunk as their two ships bobbed on the swells, all alone in the middle of the Gulf of Aden.

It was a grand time, exactly the kind of floating brouhaha that would be unheard of in the legitimate maritime trades, the sort of thing that made the sweet trade so very attractive. The men wished to go on a spree and they did, and there was no one who could tell them otherwise. Not Marlowe, not Billy Bird, no one.

In the *Bloody Revenge*'s great cabin, which Elizabeth knew so well, the festivities were a bit more subdued, but not much. Along with the four guests from the *Elizabeth Galley*, Billy Bird invited in Quartermaster Vane and Hunter Reid, the *Revenge*'s first officer, whom Elizabeth had not met.

Like the men forward and on board the *Elizabeth Galley*, they ate and drank to excess, and the talk was loud and boisterous. The Galleys told the others of their adventures on St. Mary's. The *Bloody Revenge*, it turned out, had called there three weeks before. They declared Lord Yancy mad, and the conversation moved on.

Through the night the party continued, and it was only as the sky was growing light in the east that the men began to collapse in drunken exhaustion. For most of the day the two vessels floated there, hove to, while all hands slept off the night's drunk.

When at last the companies of both vessels were awake and somewhat sober, there commenced some debate as to whether they would do it all again. Given another hour for heads to stop pounding and stomachs to find their sea legs once more, they might have started afresh, but as it was, they voted to eschew their pagan rituals for the time and go off hunting the Moors.

They would work in concert, they decided, the *Bloody Revenge* sticking to the northern part of the mouth of Bab el Mandeb and the *Elizabeth Galley* to the south. By remaining within sight of one another, or at least within range that a signal cannon could be heard, they each doubled the territory they could cover, and each could come in support of the other when the fighting got hot.

There was little concern over sharing out the booty between two companies of men. It was well known that the Moorish ships carried enough to make them all very wealthy indeed.

And so with much difficulty and many aching heads, the two ships squared away and set more sail, with the *Bloody Revenge* sailing a little north of west and the *Elizabeth Galley* a little south, off to take up their stations for the great hunt.

On the *Galley's* quarterdeck Elizabeth and Thomas and Francis Bickerstaff enjoyed the evening air, the regular motion of the vessel underfoot. They felt content, happy, full of anticipation. They had made their way from England to St. Mary's to this place, and save for their troubles on that island and the hardships inherent to any ocean passage, it had been half a year of generally pleasant voyaging.

And all that time, and right in their wake, Roger Press had been following them like a shark on a trail of blood, and they had not known it.

And they were no more aware, on that night, as they closed with the narrow entrance to the Red Sea, that the shark was there still, closing, pursuing them now with purpose and wicked intent.

Chapter 20

ELEPHIANT, Lord Yancy, sat on his temporary throne and stared out over the top of the stockade, out over the sharp cut of the valley, deep green with its blanket of jungle and shadow, out over the flashing ocean and finally to the low, blue-green, irregular line that was Madagascar in the distance. He held a glass of brandy in one hand and took desultory sips from it. He listened.

To his right, in a slightly shorter chair, sat the ursine figure of Henry Nagel, drinking rum. Nagel was still dressed in the rags of a sodden pirate thrown up on the beach. In his halting way he was relating the events of the past few days.

When he finished, Yancy closed his eyes and said, "Henry, tell it all to me again, please." He had to be certain he had missed nothing. He had to check for inconsistencies that might indicate betrayal.

"Them two ships come in on the tail of the flood," Nagel began with the great patience of a man too slow-witted to grow restless, "and they anchored by their best bowers. I knew there was no one still at the house, doing that Dinwiddie's bidding, so I got four of our lads to act like they was a boat for hire. Dinwiddie comes down to the dock, dressed like it was his fucking coronation and acting the right king. He hires the lads to take him out to the big ship, the *Queen's Venture*. Says he has to welcome the new arrival to 'his' island."

"Dinwiddie did not recognize any of the boat crew?"

"No. They was lads never met him. So they take him out, and he's welcomed aboard with a side party and all. And then Press comes out and starts kicking him around the deck. The lads in the boat, they stayed there the whole time, listening, peeking over the gunnel sometimes, and never a one noticing them.

"So Press beats hell out of Dinwiddie for an hour, and the whole time he's asking, 'Where's Yancy? Where's Yancy?' and all the time Dinwiddie's saying, 'He's dead! He's dead!' "

Yancy nodded his approval. How could Press think he would outwit him, catch him by surprise? Press was a pathetic worm, not worthy of the title "adversary."

"After an hour or so," Nagel continued, "Press stops, and then he sees the lads in the boat and near shoots them, but they got away. I'm watching from the shore with a glass. They put together a landing party, goddamned lot of men, two hundred or more, I guess.

"They come ashore, and I watched them march by. I'm laying against a wall, like I'm dead drunk, and they just march on past, nothing said. They had that dumb bastard Dinwiddie with them, leading him on a halter like a cow. They go up and take your house with no fight, 'cause there weren't no one there to fight with.

"That night a hundred men or so come back down to the town, and they search every building, going through the warehouses, the whorehouses—everywhere. And everywhere they are asking, 'Where is Elephiant Yancy? Where is Yancy?' and the only answer they get, course, is 'Dead.' "

Again Yancy nodded as he listened to Nagel's account of events unfolding just as he had set them up. Every man on St. Mary's who knew unequivocally that he was alive and where he could be found was right here with him. Everyone in the town below would have known about the fire and heard the rumor of his death and would have no reason to doubt it. They were the perfect people to pass the lie on to Press, because they did not think they were lying.

"But here's the damnedest thing of it," Nagel continued. "They're there . . . a day and a half, I reckon, and then next thing I know here's Press marching most of his men right back to the ship, and it's up anchor and away. The tender's left behind, and maybe seventy of the men to garrison the house, but the rest of 'em just sail off.

"I reckoned you'd want to know why, so I go up to the house, and I bring a bottle, and I start in to talking with the bastard they got guarding the gate and sharing my bottle with him. Tell him I figure to join in with them and can I talk to Press?

"And what does he tell me? Tells me Press is hot to kill that son of a bitch Marlowe, what was just here. I reckon Dinwiddie told Press Marlowe was here and where he gone. Turns out they go way back, Press and Marlowe. So he's off to hunt Marlowe down, and when he catches him, he's bound back to St. Mary's and reckoning he'll make himself lord of the island. Like he could take your place, my lord."

Hot to kill Marlowe? Yancy thought. *How very odd.* He recalled how Press had been obsessed with killing the man named Malachias Barrett, who had marooned him, left him to die. He had been there on that patch of sand eight days when Yancy found him. It did not seem possible that any living thing could have survived that long, with no food and a single bottle of water, under the blistering Caribbean sun. But Press had. He had talked endlessly of Barrett and how he would kill him.

Now he had come to St. Mary's on a mission of vengeance and was likewise obsessed with this Marlowe. Roger Press collected enemies the way a ship's bottom gathers barnacles and weeds, just by being.

Yancy thought of this new irony, smiled, and then chuckled. It was all too much. Press marches off, leaves less than half his men behind, vulnerable as a nestful of eggs. And where does he go? Off to kill the man that he, Yancy, has been thinking day and night about killing. The one man who had supplanted even Roger Press as an object of Yancy's hatred.

Perhaps Press and Marlowe will kill each other, he thought. But no, that was no good. He wanted to personally see them die, both of them.

Perhaps Press will return here with Marlowe as his prisoner. And my dear Elizabeth as well. That thought warmed Yancy extremely. And it was entirely feasible that Press would do so.

"Come, come, Henry, no time to waste." Yancy stood up, put his glass down on the small table by his chair. "It is time for us to go home."

The next morning they finished their preparations. It would take them the rest of that day to get from the mountain retreat to the big house, but that was fine, because what Yancy intended to do had to be done in the dark. Night was their ally. They did not need light, because they knew every inch of the house that would soon become their killing field, and the men who occupied it now did not.

Yancy and four handpicked men stripped off the fine clothing that they were accustomed to wearing, and donned tattered, stained, and patched-up rags. They smeared their faces with dirt and blood, then re-garded themselves in the big mirror that Nagel had brought out. The effect was perfect.

They strapped on belts with the ubiquitous sheath knives in the small of their backs and secreted daggers inside shirts and breeches, and by midmorning they were off, working their way down the long, winding trail, down from the mountain hideout, through the valley, and over the hill that overlooked the harbor, the hill on which sat the house that Adam Baldridge had built.

It was fifteen miles, and they moved quickly, but still they did not reach the crest of the far hill until an hour after sunset. There they sat and rested and alternated between standing watch and sleeping, save for Yancy, who remained awake and alert, like a deer at a water hole.

Somewhere around midnight they headed out again. As they walked along the crest of the hill, they could see lights in the big house a mile away. They followed the trail down and down toward the water, until at last it met up with the dirt road that ran along the waterfront. They trudged on, past Yancy's warehouses, past the low, ramshackle buildings in the town.

There was not a person in St. Mary's who would not have recog-nized Lord Yancy, but now as he shuffled along, his battered hat pulled low, his clothes in rags, no one paid the slightest attention to him. He looked like any of the human flotsam that washed up on the island's shore every day.

Up the familiar road, up to the big house. They could see lights burning in windows all over the building, could hear the sounds of men carrying on. Yancy remembered the words in the report that Atwood had sent. *"Consent of the queen," my arse*, he thought as he shuffled along, looking hurt and exhausted. *Bloody pirates is what they are, and no more, and all the secret dealing with the queen cannot change that . . .*

At last they came to the gate through the stockade wall, the only realistic way in. Two months before there would have been any number of rotten bits in the stockade through which they might have crawled, but by Yancy's own orders that wooden wall had been strengthened and repaired. Now even the most lax patrol would be alerted by an attempt to scale it or breech it.

No, it was in through the gate. That was the only way.

"Hold, there!" It was the first challenge to their progress, the guard at the gate. In the dark, Yancy saw him swing his musket around, saw a second guard do the same.

"Please, sir, I beg of you," said Yancy, and his voice cracked most effectively. "Pray, sir, we are shipwrecked on the far side of the island. We have walked over the mountains. Please, food and water, we beg . . ."

There was silence after that. The guards were not ready for this eventuality. "Go down to the town," the one guard said at last, taking the initiative. "They have food and water there."

"Please, sir, they will give us nothing without we pay, and we ain't got a groat betwixt us five. 'Go see the lord of the island, do you want charity,' they say."

"Humph," the guard said to that, and then, after another silence, said, "The lot of you, sit down there and keep your hands out."

He pointed with his musket to an ironwood log, a foot and a half thick and ten feet long, that was rolled up against the stockade wall and used by the guards as a sort of bench. Yancy and his men sat in a row along the log, like birds on a branch, and the guard said to the other, "Go and get Lieutenant Tasker."

They waited in an uncomfortable silence for five minutes, and then the guard was back and another man with him.

"This fellow says they was shipwrecked on the far side of the island. He's begging food and water."

The new arrival—Lieutenant Tasker, Yancy guessed—stepped toward them, looked down on them. "What ship?" he asked suddenly.

"*Betsy*, snow, from Liverpool, bound for the Bay of Antongil. We . . . we had business there, like . . ." Yancy had anticipated these questions, had his answers ready.

"What is your name?"

"Joe Benner, my lord. Boatswain. The officers is all dead, sir. We carried the captain halfway across the mountains, like to save him, but he died and we buried him. The rest and the other hands, they drowned."

Tasker was silent for a moment, and then Yancy added, "Please, my lord, we suffered something horrid. Food and water, it's all we ask, and someplace safe to sleep. We been in that wicked, wicked jungle four days now. I beg of you. You are lord of this place. Won't you see to helping some poor, desperate sailors?"

He watched as Tasker ran his eyes over the five men, assaying the risk. It would appear small, Yancy had made certain of that. Just five men, and they too weak with hunger and exhaustion to cause any trouble.

At last Tasker said, "I am not lord of this island. Captain Press is in charge here, but he is gone and left me in command."

He considered for a moment more and then said, "Very well. You may come into the kitchen and eat and drink and sleep there under guard."

"Oh, bless you, sir," Yancy began, and the others joined in with their authentic-sounding gratitude.

Tasker led them through the gate and into the house and then out a back door to the kitchen, which was connected to the main house only by a roofed-over walkway twenty feet long. Yancy stared about as if seeing the house for the first time. He took note of the guards at the entrance to the great hall, and through the open door could see that it was functioning now as a barracks, with a majority of Press's men asleep within, like deer run into a pen.

Inside the kitchen they were given food and water, and they fell on both like wolves. They were in fact ravenous and parched, since Yancy had allowed them nothing to eat or drink for the past eight hours, and the effect was complete.

For ten minutes they sated themselves in silence while the two men guarding them grew increasingly bored. At last Yancy pushed back from the table.

"Dear God, but that is good," he said to the guards. "Pray, give our thanks to— What was the good man's name?"

"Lieutenant Tasker."

"Yes, yes, of course. But say now, I had always heard there was a fellow, name of Yancy, who run things on St. Mary's."

The guard chuckled. "Yancy? There was. Captain Press come clear from England in order to knock that son of a bitch on the head. Lucky for him he had the good sense to drop dead right before we showed up."

"Lucky for him," Yancy said, and thought, *You die first.*

Yancy continued to nibble at the food that was laid out for them. It was the first meal he had had for some time that was prepared by another's hands, but of course his anonymity protected him from the threat of assassination.

As he ate, he continued to engage the guard in conversation.

The man was not of a talkative bent, but Yancy drew him out, asking him about his home, his experiences, sharing stories of places they knew in common. Soon there was something of an easy rapport between them. As he talked, Yancy imagined what it would be like when he cut the man's throat.

Finally Yancy and the four others had eaten their fill. They pushed themselves away from the table and found places on the floor to curl up and sleep. They were as genuinely exhausted as they had been hungry and thirsty, and soon the hall was filled with the bestial sounds of their snoring.

Yancy was glad of it. The guards, he knew, would not notice that he was awake with the others so genuinely asleep. He lay there motionless, eyes closed, and listened to the little sounds of the guards moving around, talking on occasion to one another, yawning.

He remained still for an hour, but he dared wait no longer for fear that the guards would be relieved. He imagined it was somewhere around two in the morning. That was a good time. Defenses were down at that hour, watchfulness at a low ebb.

He rolled over with a groan, sat up. He saw the guard straighten, reacting to the first movement in an hour or more.

"Got to piss," Yancy said.

The guard nodded. For a moment he was silent, and Yancy knew he was debating whether or not his charge needed accompaniment in that task. Finally he said, "Out that door there. Just piss in the bush. And come right back."

Yancy nodded and stood. The guard did not realize that his decision had bought him at least four more minutes to live.

Yancy walked slowly, awkwardly, to the door, as if his muscles were sore and aching. But once outside and beyond the guard's view, he picked up his pace, racing around the familiar north end of the building, down a flight of stone steps and along the dark back side of the big house. He could see nothing beyond vague shapes, the outline of the house against the stars, the blackness that was the stockade fence. But that did not matter. He was lord of the place, and he knew every inch of the grounds.

To his left, thirty feet beyond the stone wall of the house, there was a hump of dirt with a small door set in it. Yancy made a move in that direction, then stopped. He heard the crunch of shoes on gravel, a guard patrolling the perimeter.

Son of a whore, he thought. He did not have too long before the idiot in the kitchen came looking for him or raised an alarm.

Yancy waited for long maddening seconds, crouched in the blackness by the wall, as the guard came closer. He heard the man stop, pause, then head back the way he had come. Yancy waited another minute, until he could no longer hear the footfalls, then left the shadows' protection, racing across the ground in a crouch, making for that well-hidden door set in the mound of earth.

With a dozen strides he was there, feeling along the ground until his hands fell on the heavy bar that was set across the door, preventing anyone from opening it from the inside.

He lifted the bar, put it aside, and swung the door open. Movement from the darkness within, and then Henry Nagel, hunched nearly double, emerged from the tunnel. He straightened with a stifled groan, stepped aside, and then another man followed him and another and another. More and more men—big men, bearded, with weapons hanging off them—poured out of the secret entrance and spread out on the lawn, crouching down, waiting in silence.

"How many are we?" Yancy breathed the words.

"Fifty, all told."

Yancy nodded. They were the men from the compound, the original Terrors, his loyal core. Nagel had augmented their numbers with men from the town, pirates who were temporarily on the beach or who had made their homes on St. Mary's. They were always ready for a good fight and eager to join in on the side most likely to win. Nagel had convinced them that it was Yancy.

"Good. Let's go." He turned and headed back the way he had come, and behind him the sound of fifty big, armed men following, being as quiet as they could, which was not overly quiet.

Along the dark perimeter of the building and up the stone steps. Yancy guessed he had been gone five minutes at least, enough for the guard to become concerned. He hoped the man would try to find his charge by himself, rather than raise the alarm and admit he had let Yancy leave unescorted.

He moved cautiously toward the edge of the kitchen building, slowing his pace, listening.

"Benner? Benner, you son of a bitch, where are you?" he heard the guard hiss. Trying to cover his mistake.

Yancy stepped around the corner of the kitchen and stopped, twenty feet from the guard. He could just make out the man's dark shape. "Here!" he called softly. "Come and see this, you will not believe it!"

He slipped the ten-inch stiletto blade out of his shirt, held it easily at his side.

"Get over here, you bastard!" the guard said in a loud whisper.

"No, truly, you must see this. You will not believe it!" Yancy called out. He heard the sounds of the guard approaching, just audible as he stepped over the soft ground, heard him muttering.

The man's dark form loomed up in front of him, and Yancy said, "Here."

They stepped around the edge of the building and stopped in the face of the fifty pirates waiting there. The guard's mouth fell open, and he was about to say something—to yell, perhaps—when Yancy grabbed his hair and jerked his head back and with one fluid motion cut his throat, clean through to the vertebrae.

The guard made a gasping, gurgling sound and crumpled to his knees. Yancy felt a stream of hot blood lash across his cheek, and he thought of his daily pig killing.

"There. I told you you would not believe it," Yancy said to the dying man, then waved his men forward and led them on to the open door to the kitchen.

There he stopped them again and went in himself, calling to the one remaining guard. "I think your friend has need of your help," he said. "He sent me back for you."

The second guard was a cautious man, and he held Yancy at musket point and made him lead the way. But for all his caution he was not ready for Henry Nagel, waiting by the edge of the door, who grabbed him by the mouth as he walked past and jerked the gun from his hand. The guard screamed into Nagel's callused palm, thrashed like a fish in the bottom of a boat, but he could not break Nagel's grip, and Nagel dispatched him the way Yancy had done his partner.

The fifty crowded into the kitchen and joined their four comrades waiting there. Nagel handed Yancy his sword and shoulder belt, which he draped over his shoulder, and a brace of pistols.

Nagel stuck a bunko—what the Portuguese called a "cheroot"—between his lips and lit it with a lantern, then handed it to Yancy and lit another.

"Very well. Let us go," Yancy said. He marched out of the kitchen, down the walk, and back into the big house. The need for subtlety was past. They had surprise, and they had sufficient numbers. The men knew what to do.

Down the hallway to the tall doors that opened into the great hall. The sentry, half asleep, jerked up at the sound, turned toward Yancy and his force of men.

"What in hell . . . ? Who the hell . . . ?" was as far as he got before Yancy shot him and then with his second pistol shot the other guard. There was a moment's pause, a universal holding of breath, save for the ringing echo of the pistol shots.

And then, as Yancy stepped past the slumped, bleeding forms of the guards and into the great hall, panic exploded like a keg of power going off.

Men leaped up from the floor where they slept, arms grabbed for muskets, for swords, for breeches. They were dark ghosts in the light of the three lanterns that illuminated the hall with their weak light. Men shouted in alarm or confusion, shouted questions, shouted orders.

Yancy pulled the cheroot from his mouth, touched the glowing end to the fuse of a hand grenado, tossed it into this thrashing crowd of men. Nagel and three others did likewise.

Yancy watched the path of their flight across the dark room, marked by the fuses that glowed and hissed. He was watching one of them bounce at the far end of the hall when the first exploded, then the second and the third and in the same instant the final two.

The howls of confusion turned to shrieks of agony, screams of terror, and then Yancy stepped farther into the room, and the men behind him followed and spread out, and they began to empty their pistols and muskets into the crowd.

From the darkness a few muskets answered back, and behind him Yancy heard more gunfire, and he knew that the officers, who would have been sleeping in the upstairs rooms, had come rushing to the sound of the fight and had run into the twenty men he had dispatched to lie in wait for them.

The gunfire made a relentless noise, a grand orchestra of priming and powder, so that no one shot was distinguishable from another. Then through that din came the first cry of "Quarter! Quarter!"

"Hold!" Yancy shouted, and the gunfire ceased abruptly. Nearly all of the guns would be expended by now, and there was no need to engage in fighting with cold steel if it was not necessary.

"Lay down your arms!" Yancy shouted. He did not know at whom he was shouting. The brilliant light of flash in the pans and at the muzzle ends had ruined his eyes for seeing in the dark. He was aware only of the dim shapes of the high windows in the great hall, and in the circles of light thrown off from the lanterns he could see dead men and living men and pools of blood.

From the dark came the clatter of muskets hitting the stone floor. The gunfire behind him had ceased. Yancy was once again lord of St. Mary's.

He wondered what horror the dawn would reveal, once he was able to see the results of his slaughter. He wondered, but he did not care very much, and it was only a vague sort of curiosity. There were prisoners enough to clean up the mess and burn the dead.

For him it was just more preparation. He felt suddenly very weary, overcome with the strain of it all. He was ready to kill Press and be done with it.

Or rather, he was ready for Press and Marlowe to sail back into his arms so that he might begin the protracted process of killing them both.

Chapter 21

FORTUNA FORTES fauct . . . Marlowe thought. Fortune favors the brave. But still he felt uneasy.

He wondered about the nature of luck. Had he been lucky to escape from Press in London? Real luck would have been never meeting with Press in the first place. On the balance was he lucky or not?

He had been lucky to get himself and Elizabeth out of St. Mary's alive. But did that count as luck when set against the very ill fortune of crossing paths with the lunatic Yancy?

Must see what Bickerstaff thinks about all this.

This internal debate, as philosophical as Marlowe was wont to get, took place, as such debates so often did, high aloft, as Marlowe stared out at the horizon.

The horizon always made Marlowe thoughtful. It was the edge of mystery, the unknown in any direction. At sea one's fortunes, be they in the form of prizes or enemies, landfalls or foul weather, came up over the horizon. Staring at the horizon was like trying to peer into the future.

In this case it was a wild ride. The *Elizabeth Galley* was lying to under bare poles to make her top hamper more invisible to any vessel that might come up over that sharp blue line in the distance. There was a moderate swell running with the ten or so knots of wind, and without the steadying pressure of the sails the *Galley* was rolling hard in the sea. Standing on the main topmast crosstrees, Marlowe and the lookout were swinging through great arcs as the ship rocked back and forth.

It was a motion that would have made most landsmen, and not a few seamen, sick, and even climbing aloft in that swaying top hamper would have seemed a daunting task to one not bred to the sea, but Marlowe did not give it a thought. With the cry of "Sail, ho!" and the report that this new ship's bearing meant she was coming down the Bab el Mandeb from the Red Sea, the motion became nothing more than an annoyance as he raced up the shrouds, thinking only of identifying the ship, preparing to take it, dreaming of the riches in her hold.

They had been on station, waiting, for two days. South of them the dry headland of Ras Bir was visible from the masthead. To the north of their position the topgallants of the *Bloody Revenge* flirted with the horizon, sometimes appearing, sometimes dropping below the blue line. From his masthead Billy Bird should be able to see the coast to the north of his position. Between the two vessels they could watch every inch of the passage from the Red Sea.

The *Bloody Revenge* was not visible now, nor had it been for the past five hours.

Billy Bird, you son of a bitch, now where are you off to? Marlowe wondered as he once more scanned the horizon for some sign of the brig. He speculated that perhaps the Bloody Revenges had spotted a vessel to the north and headed off to take her alone, deciding in the end to deny the Elizabeth Galleys their part of the booty. Quite possible.

It was also possible that the brig was just below the horizon, perhaps, like the *Elizabeth Galley*, under bare poles and thus invisible to Marlowe and his glass. If that were the case, then they would certainly hear the gunfire from the battle that Marlowe guessed would commence in an hour or so. Gunfire would draw the pirates like sharks along a bloody trail in the sea.

He shifted his glass back to the approaching ship, hull up now. A great, fat lumbering thing, flying the colorful flags of some Moorish state that Marlowe did not recognize. She threw off bright glints of light as the sun beat down on gold trim, silver helmets and halberds, and brass cannon barrels. She was under a full press of sail, but still she wallowed, her high poop deck swaying back and forth, back and forth, like a stout woman doing her best to hurry.

Marlowe tried to temper his excitement, no simple task with the men on the deck below buzzing like the cicadas back home as they stared and pointed and counted up the riches in their heads—or out loud. This was the one. If she was not *the* treasure ship of the Great Mogul, then she was near enough.

He slung his telescope over his shoulder, climbed back down to the deck. "Mr. Flanders, the *Bloody Revenge* is not in sight. Let us give her the cannon signal, then get ready to go after this bloody great bastard! Hands aloft to loosen sail!"

He could not resist the dramatic flourish in that last statement, so taken was he with the high energy on deck. The men cheered, howled, banged the flats of their swords against the bulwarks. The sail looseners swarmed up the rigging, and also some who were not sail looseners but who wanted to see the sails set with all the alacrity the ship could manage. Flanders hurried forward, conferred with the gunners on the starboard side.

The sails spilled off the yards, and the guns went off, two in quick succession, a pause, and then a third. It was their prearranged signal, and it meant "Prize in sight, close with us." And if that did not bring them, then the broadsides that would soon follow should. This treasure ship would have to fight now; she could not outrun the *Elizabeth Galley*.

And if he does not come, then that is his damned hard luck, Marlowe thought. If Billy Bird were off chasing some other ship, to which he had failed to alert his newfound partners, than that was his business, and a sorry bastard he would be.

The Moorish ship was a good mile off at least when she began to fire.

Pathetic, Marlowe thought as he saw the puffs of smoke from her ample sides, the black streaks of the balls' trajectories, the spouts of water as the round shot plunged into the sea in a wild and random pattern, and at the same time the flat rumble of the gunfire, just catching up with the shot.

Pathetic. None of the shots had hit, of course, but none of them were even in line with the *Elizabeth Galley.* They fell into a patch of water at least an acre wide.

She was a big one, too, bigger even than Marlowe had first suspected. By his best guess, for he was too far to see with any certainty, she mounted sixty guns. And they would be big ones, thirty-two-pounders at least. The Moors did not play around with popguns.

He was likewise too far away still to see the number of people aboard her, but he imagined that her complement was massive.

The Moors lacked nearly all of the Europeans' traditional naval skills. They were not practiced gunners or skilled seamen. Their ships were not nimble or well handled. What they were was big. The Great Mogul and those who sent tribute to him and those who carried pilgrims to Mecca tried to compensate for a lack of naval tradition with overwhelming size—in their ships, in their guns, in their crews.

Generally it did not work. Marlowe's thoughts naturally turned to Thomas Tew, who had first stood on the deck of an English privateer and watched one of those fat ships roll down on him, just as he, Marlowe, was doing now. The ship Tew had attacked was even bigger than this one, over one hundred guns, if Marlowe remembered correctly. Three hundred soldiers.

Tew had told his men that despite all her guns and men, the Moors were wanting two things: skill and courage. They took her in fifteen minutes of fighting, with never a one of the *Amity*'s men even injured.

Marlowe imagined that the Moors were wanting a third thing, and that was motivation. It was not easy to conjure much enthusiasm for dying in defense of a tyrant's treasure, not a sou of which you would ever see. Put up against the highly motivated Roundsmen, the Moors were at a great disadvantage indeed, despite their numbers.

Another broadside exploded silently from the big ship's side, and again the jets of water, shooting up over a great span of sea, were accompanied by the rumble of the guns.

How long between those ragged and ill-coordinated broadsides? Marlowe wished he had timed it. It was a few minutes at least. He did not need to time their rate of fire to gauge their ineptitude.

He thought of Tew again. He had not been so lucky the second time around, his belly shot away by a cannonball, his men surrendering with no further resistance. What a hell the rest of their short lives must have been, enslaved by the Moors. Marlowe wondered to what brutal work the Great Mogul would have put his Christian slaves. Christian slaves who had tried to rob him of his tribute, no less.

Tew got off easy. Marlowe wondered what it was like to hold in your guts with your hand. He realized that his palm was pressing against his midriff, as if he were practicing the stance.

"On deck! Sail, ho! One point abaft the starboard beam! Reckon she's the *Bloody Revenge!*"

Damn. Marlowe frowned, looked to the northward. *This bloody complicates things*, he thought.

If they had taken the Mogul's ship with no help from Billy Bird, then the matter was clear: the Bloody Revenges had no claim to the treasure. If they had taken her with Billy's help, then it was equally clear: the treasure would be divided between the two ships.

But now what? What if they took her in sight of the *Bloody Revenge* but without their help? Would Billy Bird and his men expect their part? Would the Elizabeth Galleys agree? Would the two pirate crews go at one another?

"Listen here, you men!" Marlowe shouted, taking his place at the rail at the forward edge of the quarterdeck. "Looks like yonder comes the *Bloody Revenge*. If they're in sight, they got a claim to the booty, but that doesn't mean we have to do all the work for them. We'll drive this bastard north, get him between us. I don't reckon the Moors'll give us much fight, but what they do give, we'll let them other fellows share!"

This met with a cheer, the men shouting and banging, and then, like a counterpoint, the rumble of the Moors' guns. Marlowe had not even noticed them fire, did not bother watching where the shot fell.

The Moor was sailing full and bye with larboard tacks aboard. The *Elizabeth Galley* was on a dead run, riding those late-winter winds that flowed from the Indian Ocean and channeled northwest through Bab el Mandeb and the Red Sea. Twenty minutes on their generally converging courses, and they had closed to within half a mile of one another. The *Bloody Revenge*'s topgallants were visible from the *Galley*'s deck, and the man aloft was certain of the brig's identity.

"We'll give them a cannonading! It's a long shot, but give it to 'em as best as you can!" Marlowe called down his encouragement to the gunners, then stood back and fixed the Moor with his glass. He heard Flanders in the waist shouting "On the up-roll!" and felt the *Elizabeth Galley* heel with the swells, and then the cry, "Fire!" and the starboard battery went off, eight six-pounders, deafening in their proximity.

The weight of iron was pathetic compared to what the Moor could hurl with a single broadside, but Marlowe could see through his glass that more than half his gunners had hit their mark, and he knew that a six-pound ball that hits is worth more than any size ball plunging into the sea.

He looked down into the waist. Half the guns were run out again. Thirty seconds later, and they were all of them loaded and ready.

"On the up-roll! Fire!" and once more the *Elizabeth Galley* blasted her iron into the great barn of a vessel that carried the Mogul's treasure.

The Moorish captain clearly understood as well as Marlowe the relative worth of round shot that hit compared with round shot that fell into the ocean. Likewise he seemed to understand the limitations of his own ship, and clearly he knew better than to try to tack that behemoth, despite the decent wind and miles of sea room.

Marlowe watched with some amusement as the great gilded beast began her ponderous turn, the bow pointing more and more toward the *Elizabeth Galley*, the masts coming into line, the huge, ornate poop lost from view behind the courses as the Moor laboriously wore around.

The heavy yards swung in short, jerky stages as the stern passed through the wind. At last the treasure ship came up on a starboard tack with her yards braced round and bowlines hauled taut. The entire evolution had taken over ten minutes, but finally they settled on their more northerly course, away from the *Elizabeth Galley* and toward the *Bloody Revenge*, which Marlowe guessed they had not yet discovered.

"Hands to braces!" Marlowe cried, and the sail trimmers left their guns and went to the pinrails, and a moment later the *Galley* came up on a starboard tack as well, like the Moorish ship and half a mile astern. But the *Galley* sailed half again as fast as the Moor; Marlowe could pretty much choose the moment they would board her.

They chased on for another hour, the *Galley* sailing a somewhat higher course than the Moor so that they could continue to pepper her broad transom with round shot.

The *Elizabeth Galley* was a quarter mile astern when the Moors spotted the *Bloody Revenge*, a mile north of them, and turned more easterly again, sailing as close-hauled as she could, which was not very. She was a big, clumsy cow set upon by two nimble wolves, and the more she tried to flee, the more pathetic and vulnerable she appeared.

"Very well, Honeyman," Marlowe said to the quartermaster, who was standing beside him on the quarterdeck. Before St. Mary's he would have chased the man away, but now he was happy to have him there.

There was no question, of course, of a divided command. They were in a fight now. Marlowe was absolute ruler of the ship.

"Very well," he said again, "enough of this nonsense. We'll lay her alongside and board her. By the time we come right up with her, the *Bloody Revenge* should not be far behind.

"Aye, Captain," Honeyman said. He hurried forward, relaying Marlowe's words in a loud voice, in a tone untainted by excitement or fear or emotion of any kind. The boarders saw to their cutlasses and pikes and pistols; the gun captains took pains to load with the roundest of shot, and grape on top of that. The men massed in the waist and on the quarterdeck, waiting.

The *Elizabeth Galley* closed fast, with the Moor caught between the pincers of the two Red Sea Rovers. Marlowe climbed up the main shrouds halfway to the main top, shifted his glass between the Moor and the *Bloody Revenge* and back. Billy Bird was making no extraordinary effort to get into the fight. The *Revenge* would come up with them a good fifteen minutes after the *Galley* had laid alongside the Moor.

"Damn you, you bloody . . ." Marlowe muttered. The word "coward" was floating just below the surface, but he could not bring himself to voice it. It was too heinous an accusation, even to be made in private, without greater evidence than he had.

After all, the *Revenge* might have sprung a plank, or her bottom might be covered with weeds, or the men might have decided to become insensibly drunk. Any number of things might have happened that were beyond Billy Bird's control.

Marlowe climbed down, regained the quarterdeck. "Elizabeth, my dear," he called to his wife, who had been all the while standing aft, keeping out of the way. "We will be at them directly. I think it would be best were you to retire to the cable tier."

"Of course, my love." Elizabeth stepped over, kissed him. Bold as she was, they both knew that the decks would not be the place for her when the fighting got hot.

Marlowe glanced down at the two pistols thrust in her sash. "You are all loaded, then?" he asked, trying to make his voice sound as cheery as possible. He had insisted that Elizabeth take two loaded guns with her. He had explained that if they were taken, the guns were not to be used for defense.

It was not the first time Elizabeth had been relegated to the cable tier with instructions to blow her brains out if the ship was taken. Marlowe did not like it, but there was no other option. He could not get the image of Thomas Tew out of his head—his guts spilling on the deck, his crew surrendering to the Moors. The thought of Elizabeth dead by her own hand was more palatable than the thought of her in the hands of the Moors.

"Loaded and ready," Elizabeth said. She gave him an alluring smile, kissed him again, and disappeared below. If she was afraid, she would never let him know it. He knew that Elizabeth did not wish to burden him with any additional considerations, and he loved her for that and for many other things besides.

Another broadside from the big ship, two cable lengths away, and this time a few of the heavy balls hit, sending up swarms of splinters and making the vessel shudder from stem to stern, but there was no damage that Marlowe could see.

The men in the waist were silent, their previous enthusiasm waning as the Moorish ship loomed over them, her enormous size becoming more obvious and intimidating with every yard they closed. Marlowe swept the Moor with his glass. He could see the decks crowded with men. He could see white turbans and black beards and bright-colored jackets and the skirts they wore below them. He could see flashing swords and pole arms. There were hundreds of them.

"Mr. Flanders, let us have a few broadsides here!" Marlowe shouted.

That thought seemed to sit well with the Elizabeth Galleys, and they moved with a will to run out the larboard guns.

"On the up-roll! Fire!" And the world was lost in the blast of smoke and the thunder of the guns, and when it cleared, Marlowe could see gaps in the Moor's bulwarks and rigging hanging in tatters.

"Again!" he shouted, but the men were already reloading and running out. Now he could see wolf grins on their faces, and more than a few of them were shouting at the enemy.

The guns fired again, and some of the Moor's as well, the two ships blasting metal and smoke at one another over two hundred yards of water. Marlowe saw one of his men go down with a splinter in the arm, another knocked on the head by a falling block, but nothing worse than that. There were more holes in the Moor's bulwark, and two gunports had been smashed into one.

"Grape now!" Marlowe called down to the waist. "Grape and langrage, and get ready to board her!" The two ships were closing fast. Even without a glass he could see the defenders massing at the big ship's rails, which were a good fifteen feet above the Elizabeth Galley's highest deck.

"Maximum elevation, let us blow a path through these bastards!" Marlowe's blood was up now, and he was filled with the fighting madness that swept fear and even good sense away. His men felt it, too, he could tell just watching the way they manned the guns or held their weapons or hopped from one foot to another, eager to be at the enemy.

Someone began to chant: "Death, death, death . . ." and the others picked it up. That was what Marlowe was waiting for, the vaporing. He had been on both sides of that sound, and he knew how unnerving it was to a ship's company that was waiting to be fallen upon by pirates.

One hundred feet between the ships. Any closer and the *Galley's* great guns would not be able to elevate high enough to reach the massed soldiers.

"Fire!" Marlowe shouted, and an instant later came the roar of the guns, punctuated by the scream of the small grapeshot and langrage, the crash of wood as the shots hit home, the screaming and chanting of the Roundsmen as they worked themselves into a frenzy for boarding the Moor.

The wind rolled away the smoke, lifting it like a blanket, and the Moorish ship loomed over them, a great, gilded, ornate, battered cliff. There were holes in the formerly solid mass of defenders where the *Galley's* grapeshot had cut its swath.

Marlowe looked behind him. Bickerstaff had the helm, which was the only participation that he would take in what he considered to be a nefarious act of piracy. He would fight to the death to defend the ship against boarders, but he would not board another, not for a cause such as this.

Marlowe saw Bickerstaff push the helm over and turned back toward the Moor, and the two ships collided. In the waist Honeyman was up on the rail and grabbing the boarding steps on the Moor's side and racing up, Hesiod at his heels, and behind the black man a dozen screaming Roundsmen. Forward of him Burgess and Flanders were leading more men over the fore channel.

"Aft boarders! To me!" Marlowe shouted, jumping up on the quarterdeck rail and up into the mizzen shrouds. One of the Moor's great guns was level with his belly, and thoughts of Tew flashed through his mind, but then the others were racing aft to follow him, and it was time to go.

The Moorish ship was so huge that Marlowe had to climb halfway up the *Galley*'s mizzen shrouds just to get to the bottom of her main shrouds. He leaped across, landed on the channel, that platform jutting from the Moor's side, climbed up into the Moor's main shrouds.

On the deck below, the fight was fully involved, dark-skinned, bearded, turbaned defenders firing their ornate pistols and swinging their great swords at the wild men who poured over their decks. All the fighting was forward of the mainmast; no one even saw Marlowe and his band coming up behind, save for the officers on the quarterdeck and the poop. Marlowe heard them shout—a warning to the others, he guessed—but he could not understand a word of it.

He swung down to the deck, sword ready, met one of the officers coming forward. The man pointed a pistol at Marlowe, fired from ten feet, and missed. He flung the pistol away and raised his big, wide-bladed scimitar and attacked.

Marlowe thought he had an easy kill—the man was open—and he lunged, but the scimitar swung around and knocked Marlowe's sword aside. The officer brought his blade back again, but rather than retreat, Marlowe charged, hitting the man in the chest with his shoulder, knocking him to the deck, driving his sword into him before the Moor even knew what had happened.

Marlowe turned toward the fight in the waist. The men he had led over the main chains were already plunging into it, falling on the turbaned defenders from behind, screaming like the damned, and that was enough for the Moorish soldiers. They flung aside pole arms and scimitars and daggers as they fled for the scuttles and hatches or fell in supplication to the deck.

The Galleys chased them to the scuttles and slammed the hatch covers down on them or held them at sword point in little clusters around the deck. Suddenly the great volume of noise fell off to nothing. The Moorish ship was theirs. There had been little bloodshed that Marlowe could see, and what there had been had been mostly on the side of the defenders.

"Well done, men! Well done! She is ours!" Marlowe shouted, and around him grins, nodding heads, men too winded to cheer.

"Here's *Bloody Revenge*, and just in time so she don't get no one hurt," called Honeyman. The brig was a cable length away and coming down fast. Marlowe could see men on her deck. They looked as if they were getting ready to board.

"Flanders, quick, haul down that damned Moorish ensign. They might not know the ship is taken."

Flanders ran aft, tossed off the flag halyard, pulled the big, garish ensign down from the ensign staff, and let it pool on the deck.

Marlowe walked over to the larboard gangway. He wanted to see Billy Bird's expression when he found that the *Elizabeth Galley* had taken the Moor without him.

The *Bloody Revenge* was less than one hundred yards away and showing no sign of heaving to or even slowing her onrush. Marlowe looked to her quarterdeck for some sign of the flamboyant Bird, but he could not see him. He wondered if that was the problem, if something had happened, some shift of power.

Fifty yards, and they still came on. "Don't he know we already took the fucking ship?" Honeyman asked, voicing the thoughts of many. Twenty-five yards, and Honeyman leaped up on the rail, shouted, "Stand off! Stand off, ya rutting bastards, the ship is ours!"

But they did not stand off, and Honeyman jumped down, and the others fled from the larboard rail as it became clear that the *Bloody Revenge* was going to hit their prize, and hit her hard.

At the last moment, the *Bloody Revenge* turned. Her jib boom caught on the Moor's bulwark and snapped as her helm went over, and then the brig hit the bigger ship with a shudder.

"What in all hell are these arseholes about?" Flanders said, loud. And then a shout from below the rail, and they heard the sound of men swarming up the side, and then the first of the Bloody Revenges appeared over the bulwark, swords and pistols in hand.

"Hold! Hold!" Marlowe shouted. "The ship is ours, the Moors are below! Hold, there!"

It was like shouting at deaf men. The Revenges did not pause for a beat before they fired a volley into the stunned men of the *Elizabeth Galley* and then fell on them—those still standing—with sword and cutlass.

Chapter 22

THE FIGHT did not last long. It was shorter even than the battle with the treasure ship's original defenders. The Elizabeth Galleys were exhausted, stunned, and taken entirely by surprise.

A pistol ball grazed Marlowe's ribs, and it hurt like the devil, but it did not put him down. He had time enough to recover from the shock, time even to draw his sword and shout again for the boarders to hold their attack as the Revenges swarmed across the deck to fall on his men.

Even as Marlowe's sword rang with the clang of steel on steel and he turned aside an attacking blade, he could not believe the depth of the betrayal. He did not know Billy Bird well, but Elizabeth did, and he could not believe that she could have misjudged him to such a degree.

He parried the sword thrust, leaped back from the slashing dagger his opponent wielded in his left hand, lunged forward. The move was slow and awkward—like his men, Marlowe was tired—and his blade was easily beaten aside. Marlowe leaped back away from the riposte, the man's blade missing him by inches.

Billy Bird, son of a bitch! Marlowe thought, even as his eyes kept track of every move his opponent made. But he had not seen Billy come over the rail. His eyes darted around. No Billy that he could see. Had Billy Bird been voted out by a faction of his crew bent on betrayal?

The other man lunged again, a full-body attack, sword and dagger, and Marlowe had all he could do to fight him off. The man—Marlowe did not recognize him—was fast, but Marlowe could see his tendency to expose himself as he countered with the dagger, and he knew that was the weakness that would kill him.

One step back, sword held low, and the man leaped forward, brought the dagger around, and Marlowe had him right under the arm, drove his sword into his thrashing body. The man's eyes went wide, his mouth fell open, and he screamed as if the sword puncture had released the sound from his chest.

Sword withdrawn, and the man collapsed. Marlowe turned to see who was next. Searched the deck for a familiar face. He had met most of the Revenges during their floating bacchanal. But he recognized no one.

And then one of his own men threw down his sword, shouted, "Quarter!" And then another did the same, and then the fight was over, the furious, confused, stunned Elizabeth Galleys dropping their weapons, glaring at this new enemy, who looked on them in gloating triumph.

And then on the far side of the deck, up the boarding steps and through the gangway came Billy Bird. He stepped with great difficulty. His face was a battered wreck, his nose broken, both his eyes blackened and one of them swollen shut.

He stood there for a moment, swaying. And then, coming up behind him and shoving him to the deck, appeared Roger Press.

Hours before, Billy Bird had heard the signal, two guns in quick succession, then a third, and he knew what it meant. His head had jerked up from the deck, half turned toward the sound, and then Roger Press had slammed his boot into Billy's stomach and driven the breath out of him.

"What was that?"

Billy Bird, eyes wide, gasping, as if all the air had suddenly been sucked from the deck. At last he managed to draw breath. "Cannon fire, you stupid bastard . . ." he croaked.

Press kicked him again. "I know it's cannon fire. Whose? Sounds like a signal to me. Is someone signaling you, Captain Bird?"

More coughing and spitting blood, and at last Billy Bird managed a weak "Sod off . . ."

Press kicked him again, then straightened and stared out at the horizon. He didn't need Bird to tell him it was a signal; that was clear enough. Soft, muted, coming from someplace over the horizon, but it was definitely a signal.

He picked absently at his teeth with his silver toothpick.

He's no coward, this foppish little prick, I'll give him that, Press thought.

The *Queen's Venture* had sighted the *Revenge's* topgallants at first light, the first European ship they had seen since leaving St. Mary's. With the lookout's hail, Press had been consumed with hope that this might be Barrett's—Marlowe's—vessel. They had run their East Indiaman bunting aloft, closed fast with strange sail.

But she proved to be a brig, and Dinwiddie had said the *Elizabeth Galley* was a ship. So the next-best possibility was that the brig was working with Marlowe or at least had spoken to him.

The brig flew the British merchantman's ensign. They did not try to run at the sight of the *Queen's Venture*. There was no need; an East Indiaman would do them no harm.

The *Venture* ranged up alongside, ran out her great guns, overwhelming the brig with her size and firepower and the strength of her company, armed and arrayed along her deck. The brig wisely hove to, agreed to a boarding party, acquiesced to all of Press's demands with never a shot fired.

Billy Bird had tried to bluff his way through the interview, an interview that took place on the brig's quarterdeck with all the *Bloody Revenge's* company herded forward and held at bay by the muskets carried by Press's men, the great muzzles of the cannons that aimed at them from the *Queen's Venture*'s side, fifty feet away.

Bird began with hollow protests at the treatment they were receiving. But Press, wanting to put some veneer of legitimacy on what he was doing, showed Bird the queen's commission that he carried and then asked to see Bird's privateering commission. Bird produced some document issued by the governor of New York, which Press glanced at and declared invalid.

Press informed Bird he was subject to arrest. Asked him about Marlowe. Billy Bird did not know any Marlowe but had seen a sail running off to the westward just the day before, thought perhaps that was him.

Then Press began to interrogate him for real, using his fists and boots and a belaying pin taken from Billy Bird's own ship. He went at Billy for twenty minutes in that manner. The Roundsman never wavered in his story and even had the fortitude to continue to hurl back insults and abuse. And the more Billy cursed him and verbally abused him, the more punishment Billy endured, the more Press was certain that he was lying.

And then came the signal from beyond the horizon, and it did not matter anymore what Billy Bird said. Someone was out there. It was time to go see who it was.

Roger Press had it all: the *Bloody Revenge*, the *Elizabeth Galley*, the Moorish treasure ship, St. Mary's. It was the bastard's greatest moment of triumph, but Marlowe did not feel privileged to witness it. As he sat on the deck with his hands held behind his head, which was humiliating enough, he searched his mind for something that would make Press's victory less complete. But he could think of nothing.

, Press himself had taken pains to give Marlowe the particulars. Told him about his conquest of St. Mary's and all the riches there, his capture of the *Bloody Revenge*, his idea for using the brig in a *ruse de guerre* that completely fooled the men of the *Elizabeth Galley*—and their captain. And all the time the damned toothpick waggling at him.

Press made certain that Marlowe was there to hear his first officer's report of the preliminary inspection of the cargo carried aboard the captured Moorish ship. Gold and silver in coin, bar, and dust; pearls; jewels, set and loose; jewel-encrusted statues and daggers and crowns and even a saddle emblazoned with rubies and diamonds. Bundles of silks, spices, ivory. It was the booty that the Roundsmen dreamed of. The booty that for a brief moment had been the take of the Elizabeth Galleys. And now it was in the hands of Roger Press.

"Dear God, Press, you whoreson, either kill me or give me a sword and fight me like a man!" Marlowe shouted out at last, able to bear no more. "You hung back before, when your men boarded us, never gave me a chance to kill you. Just like your damned cowardice at Nombre de Dios. Play the man now, if you will, but for God's sake don't bloody bore me to death!"

He did not expect a sword. He expected a belaying pin across the head. But instead Press just grinned, poked at his teeth with his toothpick. "No, no, Marlowe. If I give you a sword, you'll just fall on it and deprive me of the pleasure of killing you. And I haven't the time to do a proper job of that now. I have all this booty to get into my ship.

"But see here, I know you have a head for numbers. I think I shall have you write out the inventory of my treasure as it is swayed out. What say you?"

"I say kiss my arse."

"Oh, indeed?" Press looked down at the quarterdeck of the *Elizabeth Galley*, fifteen feet below. "Say, ain't that the little doxy who was a stranger to you back in London?"

Someone of the *Elizabeth Galley*'s crew, thinking the Moor taken, had told Elizabeth it was safe to come topside again.

"Is she a stranger to you still, Marlowe? Have you no care of what happens to her? Or do you think mayhaps you will cooperate with me?"

In the end it was cooperation. Marlowe rummaged through the great cabin of the Moorish ship, more like a setting for some sort of harem than a ship's cabin, under the close scrutiny of three heavily armed guards. At last he found the ship's ledger books and a silver writing set. He flipped through one of the ledgers. It was crammed with items written in a tight scrawl, the Indian letters utterly foreign. But the second half of the book was blank, and Marlowe reckoned he could use that to take the inventory in English.

Press did not intend to keep the Moorish ship. He did not explain his intentions to Marlowe, but then he did not have to. Taking the ship would have been pointless; dealing with her poor sailing qualities and the four hundred or so prisoners on board would have been more aggravation than the ship was worth.

No, Press would empty her hold into his own ship, rob the people on board of whatever valuables they had, and then let them go on their way. It was the only logical plan. It was what Marlowe had intended to do.

As the hatches were broken open and the Elizabeth Galleys forced at gunpoint to go below and begin breaking bulk on the valuable cargo, Press's ship came up over the horizon. She was a fast one, and big. A former man-of-war, Marlowe guessed. He thought perhaps he had seen her on the Thames, back in London. That would make sense.

"Lovely, ain't she?" Press asked, and Marlowe cursed himself for letting Press see him staring at her.

"*Queen's Venture*. A gang of these rich bastards with the East India Company hired me to command her. I negotiated for half the prize money. But now I reckon I'll just take all the prize money. Why go back and be a wealthy gentleman in England when I can be an even wealthier king on St. Mary's, eh?"

"Roger, it's hard for me to figure anything I could care less about," Marlowe assured him.

"Yes, you always did lack direction, young sir. So here is something to keep your mind on your work."

Two of Press's men led Elizabeth onto the Moor's deck, her wrists bound in front of her. They pushed her down to a sitting position and tied her wrists to a ring bolt in the deck.

"Just a reminder." Press grinned. He held the toothpick between his teeth and waggled it with his tongue.

Marlowe looked at him, expressionless. *I am going to rip your sodding heart out*, he thought.

It took another hour for Press's men to move the *Bloody Revenge* and to maneuver the *Queen's Venture* alongside, but soon the two ships, the *Elizabeth Galley* and the *Queen's Venture*, were tied to either side of the Moor, a floating island of wood and cordage, with the *Bloody Revenge* and her skeleton crew hove to a cable length away. Roger Press's private flotilla, an armada of Red Sea Rovers.

The Elizabeth Galleys and the Bloody Revenges did the work while Press and his men oversaw the operation at gunpoint. The great wealth of the Mogul's ship was swayed up from the hold and left to hang over the gaping cavern of the Moorish ship's main hatch while Marlowe wrote down a careful description of whatever it was, along with the quantity in the column provided in the ledger book.

Press made regular inspections of his work, kept a close eye on him as he did his inventory. There was no need for further threats against Elizabeth. Both men understood how things lay.

When a guard from the hold dragged one of Billy Bird's men topside and reported that he had caught the man slipping a loose coin into his shirt, Press smiled and gave the order to hang him, then and there.

The man kicked his way up to the end of the main yard, and when he was dead, his body was left in place, like a pirate hanged in chains as a warning to honest mariners. The execution took ten minutes, and then it was back to work.

The *Queen's Venture*, being largely empty of stores after her voyage from England, absorbed a great deal of the Moorish treasure, but even her big, cavernous hold could not take it all. Once she was full, hatches were broken open aboard the *Elizabeth Galley*, barrels of food and water jettisoned, and Marlowe's former ship—Press's newest—was loaded with the last of the take.

It took two full days, bobbing along in the Gulf of Aden, to empty the Great Mogul's ship, so prodigious was the treasure she carried aboard. As the sun set on the second day and Marlowe handed his last ledger book to Press, the third he had filled, Press smiled at him and said, "An excellent job, my dear Marlowe, excellent. You know, I had thought I would kill you now. Thought perhaps I'd bugger your pretty wife in front of you and then kill you, but Lord, I am far too tired for that! So much booty!

"So I think instead I will stow you safe away and let you wonder what I am doing to your wife, and then, when we get back to St. Mary's, then I will kill you. It is far more amusing to think of you all alone, pondering your fate. You may think of me and how I sat in agony for eight days on that accursed strip of sand on which you left me. Do you recall, Marlowe? I hope so. Because I want you to think about it. You will have ample time."

He was no longer smiling when he finished his speech and waved for two of the guards to take Marlowe away.

Marlowe glared at him. He wanted to shout, to threaten, to assure Press that he, Marlowe, would kill him slowly and painfully if he touched Elizabeth. But it was pointless, and if he made Press angry, then that anger might be vented on Elizabeth, so Marlowe kept his mouth shut and let the guards lead him off.

They took him down into the cable tier of the *Queen's Venture*. It was the very lowest part of the ship, where the coils of hemp cable sat on a platform that kept them just a foot above the water in the bilge. It was a black, humid, and stinking place, with rats rushing about in the dark.

The guards sat Marlowe on a small open part of the platform and chained him hand and foot to a ring bolt driven into a heavy timber brace. They secured the bolts in the hand and leg irons, tested them, and when they found them secure, they left him.

He sat on the rough deck and tried not to let the despair sweep him away. On the Moorish ship the work was done, and Press was letting his men have their fun with the prisoners. Even so many decks down, and on board another ship, Marlowe could hear the screams of men, the shrieks and sobs of women, laughter, gunshots.

He could picture what was happening on board the Moor. He had seen it all before, on other ships and other oceans. He wondered what part Elizabeth was being made to play, but he pushed that thought aside. He would go mad for certain if he let himself think along those lines.

He contented himself with the thought that Press would not harm Elizabeth until they were back at St. Mary's at least. Press would not do anything to her unless Marlowe was watching. He assured himself that he, Thomas Marlowe—Malachias Barrett—would kill every whoreson one of them, and he left it at that. He did not consider how realistic that thought was.

At some point Marlowe passed out from exhaustion, only to be tortured by nightmare dreams. When he awoke, he was in the cable tier still, still alone. He stared into the gloom, but even with his eyes adjusted as they were to the dark, he could see nothing beyond vague shapes.

He lay very motionless and listened. There was a great chorus of scratching as the rats scurried around the place, but there was little beyond that. The bacchanal on board the Moor was over. He did not know if it was day or night, but he was quite certain from the movement of the vessel that they were still hove to.

His legs and arms were stiff. He needed very much to relieve himself. He looked up at the dark deck overhead, could see nothing. He considered shouting out, calling for the irons to be removed so he could use the head. Wondered if anyone would hear him.

But as he considered it, he realized that Press would not allow the irons to come off, not so Marlowe could use the jakes. This was part of the torment, making him wallow in his own filth. He felt the despair rising again. He fumbled to undo his breeches under the constraints of the irons, then shuffled along the deck until he was at the end of the chains and there did his business as best as he could. It was disgusting, humiliating. Torture. That was the idea.

And so Marlowe established the one spot on deck that was the head and then, at the other extreme of his chains, the place where he lay.

Back away from the latrine area he tried to stand, but the chains would not allow it, so he sat upright as much as he could. He tried to concentrate, but soon his mind began to wander, and so he let it, and when it tended toward dark thoughts, he steered it toward pleasant reverie.

He was picturing himself riding the fields at Marlowe House under a blue sky when he heard activity above, feet running, the muted shouting of orders, the creak of the rudder communicated through the timbers of the ship. He listened hard, tried to separate the sounds.

After some time he felt the ship heel over—not the wallow of the ship in the swells but the heel of a vessel under a press of canvas. He heard the gurgling note of water running down their sides.

They were under way. To where, he did not know, nor did he know with what ships they were sailing in company. He did not know if his own men were still alive, what had become of Elizabeth. All he knew was the blackness and what little he could divine from the sounds, three decks up, and that was very little indeed.

It was a full day at least before someone brought him food and water, and by then his every lucid thought was concentrated on his hunger and thirst, though the lucid ones were getting further and further between. In his croaking, parched voice he asked the man where they were, what time was it, what of his crew. But the man just set down the weevily biscuit and the half-cooked salt pork and the pewter pint cup of water and left with never a word.

And so it went every day, once a day, when some dimly seen figure appeared with the barest scraps of food and just enough water to keep him alive. After a few days Marlowe did not bother to ask.

He guessed that they were bringing his meals at inconsistent times, just to throw him off regarding day or night. He did not think it would matter. Darkness or sunlight made no difference in the cable tier. He slept, woke whenever. Prayed for the hours to pass.

But as day dragged into weary day, he found himself becoming desperate to know the hour beyond his black pit. It was a need he did not understand, but it was as powerful as his hunger or thirst. What time was it? What watch? Was it daytime or night? Something, anything beyond the darkness and the rats, but he could not find out. There was nothing, only the shadowy figure with the food and water. Once a day, he guessed. He could never predict when.

He thought of the one voyage he had made as an ordinary seaman aboard a slaver, thought of those poor people chained down as he was now. Was it better for them, to have others there? The slavers tried to mix up the tribes so that there could be little communication. Was it worse, being jammed in with others with whom you could not speak?

The slaves at least were given some time on deck, which he was not. On the other hand, the Africans had no notion of what was happening to them or where they were bound, whereas Marlowe knew exactly. Was his lot better or worse? He did not know. He knew only that he now shared with those people the bond of suffering, when before he had felt only sympathy.

After some time—a week, perhaps, perhaps more or less—he found he could not maintain a rational line of thought. He tried, concentrated on some problem or other: how to get a ship off her beam ends without cutting her masts away, where the best spot would be to clear woods for new tobacco plants at Marlowe House; what would be the ideal layout, rig, and armament for a privateer.

But trying to maintain this train of thought was like grabbing an armful of smoke, and his mind wandered off into crazy and unconnected images. He was going mad, and it frightened him more than anything ever had.

And the thing that saved him from madness, as it turned out, was also the thing that nearly killed him.

He was lying on his side, not asleep, not awake, but in that half-conscious state in which he spent more and more of his black hours. The vessel was rising and falling as it plowed close-hauled through a short chop: up, pause, down, thump as the bow hit the wave; up, pause, down, thump.

It was a rhythm that had become ingrained in him years before, through countless hours of walking the decks of vessels on that point of sail. He might not know the time of day, but he could generally guess from the motion of the ship the sea state and the *Queen's Venture's* point of sail. In his nightmare world he sometimes thought he was on the quarterdeck, sometimes thought he was sleeping in his great cabin or wounded and dying on the deck, and sometimes he recalled he was chained in the cable tier.

He lay there, eyes sometimes closed, sometimes open—it made no difference—and smelled the stink of the bilges and his own waste, which he hardly noticed, heard the scurry of the ubiquitous rats, which seemed to be even more active that night. Or day. Whatever it was.

Thomas Marlowe drifted in and out of consciousness and only slowly became aware of the cold inching over him. He felt it creeping over his legs that were sprawled down the sloping deck, a numbing chill, reckoned it was death come for him at last. It was not the sensation he would have expected.

He reached slowly down with his hand, wondering if he could still feel his legs, and his hand came down in water, and suddenly he was alert, sitting bolt upright, his eyes open, all the cobwebs of nightmare washed clean away.

"Dear God," he said, and his voice sounded odd, and he realized he had not spoken in days, perhaps weeks. He reached out with his hands in the darkness, and everywhere around him swirled cold ocean water, rushing unimpeded. The *Queen's Venture* was sinking.

"Dear God," he said again. He could tell from the ship's motion that they were not in any severe weather. She must have sprung a plank. Some rotten wood in her hull, undetected, waiting like a weak spot in a dam to go, and when it did, in came the water, fast.

The water was over the lower edge of the cable tier and creeping higher, gushing in from whatever breach had been knocked in the hull. He strained to listen for the sounds of panic topside: rushing feet, shouted orders, hatches torn back to give all possible light to the carpenter and his mates as they searched for the leak and tried to drive a plug into it. But there was nothing. They did not know.

For a moment he considered keeping his mouth shut. Let the water rise up around him, drown him, deny Roger Press the pleasure. How long would it take them to discover the leak? If he kept quiet, perhaps the *Queen's Venture* would sink, and Press would be made to endure the agony of watching both Marlowe and the treasure of a lifetime sink beyond his reach.

But he would not do that. The cold seawater had washed him clean of his ennui, had woken him from his dream stupor. The feel and smell of the ocean invigorated him, and he was ready once again to fight.

"Hoa! On deck!" he shouted, and his voice cracked and his hail was unimpressive. He swallowed, coughed, and tried again. "Hoa! On deck! Deck there! You've sprung a bloody plank! Hoa!" He shouted until he felt his throat begin to ache, but there was no response. He wondered if they thought it was a ruse, if they thought he had gone mad, if they were all gathered around the hatch, listening and laughing.

"Hoa! On deck!" he shouted again, and finally he heard the sound of bare feet on the ladder, coming down to the cable tier.

"You there, you've sprung a bloody plank, and you may want to see to it," Marlowe shouted, not so loud. There was no response. He was certain Press had told the men not to communicate with him. But the footfalls grew closer, and he could see the vague shape of a man in the dark.

He heard feet come down in the water, an intake of breath, and the man said, "Goddamn it!" then turned and raced topside again.

Another moment's quiet, and then the panic that Marlowe expected broke loose. Over the groaning of the ship and the sloshing of water inside and outside the hull, he could hear orders shouted, men racing in a hundred directions, hatches pulled off. The ship came more upright, and the water that was filling the hold, and which had been confined to the low side of the heeling vessel, washed over Marlowe, almost up to his waist in his sitting position. He knew they had hove to. They had to take the pressure off the leak until they found it.

He saw the loom of lanterns above him as the carpenter and his mates raced down from above, and then he saw the lights as the gang clambered down into the hold. He had to turn his eyes from them, the brightest he had seen in weeks.

The carpenter ignored him as he plunged into the knee-high water and made his difficult way forward. In his wake came three men carrying hammers, crowbars, and wooden plugs. They disappeared forward, and soon Marlowe could see only the glow of their lanterns, illuminating stacks of barrels and the bundles of loot that he himself had inspected.

At the same time he heard the sound of the pumps. It was another sound that was familiar to him, his having heard it on a daily basis, generally for an hour or so a day, which was not a lot. But now the sound was different, faster and higher-pitched, and he knew the men were working the pump brakes with the proper urgency.

The water was creeping over Marlowe's waist, and he wondered whether he would be released from the chains if it rose much higher. He did not think so. From forward he heard one of the carpenter's mates shout, "Here! Over here! Damn me!"

There followed the sloshing of men hurrying through deep water and then the carpenter's voice, loud with urgency: "Go tell the captain there's a plank sprung, just between the aftermost cant-timbers on the starboard side, right by the turn of the bilge. Tell him I'm going to try and plug the bastard, but he best make ready to fother a sail over it!"

The carpenter's mate rushed past and up. *Fother a sail. Damn*, Marlowe thought. The carpenter did not think he could plug the leak. It was so bad that Press would have to take an old sail and pull it over the hole from the outside of the ship and let the pressure of the inflowing water hold it in place.

Suddenly, drowning was a real possibility. But it did not frighten him. The excitement, the danger, the edge of panic were nothing but a relief to him after the darkness.

Marlowe listened intently, and with the hatches thrown open he could hear a great deal of what was taking place on the weather deck. He could hear the orders flying around as the sail was lowered over the side and the instructions relayed back and forth from the carpenter, who was still in the hold, and the officers on the deck above.

It took an hour of the most intense activity before the sail was fothered over the leak. The water was up to the middle of Marlowe's chest when at last it stopped rising and slowly, slowly receded as the pumps caught up with the inflow. The weary carpenter staggered aft and climbed back up without a glance in Marlowe's direction.

Another hour, and the water was back below the cable tier, and the *Queen's Venture* was under way, the old routine begun again. But Marlowe was no longer lost in his own misery. He was alive, alert, his mind working clean and fast.

For two more days, by his estimate, he sat chained to the cable tier. And then without warning he felt the motion of the ship change, and he guessed that they had come into sheltered water. And then hands began to pull the anchor cable up from the cable tier and ready it for running, and Marlowe knew they had arrived somewhere. He guessed it was St. Mary's.

This, he knew, was what Press had been waiting for. This was where Press intended to finish him. But Thomas Marlowe was no longer afraid or desperate or ready for death. Now he was simply ready.

Chapter 23

ST. MARY'S. It was only the second time that Roger Press had sailed into that open roadstead, past Quail Island and into the harbor, but already it felt like a homecoming. The southeasterly wind had driven his three ships easily up the channel between the little island and Madagascar, and just enough breeze reached into the harbor to give the ships steerage way as they ghosted toward their anchorage.

On the big house atop the hill and the gun batteries on Quail Island, the Union Jack flapped in the puffs of wind that blew from the sea. The lush green of the jungle spread up and away from the dilapidated town, shot through with bursts of flowers like exploding grenadoes. There were a few ships riding at their anchors, Red Sea Rovers and island traders and, of course, the *Speedwell*. It was just as he had left it. It was his home now, his kingdom.

Then, from one of the batteries at the big house, a plume of white smoke, shot from the mouth of a cannon. Press started, bit down on the toothpick. And then, a second later, the flat *pow* of the gun and a second plume of smoke from the gun next to it. *Pow*, and a third plume. No fall of shot. Press smiled. Tasker had arranged a salute. Good man.

Seventeen guns, the sound rolling around the harbor. Press let his eyes linger on the Union Jack as he rolled the toothpick across the roof of his mouth. Perhaps that was not the flag to fly. Perhaps he needed a flag of his own. Perhaps a red flag with a picture of his enemies screaming as they are crushed beneath a plank piled high with stone. Press. He smiled at the thought.

The *Queen's Venture* led the way, standing in under topsails. Up on the foredeck, former third officer, now acting first officer Josiah Brownlaw stood ready to let the best bower go. Clayford was off in the *Elizabeth Galley*, and the *Venture's* second, Mark Montgomery, was in command of the *Bloody Revenge*. They were spread pretty thin. But now they were home.

Just behind where Brownlaw stood at the cathead was the spiderweb of ropes that held the fothered sail in place. That had been a near thing, the butt end of a plank rotted clean away. If Marlowe had not called out, there was no telling when they might have found out about the leak. Perhaps when the *Queen's Venture* filled and capsized. The carpenter had been none too diligent about sounding the well, but once the leak was stopped and Press had thrashed him soundly, he had become far more attentive to his duties.

It was ironic, Press thought, that Marlowe had saved them. It would not change in the least the horrible death he had planned for his former quartermaster, the man who had marooned him. But it was ironic.

They crossed the harbor and came to a spot two cables from the old wooden pier, and Press called, "Clew up, fore and main topsails! Round up! Let go!"

Overhead the topsails rose like curtains at a play, and the ship turned up into the wind, and Brownlaw gave the signal for the seamen to let the anchor go. It plunged into the blue harbor, and the *Queen's Venture* crept astern and then stopped. Press looked over the side. He could see the anchor cable for some distance through the water, clear as glass.

To larboard and just to windward of the *Queen's Venture*, the *Elizabeth Galley* turned up into the wind and dropped her hook, moving under the expert command of Israel Clayford. Thirty feet away, and Clayford let his anchor go. Thin messenger lines, their ends tied in bulky monkey's fists, sailed across the gap and landed with little thumps on the *Queen's Venture's* decks. The men grabbed them up, hauled them aboard. Attached to the bitter ends were heavier cables to bind the ships together, and they came snaking over the open water as the men pulled them in, hand over hand.

The *Queen's Venture* was a tired ship, a battered pugilist who could no longer stand on his own, but needed to fling an arm over his comrade's shoulder for support. They would raft the two ships together, the *Queen's Venture* and the *Elizabeth Galley*, and the *Galley* would keep the *Venture* afloat. The fothered sail had slowed the leak, but it had not stopped it. If another plank gave way, then the *Galley* might be the only thing preventing Press's flagship from sinking to the bottom.

The first order of business would be to remove the booty from her unstable hold. Then careen her on his beach, set her to rights again.

Press watched the cables come across the water. Brownlaw had one of the midships lines taken to the capstan, while on the *Galley's* deck Clayford had the same done with the other. A few minutes of rigging the capstans, and then the crews of the two ships were stamping them around, drawing the two vessels together.

On the starboard side the *Bloody Revenge* came to an anchor with her main topsail aback.

Roger Press shook his head as he marveled at the sight. Two big ships, man-of-war built. The sloop *Speedwell*, the brig *Bloody Revenge*. He had a squadron under his command, the most powerful concentrated force on the Indian Ocean. Why stop at St. Mary's? He had the means now for greater conquest.

It took half an hour to raft the two ships to one another. Press, growing increasingly agitated, paced, jabbed his gums with the toothpick. He had expected Tasker to come down to greet him. Scribner, the boatswain of the *Speedwell*, who had been left in charge of the tender, had come across in a boat moments after the *Venture* had come to an anchor. He reported that all was well and that he had not had word from Tasker in some time. And that, Press imagined, was all right with the boatswain. He apparently had made no effort to contact the first officer.

And other than the salute from the batteries, Tasker had made no effort to contact his commanding officer.

Press pictured Tasker and the men in the big house, engaged in a wild drunk, or passed out and asleep. It was not like Tasker, but then Press had seen more than one man lose his wits when pirating got in his blood. It was time to see about this.

"Brownlaw, I want— Belay that, lay aft here!" Brownlaw left off what he was doing and scurried aft. "I want to go ashore. Get the longboat manned and pass the word to Clayford to man his boat as well. Thirty men from his company. I'll take seventy or so men with me. Pistols and cutlasses. Clayford will come with me."

Press was not about to leave Clayford alone with all that treasure underfoot and only a hemp anchor cable holding him in place. Brownlaw, however, was young and lacking in experience, the third son of a minor lord with enough money and sea experience to tempt Press into shipping him. He had that absurd sense of honor that all the aristocracy pretended to. He could manage things in Press's absence, but he did not have the guts or the guile to betray his captain. "You are in command of the ships until I return. We may need to do a bit of disciplining up there."

"Aye, sir," Brownlaw said, and he turned to comply, but Press said, "Hold a minute . . ."

Roger Press paused and stared up at the big house and ran the numbers over in his head. Between the *Queen's Venture* and the *Speedwell* he had somewhere around 250 men. He was taking a hundred with him. Another twenty or so were sick or injured from the fighting. That would leave nearly as many prisoners as men on board the three ships.

That would not do. Not with Marlowe and Billy Bird and that other one—Bickerstaff—still aboard. Any of those might organize the men, take back their ships and all the booty that he, Press, had captured. No, that would not do at all.

"Also, we'll take . . . fifty of the prisoners out of here, lock 'em up in the prisons in the big house. Make certain that little fop Bird is with them and Bickerstaff as well. Get Marlowe out of the hold and his doxy from the cabin."

"Aye, sir." Brownlaw hurried off to see those orders carried out.

Press liked to make a show. The couple hundred half-drunk pirates and whores who were the residents of St. Mary's would have dubious loyalty at best to anyone claiming sovereignty over the island. But Press knew their type, knew they respected power in the form of men and arms. So he would win their respect by displaying, as often as necessary, how much of each he had under his command.

One hundred armed men and fifty prisoners would do nicely.

Ten minutes, and the boats were manned. Elizabeth was brought up from the cabin where she had been held since they had set sail in the Gulf of Aden. She had not been molested in any way. Press had considered it, but in the end he had done nothing. His mind was too full of other concerns.

It was enough that Marlowe thought he was having his way with her. He would save the actual doing of it until Marlowe could watch.

Then, from the after scuttle, Marlowe emerged, hands bound before him. He looked as Press had imagined he would. Two weeks' growth of beard, filthy, pale, squinting, and limping. His clothing was torn, his stockings around his ankles, his hair was a matted tangle. He looked like what he was—a broken man. Press hoped he still had enough of a spark left in him to take an interest in his own death and that of his wife.

"Marlowe, glad you could join us," Press said, grinning, waggling the toothpick.

Marlowe looked at him, his head cocked, his eyes like slits. "I feel much refreshed, Captain Press. Are your saltwater baths for everyone or only honored guests?"

Press frowned, looked hard at Marlowe. He had not expected a flip response, had not really expected any response at all. He reckoned that Marlowe would be a jabbering idiot after two and a half weeks chained in the cable tier, with just enough food and water to keep him alive, meals served at odd hours to throw off his sense of day or night, not a one man allowed to speak to him.

But he was not a jabbering idiot, not a broken wreck. There was still a spark there, a bright one, and Press wanted to stamp it out like an ember from the fireplace that has fallen on the rug.

But time for that later. "Get them in the gig, let us go," Press said, and he climbed down into the longboat, holding his sword out of the way as he sat in the stern sheets.

It was a short pull over smooth water to the dock. Press stepped ashore, his men behind them, and they waited there as the boats went back for the prisoners. Filthy, ragged, they were led up from below, and Clayford sorted them out, organized them, and bound their wrists.

Soon Press had his army assembled behind him, with the prisoners in their midst, and he led them once more through the town—his town now—and up the hill toward the big house. He tramped on, expressionless, but his eyes moved like a raptor's over the building and the grounds in the distance.

He could see no signs of life, no party there to greet him. Tasker had to know he was back—he had saluted the squadron. So where was he?

The emotions started to roil in Press's mind. Anger, concern, disappointment. But mostly anger. He picked up his pace, his long, thin legs moving fast, and the men behind him struggled to keep up.

The big gate in the stockade was closed, and there were no guards there, though Press had instructed Tasker to keep two at least posted at all times. Press pushed on the gate. It swung open, unlatched and unimpeded, and he stepped through to the empty grounds in front of the house.

He could hear noise now, shouting and yelling and . . . singing. He cocked his ear. Yes, it was singing, coming from the great hall. "Tasker, you worthless son of a bitch," Press muttered, "letting those bastards go on a drunk."

He let his eyes move over the house and the grounds, and they fell on a figure sitting motionless by the wide landing at the main entrance to the house. He was propped against the side of the house, unmoving, and he looked unhappily familiar.

"Come along," Press said over his shoulder, stepping quickly across the open ground, his men filing in through the gate and following behind.

Halfway to the main door, and Press could see that the figure slumped against the building was Tasker. He held a bottle of rum cradled in his arm like a baby, his head was resting against the stone wall of the house. He was not moving.

"You stupid, stupid bastard," Press said and moved faster still, already picturing the swift kick he would give his now-former second in command.

Ten yards from the man, and Press slowed, then stopped. Tasker did not look at all well. His face was gray and pinched, and there was something unnatural about the way he sat. He looked, in fact, like he was dead.

Roger Press felt a sick twist in his gut, and the memory of Nombre de Dios sprang unbidden into his head. He had planned it all, executed it perfectly. Sent Marlowe and the others off to their certain death, distracted the Spaniards while he and his chosen few made off with the booty. He had only to get the take into the boats and go; he had been that close. But Marlowe had not been killed. He had appeared at the landing, and Press's whole plan had collapsed around him.

Why did that memory come to him now?

Press approached Tasker slowly, looked the motionless figure over carefully as he did. The man was dead. There was no mistaking it. What had killed him? Was the yellow jack there? The plague? Had he drunk himself to death?

Press looked around, as if he might see the answer somewhere in the compound.

And then a musket fired, the double crack of priming and powder, and the dust leaped at Press's feet, and Press leaped back, looked up. From every window of the great house men leaned out, muskets aimed down, and suddenly the grounds contained by the stockade wall became a pen to hold animals for the slaughter.

Press whirled around. More men charging in from the open gate, muskets leveled, ready to shoot down any of Press's men who reached for a pistol or unslung a musket from their shoulders.

He whirled again. More men charging from around the house on either side. Men with the look of pirates, with pistols and muskets and cutlasses. As many men as Press had. More, perhaps, and with their guns leveled and ready.

One of these men stepped forward, a big man, taller than Press even, and weighing three stone more. "Every one of you bastards, drop your firelocks or we'll shoot you down!"

Press whirled around again, turned a half circle, too stunned to speak, and before he found his voice, before he could order his men to fight to the last, they tossed aside their weapons and put their hands meekly before them. The prisoners held their bound wrists aloft to show that they were no threat.

"Over there!" the big man said, nodding with his jutting beard toward the stockade wall and pointing with one of the two pistols he held. Press's men began to back away, leaving behind a pile of muskets and pistols lying in the dust where they had been dropped.

And still Roger Press could not speak.

"Ah, Roger Press, I reckoned you'd come calling someday."

Press whirled around again. *No, no, no! It cannot be!*

Elephiant Yancy, standing next to the lifeless body of Jacob Tasker. He grinned, gave Tasker's body a push with his foot, and the dead man fell forward onto the ground.

Press felt the scream building, deep inside. "Aaaahhhh, you son of a bitch!" he shouted, the sound escalating, and then he charged forward, pushing past the big man, his eyes focused on Yancy's throat.

And then he stopped, doubled over, thought for an instant he had been shot, but in fact the big man had hit him in the stomach. He collapsed to the ground, gasping, thrashing in the dust.

"Roger, Roger, oh dear," he heard Yancy say. "You never did know how to be a proper guest. You did not when I saved you from that spit of sand, do you recall? Tried to lead a mutiny against me. I reckon you weren't such a good guest for the Dons neither. The Inquisition don't like it when someone gets out alive. Not a pirate anyway."

Press sucked air into his lungs. A thousand words crowded in his head, but none could get out. He heard Yancy's feet on the stone steps and then on the ground, and he knew the little bastard was standing over him, but Press would not give him the satisfaction of looking up.

"So you lie at my feet once more?" he heard Yancy say.

"I'll kill you for this," Press gasped, the first words to find voice.

"Yes, yes. God, but you are tiresome." Yancy paused. Press braced himself for a kick or a blow, but instead he heard Yancy gasp as well. "Oh, Roger, is it possible?" Yancy asked. "Have you brought me Thomas Marlowe, too? And Elizabeth?" Yancy laughed, his high-pitched, squeaking laugh. It always reminded Press of a rat being crushed underfoot.

"Oh, Roger, my beauty," Yancy said when he had finished laughing, "you could not have done more for me if you had brought me the treasure of the Great Mogul himself!"

Chapter 24

MARLOWE THREADED his arms through the iron bars of the cell, looked across the stone-floored alleyway to the cell facing him.

"Lord, Roger, is there any damned thing you haven't made a hash of?" he called across the open space. "You were the richest man in Christendom for . . . what? Two weeks? And then you deliver it all to Yancy like it was a tribute. Lord, what a dumb arse."

"Shut your fucking gob." The voice came from the dark cell, the speaker unseen.

They were in the prison in the big house, built into the lowest part of the building, under the first floor. The prison consisted of no more than two big stone rooms fronted with iron bars that faced each other across a six-foot-wide walk. The cells were cool and damp and lit by only a single window in each, a slit eight inches high and two feet across set at the top of the wall.

A lone flight of steps led from the alleyway up to the first floor. Two steps, a landing, and then a 180-degree turn and five more steps up to the grand entrance. A bored guard sat in a chair at the bottom of the stairs. There was no need for more. The cells were impenetrable, the iron bars thick and sound.

Marlowe, Bickerstaff, Honeyman, and Billy Bird, along with their men, those who had come ashore as prisoners, were in the one cell. Two-thirds of Press's captured men were in the cell opposite, with Press. A third had elected to join Yancy.

More than a third, actually, but Yancy was not so stupid as to allow too many men of dubious loyalty into his personal army. Yancy chose the few he wanted, locked up the rest.

Yancy had kept warring crews apart. Marlowe guessed he did not want them killing one another. That was Yancy's office. He figured that Yancy would not have locked up the officers with the men if there had been more than two cells, but there was not.

What had become of the rest of the men of the *Elizabeth Galley* and the *Bloody Revenge*, Marlowe did not know. He imagined they were still battened down aboard their respective ships, their guards waiting for word from Press. He reckoned Yancy would take them in his own time.

He did not know where Elizabeth was, but he could guess.

Marlowe wondered if his circumstances were any better or worse now than they had been three hours before, when he had been Roger Press's prisoner. His concern for Elizabeth was the greatest thing on his mind, and that had not changed at all.

But now at least he had Roger Press's profound misery to cheer him. "You should have killed me, Press. You pissed that opportunity away. Now Yancy will butcher you, and you'll never have the chance."

"Butcher me? I reckon he's butchering that little doxy of yours right now. Thrumming her good. What do you say to that, Marlowe?"

"I say he tried that before and nearly lost his whole damned house. Elizabeth can take care of herself." He spoke the words with a confidence he did not feel. But he would not let Press exploit his one area of genuine fear.

"Captain said 'shut your gob,' " Israel Clayford said. He was leaning against the iron bars of the cell he shared with Press, six feet away. He was a big bastard, and mean-looking.

"Don't you get into this," Marlowe said to him. "Captain's a dead one. You just look to your own neck."

Then Press emerged from the gloom and ran his hands through the bars, like Marlowe, and faced him. "Look, Marlowe," he said, his voice low, "I know you want to kill me much as I want to kill you. But I say let's set that aside for now, work together. Won't do either of us any good if that bastard Yancy kills us both, will it?"

Marlowe smiled, and then he laughed, and his amusement was genuine. "What you mean is, I help you save your sorry hide and then you stab me in the back again?"

"Damn your eyes, Marlowe! Don't you see that we're both dead if we don't work together, and it ain't going to be pleasant, I'll warrant. I say—"

The guard was up, and with two steps he was in front of the cell. He slammed the flat of his sword against the iron bars. Press jumped back in surprise, shouted, "You whoreson!"

"None of that," the guard growled, looking at Press and then Marlowe. "I hear one more goddamned word like that and one of you goes in the pit."

Marlowe and Press glared at the guard, and the guard glared back as he retreated to his chair by the steps. Marlowe did not know what the pit was. He did not care to find out.

How they were going to get off St. Mary's alive, he had no idea.

Elizabeth was stretched out on the big four-poster bed in Yancy's bedchamber. The space was lit softly with candles placed around, throwing off pools of light, while the rest of the big room was lost in shadow. In another circumstance she might have found the room lovely, warm and romantic.

Her wrists were bound tightly together and tied to the bed's headboard, forcing her into her supine position. She gritted her teeth and pulled, jerked at the constraints, worked her wrists under the rough cordage.

She had been struggling for twenty minutes, and her wrists were raw and bleeding in places, and she was no freer now than she had been when Henry Nagel first forced her onto the bed and lashed her in place.

"Son of a bitch, son of a bitch . . ." she muttered as she struggled and then finally gave up, let her body go limp, exhausted from the effort. "Oh, God . . ." she whispered.

Yancy had learned his lesson the last time, apparently, about letting Elizabeth wander free in the room in which she was imprisoned. She knew that as long as she remained tied as she was, Yancy was free to do as he pleased. She might be able to get in a good kick or two, but in the end he could rape her to his heart's content.

"Oh, God . . ." she said again, giving in to the despair.

She had been alone in the room for an hour. At first she had not dared move, but she lay very still and listened, hoping to hear something that would give her some indication of what was happening.

Yancy had sprung his trap, had marched Press's men and Thomas and Billy and Francis and their men off to some prison, she supposed. She had been held at gunpoint in the grand entrance while the men were led down a half-concealed stairway to a level below the house. From there she had been taken to the great hall, alone but for the three guards who stood over her.

For two hours Elizabeth had sat there before Nagel had come back and taken her to Yancy's bedchamber. She did not know what had become of the others, if Thomas was alive or if Yancy had killed him already. She did not know what would happen to her, but she could guess.

Her eyes moved again to the swords mounted on the wall. A pair of long, thin, cup-hilt rapiers, crossed and mounted as decoration, they were very like the weapons with which Bickerstaff had taught her sword work. If she could just get her wrists free and get one of those weapons in her hands, she could skewer the filthy insect as he came in the door.

She struggled anew against her bonds, clenched her teeth against the agony of her raw flesh, but it was no use. Nagel was a sailor. He knew how to tie things so they stayed tied.

Then footsteps in the hall, light footfalls, and she knew it was not Nagel. She lay still, listened to them growing closer, and she was sure that the soft, quick steps were those of Elephiant Yancy. There would be no getting out of this through brute force alone, no chance to run him through as he entered the room. She had no choice now but to play the willing lover, if only until her hands were free.

The thought of it was as revolting as that of being forcibly raped.

The footsteps stopped. The door to Yancy's bedchamber, like all the doors to all the bedchambers in the big house, had a heavy lock that could be worked from inside the room or out. Each room could function as either sanctuary or prison.

Elizabeth heard the key turn in the lock on the other side of the door. The door swung in. Half lost in the shadows was Elephiant Yancy, wearing his rich silk clothing, his long cape with its red lining trailing behind him. He stood there for a moment and looked at her, and she tried to look back in an alluring, come-to-me manner, but it was hard, being tied as she was. She reckoned that the sight of her lashed to the bed was all the allure the little prick would need.

"Elephiant, where have you been?" she asked, as if she cared.

Yancy stepped into the room, and then Elizabeth could see his thin weasel face, the carefully groomed mustache and goatee, which he stroked as he watched her, as was his habit. He believed that the gesture made him look thoughtful and intelligent, she could tell.

He turned and closed the door and locked it, set the key on the table by the door, then crossed the room, stepping with authority and confidence. "It has been a busy day, my dear, a most busy day. But I need not tell you that." He whirled his cape off, tossed it on a nearby chair.

"I have no doubt," Elizabeth said soothingly. "That beast Nagel has tied me up. Let me loose and I'll rub your shoulders. You need a soft touch."

Yancy took a step toward her. "That beast Nagel tied you up on my orders. You nearly burned my house down, when last you was here. Do you recall?"

"Me? You think that was my fault? I have no notion how the fire started, though I do recall it nearly killed me. But come, let me make it up to you."

He smiled down at her, then tossed his head back and laughed. "I am not so much a fool, you know, as to think you want me in that way!

You'll have me, want me or no, but I'll not be tricked into thinking you hold some great love for me. Someday you will. But not now."

"How do you know? You are a handsome man, and a powerful one. Perhaps I do have some feelings for you."

"Perhaps. But what will you do if I untie you, eh? Fight me? Punch me? Kick me? What will you do?" He stepped over to the bed, ran a finger down her cheek, down her neck, over her breasts. Elizabeth closed her eyes, made a purring sound as between closed lips she clenched her teeth.

"What will you do, my lovely?"

She opened her eyes. "Why don't you let me free and see?" she said, just a whisper.

Yancy ran his fingertip over her face again. "I will." He reached around his waist and pulled out his long, needle-thin stiletto, held it up, let the candlelight dance off the blade. "I am not such a fool," he said again. "But I think I will like it if you fight. These native girls are so very passive, they will lay down with never a struggle. I think I will like a bit of a challenge."

Elizabeth lay very still as he moved the knife past her face, less than an inch from her skin. She felt the tip of the blade touch her arm, as light as a feather, and Yancy ran the point gently up the length of her arm until she felt the steel against her wrists, and with a quick motion he cut the bonds away.

"Oh," Elizabeth moaned involuntarily. A great wave of relief flowed over her as she lowered her arms, gently rubbed the raw flesh on her wrists.

Yancy had made a grave mistake. Her arms and her wrists had ached so much, she had been so very helpless, that her will and her strength had begun ebbing fast away, and she had not even realized it. But now the fight was back in her.

She snuggled deeper into the bed, looked into Yancy's eyes, gently bit her lower lip. There was not much about enticement that Elizabeth did not understand.

Yancy tossed the stiletto aside. He was kneeling beside her on the bed, and she ran her hand up his thigh. She turned her head and let a wisp of her long blond hair fall across her cheek.

She did not dare look at the rapiers. But even as she caressed Yancy's leg and his waist and ran her hand up his chest, she was calculating time and distance, gauging whether she was better off going for the weapon or going directly for the door.

Yancy came down on top of her, his hands planted on either side of her, and he began to kiss her neck roughly. She shifted under him, gave a low moan, swallowed hard to try to quell her revulsion. She could make it to the door, she concluded, but she would not have time to grab the key, work the lock and get out, then lock it again from the outside. Not unless Yancy was genuinely disabled. And for that she needed the rapier.

Timing, timing, timing, it was everything, and she knew she had to endure a minute more of his insult. She ran her fingers through his hair, stretched out her neck, forced her mind to concentrate on visions of Marlowe House, her beloved garden, long rides through the fields.

Yancy ran his mouth over her neck and down her chest, and his hands grabbed at her breasts. She could hear his breathing growing raspier. She moved her hand over his back and down his leg, shifted under him. He reached up and tugged at her bodice, kissing her roughly above her breasts, getting swept up in his desire, his former caution forgotten.

Elizabeth pressed her lips together hard, slid her hand along the inside of Yancy's thigh and up. She could feel his erection under the loose fabric of his breeches. She ran her hand along it, and he pressed against her and made a guttural sound and bit her neck. She moved her hand lower, cupped his balls.

Yancy groaned, pressed closer, and then he sensed the danger. He began to push himself off her, and she squeezed him hard, crushing him with a grip grown powerful after half a year at sea.

"Bitch!" Yancy shrieked, tried to stand up on his knees, but the pain doubled him over. Elizabeth let go of his privates, rolled out of the way just as Yancy would have collapsed on top of her.

She rolled off the far side of the bed, hit the floor, and leaped to her feet. "Ahhhh!" Yancy screamed, part pain, part fury. Elizabeth raced around the bed, eyes on the door, thinking, *Perhaps I can make it . . .*

But then Yancy was off the bed, hunched over, staggering for the door, the stiletto in his hand. He was half lost in the deep shadows that filled the room, the little pools of yellow light from the candles. "Go on, go for the door, you rutting bitch! Think you can make it?" he hissed.

Elizabeth stopped, took a step back, reached up, took hold of a rapier on the wall, and pulled it free. The weapon danced in her hand, felt as natural there as her hairbrush or glass, but Yancy did not notice the ease with which she wielded it. He stood between her and the door, straightening slowly, grimacing. "Come on . . . you want to leave, you have to go through me first . . ."

She advanced on him, point of her blade at the height of his eyes. He stood straighter, and his grimace resolved into a grin as the pain subsided. "I said I wanted a fight, and, oh, you do not disappoint, do you, my dear?"

Elizabeth paused. She felt taut, every muscle pulled tight like a ship's rigging. Everything in the dim light seemed sharper, every sound distinct and clear. Yancy was grinning at her, holding the stiletto in front of him. Knife against sword, it did not seem to be such a problem.

She lunged at him, arm extended, back leg straight, forward leg bent, tip thrust at his chest, and to her amazement he caught her blade with the hilt of his stiletto and turned it aside. He tried to twist her blade, to disarm her, but she knew the trick and leaped back, *en garde*, pulling it free.

She lunged again, instantly, automatically, and that move, fast as it was, took Yancy by surprise. He could do no more than leap out of the way of her attack, scrambling around her in satisfying flight as she whirled with him, keeping the tip of her rapier pointed at his chest.

Yancy backed away. "You are no dainty little thing with a blade, I see," he said, sneering, patronizing. "Good, good. I'll cut you a little before I fuck you. Before I kill that bastard Marlowe right before your eyes."

Elizabeth pressed against the door, felt for the key on the table while she kept the tip of her rapier between herself and Yancy.

Yancy stepped back again and again, always facing her. She cursed under her breath and patted the tabletop with her hand, but she could not find the key.

Then Yancy turned and grabbed the second rapier and turned back fast, and Elizabeth could not worry about the door. He held the rapier low, beckoned with the stiletto, now in his left hand. "Come on, come on, try and stick me, you bitch . . ." He circled toward her.

Elizabeth stepped away from the door, gave herself some fighting room, as she had been taught.

Yancy paused. He was waiting for her to make a move, and she knew better than to comply, but she did not have the advantage of time. Every minute might mean someone coming to Yancy's aide. Killing Yancy would do no good if Nagel was waiting outside the door.

She advanced on him, and he held his ground, the point of his rapier on the floor. She lunged, full out, and Yancy's rapier came up and knocked her blade aside, and he slashed out with the stiletto, missing her stomach by half an inch as she leaped back.

Damn me! she thought. Yancy was fast as a snake, faster than Bickerstaff or any of the men she had sparred with. She circled around.

In a blur Yancy was on her, his rapier flicking out, and she parried him by instinct alone—lunge, parry, riposte, parry—the familiar clash of steel on steel in the small room. A slash with the stiletto that threw him off balance, and Elizabeth was able to leap away and then make an awkward lunge. She caught him in the shoulder and sank her blade an inch deep into his flesh before he was able to leap clear.

"Ahhh, damn you, you bloody whore!" he yelled, furious now. He clapped his hand with the rapier over his shoulder, and Elizabeth knew opportunity when she saw it. She lunged again, a running attack.

Too late to parry, Yancy twisted, and her blade, aimed at his chest, caught him in the upper arm and tore through flesh and cloth like a knife cutting meat, and Yancy shrieked and leaped clean away, onto the bed and over it, rolling on the sheets and coming up on his feet on the far side.

Elizabeth turned and raced for the door, tried to find the key among the shadows on the table, but she could hear Yancy coming at her from behind.

She turned back, blade up as he lunged, fully extended. She parried his sword, flicked it aside, and lunged back at him. He caught her blade with the stiletto, pushed it aside and held it down.

They stood facing each other, eyes locked, breath coming fast, both of them too close to use their rapiers. A moment of silence, motionless they stood, and it was as if a year were compressed into that one instant. Elizabeth could smell him, the sweat and perfume and garlic.

She felt the pressure come off her blade as he slashed at her with the stiletto, and she kicked him in the groin. He doubled up, still too close for her to skewer him, so she swung her hand and hit him in the side of the head with the steel cup-hilt of her weapon.

Yancy was knocked sideways by the blow. He staggered, fell, and his head hit the edge of the table as he went down. Elizabeth heard the thump, saw his head jerk in an unnatural way, and then he was lying curled on the floor and still.

She stood, heaving for breath, the tip of her rapier resting on the floor, ready to move if Yancy did. For a full minute she stood there, breathing, watching Yancy for any sign of life, listening for any sound from the hallway. She wondered that all the noise had not brought people running, but perhaps it was not unusual to hear screaming from Yancy's bedchamber.

At last her breathing was under control, and she could hear nothing beyond that. She kicked Yancy's rapier away from him, leaned her own against the wall, and picked up the stiletto. She held it down at her side, ready to strike, and prodded Yancy with her toe. He did not move. She crouched down beside him, felt his neck for a pulse. It took a few tries, but at last she felt it, the life still beating in him, and she did not know if she was happy or not.

She gritted her teeth, rolled him onto his stomach, stepped back, and waited for him to move, but he did not. Another second, then she straddled him, grabbed his hair, pulled his head back, stretching out his neck. She reached around with the stiletto, pressed the razor-sharp blade against his throat, and stopped.

Do it, do it, damn your eyes . . . she cursed herself, but she could not. "Oh, damn me for a weak fool," she whispered, letting Yancy's head drop. His chin hit the floor with a thump, and she heard his teeth snap against each other, but he did not stir.

She stood up, staggered over to the bed. She was very tired, and her body ached. She found the lashings that had held her to the bed, and a few pieces were long enough for her to use. She carried them back to Yancy's prone figure, knelt with her knee in the small of his back.

Along with sword work Elizabeth had learned a great deal about lashing things in her time at sea, it falling to her to secure all of her and Marlowe's things in the great cabin against the roll of the ship, and she applied those skills to Yancy. Round turns around the wrists, crossing turns between, finished off with two half hitches, the bitter end hauled taught betwixt them. Yancy was not going to untie that by himself. She cut off the excess, bent it onto another piece of cordage with a double sheet bend, and served Yancy's ankles out in the same manner.

That done, she tucked the stiletto into her skirt and found the key. She picked up her rapier and unlocked the door, eased it open, peered out into the hall. There were lanterns glowing dimly at either end, but in the muted light she could see nothing else. She stepped back into the room, retrieved the second rapier, then stepped silently into the hall. She closed the door, locked it, moved softly toward the big staircase.

She would find Thomas. If he was alive, she would free him and they would get off the damned island. If he was dead . . .

She pushed that thought aside, moved fast and silent down the hall, the rapier at her side, ready.

Chapter 25

ELIZABETH CAME to the head of the wide stairs and stopped, crouched down in the shadows. She had worn her silk slippers leaving the ship, had understood instinctively that she would need to move quickly and quietly and could not be encumbered by her fashionable footwear.

She waited for several minutes in that place, listened for movement: alarm, guards pacing—anything. She did not know the hour but guessed that it was somewhere around two A.M., a dead time. Nothing moved.

She took the steps, catlike and urgent, her every sense sharp, but there was nothing there but the silent building and only the tiniest amount of light from sundry lanterns illuminating it. The stairs emptied onto the big, two-story grand entrance, and across that open space with its polished tiles was the front door.

Elizabeth skirted around the grand entrance, keeping to the shadows, making not for the front door but rather for the door half concealed in the wall down which she had seen them take Marlowe and the others, hours before. Prison, torture chamber, place of execution— she had no idea what was at the bottom of those steps.

She paused again at the door, looked around, then held her two rapiers under her arm and lifted the latch, slowly, and eased the door in. She braced herself for a squeal of hinges, a creak of the door, but it moved silently. She cracked it enough to squeeze through and then closed it behind her.

It was nearly black beyond the door but for a faint glow from belowstairs, enough to see that the stairs went down to some kind of landing, then doubled around, presumably going down to the floor below.

She reached out with her toe, found the first step, and took it, then the next and the next, moving carefully toward the light. Five steps and she was on the landing. She crept up to the edge of the second staircase, darted her head around, and pulled back quick.

She looked for no more than an instant, but in that glimpse she saw a guard, another of these big piratical bastards, slumped in a chair, his back to her. The light came from a single lantern on a hook over his head. She could not tell if the man was asleep or awake, could not see what was beyond him, down the passageway.

Softly she drew in a breath, steeled herself for what she would have to do. The staircase was too narrow for the swords; she would have to use the stiletto. She laid down the long weapons gently, silently, pulled the stiletto from her skirt, and eased herself around the corner.

Down one step. The guard was six feet away, and she realized that she did not really know what she was going to do. Stab him? Could she? Another step, and her slipper crunched on loose gravel on the stone stair, like a thunderclap in that silent prison.

The guard gasped, leaped to his feet, spun around, hand on his sword. Elizabeth froze. She saw the man's face go from shock to confusion to delight at the sight of her. She turned and fled.

Back up the stairs, around the wall, and onto the landing, and she stopped, stiletto out, the guard's footsteps pounding behind her. The big man turned the corner, charging for the next flight of steps, not expecting her to have stopped dead. He brought up short with a sharp intake of breath, the needle tip of Elizabeth's weapon under his chin.

"Hold!" she hissed at him. "Back down with you."

The guard took a step back and then another, glancing over his shoulder at where he was stepping, his hands held up in front of him, never taking his eyes off Elizabeth for more than an instant. One step back, another. He paused. There were three steps down to the floor of the prison below.

"Turn around. Down you go," Elizabeth said softly, trying to sound as menacing as she was able. The man nodded, half turned. Then his hand shot out and grabbed her wrist and jerked it sideways, and Elizabeth gasped at the power of his grip, and he wrenched her arm, twisting her partway around.

She pushed off as hard as she could, using all the strength of her legs to slam into his chest, shoulderfirst. She felt him sway back, like a tree cut nearly through, and then the two of them went over.

Elizabeth had an image of flogging coattails and waving arms and clattering weapons and a grunt of surprise, and then the pirate hit the stone floor, and she fell on him, and the tight space was filled with a rendering crack and then the beginnings of a shriek of pain.

She pushed herself up, the stiletto still in her hand, pressed it under the pirate's throat. "Quiet!" she hissed. She could see the man's arm caught below him, broken and twisted at an unnatural angle, but he stifled his scream of agony for fear of worse.

Elizabeth stood slowly, keeping the dagger in the man's face. "Make one sound and I'll cut your throat." The pirate was gritting his teeth and breathing with the pain of his compound fracture, his eyes shut tight, but he nodded, and Elizabeth stepped away from him. She took the lantern down from the hook, stepped along the narrow passage between barred cells. Did not know what she would find.

Then, suddenly, right in front of her, leaning on the bars, the one thing she hoped for above all others. Thomas, her husband, looking on her with wide eyes.

"Elizabeth? My God . . ."

"Thomas! Oh . . ." She ran to the bars, took his outstretched hand in hers. His hair was wild, with bits of straw sticking to it. He looked exhausted and still half asleep, but beyond that unhurt.

"Thomas, are you . . . ?"

"I am well. And you, did that bastard . . . ?"

"No, no. I left Yancy bound, but he might be discovered soon. We must go."

"The guard had keys on his belt."

Elizabeth pulled herself away, stepped back to the guard, who was groaning as he tried to get his broken arm from under him. Hanging from a leather lanyard on his belt, a big set of keys. Elizabeth cut them free, hurried back to the cell. She picked one, fumbled it into the lock, but it would not turn.

"Try the other," Thomas whispered. Behind him, in the deep shadows, she could hear Honeyman rousing their sleeping men. Elizabeth worked the key out of the lock, inserted the other, twisted, and heard the click of the lock opening.

"You men." Thomas turned to the others, addressed them in a whisper. "Follow me. We haven't the weapons to fight our way out of here, so let us be damned quiet. Come."

He pushed through the cell, stood aside as the others followed.

"Marlowe!" a voice whispered from the cell on the other side of the alleyway. Elizabeth turned in surprise. It had not occurred to her that there might be others there. But there were. Roger Press, his face pushed against the bars.

"Marlowe! You can't leave me here!"

"Oh, no?"

"Son of a bitch, Marlowe! You won't get out of here without me and my men."

"I don't reckon I would get out *with* you and your men. You have a way of seeing to that."

"You bastard! If you don't let me out, we'll wake the whole goddamned house! You'll never make it to the harbor!"

"We'll chance it. Fare thee well, you stinking bastard. I hope Yancy lives long enough to impale you." Thomas pushed through his men, down the alleyway, and Elizabeth walked with him. He pulled the sword from the guard's scabbard and headed up the stairs.

"Marlowe! Marlowe, you bastard!" Press screamed at the top of his lungs, the noise filling the prison, frightening in its volume. Elizabeth bounded up the stairs, collected the rapiers, gave one to Billy Bird and one to Bickerstaff, and the men filed up the passage and out into the grand entrance.

Behind them Press's screams spilled from the door, but the sound was thankfully muted by the floor and heavy walls. It was not enough to wake a man, but if anyone was already awake—a guard, for instance—then it would be heard.

They filed quickly through the door, and the last man shut it behind him, and Press's shouting was blotted out.

Elizabeth and Thomas stood side by side, listening, but still the household slumbered on.

"Come along," said Marlowe, and he led them across the grand entrance and out the big front door, to the open air, to the grounds that would lead to the stockade gate, to the road that would lead to the harbor and the sea and escape from that horrible place.

Elizabeth took a lungful of the night air. It was sweet and clean and free of the odor of the big house. It was like being on the ocean, and she felt her spirit lifting, lifting, though there were still a hundred chances for bloody death between the front door and the sea.

Lord Yancy woke, opened his eyes quickly, and shouted with the pain, then whimpered with the agony brought on by shouting. "Oh, God, oh, God . . ." he gasped, closing his eyes against the flashing lights and the pounding in his head. He lay very still, let his breathing return to normal, then slowly he opened his eyes again.

He could not move his arms or his legs. He wondered if his neck was broken, and he felt the panic starting in again. He forced himself to be calm. He could feel his limbs, could feel a burning sensation at his wrists. He was bound hand and foot and lying on the floor.

"That bitch!" he yelled, and was greeted with a renewed pounding in his skull, and he had to lie quiet until it subsided. He breathed, slow and steady, braced himself, then rolled over and sat up.

The sky was still black outside, the room still illuminated by the candles, which had not yet burned all the way down. He could not have been unconscious for so very long, which meant the bitch might yet be in the house. He struggled against the ropes around his wrists, but they were solid and unyielding. His fingers felt cold and thick and numb. He was tied well.

"That bitch!" he shouted again, and this time the pounding was not so debilitating. He searched the floor. His stiletto and both rapiers were gone. There was a clasp knife in the pocket of his coat, which was flung over the far chair. He considered the difficulty of retrieving it and cutting himself free as opposed to the practicality of shouting for help. He pictured Henry Nagel finding him thus, beaten and bound by a woman, and he had an uneasy feeling that that would be the end of his reign over St. Mary's.

With great difficulty he squirmed around until he was standing on his knees. He tried an experimental hop, but the pain was excruciating, jarring him at a dozen points of agony. The pain in his head flared, and he thought he might pass out. With a groan he flopped onto his side and squirmed across the floor, the most humiliation he had suffered in memory, and he could think of nothing beyond Henry Nagel opening the door and finding him writhing there like a broken snake.

Five agonizing, embarrassing moments later and he was across the room. He reached his arms around as best he could, found the clasp knife in the pocket of his coat, and pulled it out. With numb fingers he struggled to unfold it and then held it awkwardly as he sawed at the bonds.

Four times he dropped the knife, and he was near weeping with despair when he felt a little give in the rope, and he knew that a strand had parted. With a renewed effort he sawed at the cordage, and soon he felt the rope part altogether, felt the rock-hard lashing fall away.

He let out a great groan of relief, brought his hands around in front, rubbed the raw flesh, felt a sharp tingling as the blood flowed unimpeded to his fingers. He snatched up the knife and cut his legs free and stood, shaking, to his feet.

What now, what now . . . ? Get the bitch back.

He had saved himself from the humiliation of being discovered bound like a pig for slaughter on the floor, but still it would not go well for him if the tribe he ruled found he had been bested by a woman.

Find that whore, bring her back, bloody well teach her . . .
Where would she go? The waterfront? What would she do?
She'll free Marlowe!

"Goddamn it!" Yancy said out loud. Of course she would try to free
Marlowe. "Goddamn it!"

He limped across the room and tried to open the door, but it was
locked. He cursed, looked around the table for the key, but he could
not find it. He snatched up a candle and looked closer, looked on the
floor around the table, but the key was not there.

He was locked in, but it did not matter. He abandoned the door,
limped back across the room, pulled aside an ancient tapestry that
hung from the wall on the other side of the bed. A small door was concealed behind it, and he pushed that open and stepped into the dark
passage beyond.

The air was dusty and smelled of sealed-off spaces, the odor of the
tomb. Adam Baldridge was a man of foresight; he had envisioned the
need for a second way out of the master bedchamber. But Yancy was
also a man of foresight. He understood that if he had to use that exit,
he would probably need weapons as well, and so he kept them there,
ready.

He took down the brace of pistols, their butts bound by a ribbon,
draped them around his neck. A sword belt hung from a hook, with a
sword and dagger hanging from it. He took that down next, strapped it
around his waist.

Down he went, down the steep, narrow stairs built into the smallest
possible space, his shoulders brushing either wall as he hurried down,
the candle guttering and wavering and threatening to go out.

He came to the bottom door and unlatched it and pushed it open
as best he could. It, too, was concealed behind a tapestry that adorned
the grand entrance, and Yancy had to push against the heavy cloth as
he slipped out the door and into the big open space.

There was nothing amiss that he could see. The door leading to the
cells was closed. It was silent, everything silent. Either she had not
come that way or they were long gone. He raced across the grand entrance, flung open the door to the prison, took the steps fast.

From the landing he could see the guard, passed out or dead on the floor, two steps below, his arm broken and twisted under him.

"Bitch!" Yancy shouted, jumping down the steps and past the guard. The door to the cell that held Marlowe and his men was open. The cell was empty.

"Bitch!" Yancy shouted again, his voice high-pitched, too wild with fury even to think of what he would do next.

Then a voice beside him, thick with urgency. "Yancy!" Roger Press pushed himself against the bars, looked down on Elephiant Yancy.

"Press, what happened here?" Yancy demanded.

"Marlowe's little doxy let him out. Was she not in your care?"

"She escaped from the idiots guarding her. After I was done with her," Yancy added, and then realizing how inappropriate it was to address Press as if he were an equal—or even a human being—he added, "though it's no concern of yours. You are a dead man either way."

Yancy turned and headed back for the stairs, moving fast, but Press called, "Wait! Wait, Yancy, there is something you don't know!"

Yancy stopped but did not turn, considered whether or not he should listen. Press was like a snake, and his words could be as hypnotizing as a snake's eyes.

But that was for weaker men. Yancy knew he was not fool enough to be drawn in, to be charmed and persuaded by Press's rhetoric. He turned. "What?"

"Marlowe will go for the harbor, try to make it out to his ship—"

"You reckon that didn't occur to me?"

"No, wait for it. This is what you don't know. While I was out hunting Marlowe, I captured the Great Mogul's treasure ship. My ship, and Marlowe's, is stuffed with treasure, more wealth than even you would see in a lifetime. Without my help, Marlowe will sail off with it!"

"Without your help?" At that Yancy laughed out loud. "You have been help enough, bringing it to me. I can take it from Marlowe and his pathetic little band! But thank you for telling me this."

"It ain't just Marlowe!" Press said, and Yancy heard the genuine note of conviction in his voice. "I left two hundred men aboard when I come ashore. You have the force to take on two hundred trained men? Men-of-war's men? If Marlowe gets out to those ships and convinces them I'm dead, they'll sail off with a fare-thee-well, and you can't stop 'em. Maybe they'll kill Marlowe, maybe not, but either way the treasure is gone. They have to see me alive or they'll sail, and you can't stop them. Do you hear?"

Yancy hesitated, felt himself slipping down the ways of Press's logic.

Then Press drove home the final argument. "You can have half the treasure or none of it, simple as that."

Yancy made up his mind. He would, in fact, have all the treasure. He would simply double-cross Press after the booty was secured, lock him up again. He had men enough to keep Press in check until then. He crossed the narrow alleyway, retrieved the keys hanging from the other cell door, and let Press and his men go free.

"How long have Marlowe and the others been gone?" Yancy asked as he twisted the key in the lock.

"Half an hour, thereabouts," Press said. There was an eagerness, a hint of triumph in his voice that made Yancy uncomfortable, but the lock was unlocked and the door half opened, and it was too late to close it again. "Probably clear to the harbor by now."

Yancy swung the door open all the way. "Follow me," he said, and hurried for the stairs, his unlikely allies at his heels.

Marlowe and his band were at the harbor, pulling across the harbor, in fact, spread out over four boats. They had met no resistance. The big house was asleep. The guards at the stockade gate were looking for threats from the outside, not from within.

They showed only a dull curiosity when Marlowe pulled the gate open behind them, turned to see who it was, and were clubbed down by Honeyman wielding a heavy stick he had found on the ground. They fell with no more sound than that made by a bread bag dropped from five feet. Their inert forms were dragged into the shadows and relieved of weapons.

Down the hill, down the dark road with dawn still four hours off. They moved fast, silent, and if anyone saw them, he did not raise an alarm. Marlowe realized that there would be no telling who they were

in the dark, and if anyone mistook them for Yancy's men on some clandestine mission, he would not be eager to give them away.

From the stockade all the way to the wooden wharf, they heard
nothing but quiet night sounds, saw nothing unsettling in the motionless, dark, and disinterested world.

They stepped out along the wharf, their shoes making hollow
sounds on the boards. Across the water they could make out the dim
shapes of the four anchored ships. Closest to them, anchored by herself, was the *Bloody Revenge*. Beyond her the dark mass, the seeming
tangle of spars and rigging of the *Queen's Venture* with the *Elizabeth
Galley* tied to her seaward side and hidden from the men on the dock.
And one hundred feet beyond the *Elizabeth Galley*, the tender *Speedwell*. All four ships like stepping-stones across the water. They seemed
peaceful, asleep.

Not for long, Marlowe thought.

All the boats from the *Queen's Venture* and the *Bloody Revenge* were
still there, tied to the dock, right where Press had left them.

"We can't leave any boats for Yancy to use if he tries to attack," Marlowe said. "Billy, divide your men up. Take the longboat, there, and
that gig. I'll get my men in the others. We'll all make right for your
brig, since she ain't rafted up with the other ships. I don't think there's
much of a prize crew on board, anchor watch at best. Take her, loosen
off sail. Load the guns. I reckon we can feel our way out of here in the
dark."

"Right," Billy Bird said, then hesitated. "Actually, damn the hellish
brig, I say. Marlowe, do you mean to just sail off? Leave your own ship
behind?"

"I do. Whatever are you thinking?"

"Well, there is a damned lot of booty in that beastly ship of Press's.
In yours as well. Surely we can't leave it for Yancy?"

"You are suggesting . . . ?"

"At the very least we should take that bloody *Queen's Venture*. Just
sail it right out of here. That fothered sail has held this long, it will
hold a while longer. All our men go up her side, take her, and we take
your ship as well, and then we sail them both out of here."

"And leave your ship?"

"Damned leaking bucket, with my share of that booty I could buy ten like her."

"Please, Marlowe," Bickerstaff spoke up, "tell me you are not actually considering this."

"Well, there might be some sense in it . . ."

"You are overreaching, I fear. Let it go, get out with your life."

"We cannot let Yancy have that treasure," Billy Bird argued. "Lord knows what wickedness he would get up to with such wealth! And we can't just sink the ship—the water is too shallow, and these natives can dive like fish. No, we must take her with us."

"We have three swords, two rapiers, four pistols, and a stiletto between the fifty of us," Bickerstaff reminded him.

"Oh. Right . . ." Marlowe was clutching a weapon and for that reason had forgotten that he was almost entirely unique in that.

"We'll take the *Bloody Revenge* first," Billy Bird suggested. "Should be no great task, as you said, easily done with what we have. Free my people, increase our numbers. Plenty of weapons aboard. From there we fall on the big ships."

In the darkness Marlowe could barely see Bickerstaff, though he was no more than five feet away, but he could feel his friend's sharp eyes on him. Bickerstaff sighed. It was close enough to concession for Marlowe.

"A good plan, Billy. Let us go."

They spread the men out among the boats, Marlowe, Bickerstaff, Billy Bird, and Honeyman together in the big longboat by virtue of the fact that they had between them four of the five swords. The fifth was given to Hesiod, and two of Billy Bird's trusted men were handed the two pistols. They represented the Forlorn Hope, the first into the breech, and the rest were instructed to come up behind and grab what they could—fallen weapons, belaying pins, handspikes—and join in the fray.

Across the harbor like giant water bugs, the oars squeaking in the tholes, no time for such niceties as muffling them. Fifty feet from the *Bloody Revenge*, and the not overly watchful anchor watch finally caught sight of them.

"Hoa! The boats, ahoy! Who's there?"

"Captain Press!" Marlowe shouted through cupped hands.

"What? Captain Press is aboard?"

"Captain Press!" Marlowe called again, ambiguous and unhelpful.

Silence. The oarsmen leaned into the oars. Thirty feet off. Marlowe could almost hear the confusion in the anchor watch's head. Then, "Stand off, there! Stand off, I say!"

Twenty feet, and the anchor watch began to shout, not at the boats but at his shipmates, "Turn out! Turn out!" Bare feet ran across the deck, a muffled voice shouting down a hatch, "Turn out! To arms! To arms!"

The longboat thumped alongside, and Marlowe raced up the boarding steps, accidentally kicking Billy Bird as Billy scrambled up close behind. They burst through the gangway and ducked right and left, and the anchor watch fired a blunderbuss into empty space, illuminating the deck and himself, and then one of Billy Bird's men armed with a pistol shot him down.

Sleepy and surprised men raced up through the scuttle, one at a time through the narrow passage, and Honeyman and Burgess and Hesiod were there to greet them. Not with cold steel but with belaying pins that made no more than a dull thump as the three men laid out the unwary crew, one by one.

More men came charging from under the quarterdeck, and Marlowe and Bickerstaff and Bird met them, blade against blade, but the half-dressed men, startled from deep sleep, were no match for the desperate and ready boarders. A minute of fighting, and they threw away their swords and called for quarter.

More and more men came pouring over the side from the boats below, and they herded the prisoners forward and dragged those wounded or unconscious out of the way.

"That was well done," Billy Bird said, leaning on his rapier.

Marlowe nodded. "We best move quick. They'll be alerted, aboard the *Queen's Venture*. But with luck those bastards at the big house are still asleep. They won't have heard the gunshots in any event."

Then from aft, from the dark under the quarterdeck, came a sputtering and hissing. The two men turned. The powder train burning in the touchhole of a cannon, there was no mistaking it. In the dim light that the sparks threw off they could see the figure of the man who had lit it, scurrying away.

Billy took one step toward the gun, and then it went off, a great blast of red and orange flame shooting out its mouth, lighting up the water and the boats. The gun flung itself inboard against its breeches. The blast echoed around the harbor.

The noise subsided until it was no more than a ringing in their ears.

"They bloody well heard that," Billy Bird said.

Chapter 26

JOSIAH BROWNLAW had just fallen into a fitful sleep, the weight of his responsibility pressing on him, when he heard the small-arms fire, the shouting men and running feet.

He jerked into a sitting position, whirled out of bed, and grabbed up his sword and pistol. The shots had been fired not aboard the *Queen's Venture*, he realized, but aboard one of the others, the *Bloody Revenge* or the *Speedwell*. It did not matter. All the vessels there were his responsibility.

He crouched under the low beams of his tiny cabin, took the two steps to the door, and raced out under the quarterdeck, nearly colliding with the man sent aft to fetch him. Brownlaw shoved him aside, ran into the waist, then up the steps to the gangway.

One of the hands on anchor watch was there, the man that Brownlaw had charged with keeping an eye on the lashings on the fothered sail. They had to be monitored closely. If one of the ropes parted or even came loose, they would have to know it and fix it, immediately. If the fothered sail came off, the water would quickly overtake the pumps.

But the man was not looking at the lashings now. Rather, he was staring out over the water at the *Bloody Revenge*, and his face looked worried and uncertain.

"What has happened?" Brownlaw demanded.

"Small-arms fire, Mr. Brownlaw, from the brig . . ."

They stood and listened. They could hear the clash of steel on steel, running feet. Brownlaw addressed the man beside him. "Turn out the men, pistols and cutlasses. The men from the other ship, too." The *Queen's Venture* was still tied tight to the captured ship, the *Elizabeth Galley*.

The anchor watch ran off, and Brownlaw stared across the water and chewed on his fingernails. *What is happening, what, what, what?* It could be an attack from the shore or a mutiny or the prisoners trying to take the ship.

It seemed to grow quiet on the brig, quiet enough that Brownlaw could not hear anything over the sounds of his own company turning out below and charging up on deck, the clatter of weapons, the loud talk of confused men.

Then, from the far side of the brig, a cannon fired, one of her great guns, blasting flame out over the water. The report made a famous echo around the harbor, and Brownlaw leaped clean off the deck in surprise and nearly dropped his pistol over the side.

"Damn!" he shouted. A single gun, that was the distress signal as specified in Press's standing orders.

Of course they are in bloody distress, you fool! Brownlaw chastised himself. *They're bloody fighting someone! Make a decision, make a decision, goddamn it!* He found himself near paralysis.

Find out what's acting . . .

"Hoa, the brig, ahoy! Hoa!" he called, and as he did, he realized that it was stupid to think someone would respond, but to his surprise someone did.

"Holloa! Mr. Brownlaw, is that you?"

"Aye! Johnson?" Johnson was the master's mate who had been left in charge of the *Bloody Revenge*.

"Aye, sir!" He sounded upset. His voice wavered.

"What's acting, Johnson?"

"Prisoners tried to break out, sir! Got their hands on some weapons, don't know how. I reckon we got 'em secured now!"

No wonder Johnson's voice wavered so. Damned frightening. "You need some more men there? To help guard them?"

That was met with a long silence, then, "Aye, sir! We've got some hurt ones here. What can you send?"

Brownlaw had sixty or so men on the two big ships and another twenty on the brig and twenty more aboard *Speedwell*. But nearly all the boats were ashore; he had only the barge. "I can send twenty-five," he announced at last.

"I'm grateful, sir!" Johnson called out. Brownlaw turned to the men in the waist below him. "You heard Johnson. They've had some trouble with their prisoners. Twenty-five of you in the barge, go over and lend a hand."

That was all he needed to say. The men were well trained and used to working together. They quickly sorted themselves out, and twenty-five of them piled into the barge.

Brownlaw watched them as they pulled over to the brig, and he felt a great relief, an almost-giddy sense of joy. Here he had been terrified that he would make a hash out of his responsibility. But instead a prisoner revolt had been put down on his watch, and he had dispatched more men to see it dealt with proper.

A voice from the *Speedwell*, riding at her anchor, less than a cable length away. "Brownlaw!" It was Scribner, the *Speedwell*'s bosun, in temporary command. "Brownlaw, what's acting? What are those guns about?"

"It's nothing, Scribner. Prisoners trying to break out. I have everything under control!"

And he did. Brownlaw smiled to himself. Even that bastard Press would find no fault with his leadership.

Yancy was still getting the men assembled in the open ground outside the front door when the gun went off and echoed around the high hills. Seventy of his men, fifty of Press's, and they all looked up as if their heads were controlled by a single string.

"What in hell was that?" Yancy demanded, his voice near a shriek.

"Cannon," Press said.

Yancy's head jerked around, glared up at the pockmarked face that stared with insouciance out toward the harbor. "Don't you play it coy with me, you whoreson, or I'll have you impaled here and now."

Press looked down at him, flicked the silver toothpick between his lips. Yancy had ordered that damned thing taken from him. He must have had another concealed in his coat. "I don't think now is the time to impale me, Yancy . . ."

"Lord Yancy."

"Forgive me, Lord Yancy." Press drawled the words. "My men have standing orders to fire a gun in case of any trouble. If I am not wrong, I believe Marlowe has reached my ships."

Yancy clenched his teeth, looked out over the harbor. Press stood a good foot taller than he did, and Yancy hated to stand next to him. Considered forcing him to walk on his knees. "My ships, Press. Not yours," he corrected. Press had already grown too cocky.

"Then let me suggest we get down to 'your ships,'" Press said, but by that point Yancy was too swept up with his growing sense of urgency to slap him down for his impudence.

"Come along, men! Down to the harbor! Hurry now, there's a goddamned fortune to be had!"

Those were the most motivational words that Yancy could have said to that crowd. They surged forward, Press and Yancy in the lead, and in their quick step crossed the grounds, poured out the gate—the unconscious guards unseen in the shadows—and raced down the hill toward the harbor below.

"Here they come, under the counter," Johnson said, just a whisper, and as he spoke, Marlowe could make out the dark outline of the boat pulling for the *Bloody Revenge*.

By way of rewarding Johnson for his good work, Marlowe removed the barrel of the pistol that he had been pressing against Johnson's lower spine and held it aside. He could smell the sweat on the man, an unhealthy smell of fear.

"Burgess," Marlowe whispered, and the boatswain appeared at his side. "Take this pistol. When the men in the boat come up the side, Johnson here will send them below, tell 'em that's where the prisoners are being held. We'll take them as they come down the scuttle.

"If Johnson gives an alarm, shoot him. Not in the head, right through the spine, here." Marlowe jabbed Johnson's lower back with his finger, more for Johnson's benefit than Burgess's.

"Aye, through the spine. Bloody mess that'll make. Seen 'em live for weeks that way," Burgess said, taking the gun and pulling his cocked hat low over his forehead. Burgess would be a lot less conspicuous standing beside Johnson than Marlowe would be.

Marlowe crossed the deck, went down the scuttle to the tween decks, waited with the others. A few moments, no more, and the boat thumped alongside and feet clumped and padded up the side, and Johnson's voice, tight with fear, directed them below.

Across the deck overhead and down the ladder to the dimly lit tween decks, Roger Press's men stepped right into a ring of muskets aimed at them. Thomas Marlowe, his finger to his lips, urged them to silence. It was a warning they heeded, making not a sound as they were relieved of muskets, pistols, swords, and sheath knives and then were battened down in the dark place where just half an hour before, thirty of Billy Bird's men had been imprisoned.

The hatch was closed and secured, and Marlowe nodded, looked around at the assembled men. The *Bloody Revenge* was theirs, the *Queen's Venture* assured that all was well, and her defense now weaker by twenty-five men.

Dawn was an hour away. At first light they would have to run the gauntlet of the batteries at the harbor mouth. Yancy and his men were no doubt rushing to the waterfront at that very moment, summoned by the great gun that some hero had fired off.

I have been in worse places, sure, Marlowe thought, but he did not have time to think of when.

Yancy had set the pace at first, walking fast down the hill. But Press's long legs carried him half again as far as Yancy with every stride. Soon

Yancy was jogging to keep pace with Press, and that made Press break into a half jog, and then the men did likewise. Yancy could not order Press to slow down—it was as much as admitting he could not keep up with the gangly bastard. He could not let Press move ahead.

By the time they reached the dock and clattered out over the worn boards, they were all gasping for breath—Yancy, Press, the heavily armed men. For a moment they could do nothing but breathe.

". . . Must get out to the ships . . . Where are your boats?" Yancy spoke. His breath had not fully returned, but he had to speak first.

Press straightened, made a great show of placing his toothpick in his mouth. "Had four boats tied up here. Marlowe must have taken them."

"Goddamn it! Nagel, where in bloody hell are you? Nagel!"

Henry Nagel ambled up out of the dark. He seemed to have little of the deferential snap he generally displayed.

"Lord Yancy?"

"We bloody need boats, Nagel!" A scream, barely suppressed. Yancy heard the high pitch of his voice, very uncommanding, and made a note to watch that.

"Some of them lads, the ones come from Press's ship, they say there's the treasure of the Great Mogul hisself aboard them ships," Nagel said. It was a mere statement of fact, spoken plainly, but it had the weight of accusation.

"Yes, there is. Which is why we need bloody boats!"

"Some of the lads was wondering, how come we didn't know that?"

Yancy frowned, took a step closer to Nagel, until he could make out the man's face in the dark and hoped Nagel could make out his. "Don't you question me, you son of a bitch! I tell you things when I am ready, do you hear?"

Oh, bloody hell! Yancy thought. He had just learned of the treasure himself. In the rush of going after Marlowe, Yancy had simply forgotten to tell Nagel about it, and now Nagel and the others thought he was betraying them.

That could not be happening.

He might, at some point, betray them all, but it was not possible that they should accuse him of doing so when he genuinely was not.

Nagel was quiet for a long moment. "There's the canoe, there," he said at last, nodding toward a small, leaky, half-rotten dugout tied to the dock. Then almost grudgingly added, "And there's them two big boats, with the swivel guns in the bows, tied up, up harbor."

"Yes, yes, of course," Yancy said. Two big ship's launches, he kept them armed and concealed in the event he wished to make a boat attack on a vessel in- or outbound. They were ideal.

"Get some hands . . ." Yancy began, then stopped. Send Nagel off alone to man the boats, give him the chance to capture and make off with the treasure? No, that would not do, not now. Go himself? It would take forty minutes at least to reach the boats, another twenty to pull back to the dock. Leave Nagel behind? Press?

Damn it, I must keep a weather eye on every one of these disloyal, motherless bastards!

"All of you, with me! To the boats!" Yancy led the way back down the dock, back to the road that paralleled the harbor. At least Press did not know the way. He would not be able to push ahead this time.

Johnson of the anchor watch had been held at gunpoint for some time, near an hour, and in Marlowe's extensive experience with such things, he knew that the threat of being shot would not keep the man's fear up for that long. But he still needed Johnson's help.

Marlowe climbed back up on the main deck, found Johnson sitting on the hatch, hands locked behind his neck. Burgess crouched before him, gun pointed at his chest.

"Johnson, how are you?" Marlowe asked.

"Been better," Johnson growled. The fear was gone.

Marlowe crouched beside him. "Johnson, do you see these?" He held up three gold doubloons that Billy Bird had retrieved from a secret stash in his great cabin, saw Johnson's eyes get a little wider. "I'll wager this is more than that bastard Press would pay you for the whole voyage. Do you like working for Press, Johnson? Or do you think it might be time to change sides?"

Ten minutes later, the newest loyal member of Marlowe's crew called across the water, "Hoa, *Queen's Venture*, ahoy! Mr. Brownlaw?"

"Johnson?"

"Aye, sir! All's well, got them bastards all battened down, sir! Thought I'd send your men back and come across myself, to report, like!"

"Very well. Do so," came the reply from the dark.

Johnson turned inboard. "Right, you men, in the boat!"

On that command, twenty-five of Marlowe's and Billy Bird's men clambered down the side and into the boat, taking the places once occupied by the twenty-five men whom Brownlaw had sent across and who were at that moment locked up in a lightless place in the *Revenge*'s hold.

The men made as much noise as they could reasonably make as they climbed down, drowning out the sounds of the other four boats, hidden from Brownlaw's view on the far side of the *Bloody Revenge*. Those boats, commanded by Honeyman, Flanders, Burgess, and Hesiod, were at that moment shoving off and pulling for the *Elizabeth Galley*, which they intended to board, take, and then cross over to the *Queen's Venture*.

Johnson went down in the boat, and last came Thomas and Elizabeth, who had exchanged her skirts for slop trousers and her straw hat for tarpaulin. They sat on the farthest thwart aft, the aftermost rowing station, facing Johnson in the stern sheets.

Marlowe lifted up his oar, held it straight up. "Take up your oar, dear. Hold it like this," Marlowe said to his wife softly. Elizabeth grabbed the oar that lay across the thwarts and with some difficulty lifted it so that like the others she was holding it straight up and down. With the wide-brimmed hat she wore, Marlowe did not think Elizabeth would be seen for what she was, not in the dark.

Dark. Marlowe glanced up. It was night still, but only just. He thought he could detect a general easing of the blackness, the first hints of light. It would be gray dawn in an hour.

Thomas Marlowe was well armed—the sword he had taken from the guard, a short sword, two braces of pistols—but he did not hold a gun on Johnson. Johnson was on his side now, and there was a tacit understanding that in case of betrayal he was the first to die.

Marlowe nodded to the man, and Johnson called, "Shove off! Ship oars! Give way!" and the bowman pushed the bow off. Elizabeth lowered her oar, slowly, until the weight became too much, and then she dropped it with a thump between the tholes. She cocked her head toward Marlowe and watched him and imitated his movements. Lean forward, blade down, pull and lean back, blade up, forward, down. She looked by no means as if she were an old hand with an oar, but she did well enough that she would not stand out.

They pulled slow for the *Queen's Venture* to make it easier for Elizabeth to keep the rhythm and to give the others more time to pull around the far side of the rafted ships.

The *Queen's Venture* appeared at last on the edge of Marlowe's vision, facing aft as he was. They made for the boarding steps, and Johnson called, "Toss oars!" and all the oars came up at once, save for Elizabeth's, as the order had taken her quite by surprise. But she managed to get the oar aloft before it caught on the side of the ship, and there was no comment made.

The boat glided against the *Venture*'s side, and Johnson climbed up the side and disappeared from Marlowe's view. Marlowe had given him careful instructions to make his report to Brownlaw there on the gangway, within earshot. "The minute I can't hear what you are saying, we board," he said, the threat there, the placement of the first bullet.

But Johnson had the fidelity of a true Roundsman, loyal to whoever could do him the most good, and from the boat Marlowe could hear him clearly. "Mr. Brownlaw, sir! Lord, I had thought to never be speaking to you again! Those prisoners, I finally smoked it, knew of a secret way out of the hold. A passage through the forward bulkhead, sir. They bided their time, till they knew all but the anchor watch was asleep . . ."

Johnson talked loud and fast, a man excited by the events of the night, not letting Brownlaw get a word in, not letting him ask why the others did not come aboard, not letting him hear the sounds of the other boats.

But Brownlaw was not the only man awake. From across the deck, from the *Elizabeth Galley*, a shout of surprise, someone yelled, "Hey, there!" and another "Boarders!" and a gun went off and another, and Marlowe was on his feet.

"Now, men, away! Away!" he shouted, then grabbed on to the boarding cleats, scrambled up the side, and burst through the gangway.

Johnson, unarmed, was standing to one side. The fellow that Marlowe guessed was Brownlaw was charging across the deck, waving his sword and shouting, "To me! Queen's Ventures, to me!"

There were a lot of men on deck—nearly sixty of Press's horde, Marlowe guessed. But he had as many, and he had surprise.

The men from the boats were swarming over the far side, rushing along the *Elizabeth Galley*'s gangplanks and meeting her defenders with sword and pistol. The flashes of the muzzles lit up the place like a washed-out painting of a battle, men frozen in various attitudes: aiming, hacking, defending, falling, and then swallowed again by the dark.

The twenty-five men from Marlowe's boat were all aboard. "Come along! Shout like the devil!" Marlowe called, racing forward, along the *Queen's Venture*'s gangway, rushing around to the side made fast to the *Elizabeth Galley* and into the fighting there.

"Death, death, death, death!" Marlowe's men screamed, their voices curling up to a wild, inhuman, piercing shriek, and they fell on the backs of the men who just a second before had not even known they were there.

Press's men on the gangway turned, raised pistols and swords, were shot down, driven back by the onslaught. Marlowe was the first there. A pistol in his hand, he discharged it into the mob, reached for another, but before he could pull back the firelock, he found himself sidestepping a hacking cutlass that swished past him and hit the deck.

Marlowe let the pistol fall, lunged with the sword in his right hand, found only air. The man he was facing came at him and Marlowe parried the attack, pulled his short sword, which he held in his left hand, stood ready.

Another lunge, and Marlowe beat down the blade with his sword, lashed out like a snake with the short sword, caught the man in the shoulder. The man shouted, drew back, and Marlowe hit him again with his sword, stepped into him, shoved him hard off the gangway.

With flailing arms the man plunged down into the waist, and Marlowe heard the thud that he made on the main hatch as he turned to meet the next man.

A big man, he loomed in front of Marlowe, cutlass moving as if it were made of paper. Marlowe met the blade, felt the ringing shock go through his arm, stepped back from the counterstroke. A dangerous one. Marlowe took a step back, held the short sword ready.

The big man was no subtle fighter. He plunged at Marlowe, cutlass cleaving the air. Beside him someone fired a pistol, lit the man up from below.

"Hesiod!" Marlowe shouted, thoughts of further betrayal crackling in his head, but Hesiod stepped back. "Marlowe?"

"Aye!"

" 'Vast fighting! 'Vast fighting!" Hesiod and Marlowe shouted together, and the sounds of the fight faded. The Elizabeth Galleys had pressed the defenders between them, scattered them, run into one another.

"Some of them fellows has gone aloft!" a voice shouted from the dark, then Honeyman's voice: "Some has gone down the after scuttle."

"Very well, we'll ferret them out directly." The deck that a second before had been a battlefield was now quiet, waiting on Marlowe.

From the other side of the waist, Johnson's voice: "Brownlaw, you stupid bastard, give it up!"

Marlowe turned, they all turned. The figure of a man—Brownlaw, apparently—stood on the foredeck opposite, near the bow. He was little more than a silhouette, but Marlowe could see the sword he held in his hand.

Billy Bird stepped forward. He had a knack for sounding like the universal friend, the cheerful voice of reason. "Come along, there," he called. "The ship's taken, but you and your men won't be hurt if you give us some cooperation here. Not so much to ask."

They watched the figure of Brownlaw backing away, the sword held up.

"Come on," Billy tried again. "Not bloody much you can do with that sword!"

Then Brownlaw turned, and with three wild strokes he cut away the fothered sail.

Chapter 27

"OH, THAT'S bloody done it," Billy Bird said.

With a curse Marlowe pushed through the men, raced down the gangway and across the foredeck to where Brownlaw was backed up against the bulwark, sword held uncertainly before him. The frayed ends of the lashings lay limp on the deck.

Marlowe peered over the side. He could see the water below and realized the sky was growing lighter. He could see nothing of the sail or the severed lashings. The whole issue must have sunk to the bottom of the harbor. There was no retrieving it now.

Marlowe, furious, like an injured wolf, turned and growled at Brownlaw. Brownlaw pushed harder against the bulwark, tossed his sword to the deck, a gesture of supplication. Two steps and Marlowe was on him, grabbed him by his collar, jerked him close. Their faces inches apart, Marlowe looked into the man's frightened eyes. Brownlaw was shaking his head side to side, a mute plea for mercy, and Marlowe realized that he was not going to hurt the man.

Fifteen years before he would have killed Brownlaw, just on principle, the principles that he held then, but now he would not. He was too old, had done too much bloodletting.

You are one lucky bastard, Marlowe thought as he shoved Brownlaw away. The young officer stumbled, and then Marlowe heard a shout, a cry of despair—"You stupid, stupid whoreson!"—and he saw Johnson, just a shadow, snatch a pistol from the man next to him, cock it, and fire.

The flash lit up Brownlaw's face, eyes shut tight, jaw clenched, the fine spray of blood and bone from the back of his skull as he was flung against the bulwark, already dead, and his body crumpled to the deck.

Johnson, Marlowe's newest recruit. Apparently he did not care to see riches come and go so quickly.

Marlowe had no thought to spare for either man, living or dead. He turned to meet Billy Bird, who was hurrying up beside him.

"Sail's gone. She'll fill quick," Marlowe said.

"I could get the lads on fothering another. A lot of good hands here."

Marlowe recalled the cable tier, the cold water rising fast around him. "No time. She'll sink before they're done. Pass some more cables to bind the ships together. Bowse them up good and tight. Then break open the hatches, we'll sway as much as we can aboard the *Elizabeth Galley*, then cut this bucket away, make off as soon as it's full light." He looked to the east. The mountains were black against a low band of dark gray sky. "We have an hour. Whatever we can salvage in an hour, that is our take."

There was silence on the deck, and it lasted three seconds. Then Billy Bird turned and shouted, "You heard him, lads! We've an hour to get what we can, so turn to! There's our own people still locked down below! Get them up and set these bloody prisoners to work, and let's clean this filthy bucket out!"

The men on deck scattered in ten different directions. It was like nothing Marlowe had ever seen, like the companies of three men-of-war all clearing the same ship for action. He had never seen sailors move so fast, work so efficiently and with such cooperation.

The wedges were driven from the main hatch of the *Queen's Venture* and the *Elizabeth Galley* as well, hatch covers pulled back, gratings lifted off. Another gang of men cast off the stay tackle. They laid the falls of the tackle along and saw them manned. Still more were ripping off the after hatches, and on the *Queen's Venture* they were using axes to widen their openings.

Up from below came bedraggled, filthy prisoners, Marlowe's men and Billy Bird's men, those not taken ashore. They were half starved and confused and trying to understand this sudden change of fortune, this shift in circumstance. Like sleepwalkers they were directed toward the falls of stay tackles and yard tackles to add their meager strength to the effort.

Also from below, the better-fed men of Roger Press's command, driven topside at the ends of pistols and cutlasses. They were the men who had forced the Roundsmen to load the *Queen's Venture* with booty, and now they were made to unload her again.

It was an astounding effort, all the more so because it was carried out with never an order from Marlowe or Billy. Honeyman was there to coordinate efforts, and Burgess and the *Revenge*'s boatswain as well, but for the most part they just fell to. They were seamen to a man— not man-of-war's men, trained to a single task—but Roundsmen, whose death or fortune rested on their own initiative. They knew what to do, and they did it, fast and efficiently.

By the time the first iron-bound box of booty rose from the *Queen's Venture*'s hold, twisting at the end of the stay tackle, the morning light was enough that Marlowe could see the activity on the deck of his own ship, lashed alongside. The men there were working the stay tackle as well, emptying the *Elizabeth Galley*'s hold of whatever they could— food, water, supplies—to make more room for the treasure.

Across the deck of the *Queen's Venture* went the boxes, across the deck of the *Elizabeth Galley* and down through that ship's main hatch and down into her hold. Then, fast as could be done, the tackle was retrieved, and then the next chest of treasure or bundle of silk or barrel of spice was hove up from below and swayed across, *Queen's Venture* to *Elizabeth Galley*.

Marlowe paced back and forth on the *Queen's Venture* foredeck. There was little for him to do but wait. Wait until they had secured all the treasure that they could, wait until the moment when he had to order the men to leave the rest, to set sail and slip the cable and cut away the ropes that bound the *Galley* to the *Venture*.

Just as he was thinking about that very thing, the *Queen's Venture* gave a little lurch, tilted away from the *Elizabeth Galley*. The ropes groaned, made tiny popping sounds of fibers snapping. She was listing already, lying at an odd angle, a few degrees off an even keel.

"She's filling. Fast," Marlowe said to Billy Bird, and Billy nodded.

"We've a bit more time, I should think," Billy said.

Then, across the water, from the deck of the *Speedwell*, clear even over the commotion of emptying the *Queen's Venture*'s hold, the order "Fire!" and the gray dawn was torn apart as the tender fired her full broadside into the *Elizabeth Galley*.

On the top of the hill, below the big house, in the back of the cell formerly occupied by Roger Press and his men, entirely forgotten by everyone save for the jailer who brought him his twice-daily food and water, Peleg Dinwiddie stared at the open iron-bar door.

For week upon week he had sat alone in the cell, alone with his own thoughts, the worst torture of all. The rack, it seemed to him, would have been welcome, the thumbscrews, branding, flogging—anything. Any of it would have meant human contact and pain to blot out the thoughts, the constant, unchecked thoughts.

Weeks of nothing, and then the most extraordinary series of events. First Roger Press and Thomas Marlowe, both marched down as prisoners. Dinwiddie recognized most of the men who were put in the cell with Marlowe. They were his former shipmates, men under his command. Some he did not recognize, such as the foppish fellow whom Marlowe called Billy.

But they were put in the other cell, and Press and his men were put in the cell that Dinwiddie occupied. Peleg had kept to the back, to the shadows, did not wish to be noticed. He was noticed, of course, not by Press but by others, and those men who did see him did not say anything to him. They just looked him over, turned away.

He was filthy, his once-fine clothes nearly rags, almost two months' growth of beard on his face. He reckoned he looked like some madman, locked away, and he was not certain he wasn't.

Dinwiddie had sat as silent and unseen witness to the fast-changing situation, as first Marlowe had been released by Elizabeth and then Press by Yancy. The cells had been emptied, the door left open, and still Dinwiddie sat there, unmoving, staring.

But now his thoughts were off on a new tangent. Marlowe was there, free, on St. Mary's. It could mean only that he was heading for the *Elizabeth Galley*, making sail for home.

Home. In his dark madness Dinwiddie was not even certain what that meant. Some mythical place, some land where there was something besides a stone cell and the endless self-flagellation.

Marlowe, *Elizabeth Galley*, home. It took him two hours to stand up and take a step toward the door. He paused, listened. The guard with the broken arm had not made a sound in over an hour. Nothing happened, nothing moved. Dinwiddie took another step toward the door.

Whoever was in command of the tender *Speedwell* had smoked what they were about. Marlowe did not know how.

Perhaps one of Press's men had swum over there. Perhaps they had sent a boat, unseen in the dark, to reconnoiter. Perhaps they were just guessing. It hardly mattered. They were loyal to Press, and they had figured out that his booty was being carried off, and now they were trying to prevent it.

Iron slammed into the *Elizabeth Galley*'s side, and Marlowe could feel the impact even on the *Queen's Venture*'s deck. It screamed through the air, and the stay tackle was shot through. The iron-bound box that hung from the end of the tackle plunged to the deck, fifteen feet, hit with the impact of a cannonball. The box burst open, and a cascade of gold coin spilled along the deck, but no one paid it any attention. There were more important things at the moment.

"You there!" Honeyman pointed to the gang of men holding the now-useless fall of the stay tackle. "Reeve off a new tackle, quickly! You" — he pointed to another gang by the main hatch — "get the girtline down there. We can use that for the lighter stuff."

Billy Bird stepped up beside him, and Marlowe said, "This fellow has loyalty and courage, if not so much sense, firing on us."

"Perhaps not so much loyalty or courage either," said Billy. "I perceive two boats pulling for us, and it takes no art to guess who is in 'em."

Billy pointed forward, and Marlowe followed the gesture. Far off, up the harbor, two big boats coming bow on, their oars like flickering shadows moving in the odd mechanical way oars do. They were just visible in the dawn's light. If they had not been painted white, they would not have been noticed.

"Damn it," Marlowe said, and he ran around the gangplank and over to the *Elizabeth Galley*, then down into the *Galley*'s waist. Flanders was directing the men who were emptying her holds, and there was Bickerstaff, hauling with the men on the *Galley*'s stay tackle. "Flanders, belay that for now!" Marlowe shouted, and the *Speedwell* fired again. The *Galley* shuddered, a section of bulwark ripped apart, the men inboard of it tossed aside. The clang of round shot hitting one of the *Galley*'s great guns, from the *Queen's Venture* a prolonged shriek, and then nothing.

"We'll have to man the guns, give these bastards something in return. Francis, will you set some men to handing out powder?"

"I will." This was not piracy, this was defense of their own ship, and Marlowe knew that Bickerstaff would have no qualms about joining in.

Flanders dispatched men to the guns, Bickerstaff took a half dozen below to the powder magazine. Overhead, more booty came swinging across, a great bundle of ivory tusks hanging from the *Venture*'s girtline, over the deck and down into the *Galley*'s hold.

On the *Venture*'s foredeck men swarmed around the stay tackle like ants on a pile of sugar, reeving off a new line, getting it back into action, eager to get every last groat they could out of the hold of the sinking ship.

The *Queen's Venture* shifted, rolled another foot away from the *Galley*, the bar-taut ropes binding the vessels together groaning, the wood creaking, and Marlowe could picture the water rising higher and higher. It would be almost waist deep by now, to the men working in her hold. If the ropes holding the two vessels together were to let go, then the *Venture* would roll right over and take them down with her.

They had to realize that. And no doubt they did, but greed was stronger even than their sense of self-preservation.

Up and down the *Galley*'s waist the guns' lashings were cast off, the guns rolled back, the match lit and ready to touch off powder. Up from below came the men, dispatched by Bickerstaff, bearing cartridges of powder in long leather tubes. Powder, shot, wadding—it was all rammed home and the guns trundled out again.

Marlowe sighted down the barrel of the closest gun. The *Speedwell* was growing more distinct as the dawn spread across the sky, her upper rails no longer shades of gray and black but dull red, dull green. One hundred feet away, half a cable length, point-blank range, the muzzle of the gun seemed to rest on the side of the tender. No wonder their fire had been so devastating.

"Don't wait on me!" Marlowe shouted. "Fire fast as you can!"

Crews stepped back, gun captains took one last sight, match came down on powder train, and all along the *Galley*'s waist the six-pounders fired their devastating blast of iron. The guns were just coming to rest at the end of their breeches when the *Speedwell* fired. The hull shook, two shrouds parted and hung limp, a spray of splinters exploded from the mainmast. But the tender's guns sounded smaller now, less impressive, after the *Elizabeth Galley*'s larger battery. Marlowe could see at least two of the *Speedwell*'s guns that did not fire, and he hoped the *Galley*'s broadside had managed to knock them out.

"All slack! Ease away, handsomely, handsomely!" came the shout from behind, and Marlowe turned to see a big chest, bound with iron strapping, easing from the *Queen's Venture*'s newly rove stay tackle to the *Elizabeth Galley*'s. A moment's pause as the *Venture*'s tackle was cast off, and then the chest sailed down into the *Galley*'s dark hold, a controlled plummet, where it was received by unseen hands three decks down.

The *Elizabeth Galley*'s stay tackle had not yet emerged from the hold by the time the next chest was heaved up from the *Queen's Venture*.

Oh, Lord, Marlowe thought, *we shall be wealthy, if we are not dead.*

*   *   *

Peleg Dinwiddie grew bolder with each step. Out of the cell, past the guard who did not move, up the narrow steps. He emerged into the grand entrance and listened for a long time, but the house seemed absolutely deserted.

My house, he mocked himself, *given me by Yancy, when he died*. He could not stop himself from doling out the emotional beatings, like probing at a sore tooth with one's tongue.

Across the big space and out the door. It was early dawn, light enough that he could see the harbor below in grays and browns and pinpoints of bright light. Cannon fire. The *Elizabeth Galley* and Press's tender, blasting away at each other. Marlowe would not remain long at his anchor, not once the firing started.

That thought drove Dinwiddie forward, and he humped across the grounds, through the gate swinging in the offshore breeze that was building with the rising sun.

He stumbled and ran down the road from the big house to the dock. A mile distant, it seemed like twenty. The cloud of smoke piling up between the ships looked nearly solid, and through the cloud, pinpricks of muzzle flash, and under it all the distant muted thunder of the guns.

God, how he ached to be aboard the ship! To walk the deck with the iron flying all around, to be cleansed by the physical danger and selfless defense of the ship and company! There was redemption, there his sins could be burned away by the battle fire. He ran faster.

Heaving for breath, stumbling, at last he clambered out onto the dock and stopped. He was eye level with the ships, could see them clearly. A cannonball screamed by, not far over his head. The sky to the east was orange and blue, and the only gray overhead was far to the west. The broadsides had not stopped, the constant roar of the guns, the smoke piled on smoke, all but hiding the tender from Dinwiddie's sight.

The men on the *Queen's Venture* were desperately unloading her hold, and Dinwiddie could see why. She was listing hard. He imagined that the ropes binding her to the *Elizabeth Galley* were the only thing keeping her upright. He had to get there, but all the boats were gone. So close, so damned close.

He ran to the edge of the dock, looked around, under, for any kind of conveyance. Nothing. He ran to the other side. There, tied to one of the pilings, half full of water, was a dugout canoe, a crude paddle floating in the four inches of water in her bottom. She was as unseaworthy as a vessel could be and still float, but to Dinwiddie she looked like the royal yacht.

He untied the painter, led the canoe the length of the dock, and pulled it up on the beach. He stepped awkwardly down through the sand to his boat, tipped it over, and let the water pour out. He shoved the dugout into the harbor, waded in knee deep, then carefully, carefully, eased his large body into the unstable craft. He sat for a moment, got a feel for the balance of the thing, then dipped a tentative paddle into the water and stroked.

The dugout moved ahead easily, and Dinwiddie took another stroke, felt the momentum build. The boat bobbed and dipped in the little waves that came in around the point, but there was shelter enough that Dinwiddie felt he had a chance.

If the canoe swamped, if it sank or capsized, he was dead. He could not swim.

Out past the dock, his eyes were fixed on the *Elizabeth Galley*, and he grew bolder with each stroke. The dugout moved easy despite the occasional wave that lapped against the bow and spilled water over the low freeboard. Stroke, stroke, the ships growing closer.

Dinwiddie, the mariner, with his practiced weather eye. He caught motion to his left, something moving on the water. He turned, careful, looked across the harbor.

Two big boats, carrying fifty men each, it seemed, swivel guns on their bows, also pulling fast for the *Elizabeth Galley* and the *Queen's Venture*. It took little imagination to guess who they were.

Dinwiddie groaned out loud. It was a race, him in his little canoe against Yancy and Press in their big boats, all pulling for the *Queen's Venture*, all racing to get there before Marlowe could cut and run.

A puff of smoke, a flash of light from the bow of the nearest boat, and the bang of the swivel gun. Yancy was going in shooting.

"Oh, God!" Dinwiddie said out loud, digging in harder with the paddle. The canoe shot forward, its low bow cleaving through a small wave, sending gallons of water over the gunnel, knocking the small boat off course.

"Damn!" Dinwiddie swung the paddle over to stroke from the other side, bring her head around. Another wave slapped the bow, but more broadside. The canoe began to tip. Dinwiddie shifted hard to keep it upright. And then the boat rolled clean over.

Chapter 28

YANCY STOOD in the stern sheets, screaming at the men, "Pull, you bastards, pull!" He glared at them, saw the sweat pouring off their brows, even in the cool morning air, saw the muscles stand out on their necks and forearms, their teeth clenched with the effort of pulling oar.

"Pull, you lazy, worthless bastards!"

At first he had just wanted Marlowe back. And Elizabeth. To punish her, take her, show her that he was a man. Teach her. But now that was only a part of it, a small part.

Running down the hill, Yancy had had the chance to really see the ships at anchor. Two big ships, a sloop, a brig. A powerful armada. With such a fleet he could be ruler of much more than tiny St. Mary's.

He heard Press's words over and over in his head: "*While I was out hunting Marlowe, I captured the Great Mogul's treasure ship.*"

Those words had not impressed him at first. It was only money, and money he had. He wanted Marlowe, and Elizabeth. He wanted vengeance.

But those words kept coming back to him, until at last their real significance took hold: "*The Great Mogul's treasure ship.*" That was not wealth. Wealth was not the word. That was empire, and it was his for the taking.

Yancy glanced down at Press, sitting beside him in the stern sheets. Had to keep Press near him, but the smug look on Press's face was like a sliver under his thumbnail. He wanted to slap him, looked forward to the moment, the very second, when he did not need Press anymore.

"Nagel!" The big man was in the bow, attending to the swivel gun. Yancy had to keep his eye on him now as well. "Hurry with that goddamned gun, or I will run my sword up your arse, do you hear me!" His voice was shrill, almost a shriek, a most undignified sound, but he was beyond caring. Every tiny fiber of him was focused on reaching the ships and taking them.

Nagel scowled, stepped back, touched off the powder in the touchhole. The gun fired, langrage and round shot. They were half a mile from the anchored ships. It was entirely possible that the small gun could not even shoot that far. But that did not matter. The shooting might unnerve the men on the ships. And Yancy had to do something.

The gunfire from the *Speedwell* had dropped off, and the *Elizabeth Galley* was still blasting away, with only one of her great guns and four of her men knocked out. Overhead, the squeal of blocks, the strain of rope, as crate, barrel, bundle were lifted from the *Venture*, swayed aboard the *Galley*. The thick, choking smoke from the guns swirled around the deck, partially obscuring the growing daylight.

Bickerstaff was on deck. "I've left one of those fellows in the magazine," he reported to Marlowe, "handing the cartridges out. I thought I might be of more use on deck."

"Quite. I—" Marlowe began, and then a shout from the *Queen's Venture*. Billy Bird. "Marlowe! I don't reckon we have much longer!" His words were punctuated by a groan from the *Venture*, a creaking as the two ships ground together. The *Queen's Venture* listed farther away, the ropes binding the ships together and the fife rails and bits to which the ropes were made of groaning in agony.

Marlowe looked up through the smoke. He could see the crazy angle of the *Queen's Venture*'s masts. "Good Lord!" he shouted. With the distraction of fighting, he had not kept a watch on how far the ship had gone down. He could hardly believe she was still floating.

"Get the men out of her hold, we have to go! That's all we get!" Marlowe shouted. Then, from beyond Billy Bird, from over the water, came the sharp report of a gun, smaller than a cannon but bigger certainly than small arms.

The boats. The two boats pulling for them. In the heat of it, Marlowe had forgotten them entirely, but now a new front was opened up.

Marlowe raced up the ladder to the gangway and then around to the far side to which the *Queen's Venture* was tied. It was a jump now to the other vessel's deck, listing as she was away from the *Galley*. Behind him the *Elizabeth Galley's* guns blasted, the *Speedwell* answered, sending the shot screaming over deck, smashing woodwork, rigging, toiling hands.

Marlowe moved to the *Elizabeth Galley's* foredeck, and Bickerstaff and Billy Bird joined him.

"There," Bickerstaff said, pointing to the east end of the bay. The boats had halved their distance, and now in the full light Marlowe could see how fast they were coming on.

"I don't imagine they are coming to our aid," Marlowe said. The bow gun from one of the boats fired, and the water twenty feet short of the *Queen's Venture* was marked with the falling shot, like a sudden isolated burst of rain. They were firing langrage or case shot, both loads consisting of hundreds of musket balls or bits of twisted iron scrap, designed to tear apart a packed mass of men.

"Once they reach us, our prisoners will throw in with them and they will overwhelm us for certain. We have to get these prisoners off," Marlowe continued, talking over the soft thud of the distant gun as it finally caught up with the shot. "Honeyman!"

The quartermaster came running up. "Get the oars out of the boats, and we'll set the prisoners adrift. That should keep them out of trouble for a while."

"Good thought," Billy Bird said, and then Bickerstaff said, "Whatever is that?"

Marlowe followed Bickerstaff's finger. There was something or someone thrashing in the water, fifty yards away. He could not tell what it might be.

"Here." Billy Bird offered up a small telescope. Bickerstaff took it, pulled it open, trained it at the thrashing creature. A moment's silence, and then Bickerstaff said, "It is Peleg Dinwiddie. He is clinging to a log or some such."

Peleg Dinwiddie? How odd to hear that name. Marlowe had entirely forgotten about his former first officer. It seemed a hundred years since he had last seen him. What had become of him? What was he about?

Bickerstaff offered the glass to Marlowe, and Marlowe took it, trained it on the man in the water. It was not a powerful telescope, but strong enough that Marlowe could make out Dinwiddie's form, the features of his face, even under a growth of beard. "Another bad choice for old Peleg, I reckon," Marlowe said, snapping the glass shut. "Billy, set your men to rounding up the prisoners. I'll get Burgess on the sweeps."

"Marlowe." Bickerstaff stopped him just as he was stepping away. "You don't intend to leave Dinwiddie, do you?"

"Leave him? No, he left me. Told me to sod off, you may recall. I am doing as he wished."

"He is obviously trying to reach the ship."

"And doing a piss-poor job, just like he did as first officer." Marlowe made to step away again, but Bickerstaff grabbed him by the arm, hard, turned him back around.

"You cannot abandon him," he said, a simple statement of fact.

"Damn him, I say."

"Marlowe, whatever temptation Yancy lured him into, whatever he put in his head, you were still the one that brought him here. You were the one who recruited him, convinced him to sail the Pirate Round. He was loyal to you once, and you to him."

Marlowe held Bickerstaff's eyes, furious at this defense of his faithless officer, furious at this interruption at that critical juncture. The ropes holding the *Queen's Venture* groaned again, and the *Elizabeth Galley*'s battery and the *Speedwell*'s battery went off, clouds of smoke rolling over them, the deafening noise of the guns, the shot smashing rigging, rail, men, the shouts of the men at their tasks, or fighting, or dying, and on that little patch of deck, silence, the two men holding one another's eyes.

And Marlowe found himself conjuring up the picture of Dinwiddie—stolid, unimaginative, impressionable Dinwiddie—at race day at the Page place. The look in Dinwiddie's eyes as he dangled Madagascar in front of him. Ingenuous Dinwiddie in his silly best dress, preparing for the governor's dinner.

I set that poor bastard up from the onset. I am as guilty as Yancy.

"I cannot leave now. We are in the middle of a bloody sea fight!"

"I do not want you to leave, Marlowe. I want you to give me leave to go. And a manned boat."

Marlowe glared at him. Bickerstaff was not asking him to be a hero, or even a decent human being, just asking that he, Bickerstaff, be allowed to be one.

Around them the great guns blasted, the vessels shook with the impact, the smoke choked them, made their eyes water. The noise was unbearable. *Why must I bloody bother with this?* Marlowe wondered.

But Marlowe could not do it. He could not let Bickerstaff go alone, into that kind of danger. Nor could he order another of the officers to go with him.

A cry of exasperation built in his guts. "Ahh, goddamn you!" He looked away, looked back. "Very well," Marlowe said at last. "We'll take the gig . . . no, we'll take the longboat." He turned fast, stepped across the deck to the starboard side where the pilot ladder hung down to the boats.

"You do not have to come," Bickerstaff shouted, following behind. "You have your duty here."

"Billy and Honeyman have things in hand, but if those boats reach the ship, we're done for. Perhaps I can help draw them off." It made it more palatable, thinking of a genuine tactical reason for what he was doing, not just saving Dinwiddie's dumb arse.

They stopped at the head of the ladder, and Bickerstaff said, "You are doing the right thing."

"Yes, yes, always doing the right goddamned thing." Marlowe

turned. "Billy Bird, you will be in command in my absence. Get everyone clear of the bloody *Queen's Venture* before she rolls over. Hands
aloft to loosen sail." He turned again. "Honeyman, get some men in
the longboat. Muskets if they got 'em, but don't waste time looking for
them. Set a swivel gun in the bow. There are four of them aft on the
quarterdeck, and I see powder and shot beside them. Go!"

Honeyman began to shout orders, Billy Bird began to shout orders.
Marlowe directed men down the ladder and into the longboat floating
below.

Low in the water, the boats had been mostly spared from the inces-
sant fire from the *Speedwell*. The barge had a neat hole clean through
both sides, and the very tip of the stem of one of the longboats was shot
away, but beyond that they were intact.

Across the deck, running, led by Duncan Honeyman, came twenty
men. Burgess carried a swivel gun, cradled like a baby in his arms. The
others carried muskets, pistols, cutlasses. They swarmed down the side,
handed the swivel down, set it in place, took their places on the
thwarts, set oars in tholes.

Marlowe and Bickerstaff came last, sat in the stern sheets. The
Speedwell fired, the round shot slamming into the hull mere feet above
their heads, showering them with a fine spray of splinters.

"Give way!" Marlowe called, and the oars came down, and the men
pulled with a will, eager to put the *Elizabeth Galley* between themselves and the *Speedwell's* broadsides.

Stroke, stroke, they pulled under the *Galley's* counter, around the
Queen's Venture's stern, and the *Speedwell* was lost from sight. Marlowe pushed the tiller over. He could see Dinwiddie now, clinging to
whatever that was he was clinging to, could see the two big boats
pulling fast for the *Queen's Venture*. This was going to be a close thing.

The men leaned into the oars, driving the big boat across the harbor. In the bow Burgess loaded the swivel, poured powder from a horn
into the touchhole.

"There!" Bickerstaff pointed. One of the big boats had broken away,
was making for them. He had drawn off half the attacking force, and
he took some comfort from that.

"Probably don't know what we're about, but figure to stop us anyway!" Marlowe yelled over the gunfire.

Fifty feet from Dinwiddie, and the other boat was closing fast. A bang of a swivel gun and case shot tore up the water, crackled into the side of the boat, and smashed into the arm of the man at number-two oar, who let go of his sweep, screamed in pain, clapped a hand over the spurting wound.

"Let 'em have it, Burgess!" Marlowe shouted. Burgess already had the swivel trained on the approaching boat, aimed straight on at their bow, straight at the man feverishly reloading their swivel.

Burgess snapped a pistol over the train of powder in the touchhole. The sparks drifted down, tiny, delicate points of light, and then the powder flashed and the swivel roared out, pushing the whole boat sideways, and the man at stroke oar in the approaching boat was blown away, tossed back into his shipmates as he disappeared below the gunnel.

That should cool their enthusiasm, Marlowe thought. And then from beyond the bow, a voice like a memory, like something out of a dream, floating through the gunfire: "Help! Help! Here!"

Peleg Dinwiddie.

Marlowe half stood, looked beyond the bow. Dinwiddie was clinging to an overturned dugout, and he was slipping. Two boat lengths ahead. Another stroke. "Backwater! Backwater!" The oars came down, the tholes creaking with the pressure as the momentum of the heavy boat was checked, and then they were dead in the water, and Marlowe was looking down into the bearded, gray, terrified, wide-eyed face of Peleg Dinwiddie. He was a frightening sight.

One of the oarsmen reached out with his blade, and Dinwiddie grabbed it and pulled himself over. Eager hands reached down and grabbed handfuls of clothing and hauled his tired and near-limp form over the gunnels.

Bickerstaff, beside him in the stern sheets, had snatched up one of the muskets. He trained it over the side at the approaching boat, fired, began to load it again. In the bow Burgess let go with another blast from the swivel, and several men jumped, cursed in surprise. Dinwiddie was deposited in a heap in the bottom of the boat, gasping, water streaming off him.

"Give way, together!" Marlowe shouted. He had done his moral duty, the Gospel According to Francis Bickerstaff. Time to get the hell out of there.

The men fell in, pulled. Marlowe put the tiller hard over. The longboat turned in a great, elegant arc away from the approaching boat, away from the half-sunk dugout, back toward the *Elizabeth Galley*.

Marlowe looked at the other boat. One hundred feet back, the swivel belched out its smoke and flames and case shot. The blast tore up the water, but the gun had been aimed too low, and none of the shot struck.

Marlowe pulled his eyes from that threat, looked up at the *Elizabeth Galley*. Her hull was nearly obscured by smoke, but rising from the gray cloud he could see her topmasts and topgallants, straight as ancient trees. Beside her the spars of the *Queen's Venture* jutted out at a crazy angle as the ship tried to sink and the ropes binding her to the *Galley* held her up.

He could see men along the *Elizabeth Galley*'s yards. The tight bundles of furled sail tumbling down, ready to be set. He could hear that the great guns had slowed considerably, and he wondered if the *Speedwell* had had enough.

The land breeze was filling in. It lifted the smoke in a big blanket, pitched it forward, rolled it away. Behind the two big ships Marlowe could see that the *Speedwell* had indeed had enough. She had slipped her cable, set a topsail, and was moving out of the range of the *Galley*'s great guns. Defeated or driven off, it did not matter, as long as she had stopped fighting.

"Thank you, Marlowe! Bless you, bless you, thank you." Dinwiddie was on his knees now, like a supplicant, hands clasped. Marlowe could see that his clothing, torn and filthy, had once been highest quality, better than anything Dinwiddie had carried on board the *Galley*. He was thinner, his face covered with sprawling beard. Marlowe wanted to kick him.

"Don't thank me. Thank Bickerstaff. I'd have left you to drown." He turned his attention elsewhere.

"Captain!" Burgess, standing in the bow, half turned around. They were pulling for the *Galley*, the attacking boat on their larboard quarter, and his swivel gun would not bear. "Captain! One last shot!"

Marlowe nodded, pushed the tiller over, and the longboat turned away from the *Galley* until Burgess's gun could be trained on the attacking boat. Marlowe looked over his shoulder. The others, Yancy's boat crew, were pulling like men possessed. Fifty feet away a man like Burgess's mirror image bending over their swivel just as Burgess was bending over his.

They fired in the same instant. Marlowe saw the flame jump from the other gun, but the sound he heard was Burgess's swivel going off, a deep-throated sound, and Marlowe thought, *He's fired round shot*, and then the case shot of the attacking boat hit them broadside.

Men were knocked off their thwarts, oars dropped and disappeared over the side, men shouted, clutched bloody gashes.

Marlowe coughed in the smoke blown back from the gun. There was a pulsing, dull ache in his right hand. He lifted it up, stared at the place where he felt the pain. The agony grew sharper, sharper, like an image in a telescope coming into focus, and he realized that two of his fingers, his little finger and his ring finger, had been shot clean away. Blood ran down his palm, down his arm.

"Ahhhh, goddamn it!" he shouted, giving voice to the pain and the horror. He gritted his teeth, clapped his hand under his arm, put pressure on the wound.

He turned his head to see how long they had before the other boat was on them, but he was surprised to see the boat stopped in the water, men leaning on their oars, more men swarming around the bows. There was a hole shot clean through, right at the stem, and they were close enough that Marlowe could see men stuffing jackets and rope and whatever else they had into the hole.

And he remembered. *Round shot*. He looked forward to call to Burgess, but the boatswain was crumpled over his gun, and from the looks of him he had taken most of the cast-shot blast.

Bickerstaff appeared, blood smeared on his cheek. "Francis! You're hit!"

"A scratch! But you've lost fingers! Let me see!"

Reluctantly Marlowe brought his hand out from under his arm. Once he let the pressure off, the pain shot right up through his shoulder.

Bickerstaff took the hand in his, examined it, but Marlowe had to turn his head. Even after all the bloody mutilation he had seen—and caused—he could not endure the sight of his own fingers blown to stumps.

He felt a pressure at the base of his fingers, forced himself to look. Bickerstaff had lashed spun yard around them to stanch the bleeding.

"Thank you," Marlowe said, then in his commanding voice called, "Come along, you men! Push the wounded ones aside, them that can't pull an oar! See how they loosen off sail, yonder! Let's get back to the *Elizabeth Galley* and quit this damned place!"

That seemed to rally the stunned men some. They pushed aside the wounded and the dead, took up the sweeps that were still there, pulled for the ship. Bickerstaff took an oar, and Dinwiddie, who had been lying in the bottom of the boat and had escaped any injury, took one as well.

One of Yancy's longboats, the one that had come after them, was knocked out, but the other had not swerved in her course for the *Queen's Venture*. Now that longboat and Marlowe's were converging, and it looked as if they might reach the listing *Queen's Venture* at the same time.

"Come on, pull! Pull!" Marlowe urged. He did not know if there was fight enough left in his men to do battle with another boatload of armed brigands.

Right for the low rail of the sinking *Venture*, that was where he aimed the bow. Run the boat right against the side of the ship, help the wounded up and over the slanting deck, onto the *Elizabeth Galley*, cut the ropes, and go. Sail loosened off. Cut the cable.

He looked to his left, saw the other boat closing, both making for the same point on the *Venture*'s rail. But Marlowe could see now that his own boat would get there first, beat the other by a good minute.

"Pull! Pull!" It was the kind of silly, useless order that he disdained—they could not pull any harder than they were—but he could not help himself.

Four minutes, it seemed like an hour or more, and Marlowe's longboat swooped up alongside the heavily listing *Queen's Venture*. The men flung away their oars, no need for them now, and grabbed hold of the low rail of the ship. The uninjured or slightly injured leaped over the gunnel, onto the ship, turned to help their shipmates.

Marlowe and Bickerstaff stumbled forward, lifted the still-living men out of the boat and over the rail, handed them into the arms of their shipmates, who pulled them or carried them up the slanting deck to the sanctuary of the *Elizabeth Galley*.

Dinwiddie climbed out next, stood on the rail of the sinking ship, offered a hand to Marlowe, which Marlowe ignored. He climbed out himself, turned. Yancy's longboat was thirty feet away, close, but too far to catch them now.

Marlowe reached out his arm, and Bickerstaff reached out to him. Bickerstaff's hand clapped onto Marlowe's forearm and Marlowe's onto Bickerstaff's, and he helped his friend from the boat just as the man in the longboat fired the swivel in the bow.

Marlowe's head was filled with a horrible screaming, a rushing concussion of sound, and he felt himself spinning as though someone had twirled him on a dance floor. His eyes were filled with red, he could see nothing but red. He hit the deck, slid, came to a stop against the rail. He felt a burning agony all through his right side.

He opened his eyes and was surprised to see that everything was just as it was—the water, the deck, the sky now robin's-egg *blue overhead. He looked down at his arm, the arm that had been holding Bickerstaff's. It was not an arm anymore, just a shredded mass of bone and flesh and blood-soaked cloth. He looked at the deck. Bickerstaff was there, wide-eyed. A dozen or so holes in his chest. A pool of blood below him, running into the scuppers.

"Francis . . ." Marlowe said. "Francis, what have I done . . . ?" It was no more than a whisper. His mind could grasp nothing beyond that question.

"Come on!" Dinwiddie shouted. He grabbed Marlowe's collar, tried to make him stand.

Marlowe looked up at him. "We came for you," he said. "Francis, he said we had to. We came for you. And now he is dead."

"Come on!"

Marlowe saw Dinwiddie grab Bickerstaff's lifeless body, drape it over his shoulder, and push his way, grunting, up the steep deck. He passed Bickerstaff's body across the wide gap, half ran and half slid back, pulled Marlowe to his feet. Everything felt heavy, dull, the edges of Marlowe's vision going dark. He was aware only of the pain, the incredible pain in his arm, the anguish.

Dinwiddie eased him over the rail. He saw the Elizabeth Galleys reaching out for him, pulling him the rest of the way to the *Elizabeth Galley*'s deck.

Marlowe felt his head swimming, knew he was losing a lot of blood, reckoned this was the end. Francis dead, he did not want to go on. Swimming, swimming, the tall rig overhead whirling around. He closed his eyes, felt the warmth of the deck below him.

Peleg Dinwiddie watched them lay Marlowe's pale form down on the deck, Bickerstaff's bloody and lifeless body beside him.

Close his eyes! Dear God, will someone close his eyes? Dinwiddie thought, but he could not do it himself. He could not put his hand on those accusing eyes.

"We came for you. Francis, he said we had to."

Of course. Marlowe would not have risked everything to save him. But Francis was a true man, a real friend, a decent and moral being. So of course it was Francis who took the case-shot blast. Not Marlowe. Not him. Francis. The good ones always got it.

Dinwiddie felt the agony like a hot coal inside him. He was back on the *Elizabeth Galley*, he was in the midst of fire, he had helped his shipmates back on board. But he was not cleansed, not by far. He felt dirtier than ever.

To his left, down the sloping deck, the longboat was twenty feet away and closing, fifty armed men ready to swarm up the deck of the *Queen's Venture*, over the *Galley*'s rail. Fling themselves with loaded weapons and drawn swords at his shipmates, and his shipmates, disorganized, with no arms at the ready, might well be taken.

He looked down. An arms chest at his feet, and he knew what was in it, had inspected it a hundred times back when he was first officer, a lifetime or two before. Smoldering match by the guns in the waist below. He moved without thinking, just acting on nebulous emotion, a sense for what would make things right.

Ran down into the waist, grabbed up the match. Forward, men were hacking through the anchor cable, no time even to slip it through the hawsepipe. Back up to the gangway. Flip open the arms chest. To one side, a neat row of hand grenadoes with their uniform wooden plugs and curling fuse.

He snatched one up, touched the matched to it, held it there until the fuse was hissing and burning well. Picked up another one and held that fuse to the match until that was also well lit.

Below him the boat was just bumping up alongside the low, nearly submerged rail of the *Queen's Venture*, the first of the armed men leaping out of her.

Dinwiddie jumped across to the *Queen's Venture*'s gangway and ran around the open waist, then down the deck, slipping and stumbling with the sharp angle, screaming as loud as he could. It was a scream from his heart and from his bowels, his final sound, and all his life and all he had been or done, all the horrible mistakes he had made in the past half year or ever before that—all of it went into that shout.

He saw heads snap up in surprise, saw pistols leveled, but it was too late for them. He slammed into the few men on the *Venture*'s deck like a ball in a game of ninepins, knocked them aside, launched himself into the longboat.

He fell across the thwarts with a painful crash, the breath knocked from his lungs, but he clutched the grenadoes tighter still. He heard shouts of surprise, cries of "Grenado! He's got a grenado!" Hands pulled at him, tugged at his arms, beat him. He closed his eyes tight, clenched his fists around the metal balls, then rolled over fast so he would not smother the blast with his body.

More shouts. Through clenched eyelids he saw a bright flash of red.

*   *   *

Billy Bird, watching from the *Elizabeth Galley*'s quarterdeck, saw the scene unfold with a strange combination of horror, admiration, and disgust. That fellow—Billy had no notion of who he was—had charged into the boat with two lit grenadoes, had fended off all hands reaching for him, had exposed the bombs at just the right second.

"Hoisted by his own petard, and by choice, for all love!" he shouted.

The two explosions, less than a second apart, had torn the man holding them to bits and shredded half the crew of the boat. Billy Bird could hear the scream of the shrapnel through the air, could see the bloody spread of flying metal as it plowed the men down.

Billy had had a plan, and that was to cut the *Queen's Venture* away and let it roll over the attacking boat, but then Marlowe had reached the *Venture* first and spoiled that idea.

Then Yancy's boat had reached the *Venture*'s side, and Billy thought it quite possible that those fifty armed and determined men might even overrun his larger but weary, hungry, disorganized crew, take the ship back. But now that problem was wiped out, figuratively, literally.

They had not all been killed in the blast. Some were even now crawling forward, stepping over the mutilated bodies of the shipmates, making for the deck of the *Venture*, still determined to carry the fight forward, still whipped into enough of a frenzy that they were willing to plunge into it, even with their decimated numbers.

But this was not a problem.

"Honeyman, now!" Billy shouted. The anchor cable parted under the blow of an ax, and all along the larboard side of the *Elizabeth Galley* men fell with axes on the lashings binding her to the *Queen's Venture*. It was like cutting cordwood, so taut were the ropes, and with a few strokes they began to part with the sound of small-arms fire. A gunner's mate who stood imprudently close to the rope was caught with the snap-back and flung clean off the gangway and into the waist.

The last half dozen ropes did not need cutting. With all the weight of the ship on them, they parted one after another, right down the line from forward aft as if it had been orchestrated.

The *Queen's Venture* gave a shudder and a sound like a deep moan, and over she went. Her masts came sweeping down to the water like felled trees, her larboard side disappeared, and from the *Galley*'s deck all they could see was the great white, weed-covered bottom as the ship turned on her side.

The pressure of the *Venture* rolling and pushing against the *Galley*, and the water she pushed as she rolled, served to drift the *Elizabeth Galley* away from the dying vessel.

"Sheet home topsails!" Billy shouted, and the men waiting eagerly and anxiously at the pinrails let fly buntlines and hauled on sheets, and the big sails were pulled down and out.

"Run away with your halyards!" The yards began their steady climb up the topmasts, the sails catching the breeze as they spread, the *Galley* coming to life, inching away from the *Queen's Venture*.

The *Venture*, in turn, was settling in the water. For some seconds she remained on her side, as if she were just resting, and then the hull started to sink. Her entire larboard side went down, and then her long keel disappeared under the blue-green water. Faster and faster she was swallowed up as her hull became less buoyant. The water churned and bubbled around her and rose up over her waterline, over her gunports that were now pointing at the sky, up over her rail.

At last only the upper part of her quarterdeck and poop was still visible, and then that went, and a second later the masts and yards were dragged below the water, and then there was nothing left but bits of floating debris and bodies and the ever-widening circle of rippling water.

The Elizabeth Galleys lined the rail, stared silently at the spot where the ship had disappeared. Billy, too, stared; he could not take his eyes away.

What a waste, he thought, *what a bloody waste*. It was the only thing he could think, and he was not even certain of what he meant.

Chapter 29

THE LONGBOAT bearing Elephiant, Lord Yancy and Captain Roger Press and what remained of their mutual commands, the longboat that was kept afloat through the tenuous use of jackets pushed into the gaping holes made by the round shot and half her men bailing furiously, ground up at last on the beach.

Yancy stood and pushed his way through the men and jumped down into the sand. He ignored everyone, stepped quickly up to the road and out along the dock. He stopped in time to see the poop deck and then the masts of his new flagship, the *Queen's Venture*, disappearing below the water.

He did not know how much booty was still aboard her or if it was even possible to get to it. The answers to those questions, he imagined, were "not much" and "most likely not."

Marlowe's ship, the *Elizabeth Galley*—how that name mocked him!—was under way, fore and main topsails set to the steady morning breeze and the forecourse sheeting home even as he watched.

Yancy gritted his teeth. He felt his whole body shake. Not trembling hands or shivering such as he had had before and recognized. This was something else, a tremor like an earthquake starting from his feet and spreading up and out to his extremities until his entire body was vibrating. He was suddenly afraid that something inside might give out—his heart, his brain, his bowels—something might burst from the internal pressure. He was not furious. He was far, far beyond that.

Footsteps on the wooden planks behind him, and he spun around and tried to say something, but his jaw and his tongue and his brain all seemed to be locked up, frozen in a state of paralysis.

"Dear Lord, Yancy," said Press, an amused note in his voice. He pulled the toothpick from his mouth, pointed it at Yancy. "You look as if you're like to blow a blood vessel!"

That seemed to shake something loose, and Yancy found he could think again.

His first thought was to go after them. The brig was still at anchor, and the sloop *Speedwell*. But the sloop was pretty well battered—even from the dock he could see that—and the brig would never be able to run the *Galley* down. He could not risk letting them get away.

"Nagel, you send some son of a bitch to the battery on Quail Island, you tell those bastards up there to blow that damned ship to splinters, do you hear me? Blow it right out of the water, I don't even want to see pieces of it, I want it blown apart, do you understand?"

Nagel looked around. "Send 'em in what boat?"

"Damn the boat! Send someone to swim over!"

"Aye. Stokes, you go. Get a move on."

Stokes nodded, kicked off his shoes, unbuckled his sword belt, pulled off his shirt as he ran for the water's edge.

Yancy turned his back on the others, folded his arms, watched the *Elizabeth Galley* standing across the harbor.

She would not make it. There was breeze enough, but the tide was against her. Stokes would be at the battery in twenty minutes, passing his order to fire, and five minutes after that the ship would be under their guns. There was no missing, not at that range. The gunners would blow the ship away.

Yancy wanted the ship, of course, and wanted the vast amounts of treasure that that bastard Marlowe had stolen from him. But if he could not have that, at least he could have them all dead. He could stand there and watch them as they were blasted to pieces by the battery's big guns, not a cable length from the channel down which the ship must sail. He could picture the agony on the decks as their near escape was taken from them.

Perhaps they would abandon ship. Perhaps they would row ashore. Perhaps he would get his hands on Marlowe and Elizabeth after all. He felt some small sense of optimism, where before there had been only fury.

Arms aching, heaving for breath, stumbling, Barnaby Stokes, sixteen years of age, strongest swimmer among the pirates there on St. Mary's, stood up in the shallow water near the jungle-covered shore of Quail Island and staggered for the beach.

He reached the sand, picked up his pace, jogged through the gate in the battery's wall, across the flat, paved ground, past the furnace for heating shot, past the bored gun crew who sat in the shade and drank rum and watched him with idle curiosity. He fell against the low wall along which the five big thirty-two-pounders were arranged, looking out over the water. He stood for a moment, hands palms down on the top of the wall, catching his breath, looking out at the harbor to see if he was too late.

He was not. The ship had everything set and was catching a decent breeze, but the tide was against her. It would be a good five minutes before she passed in front of the battery's guns.

Stokes stood, breathed steady, took in the scene. It was beautiful, almost too beautiful to be real. The light blue sky, the aqua blue water in the harbor, the deep blue of the open ocean beyond. The green jungle carpeting the hills, the ship a quarter mile off, like an intricate toy. It seemed too beautiful a morning to fill it with smoke and flying shot and death.

But there had been so much of that already that morning that Stokes reckoned a bit more would not hurt. Besides, it was going to be a great frolic, standing in the battery, blowing apart a ship whose six-pounder guns would be no match for the big thirty-twos.

"What's acting?" The captain of the battery came strolling up, his long shirt untucked from stained breeches.

"Yancy says to blow yon ship out of the water. Really give it to her."

The captain squinted over at the ship, spit on the ground, squinted again, and grinned. "Yeah, we can do that," he said. "Come on, lads, we've business this morning!" he called, and the others, muttering, got to their feet. They shuffled over to the low wall, looked out at the harbor. "Yancy says we're to blow them out of the water," the captain told his crew.

That perked up their interest and their spirits, and they fell to loading one of the great guns. There were ten of them on the gun crew, but that was as many as were required to work the one big gun.

They moved slowly, deliberately, rolling back the gun, ramming home powder, shot. Stokes thought that, for men who had nothing to do but man the battery and be ready to fire the guns, they were not very organized or swift, but he held his tongue. They had time. The test would be how fast they could reload when the ship was within the arc of their fire.

"Run her out!" the gun captain called, and the men leaned into the train tackles, and the gun rumbled, squealed, moved under protest up to the rampart. The captain sighted down the barrel, ordered the gun trained around, fiddled with the elevation. "That's good, lads. We'll just let her sail into it."

Four minutes they waited in silence, the only sound the song of the birds and the buzzing of insects, the breeze in the thick foliage. The captain leaned over the barrel, grinned. "Ah, here she comes, lads, right to us, the stupid bastard. Give us the match, here."

One of the men handed the gun captain the match, and they all stepped back, making a circle of men two feet from the gun, safe from its recoil, ready to leap to and reload.

"Come on, come on . . ." the captain muttered, hunched over the barrel, the match hovering over the powder train.

Men craned their heads above the wall, eager to see the damage the first shot would do. It was the most amusement any of them had had in some time.

"Here we go . . ." the captain said, and he straightened, shoved the match down into the powder. It hissed, crackled and then in one huge roar of flame and screaming metal and burning powder the great gun fired its thirty-two-pound shot, and the ten-foot, three-ton barrel exploded into a thousand shrieking fragments.

Stokes, standing ten feet away, was hurled back, knocked from his feet, skidding across the flat paving stones. His head was buzzing and ringing, his chest and stomach hurting in a way that he could not think to describe, such that when he opened his eyes some moments later he was surprised not to find some creature sitting on him, clawing him apart, because that was how it felt.

He had been tossed back into a half-sitting position against the oven. There were great rents in his chest and stomach, blood all over. He thought he could feel the bits of metal inside him, in his body.

There was nothing left of the gun save for a small fragment of the barrel still sitting on the wreckage of the gun carriage. There was nothing left of the gun crew, save for pieces and great swaths of blood, impossibly red under the bright sun.

Stokes slumped down, closed his eyes, prepared to join the others, wherever they were.

Lord Yancy watched with great satisfaction the puff of smoke from the battery, the jet of water shooting up beside the ship. They missed, which diminished his pleasure somewhat, but not so very much. Stokes had made it to the battery in time, that was the point.

As the ship closed the distance, the men at the battery would really hammer her. *Five guns firing at point-blank range, thirty-two pounders with muzzle velocities of . . . a terribly high number . . .* The *Elizabeth Galley* would be torn apart.

Yancy folded his arms, began to count in his head, *One and a hundred, two and a hundred, three and a hundred . . .* curious to see how long it would take them to fire the next shot. He imagined that they had all the guns loaded and ready, would just go down the line, firing them off. They certainly had time enough.

Thirty-four and one hundred, thirty-five . . . Yancy frowned. Apparently they did not have the guns loaded beforehand. Apparently they were reloading now. Such lack of foresight did not please him.

Fifty-one and one hundred, fifty-two and one hundred . . . Yancy stopped counting. A minute to load a single gun? Lazy bastards, he would flog them all. The *Elizabeth Galley* was right under them, or appeared to be from the angle from which Yancy was watching. Now was the time to pound her. Another minute and the best shot would be lost. Another three and she would disappear around the island.

It was an awful, awful silence that filled the next three minutes. Yancy felt his guts wrenching with his mounting fury, an emotion frightening in its intensity. He tried to quash it but could not. The *Elizabeth Galley*'s headrig was lost from sight around the northern end of the island, and still nothing from the battery. The trembling began again, moving through him.

Nothing but silence from the battery. Yancy listened, his whole being concentrated in his ears. Insects buzzing, the raucous call of some bird. Feet shuffling, some whispered conversation. Nothing else.

Half the *Elizabeth Galley* was lost from sight. Yancy was ready for the battery to open up. *Didn't want to sink her in the channel*—he grasped at that straw. *Waited till she was in deep water, didn't want to make an obstruction of her, right in the channel* . . .

And then, like the sun dipping below the horizon, the last of the *Elizabeth Galley*'s stern section slipped around Quail Island and was gone.

Yancy's entire body was trembling now, uncontrollably. He clenched his fists and his jaw and his eyelids, tensed his muscles, tried to keep his brain from blowing apart. He could picture bulging veins, ready to burst, his heart swelling and growing fragile, like a soap bubble in his chest.

And then from behind him a chuckle. It built until it was a laugh, a raucous shout of a laugh, an obscene sound, and Yancy thought at first he alone could hear it, the gods laughing at him because he could not imagine that anyone would actually dare laugh at that moment. Then he realized that it was Roger Press.

He whirled around. Press's gangly form was bent nearly double, and he was laughing, while around him the other men backed away as if he had suddenly dropped with plague.

Yancy took a step toward him and stopped, did not know what to do. It was too incredible.

Press straightened, wiped his streaming eyes, rolled his silver tooth-pick across the roof of his mouth. "Oh, Yancy, this is rich! I bring you four ships, I bring you the Great Mogul's treasure and Marlowe and his bitch to boot, and you piss it all away! All of it! God, you are pathetic, you stupid little fuck."

Press put his hands on his hips, smirking, waggling his toothpick around. There were a hundred things that Yancy wanted to do and say, all at once, but all he could see was that damned toothpick. With three quick steps he crossed the space that separated them. His hand darted up, grabbed the accursed thing, yanked it from Press's mouth and hurled it aside.

Press's smirk vanished. His eyebrows came together, his lips went down into a frown, and fast as a snake his right hand came around and slapped Yancy hard across the face. "Go pick that up, you little shit. You aren't in command here anymore," Press hissed.

Yancy staggered back a few steps. A *blow!* He could not recall hav-ing ever been struck, not since the age of fourteen. Certainly not by anyone who lived to brag of it.

His hand wrapped around the hilt of his sword. He pulled it from the scabbard with a swishing sound. "Now you die," he said simply, taking a step toward Press, who took a step back.

"Give me a sword!" Press yelled to the assembled men, half of whom were his former crew. "Give me a sword!" But no one moved.

Yancy charged, two steps, saw the look of horror and surprise on Press's face as he drove the sword into Press's stomach, the razor-sharp blade meeting little resistance as it slid through his bowels, came clean out the back.

Lord Yancy drove the blade home, right up to the hilt. He saw Press's eyes, wide with shock and pain, heard Press try to yell, but his throat was full of blood, and it was blood and not words that came from his mouth, blood running over the hilt of the sword, sticky and hot on his hands.

Yancy smiled, made to pull the sword free, but Press lurched for-ward, wrapped arms like a spider's legs around him, hugging him as if he were a dear friend. Yancy felt a surge of panic and revulsion, tried to push the horrible, bleeding thing away, but Press had strength left in his arms, and he held Yancy tight.

Then Yancy felt Press's right arm reaching down as the left encircled his neck, felt the bony hand under his coat, reaching for the dagger in the small of his back.

"No, no, you son of a bitch!" Yancy tried to push away, but Press held him tight. He could feel Press's blood pumping hot over him, could smell the blood and the dried sweat on Press's body, thought he would be sick. He felt the dagger clear the sheath, pushed away as hard as he could, but he could not beak Press's grip. He screamed, closed his eyes, waited for the knife in the back.

Henry Nagel stood at the edge of the ring of men, Yancy's men and Press's, witnesses to the fast and bloody end of their leaders.

He had been grudgingly impressed with Yancy's quickness and the force he had applied to skewer Press. That took some strength of arm, Nagel knew.

Henry had reckoned the stroke gave Yancy the final victory over Press, but he was wrong. Press still had something left in him, vicious bastard; he was not going to die alone. He found Yancy's knife, pulled it, drove it into the back of his screaming enemy, pulled it free, drove it home a second time before the two men collapsed to the dock with arms around each other like lovers, blood pooling together.

The ring of men stood silent and watched. Yancy made a sound like a long sigh, Press twitched a few times more, but nothing beyond that, and then they were dead. No one said a thing.

After a moment of this, Nagel looked up, and at the same time so did Israel Clayford, the great brute who had been second to Press. Their eyes met, and each held the other's stare, and then at last Nagel nodded toward the harbor, said, "Sloop's fair shot up, but I reckon she'd make a fine Red Sea Rover."

Clayford nodded. "Brig, too. Could work together."

Nagel agreed. "Reckon we can put it to a vote, who captains what, quartermasters and the like." He looked around, spoke louder, addressing all the men there. "Any of you doesn't care to join in, don't want to sail the Pirate Round . . . well, you just walk away, and nothing will be said."

He waited a moment. No one moved.

At last Clayford broke the silence. "Finch here's a scholar, can write a fair, round hand. What say we set him to drafting articles, like?"

"Reckon so." With that, Nagel turned, clomped down the dock, and the others followed behind. He looked up at the big house on the hill. He was ready for a wet. Ready to quit that place.

Billy Bird had among his company a fellow that they called the Doctor. He was not, in reality, a physical doctor or a doctor of anything for that matter, but he had been an apothecary's assistant, and through much trial and error among the Brethren of the Coast he had learned a few things about the surgeon's art.

Even as the *Elizabeth Galley* was standing toward the harbor entrance, Billy ordered the man to see Marlowe carried below and attended to. Billy had no real hope of Marlowe's living. But then he didn't really think any of them would live to see the open ocean.

The breeze was good, but the tide was flooding, and they were having some trouble in stemming it. At the rate they were going, they would be under the Quail Island battery for fifteen minutes, long enough for the point-blank fire to sink them and then some. But Billy set the Doctor to work on Marlowe because he was by nature an optimist.

The first shot did not surprise him, not as much as the fact that they missed. He did not see how they could. But they would get their range with the second shot, and then it would be a hailstorm of iron.

He braced, waited for it, and waited some more. It was absolute torture. He felt like a mouse being toyed with by a cat. Looking straight into the muzzles of those big guns, he felt as though he were standing naked on the quarterdeck.

The Indian Ocean was opening up before them and they were beyond the arc of fire of half the battery's guns before Billy allowed a spark of hope to burn in his heart. Ten minutes later they were past the battery entirely, out of the harbor, with no pursuit that he could see and not one hit from the great guns on the island. Billy Bird did not know what had happened. He was not even very curious. He was just thankful.

Forty minutes later the Doctor came topside, his apron covered with blood. He was holding something wrapped in a bloody piece of canvas, which he threw overboard, then ambled over to Billy Bird, wiping his hands uselessly on his apron.

Billy pointed with his chin to the spot where the Doctor had thrown the bundle overboard. "Marlowe's arm?"

The Doctor nodded. "What was left of it."

"Will he live?"

The Doctor shrugged. "He's a strong one, and the arm come off clean. He's got as good a chance as any. Better than most, I guess."

Billy nodded. He knew this routine well enough. The Doctor had done what he could, and now there was nothing for it but to wait, and Marlowe would live or he would not, and there was nothing more that they could do.

Billy wondered if he might have some claim on Elizabeth's affection, some chance with her for something more lasting, if in fact Marlowe did die. And then he flushed with embarrassment that he could think such a thing, cleared his throat and looked away, as if the Doctor might guess at the callous thoughts that had crossed his mind.

They had poured some rum down Marlowe's throat, prior to the operation, and mostly by reflex he had gagged it down. Three men had held him while the Doctor did his business with knife and saw, pulling the arteries out with a tenaculum and tying them off and then covering the stump with a clean wool cap.

Marlowe passed out halfway through the procedure. Elizabeth sat at his other side, holding his still-intact hand, staring at his face through her tears. Had he been awake, she would have forced herself to be more stoic, but as he was not aware at all of his surroundings, she let her grief and her fear go, and those feelings made her eyes brim over with tears, which ran down her cheeks, soaked into her cotton shirt.

Soon after the operation was complete, the fever set in. The Doctor came below every hour, felt Marlowe's forehead, took his pulse, tried to say something encouraging to Elizabeth, who remained at his side. But he sounded less and less optimistic.

Elizabeth swabbed Marlowe's brow, spooned broth into his mouth, sang softly to him as she would have to a sleeping child. The fever raged on, and Marlowe remained unconscious.

He was unconscious when Madagascar disappeared below the horizon.

He was unconscious when they wrapped Francis Bickerstaff's body in old sailcloth, two round shot at his feet, his Bible and his folio of *Hamlet* clutched to his chest. Those were the two books, Elizabeth knew, that he would have wished to have with him for eternity, and even if Francis himself would have scoffed at the idea of such things accompanying one's earthly remains untold fathoms to the bottom of the ocean, still she felt better for doing it.

In the early-morning overcast they hove the ship to and buried those who had died during their final run from St. Mary's, and last of all was Francis Bickerstaff. Marlowe, racked with fever, did not see Elizabeth reading the sermon, did not see her break down halfway through, doubling over as if the weight of her grief were pushing her down, Billy Bird stepping over to her, gently taking the Bible from her hand, placing his arm around her, and pressing her weeping face into his chest as he read the last of the words.

"We commit to the deep the body of our friend, Francis Bickerstaff. May God have mercy on his soul."

More ceremony than was common among the Red Sea Rovers. Billy didn't really know this Francis Bickerstaff, had only met him the month before in the Gulf of Aden, but from the looks of genuine grief on the faces of the men who had sailed with him, and Elizabeth, her hand twisting his cloak, sobbing against his chest, he reckoned this was some man going over the standing part of the foresheet.

He closed the book, nodded, and the men at the inboard end of the plank lifted it high.

                                    *   *   *

Marlowe did not see the body of Francis Bickerstaff slide off the plank,
splash into the Indian Ocean, a dull white spot, circling down and finally swallowed up by the blue-black depths. He did not see it, and that
was a blessing as far as Elizabeth could figure, because the grief would
have killed him faster than the fever ever would.

Marlowe remained in a state of burning delirium for another week,
sweating and shivering, racked by wild, disjointed dreams with profound overtones of guilt and loss, liquid dreams that made no sense
save for the horrible emotions suspended within them.

Elizabeth stayed by his side, feeding him, bathing him, talking and
singing to him, sleeping in a cot set up at his side. The Doctor came
regularly, checked Marlowe's condition, bled him and applied poul-
tices and administered Peruvian bark.

Overhead, on the brightly lit deck, the ship settled into a routine of
sorts, Billy Bird in command of the *Elizabeth Galley*, Honeyman
elected quartermaster, the crew shaken down to their watches. But
Elizabeth saw little of it, sequestered below in her twilight nether-
world, stinking of disease and medicine and bilge.

Just after noon on the tenth day, around thirty-three degrees forty-five
minutes south latitude, Marlowe's fever broke. His mind was suddenly
clear, and his skin felt cool. Not the unhealthy chill that led to trembling and chattering teeth, but cool, comfortable. He opened his eyes,
turned his head, and he was looking at Elizabeth and she was looking
at him, and tears streamed down her cheeks, and he wanted to reach
out and comfort her.

He reached his right hand over to her, but there was something
wrong because move as he might he could not see his hand, or his
arm. He looked down, puzzled, looked to Elizabeth for some explanation.

She smiled, and the tears came faster, and she swallowed and
reached over to him and stroked his face. "It's not there anymore, my
love," she whispered, "but you will not need it because I am here."

She fed him, gave him water, changed his clothes. She told him what had happened and called for Billy Bird, who was pleased to see him alive and likely to stay that way. Billy filled in those parts of the fight that Elizabeth did not know.

"But what of Francis? Where is Francis?" Marlowe asked, and he was not happy to see the looks on the others' faces.

There followed on the heels of Marlowe's recovery and his finding out what had happened in those last moments on St. Mary's the blackest sort of grief, from which he could not surface. Nor did he try very hard, like a man overboard who has given up and lets the ocean take him.

He sat in the great cabin, staring out the windows at the sea rolling away astern of them, pictured Francis Bickerstaff's body sinking down, down, down to depths the likes of which no living man could go, inhabited by creatures no one could imagine. He pictured the bound body coming to rest in the sand and the blackness.

Over and over, day after day, he tortured himself with that image. He ate little, spoke little. Elizabeth stopped trying to draw him out. Billy Bird remained in command, drove the ship around the Cape of Good Hope and into the northern trades and across the broad Atlantic. They never saw more than a glimpse of a distant sail, and wind and weather were their allies the entire time.

And for the whole of the crossing, Marlowe remained in his private hell, wallowing in his half-life of grief and recrimination, and in that twilight time the only real things were Elizabeth and the excruciating pain in his arm that was no longer there.

Then one morning Marlowe felt the motion of the ship change, and the sailor in him registered the change, despite his utter lack of interest in anything, and he knew that it was not a change in sea state but the feel of water that is embraced all around by land. Still that was not enough to stir him from his seat, staring out the stern windows.

Two hours later he could see on the starboard side the familiar outline of Cape Charles and to larboard Cape Henry, and he knew that they were once again within the confines of the Chesapeake Bay.

Half an hour after that he heard Elizabeth's soft steps outside the cabin door. She opened it, stepped over to him, said, "Thomas, won't you come up on deck?" It was the first thing she had asked of him in two months, the first time she had asked him to put aside his self-indulgent grief, and so without a word he stood and followed her out.

He climbed up on the quarterdeck, ignored the embarrassed looks and half nods of greeting from men who did not know what to say to him. He stood at the weather rail, that familiar spot; it was like putting on a well-worn glove one has not put on in years. Looked forward, past the mainsail.

Fine on the starboard bow was Point Comfort, the headland that marked the entrance to the James River, the last stretch of water between them and home.

Spring in Virginia. The sky was blue, the air rich with the smell of a fertile and living land. All around them green, where for months there had been only blue.

Point Comfort. Home. Marlowe's hands began to shake, his lip began to quiver, and without a word he stamped off and down the ladder and aft to the privacy of the great cabin. He heard Elizabeth's feet behind him. Of course she would know that he needed her at that moment. He needed her at every moment.

He swung the door open, crossed to the lockers aft, and she with him, and they sat down together, and he wrapped his one arm around her and buried his head in her shoulder and cried and cried, and he thought he would never stop.

He cried for Francis Bickerstaff and for all the others and for all he had lost and for his own stupidity. He cried because he understood that once upon a time he had had everything he had ever wanted with Marlowe House, had become the man he had once dreamed of being, the man Francis had taught him to be, and then he nearly threw it all away because he thought he could be richer still.

"Oh, God, God, Elizabeth, how could I be so stupid?" he asked into her shoulder. She did not give him an answer, and he did not need one because he knew the answer, and he knew he would never be so stupid again.

It had cost him his arm. It had cost him Francis. It had nearly cost him Elizabeth, several times over. He wept for all of it, all the way up the James River, and when at last they dropped the anchor, he had cried his grief out. He came up on deck again. A new man in a new season.

They took a boat to the shore and were able to hire a carriage back to Marlowe House. They left Billy Bird in command, left it to him to divide out the booty in the hold of the *Elizabeth Galley*. They had yet to make an official count, but even lacking that, the men knew that every one of them, every man aboard, was terribly rich, that if they did not spend it all in one wild, frenzied debauch, as their type was wont to do and as so many ashore would readily encourage them to do, then not a one of them would ever have to work again.

Thomas and Elizabeth Marlowe rode in silence down the long drive that led to Marlowe House. The flowers were just showing, the young leaves on the trees almost iridescent green. The home had been well cared for, as Marlowe knew it would be. It looked as if they had been gone only a fortnight, no more.

The carriage stopped, and Marlowe got out and helped Elizabeth out. They stood in front of their home and held one another and breathed deep, smelling the flowers and the woods and the fields. Thomas smiled, the first time he could recall doing so since they had sailed from St. Mary's.

They were home. He was home. It was a home from which he did not intend to stray, ever again.

He thought of Yancy, and Press, and their struggle to be king of the island. Idiots. Like the moth beating itself against the glass of a lantern, they fought for power and money and did not even understand why they wanted those things.

What they wanted, in truth, was exactly what he had here at Marlowe House, and they did not know it, and neither did he, until that moment. The lesson had come at the highest price he had ever paid, but he had learned it at last. He had reached the confluence of two streams: what he wanted and what he had. He stood now where those floods met, and by those waters he would live his life.

Epilogue

THE SLOOP *Mercy* of Newport stood into the harbor of St. Mary's island. On her quarterdeck, Captain Patrick Quigley surveyed the batteries that leered out at him from Quail Island, big guns that could blow his vessel to bits before he had even cleared the headlands.

There was an unusual silence on deck as the others, the fifty men who had sailed with him, also stared up at those vicious guns, waiting.

There was no smoke from the battery, no flags flying from the flagpole. Nothing moving that he could see. He felt himself relax, just a bit.

As much as he tried to project a fierce and piratical nature, he was new to this sort of thing, this Red Sea Roving, and he was not at all certain of what his reception might be.

He had been informed by others, who knew, that St. Mary's was the place to call for provisions, powder, shot, information on where one might be most likely to intercept the Great Mogul's ships. He had envisioned a lively place, bustling with people, crowded with shipping, a sort of buccaneer's version of Newport, with rum flowing and buxom young women willing to do whatever a sailor far from home might wish.

He was surprised, for that reason, to find the harbor seemingly deserted. A few decrepit ships drifted at their anchors, another was half sunk and another appeared to have been hove down on the beach and left abandoned.

"Stand by with your anchor, there!" Quigley called out to the mate up by the cathead, then to the helmsman said, "Round up, right over there."

The *Mercy* rounded up into the wind, the topsails came aback, and the anchor was let go in five fathoms of water.

Captain Quigley stood aloof as the men bustled around the deck, squaring things away. He looked over the town with his telescope. He could see a few people moving around, no more than that. He looked up at the big house on the hill. Part of the roof was charred, it looked as if it had caught fire at one point, but not recently. It had never been repaired.

He started to get an uncomfortable feeling in his gut. He had expected to be greeted with saluting cannons and dipped flags and all that sort of formality. He had expected a boat to come out, inquire of who he was. "I am Captain Patrick Quigley, of the sloop *Mercy* of Newport. We are bound away on the Pirate Round!" He had been practicing those words for two months, but now it looked as if no one was going to ask.

The mate directed the hands to get the longboat over the side, and the armed boat crew took their places on the thwarts, and when they were ready, Captain Quigley climbed down and sat in the stern sheets. They pulled silently across the harbor for the old wooden dock, all eyes darting around, the men waiting for something, they did not know what. Something.

But there was nothing, nothing in the way of human greetings. Now Quigley could not even see those few figures he had seen earlier through his glass, and he began to wonder if he had really seen them at all.

The boat pulled up to the dock, and Quigley stood and hooked a shoe on the creaking ladder and climbed up fast, then stepped aside for the others.

At first he thought that someone had dropped a bundle of clothes on the planks and had left them where they fell. He took a step closer, sucked in his breath, whispered, "Goddamn my eyes . . ."

Two skeletons, still bearing the remnants of their clothes, shoes still slipped over bony feet, lay across one another. A sword through one, a dagger through the other. Quigley might have retched at the sight, but the bones had been so long exposed that they were picked clean and bleached white and had more or less collapsed into a heap, largely undisturbed, so that one could see clearly how the pair had fallen, taking each other to hell.

Quigley smiled, amused by the folly of such men. What had they gained? Around him the rest of the boat crew climbed up and spread out on the dock and gazed at the strange and morbid sight.

Patrick Quigley, having seen as much of the skeletons as he wished to see, stepped back and looked up the road to the big house on the hill. It was impressive, even from a distance, but he could see the signs of neglect: the charred roof, the wild grass sprouting around the stockade fence that was fallen down in places. Such a fine house. What a waste that it should be abandoned thus.

And then he felt the stirring of an idea, and he looked around, as if he might see whether the others were thinking as he was. He had fifty armed and loyal men with him. Not a terrific force, but stronger than any the island could muster, as far as he could see.

How hard would it be to take St. Mary's for his own? Who was there to resist him?

He had thought to sail the pirate wind, take some rich prize in the Red Sea, head for home a wealthy man. But what were the chances of that? He'd be damned lucky even to find a treasure ship, and even if he did, there was every chance that he would end up like old Thomas Tew, holding in his bowels with his hands.

But here, here he could set up as a middleman of sorts, buy and sell from the Roundsmen and the legitimate merchantmen who plied those waters. That was real wealth, and it did not depend upon luck or exposing oneself to flying shot.

He had an image of himself in that big house, looking down on the harbor just as he was now looking up. Native girls in attendance—he had heard of their legendary compliance. Suddenly the thought of returning to Newport, bitter cold, windswept, wintry Newport and his scrawny shrew of a wife and unpleasant children seemed unthinkable.

Unthinkable, certainly, in light of the realization that he had only to march his armed band inland and take the island. Then he could set up as the lead merchant there. A governor of sorts.

Governor? No, lord of the manor. Quigley smiled to himself. *Lord, hell.* He would be king of St. Mary's.

Why had no one else ever thought of this?

BOOKS BY JAMES L. NELSON

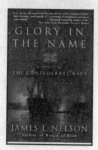

GLORY IN THE NAME
A Novel of the Confederate Navy
ISBN 0-06-095905-3 (paperback)
"By far, the best Civil War novel I've read;
reeking of battle, duty, heroism, and tragedy.
It's a triumph of imagination and good, taut
writing." —Bernard Cornwell

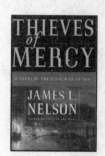

THIEVES OF MERCY
A Novel of the Civil War at Sea
ISBN 0-06-019970-9 (hardcover—April 2005)
Filled with wild characters, heart-pounding
action, and set against the bold backdrop of
the Civil War, *Thieves of Mercy* is a worthy
sequel to *Glory in the Name*.

THE GUARDSHIP
Book One of the Brethren of the Coast
ISBN 0-380-80452-2 (paperback)
A threat from Marlowe's illicit past as a
pirate looms on the horizon, and Marlowe
must choose between losing all or facing the
one man he fears.

THE BLACKBIRDER
Book Two of the Brethren of the Coast
ISBN 0-06-000779-6 (paperback)
"[Nelson's] descriptions have the ring of
truth and are conveyed with a sharpness
and clarity that even the landbound can
appreciate." —*Chicago Tribune*

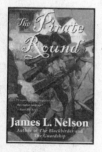

THE PIRATE ROUND
Book Three of the Brethren of the Coast
ISBN 0-06-053926-7 (paperback)
"A rousing swashbuckler filled with treasure,
sea battles, feuds, revenge, romance, and
deadly conspiracies. . . . A full broadside of
reading entertainment." —*Publishers Weekly*

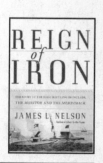

REIGN OF IRON
*The Story of the First Battling Ironclads,
the Monitor and the Merrimack*
ISBN 0-06-052403-0 (hardcover)
Nelson's rousing first non-fiction book,
on one of the great naval battles that
was a turning point in U.S. history.